TO KILL THE POTEMKIN

DEADLINE Y2K

MARK JOSEPH

St. Martin's Paperbacks

For my friend,
Nick Ellison

This is a work of fiction. Although some institutions and persons in this story resemble actual companies and people, the entities in this work were created in their entirety by the author. The real Safeway has no store on Guam Island. The real Consolidated Edison's 59th Street Station in New York generates steam, not electric power for the Metropolitan Transit Authority. The real Chase Manhattan Bank has no relationship with a firm called Copeland Solutions. The real General Motors has no subsidiary known as GM Electronics. Errors of fact cannot exist where there is only artifice.

"Wake Up Niggers" Copyright © 1970, Douglas Music Corp. All rights reserved. Used by permission.

DEADLINE Y2K

Copyright © 1999 by Mark Joseph.
Excerpt from *Afterburn* copyright © 1999 by Colin Harrison.

Library of Congress Catalog Card Number: 98-47799

ISBN: 0-312-97187-7

Printed in the United States of America

St. Martin's Press hardcover edition / February 1999
St. Martin's Paperbacks edition / October 1999

St. Martin's Paperbacks are published by St. Martin's Press, 175 Fifth Avenue, New York, NY 10010.

10 9 8 7 6 5 4 3 2 1

Stand still you ever-moving spheres of heaven,
That time may cease and midnight never come.
Christopher Marlowe, *Dr. Faustus*, 1588

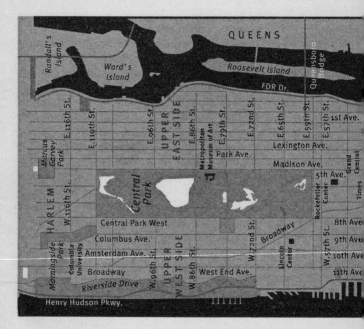

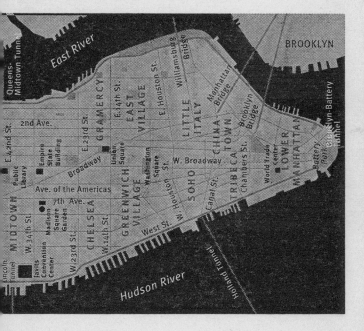

PART ONE

1991-1999

1

Venture capitalist Donald Copeland was a true believer in the power of money. During the 1980s and early '90s, his firm had financed and nurtured high-tech companies the way agribusiness husbanded livestock. Commerce was his daily bread and the global economy his steady diet.

The collapse of the Soviet Union in August of 1991 ended the Cold War, leaving capitalism to reign unchecked, a boon to Copeland's home town, New York, the undisputed center of the global economy. In New York everything was a commodity, including people, and anyone with a vision and the mental toughness to pursue it was especially valuable. Copeland drew his toughness from the granite underpinnings of the city, his bastion against the uncertain world beyond the rivers; his vision—he didn't know where his vision came from, but he never questioned it. He merely opened his eyes and saw ways to make money.

From time to time he drove to Brooklyn to admire Manhattan from across the East River. The sight of New York always inspired him, revealing ever greater possibilities of wealth and power. New York was in constant flux, the view never the same. Noticing the changes and staying one step ahead of the rate of change was the path to real riches. In the late 20th Century, change meant micro-technology.

When Copeland gazed at New York, he saw a vast network of wire and microprocessors that formed an invisible web among the high-rises. The infrastructure of the city had been completely rebuilt, automated and computerized during his lifetime. By 1991 computers ran everything from the subways to the red beacons atop the sky-scrapers. Two million people and at least as many computers occupied Manhattan, and the thread that connected the machines to the people was spun of pure gold. New York was an ocean of money that people wanted to spend on computers, and Copeland excelled at finding ways to make the financial tide flow his way. His company, Copeland Investments, had managed the financing of companies that earned millions supplying database management systems, CD jukeboxes, business software, LED displays, code compilers, electronic games, routers and switches for telecommunications, and programmable logic processors for automated control systems. Technology in and of itself meant nothing to Donald Copeland who lusted only after the thrill of the deal. Signing papers that concluded a transaction for millions was like sticking his finger into an electric socket. It charged his batteries.

One afternoon in the summer of 1991, as he was returning to Manhattan on the Brooklyn Bridge, soaking in the city, the radio babbling traffic and stock reports, a talk show host announced, "Next up, a report from the American Academy of Sciences that predicts that in eight and a half years, on January 1st, 2000, all our computers are gonna die. You heard me right, folks. Computers are going to malfunction on that date because of a nasty little programming glitch the academy has labeled the 'millennium bug.'"

Copeland took his eyes off the snarled traffic and stared at the radio dial. Twelve speakers in the Mercedes enhanced the spoken word with unnatural robustness, and the phrase "millennium bug" hung inside the computer-controlled interior like a trapped insect.

"The millennium bug is deceptively simple," the host continued.

"Most computer programs store dates with only the last two digits of the year rather than four digits. In the year 2000, computers running those programs will read 'oo' as 1900, and that's all she wrote, folks. Error! Error! Error! Crash!

"In the 1960s programmers started writing dates with two digits in order to save memory, and it became the convention. All programmers did it, and are still doing it, and none of these guys believed their programs would still be operating at the end of the century.

"They were wrong, folks. Those old programs are everywhere, and programmers are still spreading the millennium bug like wildfire. This killer computer flaw has wormed into our lives, residing patiently inside the control mechanisms of power plants, telephone systems, air and rail traffic control systems, accounting and billing programs, electronic fund transfer systems, and satellite control systems. And if that isn't enough, the bug has been burned into hundreds of millions of embedded computer chips in cars, airplanes, elevators, appliances, machine tools, and personal computers. When the year 2000 arrives, these computers are going to become confused and malfunction. We're looking at zero hour, people, the end of civilization as we know it.

"Folks, I gotta ask. Are all our computers gonna die? And if they do, then what happens? Will airplanes fall out of the sky? Do you believe it, or is it nonsense?" the host demanded of his radio audience. "Call and tell me what you think."

Only a few techno-freaks called the talk show that day, and half said the millennium bug was no big deal and easily fixed. Besides, 2000 was a long way off, and long-term planning in America meant thinking about next week. No one in radioland seemed to be paying attention except Donald Copeland who experienced a vision that appeared to him like a giant equation written in fire across the skyline of Manhattan.

He could see the future. He knew exactly what was going to happen, when it would happen, and most importantly, how to profit from his prescience. The idea of a simple programming flaw bringing the entire world to its knees was so devastating that it rocked him like an earthquake. His mind leaped from one logical step to the next at lightning speed until the entire idea unfolded like a flower at dawn.

On January 1, 2000, chaos and disaster would sweep over the land, and only those organizations that had discovered and corrected their problems prior to that date would survive. Knowing who would survive, and perhaps deciding who would survive and who would fail, would be an unassailable business advantage.

Copeland had the means and the will to pursue his vision. The means included Michael "Doc" Downs, Ph.D., a young computer engineer from California who ran Copeland Investments' department of research and development.

Copeland sped to his office, an old three-story red brick building on Nassau Street in Lower Manhattan, only a few steps from Wall Street. Bursting with his vision, he skipped the elevator, ran up to Doc's third-floor office, and knocked on the door.

He heard banging and clanging from inside. "Doc!" he shouted. "Doc, I gotta talk to you right now!"

More knocking, more banging, and then from inside a shouted, "Come in!"

Excited, Copeland ran into Doc's workspace, a computer junkyard with spidery integrated circuits, CPUs and monitors scattered around like rubbish. As Copeland stepped in, Doc clobbered a balky monitor with the butt of a heavy screwdriver. The screen popped on and the engineer grinned. "When all else fails," he declared, "I resort to the big bang theory of component repair. Hit the son of a bitch and see what happens."

A big, bearded lumberjack of a man, twenty-three-year-old Doc smoked two packs of Camels and three joints of primo marijuana per day, lived on pizza and coffee, and wore flannel shirts, blue jeans, engineer's boots and a hunting cap with pull-down ear flaps. With an IQ running on afterburners, Doc had become a hacker at the age of eight by stealing his father's password and ogling Dad's computerized pornography collection. Known as "Doc" long before earning a doctorate from Stanford at twenty-one, he was a compleat computer geek. For the last two years he'd worked for Copeland and had become his captive wizard, turning Copeland's ideas into practical, profitable products.

"The millennium bug," Copeland said. "I just heard about it."

"You're a little slow on the uptake there, boss," Doc said, tossing the screwdriver aside. "We call it Y2K. That's geek jargon for Year 2000."

Copeland repeated the acronym like a mantra, "Y2K, Y2K."

Doc looked his boss up and down, sneering at his perfectly coifed hair, impeccable grooming, Savile Row suit and Italian wingtips.

"You have that look in your eye, Donald. You smell money."

"The best smell there is," Copeland said. "What do you know about this bug?"

"Plenty. Every programmer worth his salt knows about it."

"Educate me."

"It's going to be a catastrophe," Doc said, sitting down, leaning back and resting his boots on the workbench. "People won't understand it and aren't going to believe it."

"That's what this guy on the radio said. He scared the hell out of me."

"Well, that's good," Doc drawled, lighting a cigarette. "Just for starters, take Russia, for example. A few Russian nuclear reactors will probably melt down causing massive power failures that leave millions without heat in midwinter and nothing to eat but radiation. Then things will get really interesting." Eyes twinkling, he smiled and added, "It's going to cause the kind of mischief that makes a hacker's heart go pitty-pat."

"So what can we do about it?"

"For the Russians, nothing. But for the rest of us, well—" he paused "—it depends."

Doc patiently explained that to a programmer the millennium bug was a trivial problem to correct once the flawed computer code was located. However, the bug was replicated endlessly in date-sensitive programs, and finding each instance in systems with millions of lines of code and thousands of applications was a problem of massive proportions. Furthermore, old computer programs were often improperly documented and written in older computer languages such as COBOL and FORTRAN, making the flaws even more difficult to find. Most younger programmers never learned those languages.

"Can you devise a solution?" Copeland asked.

"Sure, but I'd have to specialize. Every application is different."

"Who has the most old applications?"

"Banks," Doc replied instantly.

"No shit," Copeland said, pleased with Doc's answer. "Do the banks know that?"

"They should, but they probably don't. I mean, programmers who work for banks know, they've known for a long time, but who listens to programmers? CEO types never turn on a computer, and they sure as shit don't know anything about their mainframes or their antique COBOL programs."

"How much would a fix be worth?" Copeland asked.

Doc grinned. "That's what this is all about, isn't it?"

"How much, Doc?"

"A fortune. Hundreds of billions, maybe more. Incomprehensible numbers."

"You like the idea?" Copeland asked.

"Do you mean, do I like the idea of writing programs to kill the bug?"

"Exactly."

"It has a certain appeal," Doc said, stroking his beard. "But on the other hand, we could let all these insane corporations die when their computers fail. That appeals as well."

"Be serious, Doc. What do you think of this as a business venture? Can we make money?"

"It's a winner, Donald. It's a license to print money."

"What do you need?" Copeland asked. "Just name it."

"Well, let's see. How about a big old IBM mainframe to play with, a few hundred applications and two or three engineers."

"That's it?"

"I suppose you could buy me a bank, Donnie boy, but why bother?"

The following day they visited a warehouse in Queens and bought a fifteen-year-old IBM s/370 mainframe. Doc tore out a wall on the third floor on Nassau Street, reinforced the floor, hired a crane, installed the machine, and named it Old Blue. He spent a month testing the software that came with it, and then called Copeland in for a demonstration.

"This is what the world is going to look like on the first of January in the year 2000," Doc announced to his audience of one. "What I'm about to show you is what will happen if things are simply left alone."

Old Blue had spent its working life performing accounting services for an insurance company. The computer wasn't that old, but like many firms the insurance company had upgraded its hardware while continuing to run the same old, flawed software. Doc booted up an accounting program based on actuarial tables, reset the time and date to one minute before midnight, December 31, 1999, and gave the program a simple problem to solve, a schedule of premium payments for twenty years. Lines of orderly green numbers scrolled across the screen for sixty seconds until the clock rolled over to midnight. The machine seemed to sputter and hiccup. Old Blue recognized the date "00" as 1900, not 2000, and assumed that numbers representing the near future belonged in the distant past. Simple arithmetical calculations were no longer simple. The machine tried to divide and multiply by negative numbers. Within seconds, Old Blue tried to calculate an infinite regression, and the numbers on the screen went haywire. The random access memory quickly overloaded and the accounting program crashed. The computer was dead.

"Voilà," said Doc, lighting a Camel.

At 6:30 every morning Copeland ate breakfast in the same Upper West Side delicatessen with three old friends he'd grown up with: a cop, a grocery store manager and a heart surgeon. Copeland was excited, bubbling over with enthusiasm for his Y2K venture, and within a week his pals had banned Y2K as a subject of conversation.

"The phones are gonna go down, the Internet will die, the military will be paralyzed, no one will get a welfare check, the IRS will be all screwed up, your microwave oven won't work, but that won't matter because there'll be no electricity."

"*Enough already*," pleaded Jonathon Spillman, the grocery store manager. "For God's sake."

"You're obsessive-compulsive, Donnie," said Bill Packard, the doctor. "You should get your head shrunk."

"Fuck you, Bill. This is gonna make me rich."

"You're already rich," said Ed Garcia, the cop. "Maybe you don't remember that you got rich financing computer companies that created this problem. If it's as bad as you say, maybe you should fix it for free."

"I didn't create the millennium bug," Copeland protested. "I discovered it."

"Like a gold mine," added Spillman. "You sound like a claim jumper to me. Should we hang him, boys, or just run him out of town?"

As friends who'd known each other since childhood will do, they teased Copeland without mercy to demonstrate their wish for his success. Intelligent men, they took his predictions of doom and destruction with a healthy ration of salt, but each filed away his knowledge of the millennium bug and wondered how it might affect his life at the turn of the century.

Copeland had a hunch that Y2K would generate the biggest return of any of his ideas, so rather than create a new company with his customary financial partners, he established a wholly-owned subsidiary called Copeland Solutions and financed the software development himself.

He was patient. He understood the realities of software development, the endless trial and error and testing and out-of-the-blue insight that led to success. Doc occasionally locked himself in the computer lab, got crazy, and burned a few million brain cells with amphetamines while thrashing away at his objective. Copeland left him alone, keeping busy with his other companies that made more than enough to support his Y2K project. Sometimes he didn't see Doc for weeks.

The '90s marched on. Copeland ate breakfast with his buddies every morning, took his wife Marie to dinner at the Four Seasons and his little boy Eddie to Yankee Stadium, but these were perfunctory activities that had nothing to do with his overweening passion for making money. He grew estranged from Marie and scarcely noticed as she drifted away. Eddie was raised by nannies. Copeland traded his Mercedes for a Cadillac and then the Caddy for a Porsche. Life got faster. He could speed across the East River, catch a glimpse of the skyline and be back in his office in minutes flat. It gave him an expensive thrill. For cheap thrills, he went to massage parlors in Chinatown and on autumn weekends visited a bookie in the fish market on Broadway at 83rd to lay a hundred bucks on the Jets.

Finally, two years after Copeland's epiphany on the bridge, Doc created a software package called "Copeland 2000" that targeted the millennium bug in old legacy systems used by banks. Dependent on mainframes like Old Blue running old applications, banks and other financial institutions with millions of lines of date-sensitive computer code were extremely vulnerable to the millennium bug. Copeland 2000 went to market in late 1993 and had few takers at first, credit unions and small savings and loan companies. Then, over the next two years, as other firms began offering Y2K software and sounding the alarm, more and more major companies began to realize that the millennium bug *was* serious. The big boys began to line up, and in 1995 Copeland Solutions scored its biggest coup: the Chase Manhattan Bank.

Chase had been among the first major banks to assess the Y2K problem and arrive at the correct conclusion. With 200 million lines of infected code spread among 1,500 different computer systems running thousands of applications, Chase had to eliminate the millennium bug from its systems or go out of business. It was that simple. There was no choice. The result was a $160 million contract with Copeland Solutions.

Other banks around the world quickly followed Chase into Copeland's stable of clients. Money poured into the company, yet, having achieved success, Copeland discovered he wasn't satisfied. The high wore off within a few weeks and he found himself feeling flat and bored. He wanted a new, more difficult challenge. Without realizing it, he was a crime waiting to happen.

Despite his reputation as a bold and ruthless businessman, even his old breakfast pals believed he was honest. The truth, however, was that Copeland was primed to consider criminal activity as the next step in business. After all, the line between venture capitalism and white-collar crime was fuzzy at best. All he needed was an opportunity, and one soon presented itself.

The Chase contract gave Copeland Solutions' programmers access to the bank's most sensitive data. Every account, record, and program had to be examined for millennium bug flaws and corrected. As this process began, it was only a matter of days before Doc started noticing discrepancies.

The bank was so big it didn't know how much money it had or where it was. The first interesting account Doc stumbled across dated from 1985. In that year a programmer working for the bank had managed to pull off what later was to become one of the most common forms of computer fraud in the banking business. Every time one of the bank's computers completed a foreign exchange transaction, it converted foreign currency to dollars and rounded off the number to the nearest mill. The anonymous programmer had written a tiny program that dumped each minuscule fraction of a mill into an account that didn't show up on regular records. As it happened, the programmer was hit by a truck and died the next year, but his program continued to function flawlessly without attracting the attention of any other Chase official. By 1995, when Doc got to the account, it held more than four million dollars the bank didn't know existed.

Doc mentioned the orphaned account to Copeland, recounting the tale as hacker's lore.

"If we left that account alone," Copeland mused, "how much would it be worth by the end of 1999?"

"Seven or eight million, and I'm sure I'll find more accounts like this."

"Adding up to how much, would you guess?"

"No way to tell, but maybe as much as a hundred mil."

"That could be a lot of free money," Copeland observed.

"Hell of a joke to play on the bank," Doc said.

"If the world goes all to hell in January 2000, it would be interesting to have that much cash when everyone else was going bankrupt."

"What are you suggesting, Donald?"

"Grand larceny."

"Oh, you wicked man," Doc observed.

"Just an idea," Copeland said. "Think about it."

"The bank has auditors checking our work," Doc cautioned. "They're not idiots. Chase expects us to find these accounts and report them."

"You're smarter than they are, Doc."

"We're already filthy rich, Donnie. Chase and all these other banks are going to make us even richer."

"So what? You've been saying for years what the millennium bug will do: disaster, utter disaster. The world is going to come apart at the seams, and something like this will give us a comfortable nest egg when others will have nothing."

"You're calling a hundred million dollars a nice little nest egg? Jesus."

"Well?" Copeland said. "You have a hacker's heart. You'll do it because you can."

"That's the problem, Donald. I have to do it. You can't."

"It'll be the biggest bank robbery in history," Copeland declared, "and the bank will never know it'd been robbed. With all the other disasters at the turn of the century, who's going to care?"

"Chase, for one."

"But they'll never know, Doc."

"You're a greedhead, Donald."

"Yeah. Like the man said, greed is good."

"Are you serious?" Doc asked.

"Yes, I'm serious. I've never been more serious. What the hell, the bank doesn't even know it has this money. It's there for the taking."

"You're a scumbag," Doc stated with barely disguised contempt. "We're selling software like crazy. This company is worth hundreds of millions. And you want to . . . ?"

"It'd be criminal not to do it if we can," Copeland said, grinning broadly. "It's the opportunity of a lifetime."

2

Doc's first inclination was to quit on the spot, but he enjoyed his work and didn't want to turn his life upside down quite yet. To keep Copeland happy, he agreed to play along with no real intention of robbing the bank. Twisted by dreams of immense wealth, Copeland believed the ability to steal the money gave him the right to take it. That was the mindset of the economic engine running the global economy, it seemed to Doc. Situational ethics run amok. Grab what you can and why not; everybody else does. In theory, the heist was possible because no computer security system was foolproof, but in practical terms it was a less-than-perfect crime. The bank had 200 Y2K drudges working full time at the Metro Tech Center in Brooklyn, and more than a few were good enough to detect a theft of such magnitude. Who would take the blame? The chief programmer. But fear wasn't the reason Doc wanted no part of Copeland's scheme. Humble in his way, Doc was an honest man, a species of humanity unknown to Donald Copeland who believed every intelligent person shared his ethic of callous selfishness. Doc liked money as much as the next guy, yet he clung to the old-fashioned idea that capital could be used for purposes beyond self-aggrandizement.

Having decided to play along, he convinced Copeland that taking the money all at once during the millennium crisis was safer than milking it a little at a time. To placate the boss, he wrote a bogus program that kept a running account of mythical funds for Copeland to check every day, sometimes several times a day.

As the numbers escalated, the company's legitimate earnings skyrocketed even more quickly. Copeland Solutions expanded rapidly, selling their Y2K software packages to commercial banks in the Philippines, Japan, Latvia, Sweden, Germany and Spain. In 1996 Doc earned six million dollars in bonuses alone—not much by Wall Street standards, but enough for him to do something meaningful.

Doc had taken on the Y2K challenge because it gave him a chance to save a small part of the world from imploding. He could write source code in his sleep and truly loved computers, but deep in his heart he believed the wanton application of computers to all aspects of daily life was often reckless and misguided.

Cybernetics had caused a radical change in global demographics, dividing populations into two camps: the technologically aware and everyone else. Each technological advance pushed the two camps farther apart. Y2K was going to be a watershed event that would transform the dividing line into a perilously deep chasm. Small companies and individuals who couldn't afford to revamp their computer systems were going to perish while powerful companies who bought Copeland 2000 or similar programs would emerge stronger than ever. It was going to be a war of attrition, and ordinary people, the millions who went to work every day and trusted the systems that made their lives possible—electricity, phones, the subway, water—were going to be caught in the crossfire.

Ethical and compassionate, Doc thought the little guys should have a fighting chance. He'd done his bit to save the big boys by creating programs to save Chase Manhattan and the other banks, but $160 million worth of Copeland 2000 software wouldn't help Chase if basic services shut down and New York collapsed. Doc felt the least he could do was try to save the city from itself. He would use his money to fund a project Copeland knew nothing about. Even if it failed, it would be an amusing antidote to Copeland's wild Hollywood scheme to rob the bank.

Posing the problem was easy: How do you keep the power on, the phones working, the water flowing and the subway running in New York City when the computers that controlled those systems failed? Answer: Build an alternate control center for every system, hardwire each to its original, and at midnight on New Year's Eve 1999, seize control of the systems and run them with a computer that hadn't been corrupted by the millennium bug.

Vital control systems always had redundant backup systems that kicked in if the primaries failed. The problem was that the backup systems contained the same Y2K flaws as the primaries. Nevertheless, it was the concept of redundancy that made Doc's project feasible. In the first few seconds of the 21st Century, all the key computers in the city's vital systems had to be tricked into switching over to secret alternates instead of their own flawed backups. Was that possible? It was a large and expensive undertaking, and to do it Doc needed to buy the hardware, steal the software, and find a handful of people he could trust.

"I'm building a new computer lab for a special project at my own expense," he said to Copeland. "I'm paying, so don't worry about it. I don't want internal audits or anything like that, and I want you to keep out."

"What're you gonna do in there?"

"The world will be a mess after the century rollover. Maybe I can develop some software to put it back together."

Copeland pursed his lips and his mind clicked over. "Telecommunications, operating systems of all kinds, things like that?"

"I'm just gonna play around with a few things."

"I want a piece of that action," Copeland said.

"Talk to me in January 2000, but for now, can it, Donnie."

Reluctantly, Copeland agreed, and took off on a long tour around the world visiting clients and drumming up business. When he returned, he looked in once, asked no questions, and honored Doc's request to keep away.

First, Doc sealed off the rear sixty feet of the third floor in the building on Nassau Street and bought a brand new IBM s/390 mainframe. He divided 9000 square feet into space for the computer, a huge air-conditioner, a half dozen large workstations with dozens of terminals and monitors, a telephone switching station, a bedroom, bathroom, kitchen and lounge with TVs, a high-end audio system, and old leather couches. When everything was in order, he started to search for people.

He didn't have to look far to find his first recruit. Late one night he was working alone on a Chase terminal at the Metro Tech Center, scanning an electronic fund transfer program for flawed code. A window on his screen told him how many authorized users were using the system at that moment, which was zero. Around three in the morning someone logged on, but instead of transferring money between accounts, the user attempted to unlock the protocol files Doc was working on. It was an eerie moment in cyberspace. Doc promptly traced the call to a Chase commercial branch in Boston.

The next afternoon he hopped a shuttle to Boston, showed the branch manager his legitimate credentials as the bank's chief Y2K consultant, and asked to be introduced to the back office staff.

One of the people the manager introduced him to was a thin, relaxed, 24-year-old African-American programmer named Bo Daniels. Dressed in tidy banker's clothes, Bo stood up from his terminal to shake hands with Doc, who said, "Innumber 437 hop 22 halt bang path."

Bo's hand froze in mid-handshake. Doc had uttered the UNIX commands that had led Bo on his illicit mission inside the fund transfer protocol.

"Well, you lost me," said the manager, who excused himself and left them alone.

"May I?" Doc gestured toward a chair.

They sat in silence. Bo studied his fingernails and wondered if he could crawl into his computer and disappear.

Doc turned a beatific smile on the young man, stroked his beard, and waited. He finally said, "It was you, wasn't it?"

The programmer offered a sly smile and asked, "You gonna turn me in?"

"I don't know yet," Doc replied. "If I were going to commit computer theft, I'd go right to Innumber 437, just like you did."

"I just wanted to see if I could do it," Bo said. "If I can, then someone else can. The bank is vulnerable."

"Did you file a breach of security report?"

"No."

"Why not?"

Bo shrugged and didn't answer. "Tell me what else you can do," Doc asked.

"You want to see my resumé?"

"I don't think you'd put what I want to know in a resumé," Doc said. "How good are you? Can you write COBOL?"

They spoke geek for twenty minutes. Doc thought Bo was more than competent. He was a wickedly bright but frustrated artist hiding behind a starched shirt and suspenders. When Doc was satisfied that Bo knew enough and could learn what he didn't know, he offered him a job.

"Doing what? Y2K?"

"Something like that." Doc leaned forward and quietly said, "Here's the deal: four times the salary you're making now, a nice bonus down the line, long hours, no sleep, no dress requirements, and whatever you need to keep you going. Sex, drugs or rock and roll, I don't care. I'm leaving you a ticket to New York and a thousand dollars. You can show or not. It's up to you."

A week later Bo arrived at Nassau Street dressed like Jimi Hendrix. Doc discovered he could play a computer the way Jimi played guitar, and he was willing to play for Doc. A virtuoso, Bo could write twelve computer languages from COBOL to Java, and analyze a database management system faster than a Cray supercomputer. More than anything else, he understood how a complex series of systems worked together.

"What do you know about the generation and distribution of electric power?" Doc asked.

"Nothing."

"That's a good place to start because you won't have to unlearn anything. How long do you think you'd need to understand a power plant?"

"Oh, I don't know. A couple of years, at least."

"How about six weeks?"

"Impossible."

"Nothing is impossible to a willing heart. Disraeli said that. Sit down and look at this," Doc said, ushering Bo into a chair. He turned on a terminal, and the screen came up bright blue with simple text:

CON EDISON RESTORATION ASSISTANT
OPERATOR'S TRAINING SIMULATOR
CHOOSE INCIDENT TYPE

"This simulator is where the company trains advanced operators to deal with breakdowns and blackouts," Doc explained. "Lesson one: Bringing the power back on after a failure is called 'restoration.'"

"How'd you get this?" Bo asked, incredulous.

"There's only one way," Doc replied. "I hacked it from the ConEd command center. The simulator isn't nearly as secure as the system itself, but it contains an excellent model of the entire Northeast power grid that's updated weekly. Once you're familiar with the simulator and the model, we can go after the real thing because the model tells us where everything is."

Bo blinked rapidly, his mind whirring away. "You mean you want to hack into ConEd and steal their entire operating system?"

"More or less. Maybe a hundred or so applications. Only the parts we need."

"Need to do what?"

"Keep the power on in Manhattan," Doc answered with a wide grin, "from here."

"You're crazy."

"Correctamento, I'm crazy, but that's a given. The question is, are *you* crazy enough to become Con Edison, Bo? You have two and a half years to learn every system, every application, the location of every embedded chip. You can learn to reconfigure the system, make all the Y2K corrections, and, yes, keep the lights on in Manhattan at the moment of the century rollover. That's the idea. If ConEd can't do it, you will."

"Mamma mia. I don't know." Bo whistled and played a little air guitar. "Plus data, I suppose."

"Correct. Plus data which we check for Y2K and fix, the long, hard way. First we learn how to isolate ConEd from the grid, and then how to isolate Manhattan and the four power plants on the island plus one in Queens from the rest of ConEd. We need the operating systems of each of the five plants, plus the system operation that ties them together."

"And we're supposed to do this by ourselves, just the two of us?"

"No. We need phones, so I'm looking for a phone freak to keep the lines open, and I'm looking for a train freak to run the subway. Maybe a few more. If you make it to January 1st, 2000, there will be a bonus of a million dollars for each of you."

Bo didn't need to think about that for long. "You have that kind of money?" he asked.

"It's already in escrow. The money's there."

"What do you get out of it?" Bo asked.

"Sanity," Doc replied, reaching across Bo to the simulator key-board. He punched "Choose Incident" from the simulator menu and selected "Total System Failure."

The screen began to flash and beep a noisy alarm.

"Just do it," Doc said and handed Bo a Nike cap.

Over the next month Doc interviewed four more hackers who failed to meet his standards. They either didn't know enough, took too many bad drugs, or were so anarchic and downright criminal that he'd never be able to keep them in line. Then he discovered Carolyn Harvey.

Carolyn's idea of fun was breaking into telephone companies' computers, stealing the phone records of prominent individuals, and posting them on the Web. Doc studied her website, "Fone-Freek.com," and followed her electronic trail to a little house in Nashville, Tennessee. A big Harley was parked out front, and Doc left a note on the motorcycle.

"FoneFreek. In town searching for talent," he wrote, and added the number of his hotel. She called.

"What kind of talent?" she asked.

"Ever seen the machine code for the programmable logic pro-cessor in a DESS-5?"

"Yeah. So?"

Doc asked a few more technical questions and liked her answers enough to ask, "How would you like a phone company of your very own?"

"Ooo," she said. "That would be fun. What can I do with it?"

"Anything you want as long as you can keep it working."

"Who are you anyway?" she asked

"The Lone Ranger," Doc said. "Captain America, Yojimbo the

samurai warrior, the man with no name. You can call me Doc. Will you meet me for a drink?"

"I don't have much to do with men," she said.

"Consider me a fellow geek and nothing more," he declared. "I have real money, a legitimate company, and a job for the right person. I need someone who's interested in computers that run telephone systems."

"This sounds like industrial espionage," she said.

"It's much better than that."

They met at the Connection, a warehouse saloon for the adventurous. Carolyn turned out to be a leather-girl motorcycle dyke with a butch haircut and braces on her teeth.

"You Doc?"

"Yes, ma'am."

"What's this about?"

"Y2K."

"Ooo. I like it already. You can buy me a drink."

"Communications will be vital on the big day," Doc explained as they sat in a corner away from the music. "We'll need working phone lines, and T-4 lines direct to the power company's control center and power plants and to the subway's central dispatch center. We'll also need an in-house router hub, telcom center and interconnect. Think you can handle all of that?"

"Are you rich?" she asked.

"Got it covered. You'll have to trace the lines and physically check every switch."

"I'll need a phone company truck."

"Okay."

"Logic probes, a lot of stuff."

"Anything you need."

"This could be the biggest phone goof of all time. Wow."

"Yes, but you can't talk about it with your buddies. No bragging rights."

"I don't know about that," she said.

"That's part of the package. For two and a half years this will be your life, and the rest of the world will cease to exist."

Doc offered her the same money and bonus as Bo, a considerably better deal than her job as a lowly programmer for Bell South. The next day he took her to New York and introduced her to Bo.

"I'm Con Edison," Bo said. "Who are you?"

"I guess I'm Bell Atlantic," Carolyn answered.

Ronnie Fong was a fatally cute young Chinese woman from San Francisco with four nose rings, each of which represented a triumphant computer break-in at the Department of Defense. DOD hadn't exactly proved she'd done it, but they'd offered her a job hacking into computers at the Chinese Ministry of Defense. She'd laughed at them. When Doc called, she naturally believed he was a missionary from her nemesis in the Pentagon. He asked her to meet him at Mario's Bohemian Cigar Store, a North Beach café.

"The only reason I came," she said when she walked into the café, "is because otherwise you DOD people won't leave me alone."

"I'm not one of them," Doc protested.

"Then how did you find me? How do you even know about me?" Angry and defiant, she refused a menu, folded her arms across her chest and dared him to speak.

"You know about Y2K?" he asked.

"What about it?"

"Where are you planning on greeting the millennium?"

"At a friend's place with its own generators and solar panels."

"So you get the picture."

She shrugged.

"How would you like to spend New Year's Eve in New York?"

"Are you out of your mind? That's the last place I'd want to be."

"How would you like to be in New York and running computers for the New York City Department of Environmental Protection?

That's their fancy name for the water department." She looked at him like he was out of his mind. "You could add another ring to your collection," he added.

"This is a con job," she said. "You're DOD."

"How can I prove I'm not? If I was, I wouldn't be sitting here talking to you. I'd be taking you away in handcuffs." He handed her a plane ticket and cash. "Come to New York and decide for yourself. You'll be the water department, and just to keep you interested, we need to be kept up-to-date on Space Command in Colorado Springs. Your familiarity with military computers will come in handy."

"For real?"

"For money."

"How much money?"

Doc scribbled a number on a napkin and Ronnie counted the zeros.

"That make it worth it?"

Ronnie arrived on Nassau Street skeptical and suspicious until Doc helped her hack into a database at one of New York's fourteen sewage treatment plants. Inside the water department's computer, he took her behind the data to the machine language, a tiny portion of which he'd reverse compiled into source code written in a mishmash of seventeen different computer languages. It was a Y2K problem of the worst order containing hidden date fields, programmer errors, kludges, and previous bad fixes.

"If this isn't fixed, the city of New York will be buried in human fecal matter," Doc said. "There's no problem getting water into the city. New York has a fabulous water supply system that's almost entirely gravity-driven. The problem will be getting the dirty water out."

"What are they doing about it?" Ronnie asked.

"They?" he hooted. "There is no 'they.' 'They' is a myth. In this case, 'they' will be you. And even if you duplicate all this software and make it work, the water system has thousands of embedded chips in pumps and valves and all over the place." Doc grinned and unrolled a huge map. "This is a detailed diagram of all the pipes, tunnels, and treatment plants, the entire sewer system of Manhattan. I've traced the critical paths and marked the pumps. You can visit every one."

"Good Lord, this is a shitty job."

"You have to get your hands dirty to earn your million bucks, Ronnie."

"And when I'm not down in the sewers, I get to play with Space Command, right?"

"Right. We need to track communication and radio-navigation satellites. There's no code work involved, only monitoring. When the big night comes, we'll need to know what's working and what isn't."

"You're asking for a lot," Ronnie said.

"Yes. I'm asking for the impossible. Are you in?"

"We're close to Chinatown, right?"

"Yeah. Just a few blocks."

"There has to be a catch."

"There is," Doc said. "For two and a half years, you'll have no other life."

"This is making me thirsty," Ronnie said. "Can I make some tea?"

When Ronnie came out of the kitchen, Doc was gone and Bo and Carolyn were in the lounge.

"What kind of music do you like?" Carolyn asked. "I like anything loud."

"That's cool," Ronnie said. "You know, what I would like is some way to make this pot of tea more interesting."

Adrian Hoffman was a tubby little Florida nerd who got a thrill from bringing railroad traffic control systems to a screeching halt. Adrian's favorite trick was hacking into a railroad's signaling systems, setting all signals to red, and shutting down dozens of trains at once.

"You don't care for trains?" Doc asked via e-mail.

"I love trains. I have the world's biggest train set, Amtrak."

"Do you ever set the signals to green?"

"I don't want to kill anyone," Adrian replied.

"How old are you?" Doc asked.

"Eighteen."

"How do you feel about metropolitan transportation systems?"

"They're cool."

"Do you think you could run the New York City subway system?"

"Lots of trains. Lots of signals. Yeah, sure."

"The idea is to keep the trains running, not shut them down."

"Turnabout is fair play," Adrian wrote.

"I'll send you a plane ticket and a thousand bucks."

"No. Make it a train ticket. This is way cool. I've never been to New York."

Four days later Doc sat with Adrian in Penn Station thinking: problem child, basket case, wacko, borderline psychotic, but Jesus, does he know his stuff. Adrian looked like a classic nerd with his thick glasses and grungy long hair. He almost never spoke and brought with him a detailed compilation of every computer system used by America's six largest railroads.

"Wanna see New York?" Doc asked.

Doc didn't take him to the Empire State Building or Central Park. Instead, they spent twelve hours on the subway. Adrian stood in the front car with a view of the track ahead, and in this manner they criss-crossed the city from Far Rockaway to Riverdale, underground, aboveground, through bridges and tunnels, the trains roaring down the tracks, the signals stretched out in the darkness, green and red, an ever-beckoning stream of lights. They stopped at Grand Central and a subway yard in Queens where the platform overlooked a fleet of trains. Adrian soaked it up like a sponge, saying little, and after a couple of hours was directing the tour himself.

"This is your new train set, Adrian. That cool with you?"

"I dig it," Adrian said. "Okay."

To round out his team Doc needed an overall hardware specialist who could keep the computers and communication equipment in tip-top shape. Bo knew of a hacker from San Jose who'd stolen advanced microprocessor designs from Intel and attempted to sell them to an Indonesian cartel. His name was Judd Fernandez and he wasn't hard to locate. Doc was waiting when he walked out of San Quentin dressed in a three-piece suit that complemented his shaved head and trim goatee.

"Need a job?" Doc asked him outside the prison gate.

"I need a drink. Who the fuck are you?"

"A guy offering you a job, a real job, not one that will send you back to the joint."

"Take me to the No Name Bar in Sausalito and buy me a Bud first."

During his three-year sojourn in prison, Judd had managed San Quentin's computer system and had earned a reputation on the Net as a hardware guru.

"How much did the Indonesians offer you?" Doc asked over a beer in Sausalito.

"Not enough."

"How much is enough?"

"I'm not interested in money."

"What then?"

"Time," Judd replied. "I want time. I just gave away three years that I'll never get back."

"Okay," Doc said. "Give me two years and you'll have the rest of your life."

"I have other offers," he said.

"I know," Doc said. "You're famous."

"What's the job?"

After Doc outlined his project, Judd looked around the bar, then said, "I could go for a little New York, but you'll have to clear it with my parole officer."

A couple of days later Judd walked slowly around the IBM s/390, a vertical box of burnished metal six feet six inches tall, five feet wide and four feet deep. The mainframe. The big, bad 'puter that was going to power up New York. Inside the box were 120 central processing units, seven operating systems, and more memory than all the elephants in Africa. Lying next to the computer on the floor, an imposing stack of paper three feet high was waiting: the operating manual. Instruction one: plug it in. Instruction two: this is the "on" button. Christ almighty, he thought. He grabbed the top four inches and started to read.

3

"You are soldiers now and must conduct yourselves with military discipline," Doc said to his assembled team. "It may seem overstated and melodramatic, but it's the only way to get this project done on time."

"Do we have to salute?" Bo asked sarcastically.

"No."

"Wear uniforms?"

"No."

"I like uniforms," Ronnie declared. "Let's have uniforms."

"Uniforms would draw attention, and that's not allowed. There's only going to be one rule," Doc said. "You can't talk about what you do here. No one outside the project can ever get the slightest whiff of what we're doing. No one." Doc watched their faces as the implications of his rule seeped in. "You have friends, family, lovers, even enemies," he went on, "and you can't tell them what you're doing. It's like doing classified work for the CIA. It's secret, and secret means secret. No exceptions."

"What should we tell people, then?" Bo asked. "I talk to my mother almost every day. If I don't call her, she'll track me down and show up here."

"Tell your mother you're employed by a software company in

New York and you're working on Y2K. Don't tell them anything if you can avoid it. Anyone have a problem with this?"

"What happens if we break the rule?" Adrian asked.

"You're on your honor not to," Doc said. "I'm not going to follow you around or tap your phone."

"But what if we do?" Adrian persisted.

"Then you're gone, adios, good-bye. No money, no fun and games, no million-dollar bonus."

"How will you know?"

Doc glared at Adrian and thought he'd made a mistake. He never should have let the kid get past Penn Station. He should've bought him a return ticket and sent him back to Florida, but here he was on Nassau Street with his spacey eyes and Grateful Dead hair and, "I don't wanna follow no rules, nya nana na na." To hell with that.

"Are you going to be a pain in the ass, Adrian?" Doc snapped.

"I just don't like rules, anybody's rules."

"We can argue about anything else, and I'm sure we will, but not about this. If you don't get it, Adrian, I'm sorry. The end. You can go home right now."

Doc grabbed a phone, dialed directory assistance, and said, "Amtrak, please."

"Wait a minute," Judd said. "Let me talk to him."

"Please do."

Judd put his arm around Adrian's shoulders and drew him off into a corner.

"What's your problem?" Judd asked quietly.

"I can't stand rules."

"We're only going to have one. A hacker should understand that if you talk, you get caught and they take your toys away. Down in Florida you had one old PC. Here, you have a huge fucking mainframe and anything else you want. You don't want to lose that, do you?"

Adrian folded his arms across his chest and fumed.

"This isn't school," Judd said. "I know what kind of a guy you are, Adrian. You're the kid nobody likes, the kid people make fun of because you're so fucking smart. You use your intelligence as a weapon and tear into them, don't you? You laugh at their mistakes in school and they hate you and you hate them. Am I right? I can see it in your eyes. You screw around with the trains because it gives you a sense of power, and every time you do it and don't get caught, you feel even more powerful. But listen to this, you little shit. Doc found you, and that means sooner or later you would've been caught, and if you caused a train wreck, you'd be sent to the slammer, like me. Doc saved your ass from getting into real trouble, and you owe him. We all do. All of us have gone through what you've experienced. Bo, Carolyn, Ronnie, and me, too, we're all smart, and we've all been laughed at and teased and we've all thought of revenge. Revenge put me in prison. Doc wants us to do something important, and if you can't handle that, if you can't put away your bullshit and nerdy little thoughts of revenge and getting even, well, forget it. Are you too selfish to understand that? Are you just a little asshole? We don't have time to fuck around here. Get with the program now, or go back to Orlando."

A little wheel turned over in Adrian's mind, and he understood he was being treated like an adult for the first time. Or the last time.

"No talking, no bragging," he said. "I get it."

"I don't want to have to babysit you. Now, are you in or out?"

"I don't want to go back to Florida."

"*Doc!*"

"Yeah."

"He's gonna be okay."

They all came from places deep in the American soul, the black middle class, the barrio, Chinatown, the dispossessed working class, and had used their brains to enter the world of technology. Each had taken an unorthodox route to cybernetics and computers, and Doc had chosen them because he knew mavericks often had the keenest, most creative minds.

Ronnie Fong was the daughter of immigrants from Hong Kong who'd rejected her because she'd rejected the restrictions of their traditions. At the same time she clung to her culture. In New York she shopped and ate in Chinatown and delighted in speaking Cantonese with the fishmonger. In her heart she believed a million dollars would go a long way toward a reconciliation with her family in San Francisco.

Carolyn Harvey had been ostracized by her family because she was flamboyantly gay. Technology was her release from a world of prejudice and fear, and she'd created an identity based on defiance. Coming to New York was an act of liberation. There, in the crush of people of every possible description, she didn't have to explain or defend herself. She could just be, and she turned her back on Nashville without a second thought.

Bo Daniels' father was an accountant and his mother owned a fashionable boutique. He spoke middle-class English with a Boston accent, went to all the right schools, and had learned early on that computers didn't care if he was black or white. Chase had hired him right out of Boston College, put him in the back room of the Boston branch and left him alone. As he watched the drones in the bank being moved around like chess pieces by higher management, he'd decided he didn't want a career at Chase. Corporate culture didn't interest him unless he created it, and that wouldn't happen at Chase or any other bank. He wanted to jump right to the top and be the boss. Less of an outlaw than the others, he had an entrepreneurial spirit and saw in his new work an opportunity to go into business for himself. In the months after the millennium bug struck, he figured electric utilities would need new software to get up and running again. Bo and Doc agreed that the software they were developing for ConEd could be repackaged and sold after January 1, 2000.

Judd Fernandez's Mexican mother had raised him alone in the

barrios of San Jose. Surrounded by poverty and gangs, he had enough sense to look beyond the low-rider life around him to the neatly trimmed industrial parks that sprouted like mushrooms right next door in Silicon Valley. He wanted a job as a programmer, and there were jobs galore, but not for him. He was a punk from the barrio, self-taught, with no recognized merit badges and unskilled at writing sophisticated resumés. His talents went unrecognized. Rebuffed when he applied for work as a programmer at Intel, he decided to get even. He hacked into Intel's most secure systems and stole schematics for a dozen new chips. Then, full of himself, he took his stolen goods to Los Angeles and was snared in a sting by the LAPD. Tried in superior court, he was sent to state prison for three years. Getting caught selling the goods in no way diminished his achievement of hacking into Intel and downloading their most precious files. In hackerland, that was extreme, perhaps beyond belief, and no one would have believed it if it hadn't been proven in court.

And finally there was Adrian Hoffman whose life might have been a sequel to *Natural Born Killers*. He grew up in seven different trailer parks in Central Florida. His mom was a ticket seller at Disneyworld, and his dad drank himself to death when Adrian was twelve. Adrian was a totally dysfunctional human being from Kmart America with one saving grace. He understood the relationship between trains and computers better than anyone on the planet.

The day after Judd dressed him down, Adrian disappeared for three days. Doc was ready to replace him when he realized the kid was riding subway trains and exploring the city's private railroad.

"For God's sake, Adrian," Doc pleaded when the prodigal returned, "just tell somebody where you're going and what you're doing."

To keep him around Nassau Street, Doc bought HO scale models of the subway trains and let Adrian build a layout in the computer lab. With gentle coaxing, Doc got him to model the subway's signal system and use the toy trains to test his software patches.

Doc bought a huge condo a few blocks from Nassau Street in Battery Park City for them, and they had no choice but to learn to live and work together. Their constant proximity produced countless squabbles, two relationships and one breakup, but ultimately, using gentle persuasion, sensitive guidance and the discipline of an implacable deadline, Doc forged them into a unified team with a mission. By the end of 1997 the mission had taken possession of their psyches, and they gradually began to withdraw from the world. Outside relationships became difficult as the constraints of secrecy and silence made anything beyond small-talk impossible.

Judd helped by recounting how he'd learned to live in prison. "Just keep yourself to yourself and live in your heads," he told them, and their heads became a collective head as their ethnic and personal identifications faded away. It wasn't long before they were swept up in the urgency of their task. Two and a half years seemed like a long time, but it grew shorter every day. Nothing could be put aside or left undone.

Ronnie quickly became an expert in the city's water supply that flowed from the Catskills through hundreds of miles of tunnels, aqueducts and reservoirs. Adrian played with his model trains and took sight-seeing trips through the tunnels and into the yards. Carolyn walked the streets of Manhattan, following phone lines from junction box to building to Bell Atlantic router. Doc bought her a truck, a hard hat and genuine Bell Atlantic ID, and she went into the tunnels beneath the streets, inspected the lines foot by foot and tested every chip with a logic probe. In a year she worked her way a hundred blocks from Nassau Street to the ConEd Systems Command Center at 65th and West End Avenue, and from there to the four power plants on the island and the huge Ravenswood plant across the East River in Queens. When she finished hardwiring the lines to the power plants, she started on the lines from Nassau

Street to the Department of Environmental Protection offices in the Bronx and the subway's central dispatch office in Brooklyn.

Bo visited the bookstores around Columbia University and bought himself an education in electrical engineering for a few hundred dollars. An ordinary computer nerd would have hacked into ConEd and stolen applications without knowing or caring about the physical systems they controlled. That wasn't good enough. Bo had to know how and why and where, and in the end, who.

Six months after he started, Bo knew more about Con Edison than the CEO, Mr. Peter Wilcox, whose e-mail he could read although he didn't have time. He knew where the different subsystems worked together efficiently and where they didn't, and which sub-stations between Manhattan and the power plants were likely to blow like weak links in a chain. He'd figured out how to correct the Y2K problems and build a system that would keep the power on in Manhattan, but he had no way to trick the power company into switching over to the computer on Nassau Street. He needed secret override passwords to put his knowledge to work.

"Well," Doc asked him one day in 1998, "can we save New York?"

"Not without help," Bo answered. "I need someone inside who can give me passwords. Without the override codes, at the moment of the century rollover, I'm dead in the water. Find me a spy."

"No problem," Doc replied. "They're all over the Internet."

Finding an insider who occupied a key position in the power company's control rooms was less difficult than finding competent hackers. No one had a better understanding of Y2K problems than the hardcore professionals who sat at the controls. These men and women communicated extensively via the Internet, often using pseudonyms to hide their identities. Power plant engineers, telephone system programmers, transit system authorities, and dozens more exchanged ideas and technical information in cyberspace.

Doc logged on to the Usenet and within a month had found an engineer who posted messages under the name "Deep Volt." A senior operator at ConEd's system operations command center, Deep Volt was convinced the power grid was going to fail. Doc started sending the anonymous engineer the locations of Y2K bugs Bo had found that were missed by the company's own Y2K programmers. In exchange, Deep Volt provided secret documents, applications and system schematics. They had their insider, and from that moment on, the work progressed much more quickly.

As they got into it, they started to call themselves the Midnight Club. Ronnie had T-shirts printed with the skyline of Manhattan at night. They worked like dogs, and by the end of 1998 they'd ascertained the city's true state of readiness for the coming assault. The prospects were dismal.

After spending several hundred million on Y2K, Con Edison had the most advanced remediation program of any power company in the world, but the giant utility was at the mercy of malfunctions anywhere on the Northeast electrical grid. The interconnected systems were so complex that the chances of every company on the grid making each fix exactly right were nil. Probability studies predicted failure. If the power went down, nothing else would matter.

The telephone system had the best chance of survival because Bell Atlantic had done everything they could think of at a company-wide level to correct their Y2K problems, replacing embedded chips in routers and switches and checking every application for flaws. At the local level the work was uneven and inconsistent. Like every other system, Bell Atlantic was part of a wider network of interconnected systems, and the interconnects were extremely vulnerable and subject to failure.

The Department of Environmental Protection had one of the oldest, most decrepit computer systems the Midnight Club had ever seen. Like many city departments, the DEP was the private bailiwick of senior managers who dwelled in their own hermetically sealed universe. Their system had worked efficiently for decades and they saw no reason to change.

"We'll just have to do it for them," Doc said.

The Metropolitan Transit Authority had recognized the Y2K problem early, and the overall compliance was remarkably advanced, but the subway's train control system was ancient, having been hardly touched since the 1950s. The advantage of running an antique was that the electrical relays were mechanical devices without embedded chips. The trains would be safe, but the problems lay in the automated train boards at the MTA's traffic control center on Jay Street in Brooklyn. Adrian found undetected millennium bug flaws that would shut down the screens, and the system operators wouldn't be able to see where the trains were. They'd have to rely on the MTA's radio communication system, which was dependent on flawed chips in the radio transmitters. When the screens and communications failed, the system would come to an immediate halt.

Left alone, New York's most vital systems would break down. In midwinter, the technological overlay that made the city work would be stripped away like bad varnish, reducing New York to medieval conditions. Projecting what would happen after that depended on one's view of human nature. If people were evil and wicked, then looting and pillaging would be the order of the day. On the other hand, if the citizens of New York were concerned with their mutual benefit and survival, people would adapt and help one another. Doc believed he'd see plenty of both.

After two years, the Midnight Club had hardened into dedicated, militant soldiers of cyberspace. They were ready to take over and operate the deep infrastructure of the island of Manhattan, but they needed the essential Con Edison override passwords for the final switchover. With them, they had a chance to wrest control from the ConEd computers and save the island from a massive power failure. Without them, New York was kaput.

With six months left, they had almost everything they needed, but not quite. Deep Volt was unable to obtain an essential set of

ConEd passwords that unlocked the override controls that switched the primary system to the backup. Without those passwords, Bo's work would go for naught. Instead of switching to Nassau Street, the ConEd computers would switch to their own backup systems that contained the same flaws as the primary, and power would be lost. The passwords were kept on a locked PC with no connection to the outside world, and there was no way to hack in and get them.

"Your spy isn't worth a damn," Bo complained.

"She's doing the best she can," Doc said in her defense. "She's risking her job. If she breaks in and steals the passwords, she'll be caught and they'll change the passwords."

"There must be a way," Bo insisted. "Find a thief."

"Thieves don't advertise on the Net."

The Midnight Club was isolated from the rest of the city, but they weren't operating in a vacuum. By March of 1999 news of the coming millennium bug was beginning to reach the general public. In that month companies whose fiscal year began in March started encountering problems they hadn't expected. If no man is an island, neither is a company. The world was learning that virtually all the computers on the planet were part of one huge network that was as vulnerable as the weakest link. Firms who believed their systems were Y2K compliant suddenly found their expensive new software was corrupted by files imported from suppliers and customers who were not compliant. The technical difficulties of finding corrupted code in a maze of computer languages, lost documentation and shoddy programming became apparent. Bankruptcies mounted and panic began to creep into the financial community. Companies that had delayed the allocation of funds for Y2K because they believed the return on investment was zero realized they'd made a mistake. To their horror they discovered that no programmers were available to sort out their problems. It was too late. Every month as another round of firms began their fiscal year, the problems intensified. Billing and accounting programs went haywire, exactly the way Doc had demonstrated on Old Blue.

People looked to the federal government for leadership, but none was forthcoming. The Senate and House held hearings and experts repeated what they'd been saying for years, and the result was to call more panels of experts and create bureaucracies that argued over definitions. Every day, as the inevitable deadline crept closer, the responsible authorities argued and debated and discussed, and another day was lost. Unclear on the concept, the government foundered. Agencies such as the Social Security Administration that had been working on Y2K since 1989 learned that inadequate measures in other agencies thwarted their meeting objectives. When 2000 arrived, Social Security would be able to distribute funds, but the Treasury Department would be unprepared to cut checks. Faced with impending paralysis within its own systems, the government was revealed as powerless and irrelevant, reduced to nothing more than an obstacle and a nuisance.

Millennia, years, days, and nanoseconds are convenient ways of measuring time, and accurately measuring time is important to computers. Units of time are finite objects a computer can recognize and count, and it is the counting that allows a computer to compute. Computers count time as a way of sequencing processes. One of the first things a computer does when it is turned on is tell itself the time and date.

The millennium bug was not the only date-related problem confronted by computers in 1999. Many systems were based entirely on date and time, including the Global Positioning System, GPS, a satellite-based system of radio-navigation used world-wide by American and allied military units, civilian ships at sea, aircraft, motor vehicles and geophysical researchers. Every telephone company in America used GPS to set the clocks that ran their switching stations, billing procedures and maintenance schedules.

GPS was operated by the United States Air Force Space Command who maintained a fleet of 24 satellites, and a radio fix from three birds was sufficient to locate a position anywhere on the globe. Anyone could buy a GPS receiver, tune in the satellites and use the system. Long before the night of August 21–22, 1999, the Air Force widely disseminated the news that on that date the nature of the data beamed down from the satellites was going to change. Older GPS receivers required a new chip in order to correctly interpret the data and determine an accurate position. So many millions of craft depended on the system that failure in only one percent amounted to thousands of receivers that hadn't been upgraded.

Despite the warnings, on August 22 the world was surprised by a wave of disastrous accidents caused by simultaneous computer malfunctions all over the globe. In foggy San Francisco Bay two oil tankers collided, polluting the harbor with millions of gallons of crude. In Rotterdam a liquid petroleum gas ship rammed a pier and the ensuing explosion destroyed the pier and a railroad yard and killed 327 people. Small boats were especially vulnerable, and dozens of inexperienced sailors who depended on the system and had never learned the basics of navigation without instruments were lost at sea.

The GPS rollover was not a millennium bug problem, per se, but it was similar and came at a time when Y2K was in the news every day. People began to look at computers as Trojan horses, and all the old fears from the early days of computing were brought back to life. In the '50s and '60s the huge, cumbersome machines of that era had inspired dread. Workers had believed they would be replaced by automated machines, and they were. Students had rebelled against being treated like computer punch cards, and movies like *2001* had envisioned menacing machines making war on humanity. Cartoon characters had stalked the pages of *The New Yorker* with signs that read, "The end is near, computers are here." Computers were strange, threatening, and misunderstood, but over time they'd been accepted, embraced, and ultimately ignored, if never properly understood. As Y2K loomed nearer, the cartoons reappeared depicting a life-and-death struggle between Man and Machine. In late 1999 pundits began asking the question: What have we wrought? No one had answers that made sense. *Newsweek* and *Time* featured articles on cybernetically isolated colonies of computer scientists that had sprung up in Arizona and New Mexico. These knowledgeable men and women believed a disaster was on its way, and they'd sold their securities, withdrawn their money from banks and built fortresses to protect themselves and their families. As experts continued to contradict one another and wild predictions of an apocalypse crowded the headlines, people became confused and frightened. Every error on a bank statement was blamed on the millennium bug.

On October 1 a severe round of fiscal year computer meltdowns delivered yet another blow to the economy. On that day the federal fiscal year began, and inadequate remediation inside dozens of federal agencies became apparent. Projections failed. Planning became impossible. Government procurement agencies suddenly couldn't buy anything because they'd lost track of purchase orders and invoices. Military logistics systems lost control of entire supply chains, and the ripple effect sent a shock wave through the economy. Companies who depended on government orders saw the bottom fall out of their stock value. Technology stocks tumbled, and lawsuits, long predicted as the most expensive part of the Y2K problem, began to clog the courts as the real debate began on the issue of who was responsible for the millennium bug, and who was going to pay for the losses. The answer: everybody.

Despite all the publicity, opinion surveys in late December 1999 revealed that a third of the American people had never heard of Y2K or the millennium bug. People knew that many government computers were not working properly without understanding why. Millions of New Yorkers carried on with their lives, not completely unaware of what was coming, but uncertain as to its exact nature and what it meant. People who understood Y2K tried to explain it to those who didn't, and you either got it or you didn't. It didn't matter. It was coming, ready or not.

Those who did get it took it seriously. A New Yorker didn't need a degree in computer science to understand that a technological breakdown that started with a power blackout had severe social consequences. Previous blackouts had come as a surprise and prompted spontaneous looting. This time people were forewarned. Steel doors, window grates and security guards commanded premium prices. When guards became too expensive, small business owners bought shotguns and planned to sit in their stores themselves. In every borough, neighborhoods created community patrols and made plans for mutual protection on New Year's Eve. The police didn't object. On New Year's Eve, the department would be stressed to maximum capability even without Y2K. In the most squalid ghettos of the South Bronx, the Colombian district of Queens, Bedford-Stuyvesant in Brooklyn and Spanish Harlem in Manhattan, community leaders spread the word: Don't burn down your own house.

With one week to go, the Midnight Club had assembled a software package of 112 applications on Judd's mainframe that effectively duplicated Con Edison's system for supplying power to Manhattan. To ensure communications they'd built a state-of-the-art telephone switching station and accessed an island-wide network of wire and microwave links, every inch inspected and brought up to snuff by Carolyn. To run the subway, they'd constructed a complete train control center for seven subway lines that traversed the island and parts of Brooklyn, the Bronx and Queens. They had confidence in all their work except the sewage system. The system was simply too old, too complex, and had too many embedded chips in places Ronnie couldn't get into.

They didn't sleep much the last week. As the big day approached,

they still didn't have the crucial passwords from ConEd. Doc called
Deep Volt every day, but to no avail. The spy was able to supply
Y2K upgrades the company had developed, but no override pass-
words.

On December 30 no one left the third floor of the building on
Nassau Street, an old red brick structure with black iron railings and
fire escapes, a piece of old New York that lay just outside the pal-
isade wall that had given Wall Street its name. The wall had been
build by the Dutch to keep the British out of New Amsterdam, but
this time nothing could defend against the hostile aliens except a
tiny band of outlaws. The countdown began. The war between the
millennium bug and its Y2K antidotes was about to start in earnest.

PART TWO
December 31, 1999

4

The last day of the 20th Century dawned cold and clear in New York, a metropolis whose most horrific brush with calamity had been the cholera epidemic of 1832. History had been kind to the city. While the 20th Century had visited war and revolution on many great cities, nary a bomb had fallen on the Big Apple. The century was to end with New York pristine and unscathed, a virgin in the ways of cataclysm. If a city can be anthropomorphised into a sentient being, New York believed itself invulnerable to attack.

There were, of course, authorities charged with imagining an attack and preparing contingency plans for civil defense. During the Cold War, the dominating scenario was a nuclear strike, and the city had a comprehensive plan printed in voluminous quantities to be dragged out and distributed should a volley of Russian missiles be detected en route. In 1999, the location of the printed nuclear plan was stored on a computer that was not Y2K compliant. Likewise, plans were intact for all sorts of civil disturbances from labor strikes to ethnic conflict, and these plans made some sense because of frequent use. Over the years city planners had had ample opportunity to refine procedures for controlling riots and demonstrations. In a more sinister vein, the city was quite accomplished at preparing plans for dealing with terrorists, and for this received assistance from numerous federal agencies. On paper, chemical and biological terrorism posed the greatest perceived threat and thus received the most attention.

As the century drew to a close, the city was among the first municipalities to recognize the most imminent threat, the millennium bug, and in 1996 Mayor Giuliani established an office to deal with the problem. A preliminary assessment of municipal computers revealed 687 critical systems infected with Y2K glitches. Two years and $300 million dollars later, 453 systems still had problems. By the summer of 1999 the city began to realize that all the money in the treasury wasn't sufficient to correct the glitch. Many systems were junked and replaced, but expensive, complex new systems took a long time to install and brought new problems. Old data still had to be converted to Y2K compliance, a process full of pitfalls. New York was the most diligent city in the world in attacking the problem, but "fixing" the myriad systems wasn't good enough. It was impossible to find every line of infected code, and as always with software debugging, every four defects found and corrected by programmers resulted in a new flaw injected into the code. Among millions of lines of binary machine code, one incidence of corrupted code could kill an entire system, and in tests that's exactly what happened. The Department of Environmental Protection smugly declared it had no problems, but a preliminary test in 1999 shut down the water system in thirty seconds when embedded chips in the servo controllers froze the valves in the main Croton reservoir. The pumps were replaced and the system failed again. Twelve of the city's fourteen sewage treatment plants failed their tests. Supposedly compliant systems in accounting departments failed constantly.

No one knew what was going to happen at midnight, and if all the city's systems miraculously survived, they'd still be at the mercy of Con Edison's ability to maintain power. New York had experienced major blackouts in 1965 and 1977, but this time the giant utility company had time to prepare and write press releases full of reassurance. On New Year's Eve morning, business people and community groups who had little faith in the city or ConEd's PR department began making final arrangements to protect their businesses and neighborhoods. Flyers were posted and handed out. Portable radios were tested and deployed and weapons cleaned and loaded.

Reacting to a flood of Y2K news and the August 22 GPS debacle, the city grudgingly had drawn up a plan for total breakdown, fetching bits and pieces from older plans for blackouts and civil unrest. Given a priority considerably below the New Year's Eve fireworks and traditional celebration in Times Square, the plan was never completed, approved, or implemented, but the public relations department was authorized to say a plan existed. There were rumors that the mayor had built a secret bunker in the World Trade Center to serve as a command post if the city became a battleground. Its exact nature was a secret. The city fathers didn't want to induce panic.

They might get wholesale panic anyway, thought Captain Ed Garcia as he walked along Broadway toward his daily breakfast date with Donald Copeland and the boys. He wished the planners and commissioners would spend an hour in his precinct so he could point out the lack of stockpiled food, water, and fuel, and ask where the city planned to erect emergency shelters. If the subways went down, the city would be overrun with stranded citizens, and if Con Edison collapsed . . . what the hell. Nothing was in readiness because no one believed anything was going to happen. Garcia understood politics and didn't want to brand himself as an alarmist nut by shooting off his mouth. Not that it would do any good. Yesterday he'd uttered the phrase "Y2K" to a divisional commander who'd replied, "Why too what?"

At 6:30 in the morning Garcia walked into Bernie's Deli at 85th and Broadway, ordered scrambled and toast, and poured himself a cup of coffee. Forty-five, an inch over six feet, heavy and imposing

in his uniform with double rows of brass buttons, Garcia dropped
his hat and briefcase on a rear table as he did every day. It was a
Friday, prelude to a long New Year's Eve weekend, and the good
citizens of Manhattan were making earnest preparations to drink
too much and wear funny hats as if this were an ordinary New Year's
Eve. He'd seen twenty-five New Year's Eves as a cop, but this year,
besides the usual boozy amateurs puking in his radio cars, he had
to face millennium crazies, space invaders, and religious lunatics
predicting the end of the world, all before midnight when the electronic shit was scheduled to hit the millennium fan.

He really loved being a cop, and long ago had learned that pre-
venting a crime was far better than catching and punishing a criminal. In this case, the city, that anonymous bitch, was about to
commit a sin of omission, a horrendous crime of neglect that he
was unable to prevent.

Garcia's old friend Bill Packard arrived at the same time as his
eggs.

"Happy New Year, *comandante*," said Packard, a staff cardiac
surgeon at Bellevue hospital.

"Fuck you, too, Bill."

"You don't look happy."

"I just want it over with," Garcia said. "Walking over here I
passed three liquor stores, all busy at six in the morning."

"Well," Packard said with a big smile as he sat down, "today's
the day. You ready?"

"Gimme a break. Nobody's ready."

"Copeland is."

"He says he is," Garcia retorted. "There's a difference."

"We're gonna find out soon enough," Packard said, looking at
his watch. "In seventeen hours and fifteen minutes. Hey, Bernie!"
he shouted. "Turn on the TV, will ya?"

"Why?"

"The new year will arrive in the middle of the Pacific Ocean in a
few minutes."

"So what?"

"Just turn it on, Bernie."

"You want some breakfast, Bill?"

"Yeah, yeah, yeah."

The delicatessen owner grudgingly switched on CNN and scowled at a commercial for Budweiser, the official beer of millennium insanity.

"Expecting a big night?" the policeman asked the doctor.

"Are you kidding?" Packard replied. "I'm just glad I don't work in the emergency room, but I got problems you wouldn't believe. Do you know how many computers we have at Bellevue? Do you have any idea how many computers run every goddamn device in my ICU? Do you know how many have been checked out? None. N-O-N-E, that's how many."

"You're supposed to work on the people, Bill, not the computers."

Grimacing, shaking his head with frustration, Packard poured himself a cup of coffee and stared at the TV.

Jonathon Spillman, now the manager of the brand-new Safeway Store at 96th and Broadway, walked in and sat down.

"Don't say it," Garcia warned.

"Don't say what?"

Packard winked and silently mouthed, *Happy New Year.*

"I'm Jewish, in case you forgot," Spillman reminded them. "The New Year is in September, and the year is 5760, if you didn't know. Where's Copeland?"

"Not here yet," the doctor replied. "Tonight he'll find out if all his fancy software works. Will Donnie boy save Chase Manhattan from extinction? As if I give a shit."

"Copeland won't, but his guy Doc Downs will," Spillman said. "Doc knows what he's doing. I'm on top of this thing, guys. Safeway spent millions on this thing and Doc said we did everything right."

"The horse's mouth," Garcia said. "That's just great. The bank and the grocery store survive while everything else goes all to hell."

"Nuclear reactors," Packard said. "How many worldwide? Four hundred? Five?"

"More," Spillman said. "Nobody really knows. There's secret reactors all over the place."

"You gonna eat?" Bernie hollered at Spillman.

"Gimme a poppy seed bagel with . . ."

". . . with nothin', I know, I know."

They sat for a moment in comfortable silence, three guys from the neighborhood who'd all made good and done well. Intelligent men, success stories, and still primitive villagers. Being together made them a little less afraid.

"Hear from your wife?" Spillman asked Packard.

Leery of violence and looting in the event of a blackout, the doctor had dispatched his wife and children to the rural coast of Maine.

"Yeah. She's at her sister's place. They spent all day yesterday stacking firewood. Did Shirley leave?"

"No. That's just not gonna happen."

"Make her go," Packard said, and Garcia added, "Put your foot down."

"C'mon, Ed," Spillman said. "You know my wife. Shirley thinks the millennium is the greatest thing since Princess Di's wedding. Besides, you've never been married."

Fanfare from the TV caused them to swivel their heads toward the screen. A smiling CNN anchorman in Atlanta faced the camera and said, "Only a few more minutes, ladies and gentlemen, until the first people on earth experience the millennium. We're going live now to the Marshall Islands and Joanna Springer. Joanna?"

Old Blue now lived in the air-conditioned basement of Copeland's brownstone on West 85th Street. In an instance of whimsical cybernetic overkill, the mainframe ran the house including an elaborate alarm and security system. Old Blue began its duties at

6:30 in the morning, turning on the heat, starting the coffee, collecting e-mail and feeding a Welsh terrier named Micro. The computer called up a program that dispensed exactly one and a half cups of lamb and rice meal into Micro's bowl, and in perfect Pavlovian fashion the dog wolfed down his breakfast in forty seconds. Meanwhile, the coffeemaker brewed a cup of dark roast espresso, and at precisely 7:00 the computer turned on the TV in the master bedroom.

Copeland liked to jumpstart his day with a little hard news, and on this day of days he was awake long before the TV popped on. CNN was broadcasting live from Majuro, capital of the Republic of the Marshall Islands near the International Date Line in the middle of the Pacific Ocean, nine thousand miles and seventeen time zones west.

"The millennium has arrived, ladies and gentlemen!" gushed a breathless woman standing next to an airport runway with the lights of a terminal and a small town behind her. Fireworks were igniting above the town, the first pyrotechnics to welcome the new century. "We're only a few miles from the International Date Line, and I can't express just how thrilling this is. It's 2000, ladies and gentlemen, the Twenty-First . . ."

Static punched out her voice and behind her the lights of the town flickered before the audio snapped back, ". . . in Micronesia which lies just west of the 180th meridian, the International . . . Line. We . . . eem to be have . . . me trouble wi . . . an aircraft is appr . . ."

In the background the lights of the town and terminal blinked out and seconds later the blue landing lights on the runway disappeared. Startled, the reporter turned around, then faced the camera again, her mouth working but producing no audible sound. Above her, the exploding rockets and bright star bursts of the fireworks created an eerie illumination.

"Something . . . happen . . ."

Copeland could hear the roar of aircraft engines approaching the runway over the voice of the journalist that continued to break up.

". . . tourists who want . . . the first landing of . . . entury, but the run . . . lights . . . vintage DC3."

And then he heard a crash and saw a wall of flame before the screen went black. The television director quickly cut to the studio in Atlanta and the talking head of the anchorman.

"We seem to have lost contact with Joanna Springer, ladies and gentlemen. I don't know exactly what happened. Just a moment. Do we have audio? Yes, I believe we have audio. Go ahead, Joanna."

Her disembodied voice echoed around the world, heard by millions in every nation. "Oh my God, a plane has crashed. The runway lights went out and all the lights went out except around our satellite truck because we're running on a gener . . ."

Silence, black screen, and then the studio again.

"This is a somber moment, ladies and gentlemen. We're trying to bring you live coverage from the Marshall Islands, as we expect to bring you live coverage of the arrival of the millennium throughout the next 24 hours, but we seem to have started off with a tragedy. Excuse me, can we restore audio, at least? No? Now they're telling me the satellite connection has failed. I don't know quite what to say, ladies and gentlemen, but it appears that what we feared the most and hoped would never happen has occurred. The predictions of computer failure at this moment seem to have come true, at least on the Marshall Islands. We'll be right back after a word from our sponsors."

One of the curious things about the moment the world started to fall apart was that the entire planet heard the news instantaneously. During that first hour CNN reported four more air disasters near the International Date Line, all aircraft charted by tourists who thought they were purchasing an exotic experience by being among the first to welcome the 21st Century. Power failures disrupted dozens of Pacific islands. The technical explanations were complex and varied from island to island—old computers in some power plants decided it was 1900 and all maintenance was seriously overdue; on some islands embedded chips in automated transmission and distribution systems failed—but the results were the same. The Pacific Ocean went dark. The only exceptions were islands, like the two Midways, with virtually no computers in their electrical systems, or those with brand-new systems, like Guam, where the power company had installed year 2000 compliant software.

Copeland shouted at the TV, "I told you so, you fools! Everybody has been telling you for *years*, but no! Jesus fucking Christ."

Then he smiled. Neither shocked nor surprised, he knew this was merely the opening salvo of what promised to be a most interesting day. His vision on the bridge nine years ago was coming true, but he didn't need vindication. When you're right, you're right. What he did need was nonstop catastrophe to divert attention from the real Y2K event that would take place in seventeen hours, at midnight Eastern standard time.

As far as Copeland figured, the mighty Chase Manhattan Bank was going to suffer temporary cybernetic oblivion at midnight. He believed that when the last bits of Copeland 2000 software kicked into the bank's electronic fund transfer system at the stroke of twelve, a hidden program buried by Doc in a larger diagnostic package would instantly transfer $72 million to accounts Copeland had established in Switzerland, Liechtenstein and Panama. Seconds later, the program would temporarily destroy the bank's ability to perform electronic fund transfers, scramble the records of thousands of accounts and then self-destruct. No known monies would be missing; the bank would recover within a day or two and go on to be profitable well into the next century. To the bank, the mess would look like a millennium bug flaw that had been overlooked. Sorry, we made a mistake.

Seventy-two million dollars, half of it his. Ordinarily, he was already eating breakfast at Bernie's, but this was going to be a long day and he was in no hurry. Shower, shave, ablutions, blue pinstripe, wingtips, a check in the mirror to verify his standard-issue yuppie good looks, then coffee and exactly two minutes of frenzied affection with the dog while he read e-mail in the kitchen. Old Blue had scanned the morning papers, culled his name and that of his company from seven articles, all of which referred to a new software contract with the bank to be formally announced that day, and displayed the news on the kitchen terminal of his house-wide net. He rapidly looked through the articles, reading only the headlines.

"Copeland Solutions to Announce Another Software Partnership with Chase," declared *The Wall Street Journal*. "A Revolution in Dial-Up Banking Software to Be Unveiled by Venture Capitalist Donald Copeland and Chase Manhattan," said the headline in *The New York Times*. All the articles carried variations on the theme, and Copeland reminded himself to congratulate Jody Maxwell, his PR director, on a job well done.

It was all a charade. By tomorrow morning the world would be in such a mess that neither the *Times* nor the bank would care a whit about new software for telephone customers. Copeland's problem was getting through the day without revealing his giddiness over the robbery.

He flipped on the kitchen TV in time to see a report from Wellington, New Zealand, the first major city to be hit by the bug.

". . . and so, to reiterate, an explosion in an oil refinery on the outskirts of Wellington at twenty minutes past midnight is competing with millennium fireworks to light up this charming city. So far, local electric power here and in Auckland has remained stable, but we have reports of blackouts in outlying areas. Rural districts seem to be the hardest hit, and local authorities are broadcasting instructions on emergency power. It's not known at this time how many people in the affected areas can receive them."

"John," said the anchorman, "is it cold there in Wellington?"

"Well, we're in the Southern Hemisphere here, William, and it's midsummer, so the answer is no, it's not cold, but many people are very, very frightened. The rest are, shall we say, seriously inebriated. After all, it is New Year's Eve."

Copeland turned down the sound and watched commercials flash across the screen. The world was beginning to disintegrate, but that wouldn't stop anyone from trying to sell product. He turned back to the computer terminal and was ready to move on to personal messages when the phone interrupted his ritual. He grabbed it.

"Copeland."

"You watching TV?" asked Bill Packard.

"Yes," Copeland said. "It's quite a show."

"You predicted this," Packard said. "You were right."

"I wish I wasn't," Copeland lied. "You at the deli?"

"We're all here."

Bill Packard lived three blocks away with his wife and two kids. Partly by chance and partly by design, Copeland, Packard, Garcia and Spillman still lived in the Upper West Side neighborhood where they'd all grown up. Over the years Copeland had come close to bragging to them about his plans for Chase Manhattan. He would have loved to deal a hand of five card stud to his buddies and casually say, "Guess what I'm gonna do, fellas?" Packard and Spillman might think the scheme was clever and laugh it off, but he had no doubt Ed Garcia would put him away. It was hard to bullshit guys he'd known since he was three years old, but he'd been doing it for five years. What the hell, it would all be over in the morning.

"It's going to hit Siberia in about forty-five minutes," the doctor went on, "and two hours later, Japan."

"Fuck the Russians and the Japanese," Copeland said. "They'll get what they deserve. How are things at the hospital?"

"I'm worried. Damn near every piece of equipment in the place has embedded chips, and none of them has been checked out."

"That's crazy," Copeland said.

"I know. I gotta meet with the manager of misinformation services. These fucking bureaucrats don't understand that this thing is serious."

"Do you need help?"

"Hell, yes, but the powers that be say it isn't in the damned budget, so I can't even bring in help on my own. It sucks."

"Did you sell your stocks?"

"Yes."

"Take your money out of the bank?"

"Yes."

"Stockpile food and water?"

"Yes, and batteries, too. What is this, an inspection?"

"Don't forget candles," Copeland said. "You can't run the hospital, but you can look out for number one, right?"

"I suppose so," the doctor said. "See you tonight?"

"I don't think so," Copeland said. "I'll be in the office until well after midnight."

"Well, stop by if you can. See ya."

As soon as he hung up, the phone rang again.

"Copeland."

"Doc here. You see the news?"

"Sure did."

"It's happening all over New Zealand. The refinery, traffic lights, rural power. The water mains shut down in Auckland. You coming in this morning?"

"Just like every other day, Doc. Jody and I have a press conference at nine-thirty with the bank."

"I think the media people are going to be pretty busy this morning," Doc said. "Don't be surprised if they bail."

"Nothing is going to surprise me today," Copeland said.

"I wouldn't be quite so cocksure, Donald. Everyone will be surprised today, even you."

"I'm sure you're right," Copeland agreed, sipping coffee. "Look, these air crashes and blackouts might have some of our people upset, but I don't care. Everyone comes in today and works through midnight. This will be our busiest day ever."

"That's my Donnie boy, the slave driver. Don't worry, boss. Everyone has been briefed."

Copeland turned on his e-mail and recognized the first address as that of his ex-wife, Marie, a born-again Christian who sent an occasional message urging him to seek Jesus and read the Book of Revelation. He hesitated before opening the message. The old Chambers Brothers tune, "Time Has Come Today" was running through his head for no reason except that it often did. Tick tock, tick tock. Acutely time-conscious, Copeland wore a $12,000 Rolex to supplement the kitchen's three digitals. *Tempus fugit*, yeah Jack, you got that right. Feeling his life ticking away as though it were running on an infernal Julian clock, he'd driven himself to succeed at every enterprise he'd attempted. You only get so many hours, he frequently told himself, and if you don't impose order and discipline on every one, all was chaos. After two decades of this hard regimen, the result was a forty-three-year-old man drawn as tight as piano wire.

Copeland had become so obsessed with the delusional heist of Chase's millions that anything that got in his way disappeared from his life. Over time, the list included his wife and son. Both had grown to despise his devotion to his business, his computers, and the companies he'd created. It had been three years since Marie had gone off her rocker and joined a Christian cult in Arizona. The previous year his son Eddie, at age eighteen, had declared himself a Luddite, anti-machine, anti-computer and anti-business, and had taken his trust fund and run away to Los Angeles. As it was, Copeland had discovered he preferred living alone with Micro and Old Blue, two creatures that were capable of unconditional love.

He sighed, opened his ex-wife's e-mail and braced himself for the onslaught.

"Doomsday is here," her message began. "The Millennium arrives tonight and with it the beginning of the thousand-year reign of Our Lord Jesus Christ. Only the righteous will be saved. The world as you know it will end tomorrow. Those who worship false gods will tremble before the Lord on Judgment Day. Give it up, Donald. Turn to Jesus."

He didn't need any fruitcake, wacko shit this morning, no way. Christ, the religious right had had a field day for months, extracting every bit of mileage from millennium doom and destruction, and the irony was that they had no idea how right they were. The millennium *was* a big deal, but not the kind these goofballs imagined. Thank you, Marie, and good-bye.

Life, he thought, would be simple if you just got rid of all the people who were stuck on fixed ideas and absurd superstitions and thought they had all the answers. Computers were much better; they did what they were told and didn't preach.

A thoroughly modern man, Copeland had developed the compartmentalization of his mind into a fine art. Guilt was neatly imprisoned in one lobe at the back of his brain where it couldn't hinder his business, and the love he'd known in his life was buried somewhere nearby. He didn't know why his kid was a Luddite or his ex-wife a religious nut; he knew only that they'd disappointed him, rejected his values—but not his money—and left him to pursue his cold passion alone. They were like an airplane crash on the Marshall Islands, a distant disturbance to be ignored.

Before leaving the house, he left an electronic note for the housekeeper to order dog food. He ran a quick scan of the security system, making sure windows and doors were locked tight, and said good-bye to Old Blue and Micro. Family business taken care of, he went down to the garage to drive to work.

The Porsche burbled quietly down 85th Street to Broadway where Copeland parked in a red zone in front of Bernie's.

"If it isn't the king of the yuppies in person," Packard said as Copeland sat down.

"You've been cracking wise with the same shit for ten years, Bill."

"You gonna eat?" Bernie hollered.

"Not today, Bernie."

"Then what makes you think you can park in my red zone? Ed, give him a ticket."

"I should," the policeman said. "You gonna save the world tonight, Donnie?"

"Nope, but I'm gonna save a shitload of banks."

"You hope."

"You pays your money and takes your chances, right? Hey, I heard from Marie. The world is gonna end tonight. Be aware."

"She's right," Garcia said. "You've been saying it for years. Bill sent his wife and kids to Maine."

"Did they go?"

"Yeah."

Copeland turned to Spillman and asked, "Did Shirley leave?"

"Are you kidding?" Shaking his head, Spillman stood up. "I gotta go run my store. See you guys."

"I'll go with you," Packard said. "Let's grab a cab."

Copeland and Garcia remained at the table, and Copeland contemplated his old friend who would become his enemy in an instant if he knew the truth.

"We're malingering," Copeland said with a grin. "Is that against the law?"

"Donnie, if I didn't know you for forty years, I'd think you were a real asshole. As it is, I know you are but I don't care. You're famous. People write about you in the *Times*. You eat lunch with the mayor. You're smart and you're rich, but when the lights go out tonight, you'll be in the dark the same as everyone else."

"Think so?"

"Hell yes."

"Bet you a million dollars you're wrong."

"I don't have a million dollars."

"Okay, I'll bet you ten bucks."

"Fuck you. What's really going to happen?"

"Nobody knows, Ed. Nobody really knows."

Garcia stood, settled his elegant policeman's cap on his head, paid Bernie, and added a generous tip that Copeland matched.

"You didn't eat," the deli owner protested. "What's this for?"

"Happy New Year," Copeland said and followed Garcia out onto the sidewalk. The captain scowled at the traffic flowing by in an orderly fashion and the people walking up and down at a normal, rapid pace. Pigeons fluttered and litter swirled in a mild breeze.

"The calm before the storm," Garcia said. "What's really going to happen in our town, Donnie?"

"There'll be a run on the banks this afternoon," Copeland said. "It's been building for days, but today will look like 1929."

"What else?"

"If Con Edison has its act together and the power stays on, we'll be okay, but the subway system will die. The railroads will stop running because their control systems will crash, but they already know that. The water mains should be okay."

"Stop. I get the picture."

"It will be much worse in other places. New York will survive," Copeland said, opening his car door. "Good luck."

"See you in the morning?"

"Right here."

Garcia waved and a patrol car materialized, slid to the curb and whisked him away.

Copeland started his car, flicked on a radar detector, punched the go pedal and let 'er rip. He howled and grinned like an outlaw down Broadway, busting through yellow lights and weaving in and out of traffic all the way to 57th where traffic finally slowed him down. The streets were deceptively empty, thousands of people having left the city for the long weekend. He continued on downtown to Wall Street. His fastest time for covering the distance between the deli and the garage beneath his office was twenty-three minutes and forty-seven seconds, and every morning his daily race against the clock took him right to the edge and set the tone for the day. No compromises, no discounts, and no surprises. He drove the way he conducted his business, with control that was hardly distinguishable from recklessness, squealing the tires, pounding the brakes, exulting in the rasping exhaust echoing off the stone-faced banks and brokerages.

Wall Street was jammed. Ordinarily, many people didn't come in to work on New Year's Eve, especially on a Friday, and everyone knocked off early in the afternoon. Not today with Y2K hanging over the street like a guillotine. Untold billions of dollars were at the mercy of countless computer systems that could never be properly tested before crunch time. There was no way to run proper simulations because no one knew what was going to happen. Copeland knew it would be bad, as the early reports from the Pacific indicated, and the street was already in a tizzy. He didn't care. He'd have Chase's millions, and if Doc's software worked as well as it should, by next week he'd have more megabuck orders to repair failed systems than he could fill.

He zipped the last few blocks to Nassau Street and checked his Rolex: twenty-eight minutes flat, not great but not bad. Pulling inside, he parked next to Doc's Jeep. Doc had installed a diesel generator in the garage, a satellite dish and solar panels on the roof, ostensibly to keep his legitimate Y2K customer-support people in contact with the company's clients. If the worst happened, he was ready to transform the building into a fortress protected by barbed wire and automatic weapons, enough hardware to stop any millennium bug havoc at the property line.

Copeland rode the elevator up to Doc's third-floor sanctuary, and was striding down a corridor when Doc's office door popped open.

"Come in here," the engineer commanded.

In nine years Doc hadn't aged a day. The only thing that had changed was the clutter in his office. There was more of it.

"Take a look at this," Doc said and gestured toward a TV. "The Secretary of the Interior is issuing the first government statement of the day."

"Who's in this morning?" Copeland said, ignoring the television.

"All the customer support people are here. They've started a pool to see how many airplanes will fall out of the sky."

"Oh yeah?" Copeland said. "What a bunch of sickies. You in?"

"Sure. My hundred bucks is on number 12."

"Don't you have anything better to do, Doc?"

Doc had more to do than Copeland could ever imagine, but he shook his head and answered, "Nope. I'm gonna get stoned and watch TV all day. I haven't taken a day off in five years."

He stretched and grinned and watched the screen. He had his own charade to perform that day in order to keep Copeland from discovering the Midnight Club during the most critical hours. If the Midnight Club was going to preserve any vestige of civilization in the city, they didn't need Copeland suddenly throwing a hissy fit in the middle of a crisis.

"How'd you like the oil refinery in Wellington?" Copeland asked. "That was something. How many refineries do we have in metro New York? Four or five?"

"Eighteen," Doc said, "and they should shut them all down now, but they won't."

On TV the Secretary of the Interior was saying, "We caution people not to panic. What is happening in New Zealand and Micronesia is not going to happen here. The Department of the Interior and the Department of Energy have assurances from all the major power companies throughout the country . . ."

The television director cut away from the secretary to the anchorman, who said, "We can return to the secretary's press conference in a moment, ladies and gentlemen, but we have more breaking news. We're going . . . where? Yes, La Guardia Airport in New York City and Ellen Rothstein. Ellen?"

"Yes, William, as you can see behind me, a spontaneous demonstration has broken out here at La Guardia Airport."

The camera zoomed in on a crowd of protesters who were marching and chanting, "Not safe! Don't fly! In the sky you're gonna die!"

"Jesus," Doc said. "That's pretty funny, actually, and good advice."

"People are panicking and refusing to get onto planes," the reporter said.

"To hell with this," Copeland said. "What's up with the bank?"

An irrepressible smart-ass, Doc lit a Camel and asked, "What bank?"

"C'mon."

"Oh, *that* bank. They're waiting to hear from the Federal Reserve. The Fed wants to shut down all electronic fund transfers for 24 hours, but the big banks are protesting. When the banks suggested that two years ago, the Fed said no. Now they've switched sides. Typical government assholes."

"If they do that, we're screwed," Copeland said.

"You got that right, boss, unlesss . . ." Doc grinned, dragging out the ess and blowing smoke.

"Unless what?"

"Unless I trigger our little secret from here."

"Could you do such a thing?"

"I could, but it would seriously increase the risk factor."

"*Would* you do such a thing, Dr. Downs?"

"Just say the word, boss. Watch."

Doc turned on a custom-built computer terminal running Windows NT, keyed a few strokes, and the screen filled with a large red circle against a blue background and a caption, "The Big Red Button."

"All you have to do is touch the screen, Donnie boy, and Chase's millions are zipping their way to Panama."

"You're kidding."

"Try it, but be sure you want to do it."

"That's all?"

"Yes, sir."

"What about the risk factor?"

"What about it?" Doc said. "There are five cutouts between this machine and a modem at the bank's Tech Center. Each is supposed to self-destruct, but you never can be absolutely sure with delicate machinery and tricky little computer programs. If you don't want to hit the button, wait for midnight and it's all automatic."

Copeland ground his teeth and stared at the Big Red Button glowing like a virtual mandala. He wanted to lunge for the screen, but instead he said, "You're a diabolical bastard, Doc. You know that? Let's wait and hear from the Fed."

"You're the boss, Donald," Doc said with a grin. "You can make the decision whenever you like. Use the password 'Red,' go into DOCCM.EXE, enter 'SCREEN' and you'll have the button on your monitor."

Doc glanced again at the TV. The protesters at La Guardia continued to chant, cops were arriving at the airport, and hysterical people were mobbing taxis and busses.

"Donald," Doc said, "don't you think it's odd that the world is unraveling like a cheap sweater and all you can think of is yourself? You have a company to run. Every one of our clients will be screaming for reassurance that the software you sold them will work."

"They can all go to hell. I'm not taking any calls today. You take the calls."

"Are you going to the press conference at the bank?"

"Yes, to keep up appearances."

"Christ, now I've heard everything."

"You're a smart aleck," Copeland said and headed for the elevator and his office on the first floor. Downstairs, the staff was coming in, prepared for a long day. The news from the Western Pacific was in the air, but people were making light of it, showing only a few traces of nervousness. Copeland saw several bottles of champagne and desks decorated with gift baskets of pricey delectables. Someone blew a horn and tossed a handful of confetti into the corridor.

"Happy New Year, Mr. Copeland."

It was almost 8:00 in New York. It was midnight in Siberia.

5

Copeland's obsession with Chase's millions had made him oblivious to what the Midnight Club was doing right under his nose. Doc hoped the boss would spend the day staring at the red button, and he'd devised a few dirty tricks to keep Copeland out of his hair.

Doc thought of himself as an idealist in a culture where ideals were laughed at by most people over the age of eight. America at the end of the 20th Century was a cynical nation, but Doc didn't care. He'd kept the faith, and if a terrible darkness followed in the wake of the millennium bug, he wanted to maintain a beacon of light on an island of hope. The nearest handy island was Manhattan.

He wasn't sure why he was so fond of the overcrowded, bustling city. It was easy to badmouth New York, even hate the place, but next to New York, everywhere else was second city. New York had more money, power, influence, and extraordinary people who came from everywhere to be part of it, yet in spite of the grandiose architecture and the vastness of it all, New Yorkers managed to reduce the city to a comprehensible scale. The Big Apple was the most human of cities. People talked to one another, if not always politely. The natives turned their neighborhoods into villages and looked after one another. Doc had adapted. He loved the subway and the chess games in Washington Square. He thrived on the hustle of midtown and the hip milieu of Soho. He'd learned to order his coffee black because "regular" had milk in it. He hated the weather, but New York was a town of interiors, elegant refuges from the heat of summer and cold of winter. He often thought of the last few minutes of the Cold War nuclear nightmare movie *Fail Safe*, in which a lone United States Air Force B-52 banked over the Statue of Liberty, zeroed in on the Empire State Building and annihilated the city with a thermonuclear bomb. When America went for her own jugular, the pulsing vein was in New York.

Doc remembered a day not long after his arrival in the city when he was strolling through midtown, taking in the sights, when he saw, striding along with strong, leggy steps, a stunning six-foot-tall woman in a short Chanel skirt, Charles Jourdan shoes, Gucci bag, camera-ready makeup and hair, and an indefinable but oh-so-New York attitude as she flashed mini-gun bullets at a thousand rounds per minute from conquer-the-world eyes. Towering over the short, swarthy men who crowded Sixth Avenue, haughtily ignoring the attention she attracted, she stepped off the curb against the light directly in front of a taxi, causing the turbaned driver to hit his brakes and horn. Without deigning to glance his way, she flashed one elegant, manicured finger at his windshield and swept across 43rd Street, eyes ready to assassinate the next impediment in her path.

He'd seen mind-boggling sights like that every day in Manhattan, and perhaps that was why he loved the city and felt it was worth saving. New York was a mecca for people at the top of their game, and if they were lost, the world would lose. The millennium bug was already wreaking devastation on the far side of the globe, but if New York survived, it could lead the way to recovery.

The Midnight Club's latest projections predicted that a small utility company in Vermont called Northern Lights Electric would fail, triggering a grid-wide failure that would take down ConEd. All the time and money he'd put into the Midnight Club would go down the drain unless Bo got his override codes and isolated New York from the grid. Doc had spent a million on salaries, five million on bonuses, six million on the IBM and other hardware, and a half million on bribes to reach this penultimate step, and he was stymied for lack of seven simple passwords. By now Deep Volt would have arrived at work as day shift operations manager at the command center, and he called as he did every day for no reason except pure neurosis. If the spy actually managed to get the passwords, Doc would be the first to know.

"How's it going?" he asked.

"Things are heating up," came Deep Volt's reply. "We're running disaster simulations."

"And the overrides?"

"The supervisor will change them sometime today."

"Okay. Talk to you later."

He snapped on a bank of security monitors that presented views of different parts of the three-story building on Nassau Street. On the first floor Donald's accountants, analysts and sales people were filing into cubicles to work the phones and push virtual paper from one machine to another. On the second floor, where shifts worked around the clock, thirty Y2K customer-support people were connected to Chase Manhattan and twenty-seven other banks in eight countries, the company's clients. On the third floor a dozen nerds were arriving for work in the regular computer lab where they developed new software for Copeland Solutions and Copeland's other companies.

Doc entered a password, and a camera in the secure computer room presented a silent image of the five members of the Midnight Club watching their screens. Bo paced around his large cubicle as he watched a bank of screens that duplicated operators' screens in the five Con Edison power plants, his face a grim map of despair. Next to him, dancing to music that never stopped, Carolyn watched a Bell Atlantic display of the volume of calls at a dozen key interfaces to the outside world. In the back of the room, away from the stereo speakers, Ronnie was watching flow charts from the water department. As Doc watched, she got up from her seat and walked over to Adrian who was typing at his keyboard.

Doc snapped on the audio and heard her say, "Somebody just robbed a carload of passengers on the F Line and they have him trapped at 23rd Street."

"How do you know?" Adrian asked.

"I'm listening to 911 dispatchers. Somebody got shot."

Adrian shrugged and said, "It's not my problem."

"Just thought you'd like to know. The trains will back up."

"Ronnie," Adrian said, "I don't give a fuck what happens to the subway until midnight."

Doc commanded his screen to replicate Adrian's. Adrian was logged on to a Y2K newsgroup, a chat room for Y2K freaks who were writing furious messages trying to best one another in predicting what was going to happen. All the programmers expected to get rich cleaning up the aftermath, and Adrian was no exception. He was writing:

Hello, Joe Dinosaur, welcome to the 21st Century, only geeks allowed. This is a technoworld of microns and angstroms, solid state physics, Boolean logic—everything that makes Joe run for his Budweiser. Joe doesn't like computers. Flow charts, system analysis, COBOL, Java or diffusion furnaces have no place in his tiny mind. Here in technoland, you either understand everything and belong here, or you understand nothing, like Joe, who is wired whether he likes it or not. Joe thinks the Internet is a TV show with ten thousand channels of pornography. He doesn't get it and never will. All power flows from control of a tiny electronic switch inside a minuscule transistor which is one of 100,000 transistors on an artificial rock the size of your fingernail. Put that in your Bud and chug it, Joe. Computers control everything, and geeks control computers. Geeks rule. Party hearty, Joe. Happy New Year. When all the champagne is gone, the big clock will roll over and then you'll know what real power is.

Doc read a few more messages and sighed. Next Monday morning the status of technicians who could make things work again would be vaulted into the stratosphere, and they couldn't wait to cash in. The attitude was downright unpleasant. Unable to stand the gloating, Doc sent Adrian an e-mail—"Go play with your trains!" Chagrined, Adrian glanced up at the camera and wrinkled his nose.

At five minutes to eight Deep Volt called from ConEd.

"Doc? I'll try for the passwords again around lunch time, but don't hold your breath. I'll call you later."

He hung up, refusing to become discouraged. All he could do was wait, so he turned on the TV to watch the millennium bug push into the first of Russia's eleven time zones.

After nine years of tracking old IBM mainframes, Doc knew the authorities in the Eastern Siberian city of Magadan controlled their local nuclear-powered electrical grid with two old IBM s/370 machines. The computers were running antique software that was definitely not Y2K compliant, which meant Magadan's half million inhabitants were going to suffer a major blackout on a freezing winter's night, if not a full-blown nuclear disaster. The Magadan reactor would be the first of hundreds waiting in the path of the millennium bug, and what happened there would set a precedent for the rest of the day.

Certain that calamity was careening toward an innocent city and equally certain the Russians knew it as well, Doc hoped the power plant engineers had enough sense to scram the reactor while they still had time. Nuclear engineers were among the most careful and practical humans on the planet. You don't fool around with nuclear fission. Doc grew tense. He lit a Camel, watched the clock, and sent an e-mail to Judd, "Go online with the Russians."

He surfed the networks, looking for Siberia. CBS was still broadcasting from New Zealand, ABC and CNN were in Moscow, Fox was talking to the space station, and NBC had a man in Vladivostok, a thousand miles west and two hours behind Magadan.

The NBC reporter in fur cap and trench coat was standing in front of Vladivostok's nuclear power plant surrounded by six inches of snow.

"As you can see from the distinctive concrete towers behind me, this city and most Russian cities rely on nuclear energy to generate electricity. Worldwide, two billion people draw their ration of electricity from nuclear power plants, each with a unique computer system. The operators of this plant must be certain that each line of code in every application is free of Y2K problems, or they have to shut down the reactor. With an interior temperature of around 600°F, a reactor's pressure vessel must cool down slowly, a process that can take three days."

The camera panned over a small but growing crowd of local citizens assembling outside the chain-linked entrance to the facility.

"The people here know about the millennium bug; they know what happened in Micronesia and New Zealand, but we haven't found anyone who speaks English. Just a moment . . ."

The reporter spoke rapid Russian to a stout young woman who was carrying a bulky radio.

"Yes," she said, "some English. This radio, it is what you say? CB? Yes, citizen band, and short wave."

"Who are you talking to?"

"My friend in Magadan. It is now there—" she paused to glance at her watch "—year two thousands."

She turned up her radio and people nearby moved closer to listen. The reporter listened to the Russian commentary and offered a running translation.

"I'm listening to a short-wave broadcast from a private citizen in Magadan, Siberia, ladies and gentlemen, and he's saying they just lost their power. Yes, yes, that's right, the authorities just shut down the nuclear power plant, and it's twenty below."

A cry of despair rose from the crowd. Doc remained absolutely still as he watched the screen. The operators in Magadan had had no choice. The plant engineers had cut the steam flow from the reactor, stopped the turbines, and Magadan had blacked out along with Petropavlovsk and the entire Kamchatka Peninsula. Once the heartland of the Soviet military-industrial presence on the Pacific Rim, Eastern Siberia greeted the millennium in darkness and fear.

On screen the NBC camera captured the first few seconds of a riot in Vladivostok. Despite the danger of a computer malfunction causing an uncontrollable chain reaction, angry citizens demanding that the power remain on stormed the gates of the plant. A squad of white-helmeted militia swarmed out of nowhere and attacked the crowd with tear gas and batons. Blood flowed on the snowbanks. The audio carried the piercing sounds of shouts and screams, Russian agony, and freezing, whistling wind. Abruptly, the screen went cockeyed, then black. The bug had reached the mainland of Eurasia, and humanity had responded with repression and ignorance.

Doc flipped through the channels. All the networks were on the story right away. A shot by Fox from the space station caught a huge swath of Siberia as it went dark. The Russians aboard the spacecraft were somber, wondering aloud what was happening in their country far below and asking whether or not their ground control was going to survive the night. Doc was reminded of an incident at the Chernobyl reactor disaster in 1989. When the meltdown occurred, the power plant lost all communications with Kiev. The Soviets had had to lay a telephone line by hand from a caravan of trucks between the burning reactor and the responsible authorities, who, when finally connected, had nothing to say.

The world had made a huge mistake by relying on high technology without considering the full implications, and the millennium bug was simply a way of making it obvious to everyone. What interested Doc most was NBC's picking up the Magadan story from Russian short-wave radio. Short-wave, old vacuum tube receivers, and manual typewriters would be operating in the morning when more modern equipment failed. If things went the way he expected, the Third World would thrive while the First World went to hell overnight. If that happened, a '57 Chevy would be the vehicle of choice, a classic with no computers.

Doc called the Midnight Club and Judd answered by screaming into the phone, "Yo, Doc."

"You online with the Russians?" Doc asked.

"Got Serge online from Vladivostok," Judd replied. "He says Eastern Siberia took it in the shorts big time. There's bad news all across Russia, but Serge is no dummy. He has a generator and a dish, so he'll be ready when it hits him in another couple of hours."

"What does he know about the Magadan reactor?"

"They scrammed. They knew they had to."

"Thank God," Doc said. "How did Con Edison take the news?"

"They're frantic," Judd said. "They're watching this riot in Vladivostok and cursing the media for reporting it. Right now they're arguing over whether or not to shut down Indian Rock."

Indian Rock was Con Edison's nuclear plant in upstate New York, perhaps the world's most thoroughly Y2K-tested nuclear generating system.

"Indian Rock isn't the problem," Doc said. "It's all the equipment between there and here."

"We'll see about that," Judd said. "Got Bo's override codes yet?"

"Not yet," Doc answered. "I'm dialing."

He punched in the number of his spy inside Con Edison and she answered, "Operations."

"Doc here."

"Got nothing for you. Can't talk. I'll let you know."

Damn. Two and a half years of work, twelve million dollars, and it came down to this: hope and luck. Doc's stomach churned. He had to sweat it out. Like any good engineer, he had a backup plan, but he hoped he didn't have to use it.

Doc turned back to the TV wondering how long the networks would stay on the air. How many microprocessors between Siberia and New York had to function perfectly to transmit a signal around the world? Thousands. How many had been tested? How many embedded chips had been overlooked, never located, or improperly fixed? One bad chip and the whole thing goes kablooie.

The employee line on Doc's phone was blinking, causing him to start thinking about the phones. How many . . . ? What if . . . ? He could drive himself crazy like that. He picked up the handset and answered, "Copeland Solutions, Doc speaking."

"Dr. Downs? This is George Kirosawa from the Chase account. I'd hoped you'd be in early this morning."

"Good morning, George. Everything all right?"

"Well, no, actually. I've been watching the news, and to tell you the truth, I don't want to ride the train this morning. I hope you understand."

"The subway will be all right, George. They won't have any problems until late tonight, if then."

"I know, but my wife is terrified and my kids are upset. These reports from New Zealand and Russia have her shaking. I have to stay here with her."

"Well, I understand," Doc said. "It's all right. Happy New Year."

"You, too, Dr. Downs. Thanks."

It was starting.

As the day progressed, fear and tension among knowledgeable, rational people could be unbearable by noon, let alone midnight. Staying home was a good idea for anyone with a family.

He heard a burst of noise in the corridor and peeked out to see the public relations director Jody Maxwell slumped against the wall and uttering sighs and growls of irritation.

Jody had dressed her plump, expressive body in pale green Armani for her press conference with the bank's chief financial officer.

In her late twenties, she was the rare geek who'd crossed the line to conventional businesshood. She knew the ins and outs of successful public relations as well as she understood computers, and she had a nongeeky earthiness that Doc liked.

"What happened to you?" he asked, concerned to see her disheveled.

"I couldn't believe it," she said. "First, my neighbor stood on his balcony and threw his laptop down three stories into the street. I heard the crash and a scream and went out on my balcony, and he was right there looking like Jack Nicholson in *The Shining* with wild eyes staring down at the sidewalk. He almost hit a woman walking her dog."

"Wow," Doc said. "What did he say?"

"That's what was so weird. He didn't say anything. And then on the subway this group of about twenty lunatics crowded on and started handing out pamphlets, and when people refused their shitty little booklets, they threw them in their faces. I'm telling you, it was completely insane. *Renounce your sins*, it said. *Judgment Day is here.* They were all Asians, Koreans I think, and people got pissed off. One guy punched this woman and broke her glasses. I got off a stop early and walked. It's crazy out there. People are dressed up in paper hats and blowing horns. I saw a naked woman with '2000' painted across her tits. I swear to God."

"Want a cup of coffee?"

"How about a shot of Scotch?"

"Vodka."

"Even better. Donald in?"

"His Donaldness is downstairs and waiting for you."

"We're supposed to have a news conference with the bank this morning, but I don't know . . ." she said, her voice trailing off.

On TV CNN was reporting from Moscow where a very shaken Russian Minister of Information was announcing the imposition of martial law in Siberia.

"What's going on?" she asked Doc.

"The Russians just paid for a bad mistake," he said. "Siberia doesn't have many computers except the oil and gas pipelines and the reactors, but Russian infrastructure is a mixed bag. The telephone system is an antique with old-fashioned mechanical relays that should have no problems. Moscow and Petersburg are going to get slammed, but most of rural Russia is still in the 19th Century. The bug can't stop a horse from pulling a plow."

"Fascinating," she said, sitting down and making herself comfortable. "Horrifying but fascinating."

Doc poured her a double shot of vodka. A noisy crowd of employees came into the office, laughing and picking bits of paper from their hair and clothing. Greetings of "Happy New Year" rattled down the corridor and someone blew a horn.

"Don't you want to join the party?" Doc asked.

"Give me a break," she said. "Eat, drink and be merry, for tomorrow we shall die."

"Hail, Caesar," Doc added. "Don't worry, things aren't as bad as they look."

On TV CNN reported three spontaneous antinuclear demonstrations at power plants in Oregon, California and Pennsylvania.

"No nukes, no nukes, no nukes," the people shouted. Unlike their Russian counterparts, the American police for once looked like they believed the demonstrators had a point.

At 8:45 Copeland was in his office with one computer screen showing the red button and another displaying a chart of Y2K stock symbols and data. VIAS, TPRO, ZITL, and DDIM were companies like his that sold Y2K software and services, but unlike his they were publicly traded. These stocks had risen steadily during the last three years, but in the month of December had leveled off. With more business than they could handle, Y2K companies were unable to take on new clients because the world had run out of programmers. Copeland didn't care. In the last year he'd doubled programmers' salaries in order to keep them, and passed the cost on to his clients. Today he was merely curious. In the past week he'd liquidated every stock and bond he owned, cashed out everything, and reduced his portfolio to zero. Tomorrow, if his scheme worked out the way it was supposed to, he wouldn't need equity.

Copeland tried to distract himself by watching the stock exchanges gear up for the opening bell. Since June every major corporation in America had been put on the spot and forced to declare itself Year 2000 compliant or not. Corporations unable to prove their computers were ready for the 21st Century had seen their stocks tumble to all-time lows. Some companies threatened with Y2K liability suits had tossed in the towel, declared bankruptcy and gone out of business. The corporate landscape was being recontoured in surprising ways. IBM was stronger than ever, but General Motors was dead in the water, a ship without a rudder. Like many large companies, GM had so many computers in so many divisions and was such a bureaucratic mess that the company simply didn't know how many systems it had. One of its subsidiaries, GM Electronics, which manufactured computer chips for GM vehicles, had cranked out millions of chips infected with the millennium bug, and instead of dealing with the problem with engineers and technicians, GM had turned the fiasco over to lawyers and spin doctors. Meanwhile, computer-driven robots in GM assembly plants were poised to quit at midnight, although even if they functioned properly, they wouldn't have much to do because only a fraction of the company's 1300 suppliers were Year 2000 compliant. In the last few weeks GM had frantically tried to install new systems, but had run up against one of the harsher truths of the cybernetic world: any new system will be 100% over budget and take twice as long to install and test as any projection. The entire supply chain and sophisticated just-in-time delivery systems were going to break.

So what, Copeland thought. I drive a Porsche. GM deserves to die.

At 8:46, fourteen minutes before the stock markets were to open, America's stockbrokers, day traders, and millions of ordinary citizens who owned shares in the global economy were in their hot seats. Their computers were humming and telephone headsets chattering away with the peculiar jargon that drives the world's biggest pile of money and paper. The Internet and the floor of the New York Stock Exchange were abuzz with the usual mix of fact and rumor, though the facts had more impact and the rumors were more intense than anyone could remember. The key fact, of course, was the reality of the millennium bug, a topic that had been debated for years. Virtually everyone in the financial marketplace was tracking the bug's progress and trying to second-guess its effects on the portfolios they managed. Players were holding their breath, waiting to see what would happen next.

They didn't have to wait long. At 8:47 all the European exchanges simultaneously cut short trading and closed. At 8:49 the Federal Republic of Germany declared a bank holiday and closed all German banks. Like dominoes, the rest of Europe followed suit. During the previous year, much of the continent, particularly Germany, had persisted in belittling the millennium bug as a concoction of hysterical alarmists. They'd ignored the bug, and thousands of their mission-critical computers were not Year 2000 compliant. After all, they were Europeans, older and wiser than the rest of the planet, and they knew better. Nothing would happen. A few computers would break down, that's all. Computers failed all the time, didn't they? As the chain reaction of events steamed across Siberia, the implications of their delusions hit them like a comet: the bug was real. With the shutdown of the nuclear plant in Magadan, the Europeans suddenly woke up and started to worry frantically about the hundreds of nuclear reactors between Moscow and Lisbon. Closing the stock exchanges and banks was easy but wasn't life-threatening. Shutting down waves of power plants in the middle of winter was another matter entirely.

Copeland's phone was blinking nonstop, but he ignored it. Someone knocked on his door and he ignored that, too. His European clients were probably demanding his august telephonic presence, but he no longer cared what happened to them. On cable television's New York 1, a United Nations representative from the European Union was explaining that the introduction of the new Euro currency had created massive software problems, and that countries and companies had had to decide whether to concentrate on the Euro conversion or deal with their Y2K problems. They chose the currency because that was hard cash and something they understood. Too bad for them, Copeland thought with sage nods of his head. Now their pig-headedness had caught up with them, and he wondered why the dumbbell Europeans had taken so long to close their markets. In any event, they did close them, and the ripple effect would be a complete shutting down of the global economy until the crisis had passed. How long that took depended to a great extent on what happened to the European nuclear reactors later in the day.

In New York, the consensus was that the exchanges wouldn't open. It was obvious and not unprecedented. On days when the markets were imbued with extreme anxiety, the exchanges remained closed. The Russian declaration of martial law in Siberia had been the first indication that the markets wouldn't open. To keep things interesting, traders were betting for and against military rule being expended to the entire country. The air crashes in Micronesia provoked considerable interest as well, because wrecks always affected the market; however, a few airplanes falling out of the sky wouldn't have a long-term impact on the global economy, and neither would any event in Russia which had become an economic cesspool. Japan, however, was a linchpin of the world economic order.

At 8:52 a rumor flashed across millions of screens that declared the core computers at the Central Bank of Japan were at risk of crashing when the millennium bug hit Tokyo at ten o'clock, New York time. If Japan collapsed, economic chaos would be unleashed. With the European markets already shut down, there was no way the American markets would open.

Chaos, meltdown, and no electronic fund transfers—the key to the heist. Seething, Copeland typed in Doc's password and brought the Big Red Button up on his screen again. Should he wait until midnight and see what happened, or touch the screen? He fidgeted, pacing back and forth across the carpet, turning off the TV and then the computers. He was sick of looking at screens and hearing bad news, but he couldn't help himself. He flipped on the TV again just in time to hear the announcement that neither the NYSE nor NAS-DAQ would open. As far as the stock markets were concerned, 1999 was over and had ended with a giant bust.

Wall Street was stunned. Members of the financial community of Lower New York usually felt immune from distant events, but not this time. Buffered by the most powerful economy in the world and isolated in their private lives from the hand-to-mouth, daily struggles of ordinary people, they shared a peculiarly insular mentality fostered by a decade of nonstop prosperity. Many young brokers had never seen a down market. When the exchanges didn't open, they closed their laptops and said "Happy New Year" to one another, hoping against hope that everything would return to normal on Tuesday morning. Somehow they knew it wouldn't. Like most Americans, the brokers and bankers were abysmally ignorant of science and technology and had no real understanding of the millennium bug or the computers it was attacking. Nevertheless, however dimly, they could comprehend the effects. The global economy, absolutely dependent on computers, was vanishing before their eyes.

Jody and Doc sat quietly smoking and watching the rolling catastrophe now heading for Japan. Doc shook his head in despair. Misbehaving computers weren't to blame—ignorance was the culprit, the ignorance he encountered every day from sales clerks who knew nothing about the products they sold and couldn't make change without a calculator. The clerks were mere symbols who represented an empty, alienated, neurotic national existence, the talk shows that substituted for company, the telephone psychics, the thousands of hours of screaming advertising for products no one needed, the bad blockbuster movies with silly special effects, and the idiotic how-to-get-rich-lose-weight-and-find-your-inner-self T-shirts disguised as books. Deluged with lies and propaganda, few people knew how to distinguish truth from bullshit. The responsibility lay with corporations who hired minimum wage mental cripples and exploited them for profit. The ruling class had sold the nation's soul to a binary devil. Three and a half million people worked in the American computer industry, and they were near the top of the food chain. The rest of the two hundred seventy-five million zombies walking around were the food, and they didn't deserve what they were going to get: rampant fear and hysteria bred by ignorance. Doc hoped the millennium bug would wake them up, but he didn't believe it would.

The newspapers and TV had been full of news about the bug for weeks, and idiots who didn't know a CRT from a CPU were running around saying all the computers in the world were going to crash at midnight. They should have spent their energy fixing the damned things. Months of nonstop hype and predictions of horrendous doom and destruction had the entire planet in a state of steroidal frenzy. The cover of every magazine in America had featured the coming millennium disaster. Bank failures were predicted. Billion-dollar liability suits had already been filed against software companies and chip manufacturers, sending high-tech and financial stocks on a roller-coaster ride.

Dozens of government agencies from Social Security to the Department of Defense to the city welfare department had been issuing reassuring statements every day. Nobody in his right mind believed these agencies were staffed by competent people. While the government was mouthing platitudes that failed to inspire confidence, millennium cults were running amok. Doc had no idea what they believed and didn't care, but they scared the hell out of people by constantly screaming at the top of their lungs that the world was going to end. A huge gathering of alienists was assembled in Roswell, New Mexico, and forty thousand people were expecting imminent mass deplanetization. A much larger assembly of two million fervent Christians were waiting for Christ to appear at midnight in Hermosillo, Mexico. All over the planet people were expecting miracles, the apocalypse, redemption, salvation and the destruction of their enemies, as if the cosmos knew or cared about our faulty and arbitrary way of measuring time.

A half million people were freezing in Siberia, and that news would spread terror around the world, heralding the arrival of the bug. The citizens of New York had been advised to prepare for the millennium the way they'd prepare for a massive blackout like those of 1965 and 1977. Stock up on candles, batteries, canned goods, and bottled water and locate your gas shut-off valve. At the same time, as though the left hand had no idea what the right hand was doing, the city was gearing up for the biggest, blow-out New Year's Eve party of all time. The police had published plans to ban vehicles from several areas of the city and turn those streets over to revelers. Hotels had been sold out for months. Fireworks dispatched from barges in the rivers were going to light up the night, and if airplanes were going to fall out of the sky, everyone wanted to be in a tall building with a good view of the spectacle. Twenty-four giant video screens were already up and running in Times Square. Sometimes it seemed as though half the people in New York *wanted* the millennium bug to strike all the computers dead. They thought having everything fall apart would be amusing. Christ Almighty. New York was always crazy, but if this town went really nuts—he shuddered to think of what would happen if the ball started its descent in Times Square and then stopped halfway down.

"Doc?"

"Yeah?"

"You're talking to yourself," Jody said. "You're mumbling."

"Sorry. Just thinking."

"Can I have another vodka?"

"Sure. You okay, Jody?"

"Well, the stock markets aren't going to open. I suppose everyone around Wall Street will start partying this morning."

"They should," Doc said. "They may not get another chance for a long time. Huge parties are planned from Beijing to Washington to greet the 21st Century. Isn't that great? Doesn't that make you feel warm and fuzzy? Astronauts in the space station are hoping to see the fireworks from their aerie in the sky, and they've promised to watch out for alien spaceships as well. The world is primed for the weird, the bizarre, the wonderful and the totally insane. In New York City, dear lady, we're sure to get it. After all, this isn't Vladivostok, is it?"

6

Copeland charged off the elevator and into Doc's office. "There you are," he snapped at Jody. "Let's go kiss the ass of the venerable Chase Manhattan Bank. Are you ready, Ms. Maxwell? They called. We're on. Let's go. What are you doing? Having a drink?"

"Yes, boss," Jody replied. "I'm having a drink."

"Jesus, it's nine o'clock in the morning."

"Happy New Year," she said and swallowed her second vodka in one gulp. "I'm all business."

"I hate holidays," Copeland said. "Nobody gets any work done."

"Nobody in New York is working today, Donald," Doc said. "The markets aren't even going to open."

"I saw that. It's the big shake-out. The strong will survive and dominate."

"Like Chase," Doc said.

"That's right, like Chase, thanks to us."

"Ho, ho. Thanks to whom?"

"To you, Dr. Downs, of course."

"Thank you, Donald. And if Chase falls, we can blame you."

"You bastard."

"Let me ask you a question, Donald," Doc said, stroking his

beard. "The bank's big systems will be fine, but did anyone remember to check the time locks on the vaults?"

Copeland stammered. His face contorted and he finally said, "You were the supervisor on this project. You tell me."

"I can't remember," Doc said, cracking up. "Gee whiz."

"Come on, Donald," Jody said, standing up and setting down her glass. "Let's get this news conference over with."

"Someday," Donald said to Doc, "you'll go too far and really piss me off."

Jody grabbed his arm and pulled him out of Doc's office.

Outside, a traditional New Year's Eve day had started in earnest. With the stock markets closed, people poured out of the brokerages to join the party on the sidewalks. It was cold, a few degrees above freezing, but that didn't stop anyone. As Copeland and Jody walked toward Wall Street, Jody related her harrowing experiences of the morning, and Copeland could see she was rattled. Normally poised and self-assured, she was pale, flighty and unhappy. At her insistence, they hailed a cab.

"Where to, pal?" asked the driver.

"Chase Plaza," Copeland said.

"That's three blocks. You can walk faster."

"We'll ride, thank you."

"You know," the driver said as he turned onto Wall Street, "the freaks are out, man. It's weird out here. I seen more—"

"There they are," Jody shrieked. "The people from the train."

A whirlwind of earnest Asians was moving up the sidewalk, foisting pamphlets into the hands of passersby. Horns honked. People shouted, "Happy New Year," and "Jesus loves you even if I don't." Adding to the cacophony, across the street, in a hail of shredded paper, a bearded, wall-eyed, Bible-waving street preacher summoned up apocalyptic visions from the Book of Revelation, the ultimate source of all millennium theology, legend and nonsense.

"You gonna die, brothers and sisters, you gonna die in a worl' of agony and pain if you ain't ready for the Second Coming of our

Lord Jesus. You got less than fifteen hours to git ready fo' Judgment Day. The worl' is gonna end. The worl' as you know it ain't gonna be here no more. The ocean is gonna come right up on this street and drown all you people who don' accept Our Lord Jesus."

The driver turned around, looked at his passengers and threw up his hands just as the proselytizers reached the car and tried to shove pamphlets in the driver's window. The cabbie rolled it up, pinning an arm inside with fingers wiggling like horrid tentacles before the arm pulled free.

"The millennium, yech," the driver said vehemently. "I can't stand this shit."

"It'll all be over tomorrow," Copeland said. "One big hangover."

"I don't think so," Jody said. "Look at Russia. They've declared martial law."

"That's not going to happen here," Copeland said.

"For God's sake, Donald. What do you think this is right here right now? Look at these people. If I were governor, I'd call out the National Guard."

She gestured frenetically at the wild melange of proselytizers and horn tooters outside the cab.

"These are just the nuts, Jody. We'll be fine."

"What about all the nuclear reactors? Do you believe that every single one of those is ready? In Russia? At Three Mile Island? Jesus. Let's get this press conference over with. We're here. Let's go."

Jody scrambled out of the cab while Copeland paid the driver, who asked, "What did she say about nucular reactors?"

"Forget about it," Copeland said hastily. "Happy New Year."

As they entered the building, Donald noticed long lines snaking away from the tellers' windows in the lobby branch. It wasn't a run on the bank yet, more like a walk, but dozens of nervous people were withdrawing their money in cash.

They stopped at the lobby desk for a security check, and the attendant was apologetic. "I have to call upstairs and confirm your appointment," she said. "The computer is down."

"Good God," Jody exclaimed. "Just what I wanted to hear this morning."

"Are you all right?" Copeland asked her.

"Stop asking me that and I'll be fine."

The fiftieth floor was quiet and serene, the thick carpets and acoustic ceiling reducing every spoken word to a whisper. The male receptionist who fronted the chief financial officer's office wore a conical hat and a button that read, "Year 2000. We're Ready," the bank's new slogan.

"Mr. Edwards will be with you in just a moment," he said, "but I'm afraid I have some bad news. The press conference is canceled. All the media people have been calling saying they're just too busy this morning. The ABC crew that was supposed to be here is at La Guardia, and Channel 2 just phoned to say the president of NASDAQ has called a press conference, so they can't make it."

"Is there anything wrong with the contract?" Jody blurted.

"Not as far as I know," the receptionist answered blithely, "but perhaps you should direct your questions to Mr. Edwards."

Five minutes later the receptionist escorted Copeland and Jody into a paneled office where they were greeted warmly by David Edwards, CFO, a robust and congenial man of sixty.

"Come in, come in," he said, shaking their hands and calling them by their first names. "Sorry about the press," he added, seating them in comfortable leather chairs, "but what can one do? I understand it's a little strange outside, but I guess that's why we spent one hundred sixty million dollars, to avoid the problems others are having. What's happening is just terrible."

"You'll be glad you did, David," Copeland said.

"Oh, I already am, Donald. I suppose you know, but your people already have earned their keep."

"I'm not sure just what you're referring to," Copeland said carefully.

"Why, the lost and misplaced funds, of course. Your man Downs sent my people a final accounting just yesterday. His programs located seventy-two million dollars we never would have found without him. As they say, that's a nice piece of change, and more than enough to pay for the new package we were going to announce today. Since it already made the papers, all we're missing are the bright lights and cameras. Sorry, Jody. You were going to be the star."

"I don't mind," she said with heartfelt honesty. "I think people will have other things on their minds today. Perhaps we can reschedule for Tuesday."

"Well, Donald," said the CFO, "you should be proud of yourself and your company. The bank will be eternally grateful for all you've done."

He laid a single sheet of paper in front of Copeland who scarcely looked at it except to notice Doc's signature at the bottom. He put it in his pocket.

"Seventy-two million. Really." Copeland was suddenly short of breath and struggling to keep his composure. "I had no idea it was that much. I've been so busy, I haven't had a chance to talk to Dr. Downs."

"He's a real hero," Edwards said. "I don't suppose you'd be willing to let him go? I'd hand over the Tech Center to him if he wanted it."

"I certainly couldn't stop you or him, if that's what you want to do. Go ahead and ask him."

"That's extremely gracious, Donald, but I'm sure you wouldn't let him go without a fight. In any case, he doesn't strike me as someone who'd like to work for the bank."

"He's his own man," Copeland said, standing up. "Very much his own man."

"I'm sure we'll be hearing from him for a long time, no matter what he decides. Now, you'll have to excuse me, but I may be the only person in this building who expects to put in a full day's work today. I have a teleconference with the Fed this afternoon."

"Are they still contemplating shutting down all transfers?" Copeland asked.

"I think we can talk them out of it. After all, this isn't Russia, is it? We've got this problem licked, and I'm sure the Fed will see it that way."

The receptionist came in to usher them out. In the elevator Jody watched Copeland's upper lip develop a sudden twitch while his face went bright red, then milky white. He said nothing, and in the lobby crowded with people covered with confetti he seemed hesitant, unsure of where to go or what to do. Jody sensed that something she didn't understand had happened in the meeting.

"Donald?" she asked. "Are you all right?"

"I'm fine," he said. "I'm beginning to think things may be worse than I thought, that's all."

"A problem with the software? You've got to be kidding. The bank has been testing it for a year."

"Well, you never know until crunch time, do you?"

They reached the street where the lines of people withdrawing their deposits now extended outside and around the monumental sculpture in the plaza. Panhandlers working the lines quickly learned to hit on people coming out of the bank with their pockets stuffed with cash. A few feet away, a squad of uniformed cops shoved screaming Koreans into paddy wagons to the delight of a crowd of bicycle messengers, secretaries and financial district clones. Jody thought she'd gone to sleep and awakened inside a macabre circus.

Preoccupied, Copeland ignored the strange sights and began walking rapidly toward Nassau Street. Jody noticed long lines at every bank and ATM machine, and every few feet a stock ticker or newsstand radio was broadcasting an endless stream of news.

Transportation stocks had taken a nose-dive on the European exchanges before they closed. In Birmingham, England, a water department employee accidentally shut off the city's water supply during a Y2K test. The riots that had started in Vladivostok were spreading west across Mother Russia as people acted out a decade of frustration with the post-Soviet government. Reacting to the news, people on the street looked numbed, assaulted by body blows one after another. Copeland brushed past a man standing in the middle of the sidewalk talking on a cellular phone who abruptly slammed the phone into the concrete and crushed it.

"Donald . . ." Jody said, but he forged ahead. She gave up and slumped against a granite wall to light a cigarette. The crowd swirled around her, delirious and confused. She smoked her cigarette and walked on slowly, as befuddled as the rest.

Copeland was struggling with the growing certainty that he'd been screwed. On the day he was supposed to steal a fortune, instead of brimming with anticipation he felt like shit. The heist was his edge against the millennium bug and having it suddenly threatened gave him a bellyache. His lip twitched. It occurred to him that engaging in computer theft with an anarchistic hacker was out of his league. Christ, he'd made the guy a millionaire, although Doc would see it the other way around. They were a team. They needed each other . . . what the hell. That wasn't true. Doc didn't need him, not when he had offers like the one from the bank. At Copeland Investments, Doc had always set his own working conditions, making sure his eccentricities were pampered and appetites indulged, but he could get all that and more elsewhere. So the question remained: Why did Doc give all the found money back to the bank?

Doc's office smelled like dope when Copeland entered without knocking. The engineer grinned. "Have a pleasant meeting with the bank?" he asked.

Copeland slammed the paper onto the desk. "What the fuck does this mean?" he hissed.

Doc bent over the sheet and studied it. "Didn't I tell you about this? Must have been an oversight."

"Oversight my ass."

"Oh, come on, Donald. This was just a little surprise for you. Yeah, I gave them 72 mil because I found a lot more than that. Do you think I'm crazy?"

"Yes. How much more?"

"Enough."

"Don't play these stupid games with me, Doc. I think you got scared and backed out."

"Why would I do that? It's foolproof."

"You're afraid of going to prison, that's why. You got cold feet."

"Relax, Donnie boy. It's going to be a long day. Have a drink and be a human being. The world is going to put on a hell of a show and we have a ringside seat. Look—" he pointed at the TV. "They're closing La Guardia."

The talking head of the airport commissioner was reading from a hastily prepared text. "In the interest of public safety, La Guardia Airport is stopping all outbound flights immediately, and will be closed to inbound flights as of five P.M. this afternoon. All airlines are being notified. Flights already en route will be landed on schedule. We urge everyone, airport and airline employees and the public, to remain calm."

The notion of calm instantly vanished in a barrage of shouted questions from the press.

"Are flights being diverted to Kennedy?"

"Is Newark going to close, too?"

"Are you telling us that airplanes are not safe?"

"Were you ordered to close the airport by the FAA?"

"Will passengers get refunds? Where are you going to put stranded people? Every hotel in town is booked solid."

The airport commissioner, a deputy mayor and the chief of the airport police abruptly stood up and walked out of the conference room without answering any questions.

"Ladies and gentlemen," said the New York 1 reporter on the scene. "All we can tell you is that La Guardia is closing, and if you were planning on flying out of here today, you can forget it. Just a moment . . . I'm getting word that Kennedy and Newark airports are closing as well."

Doc shook his head and grimaced. "These people are lying through their teeth. They knew six months ago the air traffic control systems were going down, but they never said so. There's nothing wrong with the planes; it's the government's radar that's bad."

"I don't give a shit about the fucking airports, Doc," Copeland said. "What about the bank?"

"What about it?"

"How much?"

"Enough, Donald. More than you'll ever need."

On TV, the anchorman continued, "And now, from La Guardia we're going to take you to Japan. Eight thousand miles from New York, the millennium bug is approaching the islands of Japan, and the world's stock exchanges are quivering in their virtual boots. . . ."

"You should be watching this," Doc said. "The Japanese should have known better, but they've been too concerned with saving face over nonstop scandals and bad investments to take care of business. They're going to go belly-up and the repercussions will be phenomenal. I've been working out some projections in my head. Most of Asia is going down with Japan. It's the new Greater East Asian Co-Prosperity Sphere."

"To hell with Japan. Tell me about the money."

"Donald, you sold a hundred and eighty-five million dollars' worth of software to Japanese banks in the last three years. How do you expect to collect what they owe?"

"Doc, please."

"Do you really want to know, Donald? Really, really want to know?"

"Yes."

"So bad you can't stand it?"

"Jesus, we're supposed to be partners."

Doc leaned back in his chair and contemplated the stained ceiling. "Okay," he said. "I gave the money to the bank because they made me a better deal than you. They gave me a quarter of all the money I found—eighteen million dollars—and a new job. By the way, I quit."

It was a lie, but Copeland didn't know that. He didn't react at once, but his hands started to tremble. Finally, he said, "You're joking."

"Why would I joke about a thing like that? It's true. Why steal money from someone who wants to give it to me?"

"Because you like to play games and fuck with my head, that's why."

"Call Edwards and ask him. Didn't he ask you if he could offer me a job? I know he did, because I already took the job. I'm going to run the Tech Center. I start Tuesday."

They glared at each other, and then Doc cracked a grin. "Gotcha, you asshole. You believed me."

"You prick."

"I thought about it, though."

"I'm sure you did, but I still don't know why you gave the bank 72 million they didn't know they had."

"You're just too fucking greedy, Donald. I was in there every day writing new code for their lost accounts, not you. I made the decisions, and I wasn't about to discuss every single one with you. I'm telling you there is so much money left over, you'll have a hard time hiding it. People should have such problems, right?"

"You're lying to me."

"Of course. I'm pathological, I lie to everyone all the time, but I'm so smart nobody knows the difference."

Petulant, reduced to infantile frustration, Copeland muttered, "You hate me."

Doc shook his big, shaggy head and sucked a joint. It wasn't true. He despised Copeland but didn't hate him. Copeland's big brain was always full of creative ways to make money, but that was all he had. He was a cash machine with no recognizable human emotions, and Doc couldn't hate a man who was an empty shell. All he wanted was to see Copeland stew in his own juice.

"It's no wonder your wife left you, Donald," he said. "You're a child. Of course I hate you. I hate all you yuppie bastards. I hate capitalists, especially venture capitalists. Have I told you this before? Only a thousand times. You're the scum of the earth, Donald Copeland, but you're my scum. You're a known quantity, and you have just the right amount of larceny in your pathetic excuse for a soul to be interesting. Otherwise, you're a heartless prick, but that don't bother me none. I'm a heartless prick, too, worse than you."

"You know exactly how much money there is, to the penny, don't you? You keep a running account. An accurate account."

"Shut up, Donald. You're spoiling my high. I want to watch TV. Go rattle around your own office, or go play with your customer support people. They're the ones making all this money for you. You should take a few calls."

"Did the bank . . . ?"

Copeland stopped in midsentence, gave up and went downstairs to his office. He could scream and throw a tantrum, but Doc wouldn't say anything he didn't want to say. The man would play mind games on his death bed.

He turned on the red button again, but he couldn't stand sitting in his office any longer. He grabbed his coat and decided to take a walk. In moments of stress, he always visited the massage parlors in Chinatown, not far away. He glanced once more at the button that stared back like a bloodshot Cyclops. He turned it off. Shoulders slumped, the jounce gone from his step, he slinked out the door and headed toward Madam Wo's perfumed fleshpot on Mott Street.

On TV, a reporter announced a press conference with the director of the Federal Reserve tentatively scheduled for two o'clock. Doc switched channels, rocking on his heels as he stood in front of the screen. On PBS two impassioned academics were debating whether the 21st Century would begin in 2000 or 2001.

"We have no birth certificate for Jesus of Nazareth," declared a bearded pundit, "but the blessed event probably took place in the 23rd year of the reign of Augustus, and near the end of the reign of King Herod who died in 4 B.C. The crucifixion occurred in the 16th year of the reign of Tiberius, but Roman records are inconclusive and whatever Jewish records that may have existed were destroyed in 70 A.D. In any case, by the Sixth Century, Imperial Rome had fallen and the Christians wanted a new way to count years. In 525 Pope John I asked the papal archivist Dionysius Exigiuus, known to history as Denis the Little, to recalculate the calendar from the date of the Nativity, and Denis got it wrong. Alas, for fifteen centuries the world has lived with Denis' bad math. The third millennium actually commenced no later than Christmas day, 1996."

"Oh, nonsense," said his opponent.

"With all due respect," Doc said to the TV, "who cares?" He turned it off.

The phone rang.

"Doc? This is Bill Packard. I'm looking for Donald."

"Bill Packard? Dr. Packard?"

"That's right."

"What do you need, Bill?"

"Advice. We're having trouble with some of our equipment in intensive care, and I thought Donnie might be able to help out."

Chips, Doc thought, embedded chips. Every hospital in America was a depository for computer chips infected with the millennium bug. Everything from kidney dialysis machines to digital thermometers had deadly little computers inside.

"Bill, I'll tell you the truth. Donnie couldn't help you if his life depended on it, but I can."

"Do you really think you can help us?"

"You're at Bellevue, right? I'll be there in half an hour. I'll call you when I'm in front."

Doc went into his office and stuffed a bag full of logic probes and a laptop. The phones were ringing nonstop, but he ignored them and walked back through the lab, passed through two sets of locked security doors and into the nerve center of the Midnight Club.

As a joke, everyone called it the clean room because it was filthy. In place of microfilters and bunny suits, nicotine stained the walls, and junk food wrappers carpeted the floor. When Doc opened the door, thundering rock and roll hit him like a heat wave.

The five members of the club were hunched over their terminals, sweating through their T-shirts and shouting at one another as they monitored the efforts of their counterparts in control rooms all over the city.

"Bell Atlantic is running diagnostics," Carolyn shouted. "They might make it."

"Yeah, but GTE is gonna bite the dust," Judd shouted back from across the room. "Count them out. AT&T is shaky."

"Holy shit," Ronnie yelled. "My guy at the Water Department just smashed his monitor. Look at this."

"What!?"

"Yeah, no shit. Can you believe that?"

Doc walked over to the stereo, couldn't find the Off button, so he pulled the plug. The sudden silence got their attention. The Midnight Club stared at him as though he'd cut off their air.

"I need volunteers," he said. "Who can leave?"

"Nobody can leave, man, not now, not today. We're gonna be here all night," they all said at once.

"There is nothing any of you can do during the next few hours, especially since everything depends on Bo getting his passwords," Doc declared. "If you don't have it together by now, it's too late. Boys and girls, we have a mission of mercy that can help a lot of people who need it." He quickly explained the problem at the hospital and told them to turn off their terminals and grab every chip and piece of testing equipment they could locate in their piles of rubbish. "If the hospital goes down and you get run over by a drunk tonight, how will you feel? You won't feel anything. You'll be dead. Come with me and you'll be heroes. Your mothers will be proud."

Adrian refused, declaring a morbid fear of hospitals, and Bo had to stay in touch with ConEd, but Ronnie, Judd and Carolyn agreed.

"If Deep Volt calls, I'll come right back," Doc said to Bo on the way out.

"Get me my passwords, Doc," Bo said. "Or we're dead meat."

As Doc's Jeep inched across town toward the hospital on First Avenue, the streets were clogged with thousands leaving town for the long weekend, and more thousands driving in for New Year's Eve. Manhattan was turning into a 23-square-mile party in a madhouse, and it wasn't yet ten o'clock in the morning.

As soon as they hit the streets, they saw eight-inch headlines in the *Post* screaming, "STOCK MARKETS CLOSED. JAPAN THREATENED BY BUG!" The news had money people reeling on Wall Street. Men and women in expensive suits wandered around looking several steps beyond dazed and confused, their lives ruined, their electronic fortunes gone in a blaze of disintegrating pixels as the global economy collapsed in front of their eyes. Discarded cellphones and laptops littered the sidewalks as people dropped the devices where they stood and walked into the nearest bar. The saloons were overflowing, fights were breaking out, and people were tearing off their clothes and running naked through the streets to the delight of those with no fortune to lose.

Confronted by the real world, the geeks were nervous and excited.

"Whoa, dude, check it out. Dude's sitting on the curb crying like a baby."

Horns honked everywhere. Car stereos blared a dizzying array of musical styles that collided in dissonance in the bumper-to-bumper traffic. Reggae, hip-hop, techno, Garth Brooks and Beethoven all got air time on East 14th Street. Carloads of shirtless young men leaned out car windows yelling "Happy New Year!" and "Fuck you!" with the same lusty enthusiasm. From the radio they heard, "The millennium bug has reached Australia with devastating effects. Melbourne is blacked out, and Sydney suffered a momentary blackout, but power returned within the hour. Millennium festivities continued without interruption. Now this from Chase Manhattan. Are you ready for Year 2000? Here at Chase Manhattan Bank you can be sure that your funds will be safe and secure in the 21st Century. We're ready!"

Doc snapped it off. Ronnie and Carolyn were giggling at the commercial and pleaded for him to turn it back on, but he refused. On First Avenue, as they neared the hospital, sirens added to the racket, and the Jeep followed a train of ambulances into the hospital grounds. Doc called Bill Packard from a cellphone and the doctor came out with a parking permit.

"Don't want your Jeep towed while you're inside."

Packard led them to the department of information services and ushered them into an office crowded with a staff on the verge of panic. The hospital's programmers were lowlifes by geek standards, but they knew what the bug could do and were fuming with frustration over the administration's hopelessly inadequate measures. The paltry Y2K money in the city budget had gone into billing and accounting computers, not medical equipment or staff PCs.

The geeks looked around, and Judd quietly asked one of the programmers, "Don't you people have Windows NT?"

"Are you nuts? These are antique 386 machines."

"You're kidding."

"I wish I weren't."

Packard found the director of information services, a stern and uptight woman named Mrs. McCarthy who looked the geeks up and down and said, "Who's this? The band?"

"These people are programmers who are going to try to repair the computers in intensive care," Packard replied.

"Let me see the work orders."

"There are no work orders," Packard snarled, about to lose his temper. "This is an emergency and these people are willing to help us out of the goodness of their hearts."

"No work orders, no work," she said.

"You're out of your mind," the doctor said.

"We go by the rules here, Dr. . . . ." She paused to read his name-plate. "Packard, whoever the hell you are. Now, get out of my office and take these people back to whatever hole they crawled out of."

He hit her. With one punch, he knocked her cold. The other people in the room snapped their heads around, saw Mrs. McCarthy lying unconscious on the floor, and cheered.

"Aw right!"

"Let's go," Packard said to Doc. "I don't know why I bothered to stop by here anyway."

He led them across a courtyard and into another building, and within ten minutes they were tearing apart respirators and EKG machines.

"The easiest thing to do for a lot of them," Doc told Packard, "is to set the dates back four years if we can. We'll go after the BIOS chips first. If it's a flash BIOS, maybe we can reprogram it. If not, hope to God we have chips we can substitute."

"Just do what you can," Packard said, "and I'll try to keep the administrative types away. The nurses will cooperate, I'll see to that. Good luck. Need anything?"

"Coffee, boys and girls?" Doc asked.

"A no-fat decaf latte," said Carolyn.

Doc cracked up, shook his head and popped open a panel in the back of a heart stimulator. "Coffee," he said. "Just plain old-fashioned American joe, black."

7

A few minutes after 10:00, fourteen hours before its anticipated arrival, the millennium bug took a circuitous route from an unexpected direction and struck down Safeway Corporation's nationwide chain of supermarkets. The sudden infection affected 1450 stores in 37 states, including the new Safeway on Broadway at 96th, pride and joy of manager Jonathon Spillman. Safeway had wanted to move into Manhattan with a big splash, and Spillman's shiny new store was a showplace for advanced technology. Every operation from inventory control to the automatic sprinklers in the produce department was managed by computer.

Spillman had started bagging groceries as a kid and worked as a checker while earning degrees in computer science and business administration. Perfectly suited for his job, he had great empathy for ordinary people as well as a passion for computers, valuable qualities for a man who spent half of his twelve-hour workday punching a keyboard, and the other half straightening out the constant crises that were a normal part of supermarket life.

Spillman had been in his office since 7:30 wrestling with a new inventory program. Over his objections the system had been installed without thorough testing and was still full of glitches, one of which was annoying him now. He needed a hundred cases of

Ruffles potato chips, and the system was telling him the warehouse in New Jersey had no Ruffles. Smarter than the computer, Spillman knew the warehouse had Ruffles because he was talking to the manager of the Jersey facility who was standing before a mountain of potato chips.

"Put them on the truck anyway, will you, Maurice?"

"Sure, Jon, can do. Busy today?"

"Are you kidding? It's a blitz," Spillman said. "I don't know about you, but all my machines are running slow this morning. Must be the heavy load. Everybody wants everything, I suppose. New Year's Eve and all that."

"It's Y2K, Jonathon," said the warehouse boss. "Today's the day."

"Don't say that," Spillman said, a hint of alarm in his voice. "You'll jinx it."

"Don't tell me you're superstitious, Jonathon."

"We're supposed to have all this Y2K business worked out," Spillman declared. "Safeway spent fifty million dollars on these new systems. We're on top of it."

"You wish," said the warehouseman, unable to contain his sarcasm. "Tell that to my seven hundred suppliers, if you please. Half the invoices coming in here are scrambled. We may have our act together, but when I told this farmer in Maryland he should go out and buy twenty-five thousand dollars' worth of new computers, he laughed at me. Now his five tons of hot-house tomatoes don't match his invoices. According to him, he shipped his goods in 1980. That's crazy. Things are screwed up, and they're only gonna get worse. You watching the news?"

"Who has time for that?"

"You may think we have our problems worked out, but the rest of the world doesn't. They just closed all three airports."

"Oh, boy," Spillman said. "Don't worry. Gotta go. Don't forget my Ruffles."

Spillman walked into the assistant manager's office and found her watching TV.

"Amanda?"

Startled, she looked up and peered at him through her glasses.

"We have a store to run," he said gently.

"Half of Japan is blacked out," she said. "It's truly shocking."

"What?"

"Their central banking system crashed."

"What? That's impossible."

"People are lining up outside banks all over Tokyo to get their money out, and it's the middle of the night there and they say the banks won't open for three or four days, but they're getting on line anyway."

"Well, it won't happen here."

"People are scared, Jon. Have you been on the floor this morning?"

"No, I've been trying to work inventory."

"I think you'd better get your head out of that computer and have a look," she said. "I've already called the police once. A shoplifter, but a crazy shoplifter."

"You didn't tell me."

"You were busy."

Amanda opened her shades. Below, the 80,000-square-foot store was jammed with shoppers buying New Year's Eve supplies. Spillman could see long lines of anxious customers tailing away from all 24 registers, carts overflowing. The store was the focal point of an ethnically diverse neighborhood that included gays, blacks, Hispanics, and whites; rich, poor, and middle-class. Everyone shopped more or less peacefully together every day, but when the store was busy, tensions that lay just beneath the surface began to rise. Some days Spillman called it the Psychodrama Safeway, and he had four security guards on duty at all times.

This morning, with no school, the store was full of roving crowds of teenagers blowing horns and throwing confetti, and the guards had their hands full. He could see why Amanda had summoned the police to arrest a young shoplifter who'd boosted a six-pack of beer.

Shoplifters weren't the only problem. The checkout lines were slow, held up by sluggish credit card and ATM verifiers that were overburdened by busy lines at Safeway's hundreds of stores. Thousands of Safeway customers around the country were trying to clear their credit purchases at the same time, stressing the computers trying to process their requests. To make things worse, for the last two weeks the machines were rejecting more than the usual number of cards because some banks and financial institutions had issued cards that were not Year 2000 compliant. Several times a day Spillman had to go down to the checkout stands and explain to some poor soul why her credit card was rejected. Instead of babbling techno-bullshit about computer incompatibility, he told local customers to take their groceries home, don't worry about it, come in tomorrow with a check. That made him feel good, like he was a mom-and-pop corner grocery run by human beings, not a corporate monolith run by computers.

What he saw that morning in his store chilled his heart. Though the mezzanine offices were sound-proofed, he could feel the rumble of carts on the linoleum floor and the noise made by the kids; behind him, the TV droned out a litany of horror from Japan. He recalled his long conversations during the last year with Donald Copeland and Doc Downs. "Even if the computers don't fail," Doc had predicted, "people will panic anyway because of all the hysterical hype. Truth doesn't matter. Only perception matters."

As Spillman was returning to his office, trouble started in one of the express lines. A middle-aged woman clearly in a hurry to exit with her basket of fruit flashed her ATM card at the checker and slipped it through the verifier.

"Can't take that card, ma'am," the checker said as politely as she could.

"What do you mean you can't take my card?"

The checker, whose smiley-face name tag read, "Hi! I'm Denise," had come in on her day off because she knew the store would be busy. The head checker, Denise was one of Spillman's most devoted workers, but at that moment she wished she'd stayed home.

"It's not your card," she said. "It's your bank. The machine won't take any of their cards."

"Let me just punch in my PIN number," the customer snapped and furiously keyed the pad.

Denise stared at the cash register, the customer watched the digital display on the verifier and the crowd behind shifted on its collective feet. Time hung heavy as the two women slyly traded smirks. The checker was right; the card was rejected.

"I can take a check or cash," Denise said, but the humiliated customer wordlessly abandoned her groceries and walked out in a huff. With a shrug Denise punched in the code to clear the machine for the next order, but her entries into the keyboard had no effect on the register. The machine froze. The display flashed, "System error, system error."

Denise Charlotte Mathews was a checker, not a computer expert, although she spent all day working with a computer that sped the flow of commerce through her check stand. On a grand scale of her life's priorities, the computer ranked below her daughter's wedding and above the subway. She had no idea how it worked, and didn't care any more than she cared how her TV worked. Computers were a fact of life, and Denise had no problem with that. She had a PC at home in Queens and loved to log onto the Internet and research flowers for her garden. She grew roses, and paid honest money for her American Beauties by working a day shift at the supermarket where her entire existence depended on the proper functioning of a computer. At 10:13 A.M. her computer failed.

Denise lifted her eyes to the mezzanine at the far end of the store and picked up the phone. Her voice echoed through the public address system, "Computer is down. Manager, please."

When Spillman heard the announcement, his heart sank. Turning to his keyboard, he deftly called up a program that allowed his screen to duplicate Denise's register, and then another program that was supposed to disconnect her terminal from the system and then reconnect without the error. It didn't work. He couldn't disconnect.

"System error. System error."

"I can pay cash," the next customer in line said to Denise. "I just want to take my bananas and Cheerios home for breakfast."

"Sorry. I can't make change. I can't even open the drawer."

"I have exact change, or close enough."

Smiling, determined to be pleasant, Denise said, "Sure, go ahead," and put the bananas on the scale. The machine failed to weigh the fruit, and the laser refused to read the cereal's bar code.

"Nothing's working," she said. "This never happened before. The scale always works."

"Three eighty-five for the Cheerios and, say, a buck and a quarter for the bananas? How's that?" said the customer.

A gruff voice from the rear of the line piped up, "Take his money and let him go, lady. Jeez. I gotta get to work."

People continued to enter the store, the lines grew longer, and a little girl started to cry. "Mommy! I have to go!"

"All right, dear. I'll have to ask where it is."

The young mother and child left the line and were approaching the check stand when the checker in the next stand turned around and exclaimed, "Hey, Denise, my register just went down, too."

Right down the line each of the 24 checkers in sequence punched keys, banged on their machines, recited incantations and rolled their eyes. All the registers were frozen, and all the checkers reached for their phones.

"Excuse me, but where is the ladies' room?"

From the back of the store, the ominous sound of running feet welled up from the bakery department, then shouts in Spanish and in English. Two security guards raced past the check stands, heading for the disturbance.

"The ladies' room is on the right by customer service," Denise said to the woman as she reached for her phone. "But if I were you, I'd take your daughter and get out of here."

From upstairs, Spillman saw the guards running through the store when his phone rang again.

"Yes?"

"Mr. Spillman, this is Denise, and I'm in check stand one this morning. All the registers are down, and we don't know what to do. Even the scales don't work."

Before he could answer, Amanda walked into his office and announced that all three computer terminals in her department were down. She couldn't open the safe.

"What do you mean, all three?"

"Inventory, payroll and benefits, and operations, all blank, Jon. They're dead."

"Holy Moses."

The assistant manager smiled. "There's a guy outside with a sign that says JESUS IS COMING TONIGHT. Should we wait and ask for divine help?"

"I thought they took that guy away yesterday."

"He's back. Every nut case in the city is in the streets. The news is growing more horrifying by the minute. They closed the airports. The stock exchange didn't even open."

"None of that matters," Spillman said. "We have our own problems to deal with right now. The damned card verifiers have gone haywire and some kids are causing trouble," Spillman said. "It's a fucking implosion."

"Can't you get the verifier controls up on your screen?" Amanda asked.

"No," Spillman answered. "I tried."

"What can we do?" Amanda's helpless question sounded like a prayer.

Spillman shook his head and bit his lip. Decisive, the captain of his ship, he barked, "Call Jersey. Call headquarters in Pleasanton. If they don't know what's going on, we'll have to close the store. Maurice over in Jersey thinks it Y2K. Call him."

"Mr. Spillman," the telephone said a few inches from his ear, "are you still there?"

"Yes, Denise. Tell the customers our system is down. We should have everything up and running in about fifteen minutes."

"Oh, God. Fifteen minutes is like forever when it's like this. People are pissed."

"I know. The people is a beast, right? Pass the word to the other checkers. Tell them to be courteous but firm. Tell customers to just leave their carts and exit the store. Tell the guards to stop letting people in."

Days later, the supermarket manager would come to think that if he had possessed a godlike ability to freeze time and space, he would have done it right there. Before his orders could be executed, Spillman and his assistant watched as the scene unfolded on the floor below. As Denise huddled the checkers together in front of the check stands, two teenaged girls with armfuls of beer and chips burst through the express line and broke for the doors at the north end of the store, a security guard in hot pursuit. A wild chase zig-zagged through startled shoppers and grocery carts and stacks of Presto logs. At the doors the girls dropped their loot and sprinted outside, leaving the guard gasping for breath. With the commotion at the north end and no checkers at the registers, a man in a sport coat and tie pushed his loaded cart right through the check stand and out the south doors. Following suit, the next customer in line had the presence of mind to reach over the counter and grab a handful of plastic bags before pushing her cart onto the sidewalk. Behind her, two colorful Dominican gangstas, realizing that security had momentarily lapsed, walked over to a splendid display of sparkling wines, loaded their cart with champagne and headed for the doors.

"Hey," shouted a burly female guard, finally noticing the beeline of casual looters. "Hey!"

One of the gangstas stopped and with perfect form let fly a champagne bottle that zipped through the air like a Joe Namath pass and caught the guard square in the chest. As she went down with a scream, the bottle exploded and the violent noise instantly caused the first wave of panic to ripple through the front of the store. Suddenly, people stampeded toward both sets of doors only to collide with others coming in, causing more panic, pushing, shoving, screaming and fistfights. In a matter of seconds, the peaceful supermarket transformed into bedlam.

Meanwhile, at the rear of the express line, a man with twelve earrings and heavy tattoos methodically upended his cart and dumped his groceries onto the linoleum. The man in front of him shrieked with glee and dropkicked a can of chicken noodle soup into the glass doors of a dairy case, which shattered. En masse, the checkers bolted for the rear of the store and the back rooms reserved for employees. The security guards regrouped, pushed through the crowd and assaulted the south doors, trying to keep the customers inside from looting and everyone else out. In the mêlée, one of the guards pulled a gun he wasn't supposed to have from an ankle holster only to have it knocked away and picked up by a customer. With a tremendous crash, a shot demolished 400 square feet of tinted plate glass and sunlight streamed into the front of the store. It was a nice day, bright and clear, with a view of the busy sidewalk and street where chaos reigned as panicked grocery shoppers burst out of the store, overflowed the sidewalks and spilled into the busy intersection.

In front of the store, looking in through the shattered window, the ragged doomsayer with his JESUS IS COMING TONIGHT sign experienced his transcendent millennium moment. The bullet had passed through the window and through his sign, missing his head by inches. He fell to his knees and began to pray as desperate shoppers swirled around him. Two elderly Dominican ladies sank down beside him and joined in his prayers.

Inside, people were racing through the aisles, grabbing groceries as if they'd won the lottery. Screams, wild laughter, more panic, crashes. Spillman watched the entire calamity on his security monitors.

He reached for the phone, not sure who to call first, the police, the distribution manager in Jersey, or the main Safeway computer center in Pleasanton, California, three thousand miles away. Below, a brawl erupted in another line of customers, and he quickly dialed the police.

"911 emergency services. Please hold."

While he waited impatiently for the police, Spillman phoned the computer center in Pleasanton where technicians were frantically trying to understand what had happened. All their systems were down, and all 1450 stores in the chain were experiencing the same thing, although Spillman's had the only riot in progress.

Pleasanton had no answers, and it would be several days before Spillman learned what had happened to the computers. One minute past ten in the morning in New York was one minute past midnight on the Island of Guam, fourteen time zones west. Safeway had spent millions to correct its Y2K problems, but most of the money and labor had gone into domestic operations, and small international stores such as the Safeway on Guam had been overlooked. As fireworks welcomed the 21st Century in the island's capital city of Dededo, the inventory computer in the local Safeway decided it was January 1, 1900, a classic millennium bug error. As the inventory computer on Guam began its nightly routine of reviewing the day's receipts and ordering fresh goods, it discovered every item it checked was out of date. Perfectly good perishable fruit appeared to the computer to have rotted long ago. Fresh bread was declared stale. Too clever for its own good, the computer began to check random stock and decided everything needed replenishment and proceeded to write an order to restock the entire store. All this information was placed in a single file, and an inattentive clerk attempted to forward the file by satellite to Safeway's central inventory computer in Pleasanton. The Y2K software and new hardware in Pleasanton did not include an adequate firewall to protect the system from corrupted code entering from outside. No one had thought to run a simple test. When the corrupted code arrived at the central processors in Pleasanton, it trashed the core operating system and $50 million worth of high technology turned to junk. Safeway was out of business.

Technical causes were of no concern to Jonathon Spillman at ten-thirty that morning, only the effects. Computers had created his problem, but human berserkers were trashing his store. The tensions that sometimes suffocated everyone in a congested urban environment compounded by millennium hysteria and multiplied by dozens of barely civilized teenaged hoodlums added up to an explosion of frustration and violence. The Dominicans attacked the gays and the gays fought back. Then out of nowhere a gang of white kids attacked the Dominicans. Within seconds Asians and blacks were involved and all these kids were using goods off the shelves for ammunition and catching innocent citizens in the crossfire. Tomatoes couldn't do too much damage, but canned goods did. Blood flowed in the aisles.

"Emergency services."

"I've got a riot in my store and I need police and paramedics right now!"

New Year's Eve was one of those annual events dreaded by policemen. Too much booze and too little common sense meant feisty drunks and bad car wrecks, but the trouble usually didn't start until late in the afternoon. Not today, not in the 24th Precinct commanded by Captain Ed Garcia. This morning the precinct lobby on 100th Street already was jammed with excited, frightened people asking in a Babel of languages if New York was going to be blacked out, what they should do if aliens landed in Central Park, and who to sue if their computers stopped working. Of Garcia's 25 regular day shift officers and 15 extra uniforms, exactly four had a vague understanding of the millennium bug. He'd sent them to a lecture on Y2K, and they'd all slept through the presentation. Now, the baffled cops were unable to answer any of the frantic questions.

A hands-on commander, Garcia was about to go downstairs and restore order himself when the scanner on his desk blasted out a radio call for all units to respond to a riot in progress at the new Safeway on Broadway and 96th.

In a flash he was in the garage and climbing into the first car heading out.

"Go, go, go," he shouted to the young uniformed driver. "Hit it. What's your name?"

"Richards," said the driver. "Happy New Year, Captain,"

"Yeah, thanks, you, too, Officer Richards. Shut up and drive."

"Yes, sir!"

Radio crackling, siren screaming, engine roaring, tires screeching, the blue-and-white Ford flew down 100th Street to Broadway, scattering pedestrians and pigeons and dodging trucks. Two more cars were right behind, trying to keep up.

Garcia grabbed the microphone and punched the button. "This is Captain Garcia in Unit 1331. I'm on my way to 96th and Broadway. What the hell is happening down there? Anybody."

The driver was sweating and pulsing his siren as he poked through red lights, trying to make his way through the heavy traffic. AM radio stations with police scanners of their own were broadcasting reports of the riot with live coverage on the way, and several civilians altered their routes to follow the train of police cars.

"Holy shit," Richards squealed. "These idiots are right behind us."

"Nothing picks up the day better than a little police action on the fly," said the captain as he punched the microphone button again. "This is Garcia," he shouted. "Somebody down there talk to me!"

"This is Unit 1346, Sergeant O'Donahue. We have looters, Captain, and Broadway is blocked. We're going to have to go in on foot. Jesus, look at that guy. He's got a case of champagne. Hey, bud, you got a receipt for that? Christ, there's another one. They're all over the place. Stop the car, Joe. Hey, fella, hold it right there."

"O'Donahue, forget the looters," Garcia shouted into his microphone. "There's a race riot inside the store. Get in there and shut it down."

"Yes, sir."

Riots rarely came out of the blue and never at ten in the morning. The department's riot squads had orders to assemble at their division headquarters at four that afternoon for New Year's Eve duty, and most members were still at home asleep.

The police dispatcher sang the song of the city, pulling officers from wherever she could, aware that she was leaving huge tracts of urban terrain open to predators. Garcia could hear an orchestra of sirens approaching 96th and Broadway, but all the streets were blocked. The cops abandoned their cars in the middle of 96th in front of a Blockbuster Video, across the street from the Safeway where a New Year's Eve party was in full swing on the sidewalk. An uproarious chorus of "Auld Lang Syne" greeted the policemen, provoking a smile from the young cop and an explosion of rage from Captain Garcia.

"Clear the sidewalk," he shouted. "Tell them to drop those bottles and if anyone gives you any shit, cuff 'em. Richards, come with me."

Beyond the singers, the sidewalk looked like a tornado had swept across the cement. Groceries had spilled from overturned carts, cars at the curb were smashed, people were wandering around dazed, and one group was kneeling in prayer. Four people had been trampled and one customer had had a heart attack. Most of the looters had fled, and paramedics were on the scene, surrounded by gawkers as they administered CPR to the heart attack victim. The captain quickly marshaled his forces, a dozen uniformed officers, and assigned them the tasks of restoring order and helping the injured.

The store was a shambles. The liquor department was a sea of

broken glass and foaming liquid. The security guards had five looters cornered in the dental care aisle. Garcia summoned a pair of
uniforms, told the guards to put away their illegal guns, and went
looking for Spillman.

He found his friend upstairs with Amanda and Denise who were
consoling one another with glasses of champagne.

"What happened, Jon?" the captain asked. "What the hell happened?"

Spillman's face glistened with sweat and his mouth was pulled
back in a maniacal grin. For a moment Garcia thought his friend
had lost his mind, an understandable turn of events.

"Jon? You okay?"

"You want to know what happened, Ed? The impossible. What
was never supposed to happen happened. Have some champagne.
Happy New Year."

Captain Garcia softly repeated his question, "What happened?"

Spillman pointed at a blank computer screen. "Y2K happened,"
he said. "The millennium bug."

"Jesus," Garcia said, wrinkling his nose. "You and Donald talked
my ear off about that. You said it would never happen to you."

"We were wrong," Spillman said. "If it can happen here, it can
happen anywhere."

"It's doomsday," Amanda said. "All our systems are down."

"But why the riot? Damn, I know why. All the hype, that's why.
I'm going to want your security videotapes."

"Take anything you want," Spillman said. "Everyone else did."

He swallowed a glass of champagne and muttered, "Shit. They
just went crazy, ordinary people turned into maniacs."

"It was the kids," Denise said, spitting out the words. "Savages."

Garcia, who saw violence and its aftermath every day, studied
his friend and the two store employees. Jonathon Spillman was
brash, Jewish, intelligent, as cynical and jaded as any New Yorker
and usually unfazed by anything, but he was rattled. Amanda was

pale and near tears, and Denise looked like she just wanted to go home.

"Anybody hurt up here?" the captain asked.

"No, but one of my checkers had his leg broken," Spillman said, "and a guy had a heart attack."

"The paramedics are out front. They'll be okay. I think all of you should lock up and go home."

"I can't," Spillman said. "I have to clean up and stay in contact with the technical people in Pleasanton."

The policeman's radio crackled and he pressed it to his ear. "Garcia."

"Central dispatch here, captain. We have another disturbance at 99th and Amsterdam. A large assembly of people are on their knees praying in the middle of the street, and they're blocking the intersection."

"Mother of God. Okay, I'll be there as soon as I can."

"More trouble?" Spillman asked.

"I have a feeling this is going to be a day to . . ." He didn't finish the thought.

"A day to what?" Amanda asked. "What are you saying, captain?"

"Judgment Day," Garcia said, almost in a whisper, "when we find out who we are."

Outside, a siren shrieked as an ambulance carried away another casualty. Amanda burst into tears.

"Don't worry," Denise consoled her. "We've been through the worst. It's over."

"Oh, no," Amanda wailed. "Don't you understand? It's just starting."

"Go home, both of you," Spillman said. "There's nothing you can do here now."

Amanda shook her head. "How? There's no way I'm getting on a train with all those disgusting people."

"Look," Spillman said. "Go to my house. Denise, get a cab. I'll call Shirley and let her know you're coming. She's home today. All right?"

"I'll take Amanda to my house," Denise said. "I want to go home to my kids. Let's go, Amanda. It'll be all right."

"No," she said, her voice rising. "Nothing will ever be the same again."

Amanda dropped her glass, ran downstairs, stumbled, picked herself up and rushed toward the front of the store. Denise and Spillman were right behind, trying to stop her.

"Amanda, wait!"

It was no use. Amanda ran out of the store, pushed through the crowd on the sidewalk and disappeared.

Spillman saw media vans pulling up in front of the store and stopped short of the doors. "Let her go, Denise," he said. "Stay inside. We don't want to be on TV on the day the world is falling apart."

In the back of the store, the automatic sprinklers came on in the produce department. Looking fresh and delicious, the lettuce was lost in cyberspace and would rot on the shelves. Spillman rolled up his sleeves and went looking for the hand-valve to shut off the spray.

On the far side of the globe, the millennium bug was approaching the most densely populated regions of Asia. Unlike Russia, all of China occupied one time zone, and huge celebrations were scheduled at the Great Wall. Illuminated along its 1200-mile length, the wall was visible from space, and a gigantic digital clock set in the wall just north of Beijing was counting down the minutes. The Great Wall, like the wooden barricade that once ran along Wall Street, had been built to stop alien invaders from reaching the Forbidden Palace. It didn't work in the 14th Century, and wouldn't help in the 21st, either.

8

Looking over the crowd outside the Safeway, Garcia noticed that the usual I've-seen-it-all-before-so-what New York attitude was missing. Everyone appeared glazed and shocked, a rare thing on the island of Manhattan. He stuck his nose in the air and sniffed. Like every city, New York has a unique smell, and Manhattan had always smelled like ozone, salt and sweat. Garcia recognized another odor. He smelled fear.

An invisible enemy was approaching his city, and a fifth column of terror was already loose and attacking from within. He'd seen this before. As an eighteen-year-old Marine, he'd witnessed the fall of Saigon. In those last, terrible days he'd seen panic sweep over a great city and compress a million individual traumas into a single, incomprehensible conflagration. Fear makes people run when there is nowhere to go, sometimes trampling their own children. Desperation creates instant heroes and accidental villains, rends the social fabric and makes a policeman's job impossible.

Garcia decided not to make a statement about the Safeway, but before he could find his driver, microphones and cameras were thrust in his face. The cameras were rolling, and he knew some of the feeds were going out live. Eschewing the grim face the public expected from police officials, he smiled and waved at several reporters he recognized while trying to inch toward his car.

"What happened here, Captain?" came the first shouted question.

"You'll have to excuse me," he said, "but I don't have time to chat."

"Where's the store manager?"

Continuing to smile, Garcia said, "He doesn't have time for you fine people, either. He's busy cleaning up his market."

"How many people were hurt?"

"Four, I think, but I'm not sure."

"Was this caused by computers?"

"How many arrested?"

He gave in and patiently answered their questions.

One hundred blocks south, Donald Copeland had just entered the steamy reception room of his favorite massage parlor on Mott Street in Chinatown. Copeland treated sex like everything else, as a business transaction. In moments of great stress, when his mind descended to his genitals, he dealt with his libido efficiently and in great haste.

"You wan' massah?" queried the Chinese madam who knew him well.

Behind her, three young Chinese massage girls were watching TV, and without warning Copeland found himself watching the aftermath of the Safeway riot. Holy shit, he thought, his friend Jonathon Spillman was the manager of the store.

"Crazy people wreck supahmahket," said Madam Wo. "New Yawk crazy town."

On screen a cop was talking to a crowd of reporters, and he realized the policeman being interviewed was another of his breakfast buddies, Ed Garcia.

"All I know is that the store's computers went down and the

checkers couldn't handle the long lines," Garcia was saying. "People went nuts."

"Captain Garcia, we're getting reports that all the computers in the entire Safeway grocery chain have crashed. Do you have any comment on that?"

"No, I don't know anything about that. I'm sorry. You'll have to excuse me. I have to go."

Copeland could scarcely believe his ears. It had to be Y2K, but it made no sense. Spillman was a member of Safeway's Y2K oversight team. A smart company, Safeway had spent a fortune to become compliant, and they'd done everything right.

"You wan' massah or you wan' watch TV? TV talk about new disease call millennium bug. You know what it is? Is it like flu?"

"Just a minute," he said to Madam Wo, whipping out a cellphone. He punched in Spillman's private number, and the store manager answered on the first ring.

"What happened, Jon?"

"I'm tired of answering that question, Donald. I don't know. Safeway is dead, all 1,450 stores."

"That's impossible."

"Yeah, right, impossible. I thought so, too. Ed was here, but he's gone. There's another riot somewhere in Harlem."

"He's on TV right now outside your store. I'm watching him."

"Shit," Spillman said. "TV is getting people excited. I think these people who trashed my store saw all that crap on TV before they came in. They were primed. I'm thinking about going home and sitting in my house with a shotgun, you know what I mean?"

"What's wrong, Jonathon? You sound agitated."

"For Chrissake, Donnie, my store is dead, my company is dead, but across the street Blockbuster Video is doing fine. They have a window display of every disaster movie ever made, and people are going to celebrate New Year's Eve by watching ships sink and comets hit the earth. Not me. I don't have to watch a movie. I just got run over by a freight train."

"Come downtown. We can have lunch."

"Are you serious? Lunch? You yuppie bastard. I can't leave. I have to stay on-line with Pleasanton while they try to find out what happened. They got corrupted code from somewhere, but frankly, my dear, I don't give a damn. I just sent four people to the hospital. One of my checkers was trampled and the bastards broke his leg. A customer had a heart attack, and God knows what else. Ever seen a riot?"

"Only after the Superbowl, but that's just drunks."

"They could sell tickets," Spillman said. "People would pay to see what I saw today."

"Save the tapes from your security monitors," Copeland said. "Maybe you can sell them."

"That's my Donnie boy, always trying to turn a buck. For your information, Ed wants the tapes. I don't care."

"Look," Copeland said. "I'm very interested in finding out what happened to your systems, Jonathon. Mind if I talk to your people in Pleasanton? Maybe I can get Safeway as a client. Nice account. We have all these Y2K people working on the banks who won't have that much to do next week."

"I swear to God, Donnie, your mind is one of the wonders of the universe, but be my guest. Hey, if you want lunch, we got lunch. It's all over the floor, a quarter acre of it. I'll be here."

Copeland clicked off his phone, surveyed the three girls, picked the chubby one, and gave Madam Wo eighty dollars.

"You wan' special, like always?"

Copeland grunted and followed his prize down the red satin corridor.

When Captain Garcia arrived at 99th and Amsterdam Avenue, a busy intersection in a primarily Spanish-speaking neighborhood, one hundred fifty people were on their knees, praying in Spanish in the middle of the street.

Garcia's 24th Precinct stretched from 86th to Cathedral Parkway on the West Side and included some of the wealthiest neighborhoods in America, as well as some of the city's poorest barrios where less than half the population spoke English. From his friends, Garcia had learned quite a bit about the millennium bug and what to expect, and he knew damned well that many of the poverty-stricken Caribbean Islanders and Central Americans in the Two-Four didn't have a clue. What they did know was that the millennium was coming full-blast and bearing the fruit of two thousand years of mystical numerology and scrambled Christian theology.

People were spilling out of the evangelical church on the corner and into the street, falling to their knees, blocking traffic and attracting a large crowd of gawkers on the sidewalks. Garcia wasn't sure whose side they'd take if things got out of hand.

Garcia could feel another riot in the making. The mayor was in Washington for a millennium photo opportunity with the President. His Honor intended to return for another photo op in Times Square at midnight, leaving the safety of the city during the day in the unprepared hands of five borough presidents, four deputy mayors, and one police commissioner. Garcia had no doubt these politicians would barrage him with useless orders and directives. No matter what happened, Garcia would receive no help from the hierarchy because what was happening in the 24th Precinct was certain to be repeated all over the city before long. Like every other NYPD precinct captain, Garcia was on his own

The fire department was on the scene, and the fire commander was ready to turn the hoses on the crowd. Garcia knew Fire Commander Graviano as a stone-cold racist who considered the fire department a weapon in his private war against the people of New York. Graviano was willing to let a tenement burn, a process he called urban renewal.

"I'm ready to squirt 'em," Graviano said. "Just say the word."

"Let me talk to them first," the captain said.

"Talk to them?" Graviano sneered. "Fuckin' A, captain. These people don't even speak English."

Garcia moved into the kneeling crowd and found the minister, a young man in a flowing red-and-white robe who was in the throes of an ecstatic communion with the Lord.

"Excuse me," Garcia said in Spanish, using the most formal and courteous of verb tenses, "but why are you and your congregation here in the street and not inside your church? It is most certainly a church to be admired."

"We want to show ourselves to God. We want to prove ourselves as martyrs. We are waiting for you, my captain, to help us reveal ourselves to Jesus."

All the other evangelicals had stopped praying and were watching them.

"We must suffer to prove ourselves worthy," the preacher said. "Will you accommodate us, captain?"

My God, thought Garcia, I thought I'd seen everything.

"You want me to take all of you to jail?"

"Yes."

"All right, but you'll have to walk."

"Oh, no, captain, you must arrest us, put us in chains, and throw us in your dungeon."

"I'm afraid that's impossible, *padre*. I don't have the manpower," Garcia said, gesturing toward the firemen. "If you don't move, the *bomberos* will turn their hoses on you, and people will be hurt."

"So much the better, captain."

"You have women and children with you."

"We're all martyrs in the eyes of the Lord."

"I don't think so," Garcia said, shifting from the formal to the informal, trying to throw the preacher off balance. "You're going to wake up tomorrow morning and feel like an idiot. You're deceiving these people. You're under arrest. Just you, no one else."

"I can't leave my congregation."

"You can and you will."

Garcia waved over two uniforms who lifted the minister from his knees and pushed him toward a patrol car. Struggling, flailing wildly, he shouted, "It's starting, brothers and sisters, our journey to meet our Lord on Judgment Day is starting. Pray, brothers and sisters. Jesus is our witness. Jesus will see what they do to us today!"

The congregation began to writhe on the asphalt as the cops wrestled the screaming minister into the back of a patrol car.

"Take him to the precinct, captain?" asked one of the arresting officers.

"No, take him to his church. Maybe the rest will follow."

"I can't wait around here all fuckin' day," the fire commander said. "If I get another call, I'm gone."

"If we can get him out of here," Garcia said patiently, "and they don't have anyone to tell them what to do, maybe we can disperse the crowd peacefully."

"It's not gonna happen, Garcia," said the fireman, pointing to the crowds assembled on all four corners of the intersection. "What about them?"

The crowd was mesmerized by 150 people writhing and moaning in religious ecstasy in the middle of the street. Missing was the usual rumble of catcalls and jeers, and Garcia heard only a few shouts directed at the police and firefighters.

Garcia was an expert at crowd control and also had a deep empathy for the people of New York. He believed he was a public servant and a guarantor of public safety, and he hated officials like Graviano who used their authority to further their own misconceived agendas. If the firefighters turned on their hoses, the crowd would respond with rocks and bottles and rip the neighborhood to shreds.

There was another way. He gathered all the cops and firefighters around him and announced his decision.

"Okay," he said. "Set up permanent barricades at 100th Street, 98th Street, Amsterdam Avenue and Central Park West. I declare this area the Millennium Religious Sanctuary of the 24th Precinct. That's it. Do it."

"What?" screamed Graviano. "You don't have the authority to do that."

"I just did it, you stupid jerk, and I'm going to announce it to the press. Richards, get those reporters over here. I've already had one riot today, and I'm not going to have another. Commander, when I was in the Marines I learned it's much easier to ask forgiveness later than permission first. This is my precinct, and if these people are looking for God, the best they're going to get is me, Captain Ed Garcia. Let's have a little religious tolerance. These people only want to pray. They *believe*. I can't mess with that. Don't you get it? Every religious nut in New York will show up here, and we'll have them all in one place. That way, they won't be doing this all over town. Only once every thousand years do people want to pray in the streets of New York, so I say, let 'em. Get the minister out of the car, Richards. What the hell, I'll do it myself. Go back to your fire station," he said to the commander. "We don't need you anymore. Thank you."

"You'll lose your job for this, Garcia."

"Maybe, but my successor will have a precinct in one piece, at least," Garcia said as he stepped away. "Here's the media."

Garcia waved at the reporters, most of whom had followed him from 96th Street, and gestured for them to come closer.

"Ladies and gentlemen," he said in his best booming public relations voice. "I have an announcement to make. As you know, the city intends to block off several designated areas for New Year's Eve and millennium celebrations. Well, I've just added to the list. As I'm sure you're aware, the millennium has great religious significance for many people in this city, and while we may not agree with their beliefs and aspirations, we must respect them. Therefore, in the name of religious tolerance, the First Amendment to the Constitution of the United States, and the people of the City of New York, I'm closing Amsterdam Avenue to traffic as of right now from

98th to 100th. Welcome to the official Millennium Religious Sanctuary of the 24th Precinct."

The press was aghast. This was unprecedented, unheard of, almost unthinkable, but as word of Captain Garcia's decree spread among the people in the street, an explosion of joy erupted from the throats of the believers.

Garcia beamed. "Let God smile on New York City today," he said. "We're gonna need all the help we can get."

Copeland was back in the massage parlor lobby in time to see the tail end of Ed Garcia's second sound bite of the day. The official Millennium Religious Sanctuary of the 24th Precinct. Wonderful. Why the hell not? As he was thanking Madam Wo, the TV cut away from Spanish Harlem to the ABC anchor desk in Washington.

"We have more breaking news, this time from Julie Carpenter in Hong Kong. Come in, Julie."

"Bob, it's forty-five minutes past midnight here in Hong Kong, the former British colony on China's south coast, and I'm sure you can see fireworks still exploding over the harbor behind me. We've had a magnificent parade of boats and much excitement, but Bob, I have to tell you, the millennium bug is ravaging China. Astronauts on the space station are reporting a rolling power blackout across this vast nation. Only Shanghai and Hong Kong remain illuminated. The Chinese government has ordered a news blackout, but we're getting reports via the Internet and from ham radio operators."

Madam Wo and her girls burst into a flurry of excited Cantonese, pointing at the TV and looking distraught. "You go, you go," Madam Wo insisted, pushing Copeland toward the door. "We close now."

Copeland stepped into Mott Street where he was greeted by a tremendous racket rising from every building. As the news from the old country reached the heart of New York's Chinese community, a million firecrackers seemed to go off at once. He felt his chest constrict. A noisy crowd had gathered in front of an electronics store to watch TVs in the windows.

The millennium bug was shutting down the global economy, a virtual entity entirely dependent on computers and rapid communication. The Federal Reserve had to close the electronic fund transfer system without delay. He should have seen it coming and stayed in his office, and he chastised himself for thinking with his dick instead of his brain. He might be too late.

He started running, forcing his way through hordes of humanity pouring from buildings, raising a clamorous din in all the languages of earth. From Chinatown to the Battery, Lower Manhattan had become a microcosm of a planet in distress, convulsing in the shock of the first planetwide financial collapse caused by the failure of technology.

If the global economy had a spiritual center, it was Wall Street. At 11:45 A.M., with Asia crumbling in the wake of the millennium bug, the short, crooked street lined with magnificent buildings was a psychic wasteland, teeming with ghosts, chalk-faced men and women sunken into mere wisps of themselves. The illusion was deepened by half of them being intoxicated, whether with whiskey or shock didn't matter. Chaos theory had come home to roost.

Copeland had no intention of being a ghost. He tried to pump himself up and restore his confidence by telling himself that amidst the ruins, he would flourish. He would pull off the greatest bank robbery in history and get away with it. After all the mayhem was accounted for, he was going to come out a winner.

The only thing standing between him and his ultimate triumph was the Big Red Button. Hurrying along, a vision of the button began to taunt him, drawing him into its deep magenta orbit. He started to hallucinate, seeing Doc inside the red circle, then the bank's logo, then his wife and son. It was as though his entire life was surging across the screen and mocking him.

He had no idea what would happen if he launched the programs hidden behind the button. Doc could have wired the button into anything. The circuit was supposed to run through five cutouts, but where were they? He should have asked. He wasn't himself, wasn't sharp, wasn't in control. He was losing it. He was the one man in New York who should have been immune to the millennium bug, but right now as he struggled through the crowded streets, it was boring right through his heart. On the other hand, if he didn't touch the button, and the Federal Reserve shut down the banking system, the heist program would lie idle until the system was brought back on line. After waiting so long, couldn't he wait until next Tuesday or even Wednesday? But waiting might give the bank's programmers at the Tech Center a few more days to recheck the code, thereby increasing the chance, no matter how infinitesimally small, of their stumbling across the program. As Doc often said, "There is no such thing as absolute security. A foolproof system doesn't exist. There are only probabilities." Perhaps the surprise waiting in Doc's computer was that nothing would happen because Doc had guessed the Fed would close down the system. Maybe the Big Red Button was no more than a prank to torment the boss. The real trigger, if it existed, was probably locked inside Doc's laptop.

This multitude of possibilities and probabilities were enough to drive a clear-thinking businessman out of his mind. He had to stay focused, be patient, and play out all Doc's games. In the end, they'd fleece the bank and have a few laughs.

Inflamed with desire to confront the button, he burst through the front door of his building and found Jody Maxwell sitting at the receptionist's desk. A miniature TV was quietly reporting the latest millennium news.

"I thought you went home," he said.

"I couldn't even get into the subway station," she said, "and every cab was taken, so I came back to wait it out."

"Where's the receptionist?"

"She left. She's scared to death, Donald. A lot of people are."

He hadn't expected to find her there, and she was looking at him with a brazen curiosity that he found unsettling. She was appraising him, her eyes tracking him like radar, but for what purpose he couldn't tell.

"What?" he demanded. "What is it?"

"You should see yourself," she said. "You look like a wild man."

She handed him her compact mirror and he saw bulging eyes, a sweat-soaked collar, and rumpled suit. For a moment he was terrified he'd become one of the ghosts.

"Are you all right?" she asked.

"It's crazy outside," he answered, smoothing his hair and blinking his eyes, hoping to shrink them through sheer will.

"I know," she said, "but you haven't been yourself since the meeting in Edward's office. What happened this morning?"

"You were there. Nothing happened."

"Something did. Edwards gave you Doc's accounting of the lost funds and you looked like you'd been slapped in the face."

"Naturally. The sum is huge. It's a lot of money."

"Jesus, Donald. You smell like a Chinese whorehouse."

Not skipping a beat, he said, "I was in Chinatown when they announced that China was going down the millennium tube. There's a TV in every store."

"Who cares about China?" she said. "What's happening in New York is enough. Two people jumped off the Staten Island ferry, and another three went off the World Trade Center. It's enough to make you wonder."

"I'm not surprised," he said. "There'll be more."

"Are you in some kind of trouble?" she asked.

"No, of course not."

"Well, you could have fooled me," she said. "Today is make it or break it day for our clients and for us, easily the most important day in our company's history. What's going on, Donald? Is Copeland 2000 going to fail? Are we going to crash and burn?"

"Our clients are going to be okay," Copeland said. "All the banks will be fine, and we'll be fine. The software has been thoroughly tested, and there isn't anything more we can do for them now."

He started down the corridor, saying over his shoulder, "I'm not taking any calls. I'll be in my office."

She came around from behind the desk and followed. "You haven't answered my question," she said to his back. "What happened at the bank this morning?"

"You're asking questions that are none of your business," he snapped.

"For God's sake, Donald, I'm worried about you. For once in your life, stop being such a jerk."

"You think I'm a jerk?"

"Give me a break. You're upset, and not because the world is falling apart because you knew it was going to happen. You drummed it into our heads around here a zillion times."

"It was all theoretical then," he said. "Now it's real."

"You mean something actually touched you, Donald? I'm amazed."

"Listen, Jody, I appreciate your concern, I really do, but I need to get in here and get on-line. The Federal Reserve system is about to close down, and I have to stay on top of the situation."

He could feel the walls closing in, suffocating him. He pushed through the door and shut it, leaving Jody standing in the corridor.

His monitor was blinking, the red circle pulsing like a heartbeat. He didn't know what to do, whether to touch it or not. He forced himself to calm down and think rationally and decided he had to ascertain the status of the Fed. He quickly booted up another computer and accessed the Fed's web site. Within seconds he learned the Fed was shutting down all transfers at noon, in three minutes. He felt sick. His lip twitched. He groaned.

Jody knocked on the door. "Donald," she shouted, "are you all right?"

As he reached out to touch the screen, his hand froze inches from the glass. He could feel the electromagnetic vibrations of the cathode ray tube, and through them Doc's invisible hand. What the hell. He leaned forward and with great trepidation pressed his finger against the screen just as the door burst open. The monitor fizzled and popped and exhaled a cloud of pungent yellow smoke. The room's overhead lights flashed off and on and the opening notes of Beethoven's Fifth blared from hidden speakers. Jody choked off a scream, staring at the machine and her boss who looked ready to explode.

The music abruptly cut off, and a curl of smoke rose from behind the monitor, the result of a smoke bomb. Numbers and symbols that both Copeland and Jody recognized as source code from Copeland 2000 were scrolling down the screen.

The scrolling code stopped after a few seconds and was replaced with a list of eighteen Copeland 2000 programs that would launch at midnight in different places in the bank's vast computer system. Each program was listed with the number of lines of machine code, the binary instructions that tell the computer what to do, followed by the number of lines of code in each program cross-checked by programmers at the bank. In the first seventeen programs, the numbers matched, but in the last one there was a discrepancy.

Copeland 2000 diagnostics—electronic fund transfers

Diagnostic 18B

File 437

Lines of machine code   2201

Lines of code checked by   CMB 2119

Memo from Doc: Dearest Donald, can you get
over to Metro Tech and find it before they do?

Happy hunting.

"What the hell is this?" Jody blurted.

Copeland's heart dropped. Doc was telling him the theft program was buried in 82 lines of hidden code, and also telling him he had to go to the Metro Tech Center, but he wouldn't know why until he got there. It was a code slinger's scavenger hunt.

"It's a classic Doc Downs trick," Copeland said. "If the bank finds this code, they'll suspend the new contract and sue the living shit out of this company. Everyone who works here will be out of a job. I've been had. I have to go to over to Metro Tech now."

"Take me with you," Jody said. "I'm as good at code as you. Maybe better."

Copeland didn't object, but was wondering what else could go wrong on this mangled, convoluted day. Why was Doc doing this to him?

As the clock struck noon, the millennium bug struck India and Southeast Asia. Buddha winked. Time did not exist.

ק

The flood of international news affected the media like the outbreak of war, and by noon word of the approaching millennium bug had reached every corner of the city. New York was not a quiet place, and New Yorkers eagerly expressed views and exchanged opinions. By midday, millions of ordinary citizens had gathered over lunch to yak about the electronic plague advancing across Asia. The computer meltdown in the Far East had hit Lower Manhattan like a tornado, but farther uptown the note was more upbeat. A lack of understanding of the technological nature of the infection didn't stop anyone from repeating the latest sound bite gleaned from the media. The news was the news. It was TV. It was far away.

During the late morning the temperature rose to an unseasonable 45° Fahrenheit, the warmest New Year's Eve in New York anyone could remember. Some blamed the unusual weather on El Niño; others faulted global warming precipitated by excessive methane from bovine dung and the burning of fossil fuels; still others claimed that Jesus had heated the city in preparation for his imminent Second Coming; the more scientifically minded—anyone with a TV and the Discovery Channel—blamed the millennium bug.

———

At Bernie's Delicatessen on Upper Broadway, Bernie's lunchtime customers didn't want to talk about anything but the bug.

"Hey, Bernie," said Vince, a butcher who ate lunch there every day. "You hear about this thing? This whatchamacallit?"

"The bug, yeah. I heard about it. Guys come in here in the morning talk about it all the time."

"Whaddaya think?"

"I think I'm gonna go home tonight and watch the fireworks from my roof. That's what I think."

"People are takin' their money outta the bank."

"They'll get mugged."

To a lot of people, the advancing threat seemed about as interesting as the latest fashion trend or the chances of the Jets in the NFL playoffs. On Staten Island and deep in Queens, events in Manhattan were as remote as happenings in China. People heard about a riot at some grocery store, but nothing had happened at the store in their neighborhood; the stock exchange didn't open, but they didn't own stocks; the airports had closed, but they weren't going anywhere; some loony cop let a bunch of religious nuts block off a street on the Upper West Side, but *those people* were crazy anyway.

"Bernie, you own any stocks?" Vince asked.

"Nah. Wait a minute. I got a pension plan, and I think those guys buy stocks."

"No, that ain't right. They buy that other thing, mutual something."

"Mutual funds."

"Yeah, and that ain't stocks, that's something else, otherwise it would be called mutual stocks, right?"

"Right."

"You think the lights are gonna go out? I heard they went out in China or some damn place."

"Nah."

In reality, Bernie's pension plan owned thousands of shares in a multitude of high-tech companies whose profitability depended on selling goods in lucrative Asian markets. The American economic resurgence in the late 1990s had been led by software companies who sold ninety percent of the software purchased worldwide. In the last few hours their Asian markets had evaporated. The plan also owned shares in blue chip companies who were absolutely dependent on automated international communications. An American clothing company with plants in Indonesia, Malaysia, Taiwan and Hong Kong could no longer communicate with its Asian factories. Oil companies that sold crude in Yokohama couldn't collect payment. Neither could IBM, Virgin Records, or anyone else. Bernie's pension plan was in for a bumpy ride, but he wouldn't know about it for several weeks.

Until that day, many Americans thought of the "global economy" as a buzzword, a term that was little more than a figure of speech. Their Hondas burned gas from the Persian Gulf; their champagne was French; they ate Israeli oranges and Peruvian mangoes, wrote documents on computers assembled in Mexico with parts from Korea and China, and wore clothing manufactured from cotton spun and woven in India and sewn together by illegal immigrants in sweat shops in New York, yet they rarely thought about the electronic web that knitted all the pieces together. The planetary fabric that connected everybody to everybody else was being shredded.

On TVs, radios, newspapers and the Internet, New Yorkers tracked the bug's advance across Asia as it attacked computers and devastated systems already weakened by recession. The economic downturn in the Far East that had started in 1998 had slashed Y2K budgets to the bone, and many companies and governments that were fully aware of the problem had been unable to afford a fix. The priorities were correct, but the money wasn't there. In Asia, the problems were concentrated in cities subject to infrastructure failure while vast rural areas remained untouched. With few computers in rice paddies, ancient agrarian economies continued to function as they had for centuries, while the technology-dependent corporations that had spearheaded the emerging Asian economies were transformed into unwieldy beasts.

By noon Eastern standard time, Japan was two hours into the new year, and Tokyo's fifteen million residents were in the throes of agony. On a night when the weather in Tokyo was just below freezing, the western two-thirds of the city was without power, and all of Tokyo was drunk.

The Japanese government had planned a huge millennium celebration in order to boost the confidence of a nation wracked by economic insecurity. A grateful nation had poured into the streets to participate in a showing of national face. At midnight, in spite of the recession and oblivious to the night chill, three million people were enjoying a rip-roaring party when a sea of lights stretching from Tokyo Bay forty-five miles into the Kanto Plain went dark. Japanese nuclear plants were fully Y2K compliant, but computer malfunctions in the electrical grid blacked out everything west of the Imperial Palace. The city was stunned. The people had heard about Magadan and Vladivostok, but this was Japan. This was Tokyo, the most technically advanced city in the world. This was impossible.

When the lights went out, millions of citizens jumped in their cars and drove like moths toward the illuminated eastern part of the city, site of the Imperial Palace and the heart of the modern capital. Inside half an hour the entire metropolis was in gridlock. Sitting in their cars, the Japanese heard the news broadcast by radio. The National Railway had stopped all rail traffic. Water was suddenly in short supply. The airports closed. The Central Bank declared a "national bank holiday of undetermined length" that provoked a wail from millions of tinny, high-pitched automobile horns adding a final, mournful note to the New Year festivity.

Credit cards and ATM machines were useless. Checks couldn't be cleared. As microwave transmitters went down with the power outages, phone service became erratic. Cellphones went lifeless. In post offices throughout the country, mail-processing machines started stamping everything with the date "January 6, 1980." Gas pumps rolled over to the wrong date and locked. In a Honda Motors factory, robots in the paint shop began painting all the cars blue. Two of the city's four primary water mains closed down when embedded chips in a series of critical pumps decided the pumps were 100 years overdue for maintenance and turned them off. The replacement pumps had the same chip, and the chip manufacturer had gone out of business. The head of the municipal water district promptly killed himself. At one in the morning, three of the five *zaihatsu*, the huge industrial conglomerates known to the world as Japan, Inc., unofficially declared bankruptcy and their chief executive officers committed suicide.

Someone had to take the blame. Many xenophobic Japanese were loath to admit they'd caused their own problems. The complexities of Y2K didn't matter. Government ineptitude and corporate greed didn't matter. Since most software that failed was American in origin, a rumor swept through the city that the Y2K crisis was an American plot to destroy the Japanese economy. At 2:00 in the morning a crowd of angry demonstrators appeared in front of the American Embassy, throwing stones and chanting anti-American slogans. In the Ginza, sixty executives from IBM who'd rented a bar for New Year's Eve were turned out by an angry proprietor who believed the rumors and blamed them for the crisis. It didn't matter to him that IBM wasn't responsible, they were Americans who worked for the most recognizable computer company in the world, and that was enough. Thrust into the street, the men and women from IBM were attacked by gangs of *yakuza* thugs on an antiforeigner rampage. In the mêlée, four Americans and two Japanese died. Martial law was declared in the metropolis of Tokyo at 2:30 A.M. At 3:00, the Emperor opened the grounds of the Imperial Palace and instructed the army to provide tents for anyone stranded in the city, including foreigners. Only half the country heard his broadcast.

In Japan, like everywhere, though many disastrous consequences of malfunctioning computers were readily apparent, most effects didn't show up immediately. Defective computers didn't necessarily crash, as Old Blue had done; they generated inaccurate data that in turn caused unpredictable behavior in the systems they controlled. There was a ripple effect. The power outage in Tokyo was caused by one computer in a major substation sending messages to the grid to step up the power while an override computer demanded a cut in power. The system couldn't handle the conflict and shut down power to most of the city and stepped it up to the rest.

A different malfunction halted rail traffic on the Japanese National Railways. Electric power to the railroad's overhead catenaries was supplied by Y2K compliant nuclear power plants, but the railroad operators kept track of the trains with telemetry data radioed from the locomotives to a central control center. The telemetry computers lost track of the time and date, and engineers were ordered to stop their trains where they were, freezing the entire system. Eleven passenger trains were stopped in tunnels and the passengers had to walk out.

In many places where electric power faltered, redundant back-up systems kicked in and operated successfully. Phone traffic was rerouted, but the lines that remained open were swamped, first crippling military and diplomatic communications, then snarling normal domestic and commercial communications and heightening anxieties among people desperate for information. Data streaming, the life's blood of the global economy, became a data trickle in the eastern hemisphere.

Japan suffered the most because it had the most computers, but the rest of Asia experienced monumental devastation as well. Weakened by dissident strife and political turmoil, Indonesia was swept away as before a typhoon. As the world's fourth most populous nation, Indonesia represented a huge chunk of the global economy that abruptly was unable to produce or buy goods. In contrast, tiny Singapore survived intact, well-lit and uniformly compliant, having had compliance ordered by mandate, but the wealthy, thimble-sized nation was cut off from the rest of Asia when communications failed. In the Philippines the central computers at the bank of Manila survived the time rollover with the aid of Copeland Solutions software, but the bank lost contact with other banks throughout the country when the local phone system collapsed. By early afternoon in New York, the Koreas, Vietnam, Laos, Thailand, Cambodia, Malaysia and three more time zones in Russia fell under the shadow of the deepening crisis. A railroad signaling system in Northern China failed and caused three terrible train wrecks. Air traffic control failure in Bangkok resulted in six fallen airplanes, the worst air disaster of all time. Under normal circumstances, this event alone would have dominated headlines for days; as it was, it would rate a small box on page three.

At 12:30 Jonathon Spillman closed the Safeway, sent the few remaining employees home and trudged down Broadway toward his apartment, a few blocks away. Numbed, momentarily unable to process any more disastrous information, all he had on his mind was his wife Shirley's collection of Official Millennium Paraphernalia. Shirley thought the millennium was the greatest event of her lifetime, better than the 1976 Bicentennial or the wedding of Princess Diana. When Spillman had suggested she leave the city to avoid possible civil disturbances, she'd shrieked, "Are you outta your mind? You think I'm gonna miss this?"

Spillman came upon a crowd surrounding a street vendor selling battery-operated, walking, talking blond Jesus dolls at 86th and Broadway.

"Gitcher millemium doll quick now they goin' fast. He walk. He talk. He say, 'I'm a two-thousand-year-old man. I'm a two-thousand-year-old man.' Thass right. Eighteen dollars. Listen up, ladies, only eighteen little ol' dollars for a ton of millemium fun. He be walkin' from here to e-ter-no-ty."

The doll was manufactured from hard extruded plastic with stamped blue eyes, a golden halo, stiff nylon hair, a white robe with blue piping, a jerky, precarious walk and an oversized button on its chest that read, "2000 Years of Good News." In a squeaky, distorted voice the loop of tape inside the doll actually said, "My name is Jesus. I love you."

In the crowd two elderly black ladies were enthralled by the doll.

"My grandbaby is gonna love this," Mrs. Gordon said to Mrs. Henderson. "Fedex can deliver it before her birthday, and I know she'll send me the cutest e-mail." She turned a withering smile on the merchant and asked, "How much you want for this?"

"Eighteen dollars, ma'am."

"Go on. I'll give you ten."

"Ma'am, this here is a *Jesus* doll. You wouldn't want to rob me just to get next to the Lord? This is a' action figure. You gonna pay twenty-five at Toys-R-Us, plus you get yourself a 2000 Years of Good News button. This is a special, one-of-a-kind genuine millemium doll."

"Hmmm," Mrs. Gordon said. "It's pronounced 'mill-enn-ium.' I bet you don't know what the millennium is, fool."

"Ain't that the truth," Mrs. Henderson agreed, solemnly nodding her head.

"It *New Year's Eve*, that's what it is," the vendor declared. "Got a new name fo' New Year's Eve. Damn. I ain't ignorant."

Mrs. Gordon wagged her finger at the vendor. "What you say, fool. Ha! Don't you know that Jesus don't have blue eyes and blond hair? Jesus was a Semitic man of the Jewish faith. He looked more like a A-rab than a Barbie. Didn't you know that? The millennium is Our Lord's two thousandth birthday."

"You mean it's Christmas?" the vendor squawked, surprised.

"No, it isn't Christmas. It's . . . it's . . . I cain't help it if you don't understand."

"I don't know nothin' about no millemium and I don't care, neither. I got these here dolls to sell today and they look like Jesus to me. They *cute*. They make a little girl happy. That what matter to me."

"Getting your money is what matters to you."

"That, too. There ain't nothin' wrong with that."

"When was the last time you were in church, young man?"

"I got church right here on this street every God damn minute. I don't need no church. You gonna buy a doll or you gonna rag my ass?"

Laughing, Mrs. Gordon and the doll salesman settled on fifteen dollars, batteries included. Meanwhile the Official Millennium Clock ticked down a few more minutes toward the 21st Century, and commerce moved on, another sale racked up, charged to Y2K.

Spillman bought a doll, took it home and installed it in a place of honor in the Official Millennium Display Case in the living room. The plastic Jesus overlooked an Official Millennium Monopoly board. Opposite him was an Official Millennium Barbie who had one hand in a bowl of Official Millennium M&M's. Barbie offered Jesus an Official Millennium Budweiser.

Spillman spent the next three hours watching TV with a loaded shotgun across his knees. In a state of deep denial, Shirley puttered around the apartment and kvetched. She didn't care much for the Official Millennium Jesus, but she believed the Official Millennium Display Case should be nonsectarian. She didn't care about news from Japan, either. She wanted fireworks, not more tragedies. The world had suffered enough. Princess Di was dead, and nothing could be worse than that.

Downtown in Bellevue Hospital, Doc was on his back under a blood analysis machine when his pager went off. He struggled to extract it from his pocket and read the display with a pencil light: BUTTON ACTIVATED. He chuckled. Copeland would be half out of his mind by now and in a few minutes would be caught in traffic trying to fight his way to Brooklyn. Excellent. Keep the boy busy. Make him pay for his sins. This was Judgment Day, a day of redemption and salvation, and he, too, would have to pay.

The news hammering New York had created an epidemic of heart attacks, and the cardiology ward was full. Bill Packard was in the emergency room helping out with admissions. Always stressed to the max on New Year's Eve, the emergency room was exceptionally busy much earlier than usual.

At 1:30 Doc sent Judd, Ronnie, and Carolyn back to Nassau Street in his Jeep. Y2K conditions in the ward were so bad, the programmers had been able to do little beyond test chips, locate the most defective devices and tell the nurses which machines presented life-threatening problems.

The cardiac unit was filling up. Heart attack was the disease of choice among those most affected by the economic crisis. Doc was reconfiguring the programmable chip in the blood analyzer when the two cops and the hospital director of information, Mrs. McCarthy, her nose heavily bandaged, burst into the room where he was working. He ignored them.

"What are you doing here?" she demanded. "Where's that bastard who hit me?"

Doc kept his eyes on his laptop and handed an integrated circuit board to one of the cops. "Hold this a second, would you please?"

"Oh, sure," said the cop, taking the delicate device.

"That chip will cause this machine to mistake blood type O positive for O negative," Doc said casually. "What blood type do you have?"

"Uh, O positive."

"You wouldn't want the machine to make a mistake, now, would you? This could be your blood in here if you needed a transfusion right away."

"No, sir, no way."

"Good," Doc said. "You're looking for Dr. Packard? He's somewhere around here saving lives."

"This lady has filed a complaint."

"I'm not surprised," Doc said. "Dr. Packard asked me to come in here and work on these machines. This lady objected. He let her have it. Have you guys been listening to the news? You understand what's happening in the world today? It isn't just New Year's Eve."

"Yeah, sure."

"Hear about the hospital in Shanghai where machines identical to this one killed nine people earlier today?"

"No. Didn't hear that one."

"Well, I think it's a good idea that it doesn't happen here. I'm going to try to fix this thing or take it out of service as Dr. Packard asked me to do. You can stop me if you like. You have badges and guns and you also have brains. Your choice."

"Arrest this man," Mrs. McCarthy demanded. "Get him out of my hospital."

The two cops looked at one another, nodded their heads and walked out of the ward, leaving Mrs. McCarthy sputtering with rage.

"Excuse me," Doc said, crawling back under the machine. "I'm busy."

In the police station on 100th Street, Captain Garcia unfastened the top buttons on his tunic and drank coffee as he argued with his superiors downtown. No, he wouldn't remove the barriers on Amsterdam Avenue. He had four thousand deliriously happy people dancing in the street to a Latin band playing on a flatbed truck. He had more soap boxes than Hyde Park and from each a preacher was delivering his version of the Book of Revelation. It was a revelation, all right, and the merchants weren't complaining. He was sorry about diverting traffic over to Central Park West, but that was too damned bad.

The divisional commander was so busy with problems created by the closure of the airports that he had to leave the administration of his precincts to the commanders. When the airports closed, about fifteen thousand people returned to midtown and discovered there was no place to stay. It was New Year's Eve and no hotel rooms were available at any price. New York found itself hosting an army of suddenly homeless visitors.

Hordes descended on the train and bus stations demanding instant transport to anywhere, USA, but all the trains and busses were sold out. Abandoned, stranded and unorganized, the bereft presented fifteen thousand unexpected problems for the city to absorb. Another thirty thousand innocent people with air tickets on planes that weren't going to fly were forced to check out of hotel rooms to make room for other guests with reservations made months in advance. Since rooms in New York were commanding fabulous prices, the bidding started with money and quickly escalated to forced evictions, fights, disruptions and the police. An unseemly disturbance occurred in the lobby of the Plaza when the junior senator from the Commonwealth of Virginia was informed he had to vacate his suite. He took a roundhouse swing at the manager, missed, and was promptly twisted into a pretzel by a security guard. At the Chelsea Hotel on West 23rd Street, a visitor from New Orleans was asked to quit his room, which he did without removing his effects. An hour later he returned to collect his clothes and walked in on the new occupants *in flagrante dilecto*. The gentleman in bed with a lady who was not his wife thought the intruder was there for a very different reason, pulled out a pistol and shot the man from New Orleans dead, creating a passionate moment of naked, bloody chaos and a headache for the divisional commander.

At the same time the bridge and tunnel crowd of zesty youth was pouring into Manhattan for the big party. With the official celebration still twelve hours away, a river of booze was already flowing down the Great White Way to Times Square. New York was tanking up. It was New Year's Eve.

En route to the Metro Tech Center in Brooklyn, Copeland and Jody joined the crowd pushing into the Wall Street subway station. The overheated platform was packed, stinking with stress radiating from people fleeing the financial district. Thirty TVs suspended from the ceiling bombarded the restless crowd with news from Asia, but things were happening at too dizzy a pace for most to comprehend, including the New York 1 reporters who were clearly shaken by the scope of events.

"In the People's Republic of China, a huge millennium celebration at the Great Wall just outside Beijing turned to tragedy when two government helicopters crashed in midair and fell into the crowd of more than one million. The cause of the crash remains unknown, and the number of casualties is estimated in the hundreds.

"Here in New York, if you're planning a trip to the bank today for some holiday cash, you can expect a wait. A spokesman for Citibank told us just a few minutes ago that all branches are well supplied with cash to meet the needs of customers; however, we have reports of depositors lining up at New York's 3500 bank branches and 12,000 ATM machines. Unfortunately, armored cars delivering cash to the banks are stuck in traffic all over town.

"Now we turn to national news. In Charlotte, North Carolina, this morning, a branch of NationsBank was the scene of a fatal shooting when a man who was next in line when the branch ran out of money shot a teller and two security guards before being killed by police."

The reporter paused, silently reading the teleprompter, looked away and then back at the camera. "I think we should take a break," she said. As the camera cut away to the co-anchor, she said off-camera, "I don't want to read that," and the director went to a commercial.

"Ski Utah!" blared the TVs. "The holidays are here and you can be spending them in a winter paradise . . ."

On the opposite platform a cohort of drunken college students started a chorus of "Auld Lang Syne."

"My God," Jody said to Copeland. "I wonder what she—"

"They're going to have to close the banks," Copeland interjected. "It's the only thing that makes sense."

"That will just make things worse," Jody said. "Look at what happened down in Charlotte, and God knows what the next story was. I've never seen a reporter act like that."

The rails began to vibrate and headlights appeared in the tunnel as the subway train approached. In defiance of the new, improved, graffiti-free New York, an artist had sprayed the front of the lead car with a flashy "2000." The heavy train clanked into the station, wiping out all sound from the TVs. Copeland and Jody squeezed into the third car.

The passengers were more talkative with one another than usual. People exchanged worried but sympathetic glances. A middle-aged Hispanic woman tried to comfort a young mother sitting next to her with a baby on her lap.

"It can't be that bad, can it?" the elder woman said to the weeping stranger.

"I don't know what I'm going to do. The lines at the bank were so long, and I have to get home and feed my children, and my boss said he didn't know if he could pay us next week or not."

"Trust in God, my child."

At the rear of the car a man started shouting into a cellphone, "God damn it, Ira, I told you sell every Jap stock this morning. What do you mean, you can't get through? What the hell do you think I pay you for?"

"Hey," shouted another voice. "Watch your language there, mister."

"Shut the fuck up and get away from me. Hey! *Hey!*"

"Maybe you'll think again before you call somebody a Jap."

The crowd surged away from the confrontation, compressing the passengers toward the front as the train rattled into the next station. When the doors opened, Jody caught a glimpse of a man lying on the floor, his glasses shattered, his nose broken. He groaned, but the mood in the car had instantly shifted. No one moved to help him, and his assailant was gone. The car filled up again, the new passengers gazing upon the fallen man like a piece of litter.

Copeland stared out the window at a huge advertisement boosting Chase Manhattan. "Year 2000. We're ready." As the train began to move, the ad dissolved into a computer screen, the red button, the face of Edwards the CFO of the bank, and then the images were replaced by the dirty white tile that lined the station walls. The dark tunnel swallowed the train and his mind went blank, dangerously close to shutting down completely.

The Metro Tech Center was on Myrtle Avenue in central Brooklyn, a twenty-minute subway ride from Wall Street. At each stop more people got off than got on, the car thinned out and left a few vacant seats. Somewhere along the way the man who'd been assaulted, the young mother, and the gracious Hispanic lady exited the train, and Jody sat down. Copeland remained standing, clutching the overhead bar with both hands as he tried to imagine what he would find in the Tech Center's computers. Rolling under the city, he wished the train would never stop. He wanted to continue right to the end of Long Island and across the Atlantic Ocean to Europe and just keep going in the opposite direction of the millennium bug, reversing time, reversing all the flawed code, undoing all the damage and putting things back together the way they were. Yet in his larcenous heart he knew things would never be the same. His belief system was shattered, as scrambled as data spewing from an infected computer. He'd believed in money and technology, and they'd betrayed him. He'd thought himself above the fray, but the implacable rotation of the planet meant that when the subway ride ended, the bug would still be moving toward New York, decimating time zone after time zone, destroying economies without regard to race, creed, religion, history or anything else. The bug was the great leveler, treating rich and poor with equal disdain. Even him.

It came to him in a moment of great clarity that he was just as responsible for the bug as anyone else, perhaps more so, although he certainly had done his share to fight it. For his own profit, of course, plenty of profit, oodles of profit, but there was nothing wrong with that. He was rich, but Doc was right. He was greedy. He wanted too much, and what was waiting for him in the Tech Center was the police. The train ride would end in jail. He was convinced Doc had set him up to take a fall.

"Donald?"

Jody was shaking his shoulder.

"Donald? Our stop is next."

The station flashing past the windows seemed to awaken him from his reverie, and Jody led him off the train, through the station and into the clear light of Brooklyn.

On the surface life appeared normal. Traffic moved, the shops and stores displayed New Year's trinkets, pigeons fluttered overhead. Along Myrtle Avenue, banners strung between the streetlights read, "Brooklyn Welcomes 2000."

Across the street four unremarkable office buildings composed the Metro Tech Center, innocuous structures with no identification. Copeland had been there many times and had a security pass, but he hesitated before heading for the entrance.

Jody directed them into a coffeehouse and ordered double espresso for each of them. A languid waiter collected newspapers from empty tables. In a corner booth, a young woman in black turtleneck, black jeans, and silver jewelry studied the classifieds, gave up, rested her chin on her hands and scrutinized three young men with laptops at the next table.

"Code," Copeland said, stirring his coffee.

"What code?" Jody asked, puzzled. "The 82 lines in Doc's message?"

"I should have learned more code," he said in a rambling voice. "It's not a good idea to have employees who can do things you can't supervise."

"What are you talking about, Donald?"

"Doc," he said. "He goes into his private computer lab with his

weird people for hours at a time, and they're in there writing code to do I don't know what. You know, I've never been in there. Maybe that was a mistake."

"Drink your coffee. It's good," Jody coaxed. "Doc doesn't let anyone in there except his freaks."

"I don't know what they do in there."

"Donald, what are the total sales of Copeland Solutions 2000? From the beginning."

"About 400 mil."

"Doesn't that answer your question? Doc's people wrote the software that made you one of the largest vendors of Y2K software in the world. What's your problem?"

"You sound like a PR lady."

"I am a PR lady, but right now I feel like a psychiatric nurse."

"How would you know what that feels like?"

"My mother is one," Jody answered, pleased to hear an echo of Copeland's usual acerbic tone. "Are you going to tell me about these 82 lines of code before we go over to the Tech Center, or what?"

He sipped his coffee, ran his fingers through his hair and asked, "What do I look like?"

"You're a mess," she replied. "So am I. So what?"

"I haven't been in the subway in years. When did they put in the TVs?"

"Focus, Donald. 82 lines of secret code. What are we looking for?"

Copeland stared at a copy of the *Post* that lay on the next table. "JAPAN INC. SINKS," announced a headline on the front, right under, "JETS 12 POINT UNDERDOGS ON SUNDAY." He started to laugh. All his tension welled up and poured out as gleeful peals of hilarity. People in the café stared, and Jody flushed with embarrassment. After all the cockeyed craziness she'd seen that day, watching Donald Copeland lose his mind wasn't her idea of fun.

"You knew this was coming, didn't you?" she said.

"Yes."

"That's why you advised everyone in the company to put their money into cash or gold and hide it under the mattress."

"Yes."

"You're a smart guy, Donald. You must have an edge here. If there's a way to make money out of these disasters, you figured it out."

"No one could really predict what was going to happen," he said with a shrug.

"So, did you put your money under the mattress?" she asked.

"Sure, only my mattress is a safe deposit box somewhere."

"I see. Now, the 82 lines of code."

Copeland looked at her with cool, level eyes and she saw that whatever psychotic cloud had fogged his mind had lifted. He had the sly look of the Donald she recognized when he lied to someone he wanted to manipulate, and she didn't like it.

"Doc's code will probably be a reminder to get one of the techies at the bank to check a laundry list of programs," he said. "I think Doc wanted me away from Nassau Street so I wouldn't go nuts. He prefers that I go nuts in . . . Brooklyn, of all places."

"You're full of shit," Jody said with a forced smile. "I know when you're telling the truth and when you're not."

"Then I should either fire you or make you a partner in the company," Copeland shot back.

"Given the choice," Jody said, standing up, "I quit. I don't think you know the difference between a lie and the truth, Donald. I've spin-doctored so much shit for you, made you look good, protected you, done everything for you but get down on my knees and kiss your ass. I don't know why I came all the way out here with you this afternoon. You and Doc have some kind of game going on between you, and I don't care what it is. You and your 82 lines of code can go to hell. I'm going home. Happy New Year, ex-boss."

She stepped toward the door. Desperate, he pleaded, "Wait a minute. Please."

"Why? You said the bank might slam you with a lawsuit. Maybe you deserve it."

"Maybe I do," he said, perilously close to a confession. Choking on guilt, he couldn't quite utter the incriminating words.

"For what?" she asked. "Deserve it for what? What did you do?"

He took a deep breath, sipped his coffee and asked, "Have you ever discovered, all at once, that nothing you believed was true?"

She thought about that. "Not until today," she said, "and right now I'm not sure what to believe, except I'm pretty sure you're nuts."

"I think Doc is trying to rob the bank," he blurted.

Her jaw dropped. She sat down and stared at him, blinking several times in rapid succession.

"Why the hell do you think I'd ride the damned subway to the middle of nowhere fucking Brooklyn?"

"Oh, shit," she said.

"I think that's what he's been doing with his secret project."

"I don't think Doc is that kind of guy," Jody protested. "He's straight arrow."

"The perfect crime," Copeland said. "A robbery committed by someone no one suspects who has access to the most sensitive financial data and the ability to outsmart the smartest computer nerd at Chase Manhattan." Copeland was beginning to recover his normal, smarmy temperament and warm to the subject. If Doc had set him up to take a fall, he reasoned, he could turn the tables and point the finger at Doc. "This morning you were there when Edwards said Doc recovered 72 million bucks in lost funds."

"Yes, and you turned white as a ghost."

"Because the truth is there was over a hundred million."

"Oh, boy. Oh, shit. Oh my God."

"Yes," he said.

"Where's the rest?" she asked.

"I don't know. Probably Panama."

"And Doc knows you know?"

"Yes."

"And you haven't turned him in."

"It's blackmail. If I don't cooperate and do what he wants, at midnight he'll bring the bank down and make it look like a Y2K screw-up. I have to go into the Tech Center now and make sure Chase's people haven't discovered what he did. If they did, they could very well arrest me when I walk in, and he'll disappear."

"Doc did this?"

"He's a very clever man, Jody. You know that."

"So are you," Jody said. "You've just concocted a hell of a pot-boiler."

"You don't believe me?"

"I said I didn't know what to believe, and I still don't."

"Believe this. I'm going across the street. Coming with?"

He left the café and stood on the sidewalk looking at the Tech Center, an anonymous mass of gray stone with a cluster of micro-wave and satellite dishes on the roof. Inside, the electronic brains of Chase Manhattan consisted of twenty mainframe IBMs, 1600 ter-minals, 3200 phone lines, 400 PCs, two satellite dishes, high speed microwave transmitters, a bank of generators and emergency bat-teries in the basement and a brand new fully Y2K compliant tele-phone switching system. Most of the $160 million Chase paid to Copeland Solutions went into applications running on the IBMs in air-conditioned rooms on the second, third and fourth floors. The Y2K data conversion and remedial software had been thoroughly tested for a year, and Chase was as Y2K compliant as any enterprise of its size anywhere. Doc's programmers and 200 bank employees had gone through 250 million lines of code using the most exacting methods and working to the highest standards. More than 800 ma-jor applications had been completely rewritten or replaced. The project was so massive there were bound to be mistakes, but Chase knew that, as did Lloyds of London who insured the bank against liability. Everyone believed the bank would pass through the date rollover without a major glitch. Already that day, the Bank of Manila and three Japanese commercial banks using Copeland software survived even though the Central Bank of Japan failed. He'd offered the Central Bank Copeland Solutions 2000 at a big discount and they'd turned him down. Too bad for them. Too bad for everybody.

He walked to the corner and waited for the light. A newspaper delivery truck pulled up to a newsstand on the corner, and the driver tossed out a bundle of the latest edition of the *Post*.

"FED SHUTS BANKS," read the headline in six-inch type.

Tick tock. It was almost two o'clock. Just over ten hours to go.

"Okay," Jody said, appearing beside him. "Coming with."

10

The rash of heart attacks in the Bellevue emergency room slackened in the afternoon, only to be replaced by a wave of patients so frightened by the millennium bug that they'd hurt themselves or someone else. After watching the news all day, dozens of unstable personalities suffered psychotic episodes, slashing themselves, jumping in front of busses, committing self-defenestration or lashing out at anyone close—wives, children, strangers. The waiting room overflowed with weeping injured and disoriented friends and relatives.

Near the administration window, a teenager tuned a portable radio to an all-news station, and the wounded and distraught were forced to listen to a tidal wave of nerve-wracking stories from around the world. In Bangladesh, violence exploded between Hindus and Muslims who blamed one another for a rural blackout. In Jerusalem, zealous Christians who'd journeyed to the holy city to celebrate the millennium and await the Second Coming were fighting with Palestinian and Israeli police. Rioting and martial law had spread across Siberia, but reports were raw and unedited, the reasons for the disturbances unclear: fear, freezing cold, religious fervor, six hundred years of Russian angst and brutal oppression. In

Hermosillo, Mexico, cholera broke out among the two million gathered to witness the Second Coming. A man in Chicago held thirty children hostage in a daycare center and threatened to kill them all before the world ended at midnight, Central standard time. As the stories piled up, the cumulative effect was too much for people to bear. Finally, a man walked over to the kid with the radio and asked him to turn it off. When he received a sullen stare in reply, he grabbed the radio and the kid pulled back. Punches, shouts, security guards, and the bug moved ever closer.

By 2:45 congestion in Manhattan was impeding ambulance traffic into the hospital, slowing the frantic pace in the emergency room. If this is the calm before the storm, thought Bill Packard, scrubbing down after a grueling stint performing emergency cardiac surgery, it's time to batten down the hatches. He changed out of his surgical greens and ran over to the cardiology ward to see how Doc was doing.

Having done all he could, Doc was collecting his gear at three o'clock when his pager signaled a call from Deep Volt. He immediately phoned her back at the command center.

She answered, "Operations."

"Doc here. Have something for me?"

Her voice dropped to a barely audible whisper. "Operator security codes," she breathed.

"All of them?"

"No, but you'd better take what I have."

"What format?"

"Zip disks. Meet me at the northeast corner of First Avenue and 14th Street in half an hour. I'm going over to the East Side power plant."

As he clicked off the phone, Packard came into the ward and asked, "How's it going?"

Doc shook his head. "This is one ward out of a hundred," he

complained bitterly. "Get the nurses and I'll tell them what they have to do. Did Mrs. McCarthy ever find you?"

"Mrs. McCarthy is under sedation," Packard replied with a sly grin. "She stormed into a surgical theater looking for me, and to use precise medical terminology, she lost her marbles."

Before leaving, Doc explained to the staff which machines had been jerry-rigged to perform adequately, and which dangerous devices had been turned off. "After midnight, anything automatic has to be monitored," he told the nurses. "If an IV is programmed to deliver medication on a timed basis, make sure it does. Don't trust any automatic equipment tonight, and you should be okay."

Handshakes, hugs, thanks, and Doc was walking rapidly down First Avenue, his mind buzzing with electricity. The juice! Volts! Power plants! A million miles of cable and wire, routers, switches, rectifiers, transformers, circuit breakers, steam turbines and hundred-car trains of West Virginia coal to feed the bright furnaces that turned heat into vital electricity.

The generation and distribution of electric power was staggering in complexity, and computers controlled everything from safety procedures at power plants to route selectors at local substations. Between the nuclear plant at Indian Point in upstate New York and a wall socket in Manhattan, current passed through seven thousand systems directly controlled by computers. Being computers, these machines failed frequently, and utility operators had plenty of experience with breakdowns and blackouts. Nevertheless, they'd never been subjected to multiple failures in many parts of the system simultaneously.

In 1900 electricity had been sexy. Voltage was hot. Every young boy with a face that belonged on the *Saturday Evening Post* wanted to be Thomas Edison. The great man himself transformed New York into the world's first electrified city. At the turn of the 20th Century, if you were hooked up to Edison's wires, people came to your house and stared in awe at your lights. Electricity made you superior, closer to God, in step with progress. Electricity spawned countless technologies over the next hundred years, from illumination to computing, and people no longer thought of the reliable flow of electrons as sexy. Electric power was basic and dull and taken for granted.

At the other end of a wall socket in New York was a pool of oil beneath the Gulf of Mexico. All the power plants in New York burned fuel oil, minimally refined light crude petroleum extracted from the earth in an automated pumping operation whose machinery included hundreds of embedded chips. The safety of the oil riggers depended on monitoring equipment that processed data in date-sensitive applications. As the oil was pumped into ships and pipelines, computers were involved in every step. They kept track of everything from barrels pumped to overtime pay for riggers.

Fifteen million barrels of fuel oil were stored next door to the East River power plant on 14th Street. Pipelines delivered oil from these storage tanks to the other plants in the city. The reliable supply of fuel oil was the first link in the automated process that transformed petroleum into electricity, and the flow of oil through the pipes was controlled by date-sensitive computers. At the power plant, using computers at every stage in the process, oil was weighed, tested for quality, processed with additives, transferred to furnaces and burned, heating boilers in which water was turned into high-pressure steam that pushed against turbines spinning at dizzying speed, rotating generators and producing electricity. The average fossil fuel power plant had 600 computer applications running on forty systems. Five thousand embedded chips controlled valves, sensors and gates. The electric current manufactured by the plant was transmitted, distributed and blended with the output of other plants through a matrix of systems, substations, transformers, rectifiers, relays, and switches with computers at every step. The grid connected the power plants together into one unified system that made the most efficient use of the moment-to-moment capacity of the grid as a whole. At the same time, the computer-controlled connections between components of the grid were the part of the chain most vulnerable to the millennium bug and the least tested. Large utilities that had spent hundreds of millions on Y2K remediation could be pulled down by smaller companies without the resources to become fully compliant.

Doc and Deep Volt had exchanged e-mail for a year before they met, then played cloak-and-dagger games, meeting in odd places, passing information back and forth, learning to trust one another. An outspoken but thoughtful systems operator, her name was Sarah McFadden, an overworked, good-humored, middle-aged African-American mom with four kids.

On 14th Street, Doc leaned against a wall to scan the crowd. The intersection was jammed with traffic, the twelve-foot sidewalks bustling with urgent errands. Harried people crowded into little groceries and delicatessens to buy as much as they could carry. Doc guessed half were preparing for New Year's Eve; the others were laying in supplies for a siege. There was an end-of-the-world giddiness in the air and an edge in people's voices. If the power went out, it wouldn't be like Tokyo. People in New York owned hundreds of thousands of guns. In the 1977 blackout, looting had started seconds after the lights blinked off. Mayor Giuliani's new, improved, polite New York was a thin veneer of civility that could vanish in an instant.

No one was shooting yet. Instead, music was in the air, a weirdly incongruous country and western tune blaring from a car radio about a hard-luck truck-driving man whose woman still loved him no matter how bad he screwed up. "Oh, America," sang the cowboy, "you know how to forgive. You are vast and have room for us all, even sinners like me." Doc tapped his boot to the simple beat as he searched the stream of faces for Sarah.

To his left Doc could see the red brick stacks of the East River Power Station, a key component in his plan to keep power up and running in Manhattan. Left on its own, the plant would fail. Bo had broken into every system, copied every application and database, and found fatal errors he knew were not corrected. At one minute after twelve, the Midnight Club's first order of business was to take control of the program Con Edison called "the functional override" that transferred operational control from the primary to the first backup. Authorization to open the functional override file required the missing password.

Deep beneath the sidewalk, an accelerating subway rattled the concrete, and a flood of humanity issued from the exit. Sarah was among them. A quintessential New Yorker, she carried herself with a magnificent confidence that reminded him of the tall woman he'd seen that day in midtown. It made no difference that Sarah was five-six and weighed two hundred pounds. Her eyes shined with intelligence, and she never lost her smile.

"There are some passwords I just can't get," she said. "The functional override controls are among them."

"We'll manage," Doc said, disappointed.

"I don't see how." Sarah's brow developed a tiny furrow, the closest she ever came to a frown.

"Maybe I'll break into the control room with a machine gun and say, 'Hands up! Give me the password or eat hot lead!' Just like in the movies."

"If you do, I'll let you in," she said with a chuckle. "We could use a little cowboy action to get people off their asses. Otherwise, Bombay."

"India? What about it?"

"Haven't you heard? Bombay is on fire."

"Jesus Christ."

"They lost everything, power, phones, water, and fires started that they can't put out."

He saw it in his mind's eye, Bombay and all of India and its billion people and their unique interpretation of the chaos engulfing them. The wrath of Shiva, the wrath of Allah, the wrath of all the gods the world had ever known. He shuddered. "What do you think, Sarah?" he asked. "Is this the Apocalypse?"

"Doc," she said, "tomorrow the whole world may be on fire, and if it is we'll just have to find a way to put it out. And we will. Keep the faith." A twinkle danced in her eye. "You know, I've figured out what you're trying to do."

"How's that?"

"You have a mainframe somewhere, and you think you can simulate a ConEd backup system when the primary connection to the grid crashes."

"That's about the size of it, yeah."

"I don't care who you are, but I wonder why you're doing it? Is somebody paying you?"

"No. I'm paying other people. I can pay you if you like."

"I'm not doing this for money."

"I didn't think so," Doc said.

"I'm just glad to learn you aren't, either. I wish I could do more. I'll keep trying to get those passwords."

"Sarah," he said, "it may come to that. There may be much more you can do if things look bad. I've told you about Vermont, right?"

"Yes. I called them. They don't have anyone qualified to work on capacitors or voltage regulators. They said they checked them."

"Are you prepared to isolate ConEd from the grid?"

"I am, but the company isn't. They've been arguing about it all day. I have to go. God bless you, Doc, whatever it is you think you're doing."

She handed him three Zip disks and disappeared into the crowd.

Crossing Washington Square, an urban oasis with trees, chess players and a children's playground, Doc sat on a bench to watch a young father push a two-year-old on a swing. Back and forth, back and forth. The toddler giggled with delight. Somewhere nearby a dog barked. Cars milled around the perimeter, hunting for parking. Tranquil and unassuming, the park beneath the triumphal arch at the foot of Fifth Avenue was heedless of the coming storm.

Things were either deadly serious or so trivial they were laughable. There was no middle ground. Bombay was ablaze and with it probably half of India. He could walk over to the newsstand on the corner and find out, or go back to Nassau Street and watch TV, or sit in the park and watch a guy push his kid on a swing. He could think about this being a perfect moment for a military strike. India's computers were malfunctioning, her communications failing, her populace in massive disarray. She was weak and vulnerable. Her hostile neighbor Pakistan had a two-hour window in which her systems would be in order while India's were breaking down, giving the Muslim nation an advantage over her Hindu rival. Pakistan could attack India with a preemptory strike without fear of immediate retaliation.

Doc was certain every nation was on yellow alert, including the United States, and bracing for the worst. The worst wouldn't happen. If men wanted to wage war on this day, they'd have to kill one another with small arms, broadswords and bare hands. A modern nation's ability to make war and defend itself depended on computers. Military computing was several generations behind civilian technology for the simple reason that military computers had to be exceptionally reliable. Anything that worked was never replaced. As a consequence of this inherently practical conservatism, military computers running old software were extremely vulnerable to the millennium bug. An F-16 was a maze of cybernetics. A tank had a dozen computers and hundreds of embedded chips, a ship several thousand. Guns, rockets, missiles, helicopters, torpedoes, radars, sonars, mines, bombs and communication devices all depended on computers. Some would work, but enough were infected with the bug to reduce the world's military capability to the lowest level in a hundred years. That, thought Doc, will be our saving grace in the days to come.

The bug was producing only the first of the 21st Century's computer meltdowns. Such a tiny bug, and it wasn't a bug at all in strict computer parlance. A proper bug was an inadvertent programming error. The millennium bug was a deliberate programming decision made for financial reasons. In 1960 a megabyte of memory cost three million dollars, and dates ate memory. Drop the "one" and the "nine" and save dough. That's all there was to it. Cost considerations. The millennium bug was about money from the beginning, and it was going to be about money in the end. It was burning Bombay. It had ravaged Tokyo. It had left a half billion people without heat on a freezing night, all because the world had adopted the American way: save a buck today and to hell with tomorrow.

Tomorrow would arrive like a firestorm in less than nine hours. Tick tock. It was after 3:30 and counting.

Bo needed the files on the Zip disks, so Doc reluctantly left the park and walked south toward Nassau Street. If he didn't get the override passwords, it was Plan B. Life didn't arrive with operating instructions, or if it did, he'd thrown them away.

Copeland and Jody entered the Chase Manhattan building in the Metro Tech Center and approached a granite desk staffed by two women in blue security uniforms. On the counter behind them Jody spotted a six-inch ball of white fuzz, a toy polar bear wearing a tiny T-shirt inscribed, "Year 2000. We're Ready."

"Donald Copeland and Jody Maxwell to see Dr. Schwarz."

"Welcome to the Tech Center, Mr. Copeland. I have badges ready for you."

"We're expected?"

"Oh, yes, by all means."

A clipboard appeared and they signed in. A guard clipped plastic visitor ID cards to their lapels, and at the elevator another guard checked their badges. A moment later on the fourth floor their IDs were inspected again. Copeland led Jody down a corridor lined with heavy security doors marked with incomprehensible acronyms. Suddenly a pair of doors swung open and Jody glimpsed rows of computer screens, a crowd of people in New Year's Eve hats, balloons, confetti and a blue-and-white banner stretched across the room, "Year 2000! We're ready!"

The day shift of sixty-five Y2K programmers stood at their terminals and broke into applause.

"Cope-land, Cope-land," they chanted like a herd of college sophomores, whom they resembled.

"Did you know about this?" he asked Jody.

"I had no idea."

Two older women in business suits emerged from the crowd and came toward them, Dr. Schwarz, head of the Tech Center, and Dr. Neiman, chief of the Y2K group.

"Donald! Welcome," gushed Dr. Schwarz. "We've been expecting you. Dr. Downs said you'd drop by today. And this lovely lady must be Jody Maxwell. Hello, dear, welcome to the Tech Center."

At first stunned, nonplussed, amused, then thrilled, Copeland beamed like a movie star at the applauding crowd and held up his hands to receive the accolades. Introductions were followed by champagne and a rendition of "For He's a Jolly Good Fellow." Dr. Schwarz pinned "Year 2000. We're Ready" buttons on her guests, and Copeland, feeling ready to die of anxiety before he discovered what was in Doc's hidden program, had to endure an impromptu receiving line, accepting congratulations and shaking hands with the troops. Someone took his overcoat and handed him a glass of champagne.

"You did a great job, Mr. Copeland."

"Thanks."

"I heard the Bank of Manila came through with flying colors."

"Thanks."

He forced himself to make nice and answer a battery of technical questions. Finally, he whispered tersely to Jody, "Find a terminal, access diagnostic 18B and have it check File 437 in the EFT subset. Can you do that?"

"Give me your authorization code."

"Use yours."

"No."

He hesitated, then hissed, "Micro."

"That's your dog's name."

"Go on, Jody. Do it."

He nudged her toward the work area, and she wandered among the rows of cubicles that filled the windowless room. Curiously, she saw no TVs or radios and realized the Tech Center was isolated from the bedlam rushing toward New York. Not completely isolated—she spotted a *Daily News* someone had brought in from lunch—but buffered. The people surrounding Copeland had been cooped up all day. When the swing shift came in at 4:00, things would be different. They'd been at home watching TV.

In the last row of cubicles she found a schoolmarmish young woman still working.

"Too busy to party?" Jody asked.

"Some things can't wait. This is the daily close-out."

"How's it going?" Jody asked, peering at the woman's ID badge, "Martha?"

"Slow," Martha replied. "The Federal Reserve closed the banks and all our branch managers are totaling out for the day, so it's slow. It's always like that at the end of the day, even if the day ends early. Do you work here?"

"No, I'm from Copeland."

"Oh, gee, your people have been great."

"Thanks," Jody said. "Do you mind if I run a diagnostic on your terminal when you're finished? We've been meaning to test one here."

"I guess so. Sure. This is over now."

Jody glanced at the screen and saw a fireworks screen saver and a message, "Hello, Martha. Happy New Year."

"Do you mind?" Jody said as she eased her away from the terminal, hit the keys and brought up Diagnostic 18B. The screen asked for authorization, and she typed in "Micro." The monitor went black and then the fireworks popped up and, "Hello, Donald. Happy New Year."

Jody thought: Oh shit, what next? and Martha giggled. "It's been doing that to everybody all day. Is your name Donald?"

"He's my boss," Jody said. "Donald Copeland."

"*The* Donald Copeland?"

"The very same."

"Are you sure you can use his password?"

"He's here," Jody said. "Let's ask him."

Jody went back into the crowd and returned with Copeland in tow. He stared at the screen and blinked several times, his mouth frozen in an idiotic, toothy grin.

"Well?" Jody asked. "Should I run it?"

Intrigued, the tech center's senior staff had followed him to the terminal. He glanced at them crowding around, full of good cheer and sipping champagne, and their closeness made him feel light-headed, as if he were being led to his execution. For all he knew, Doc's program could kill the bank right then and there.

"What is this, Donald? A little preview?" asked a smiling Dr. Schwarz.

"It's just a minor diagnostic," Jody said. "We don't want any surprises, do we?"

Copeland was white with terror, but he said, "Run it."

Jody accessed file 437 and hit "run."

The diagnostic file presented a simple graph that showed the number of lines of code to be checked and the percentage checked. The number quickly jumped from 1% to 12 to 35 and right up to 100%, and then presented a message:

Code Compliance 100% Verified

For reverification go to Old Blue

Reverify now? Y/N

Copeland fainted, crumpling to the floor as if he'd been shot. The crowd gasped. Eyes flicked back and forth between the fallen man and the screen. Within seconds he regained consciousness, and when he opened his eyes, Jody was leaning over him.

"Donald?" she said, her voice trembling with panic. "Donald? Are you all right?"

The message was reverberating in his head, "Old Blue, Old Blue." Doc was sending him home to his pet computer after bouncing him to Brooklyn as part of a ridiculous practical joke. There was nothing he could do about it. Perhaps, he thought, he deserved to be the victim of Doc's morality play.

He blinked. Jody's face was inches from his and he noticed her look of alarm. He asked, "Why am I on the floor?"

"You passed out."

"I what?"

"You went out like . . . like a Russian power plant."

"Are people staring? Oh, God," he groaned. "I did. I've made a fool of myself."

"It's a good day for that," Jody said. "It's perfectly understandable."

"He fucked me," Copeland muttered. "The bastard fucked me."

"Shut up, Donald," Jody hissed. "Just be quiet."

"Is he all right?" several people asked at once.

"Yes," she said, turning to face them. "He's okay."

"The code isn't here," he said to her. "It's in Old Blue."

"Will you be quiet?" she whispered forcefully. "Can we talk about this later?"

"They'll know. They'll all find out."

"Shut *up*, Donald, for God's sake."

"What happened, Ms. Maxwell?" asked Dr. Schwarz, coming over and helping Copeland raise himself to a sitting position.

"I'm not sure," Jody said, thinking to herself, by God, I'm covering for him again. "It's been a very stressful day. I don't think the champagne was a good idea."

"What does this mean, go to Old Blue for reverification?"

"I can tell you," Copeland said. "Old Blue is a proprietary internal diagnostic we use to verify the diagnostic programs themselves. Jody must have used a Copeland password instead of a Chase authorization. Hit 'Y' for yes and you'll see the program. You have it under a different name."

Martha punched the button, and the computer ran a conventional verification program with no surprises, as he knew it would. He pushed himself to his feet and tried to recover his dignity, but it remained on the Tech Center floor.

He walked unsteadily to a chair, sat down, asked for a telephone and dialed Doc's cellphone.

"Doc here."

"I'm at the Tech Center," Copeland said.

"That's a nice place to be. Having a good time?"

"What's the point to all this, Doc?"

"Go home to Old Blue and find out."

"And if I don't?"

"Then you'll find out something else," Doc said.

"Don't you have anything to say?" Copeland whined.

"Nope. I'm busy."

"Where are you?"

"Not in Brooklyn. Call me when you get home, as I'm sure you will. Bye, Donnie."

Click, dial tone. Copeland stared at the phone and hung up, defeated. Jody forced him to drink a cup of coffee, be polite, say thank you and good-bye before hurrying onto the elevator, past the security desk where they turned in their badges, and out of the building.

"I'm going to kill him," Copeland shouted at Myrtle Avenue. "I'm going to murder the son of a bitch."

Copeland was so enraged and Jody so concerned that neither noticed immediately that no traffic was moving on Myrtle Avenue. A stillness filled the air, pierced by the wail of a police siren not far away. Then came the crackling din of firecrackers. The acrid sting of tear gas caught them by surprise. Jerked to their senses, they looked around and saw a blue line of police in riot gear and gas masks stretched across the four-lane avenue and moving at a steady pace from right to left toward Cadman Plaza, a block away.

The plaza was filled with smoke and gas, and they heard shouts and more firecrackers detonating in the distance. A white van painted with the logo of New York 1 cablevision followed ten yards behind the cops.

Copeland ran into the street and shouted at the driver, "What's going on?"

"Drunks. College students. And what, Marty?" the driver asked his passenger. "Oh, yeah. Russians. Was it Russians or Russian Jews? I dunno. Anyway, Moscow went dark a little while ago and all these Russian immigrants showed up at Borough Hall. There was some kind of demonstration, and at the same time about how many, Marty? Maybe three hundred college kids from all these colleges around here start having a New Year's Eve party in the plaza with kegs of beer and probably Ecstasy and you know what that's like, right? Then the news comes in about Bombay, India, and some peabrain sets a trash can on fire and then a car on fire, and then the demonstrators mix it up with the drunks and somebody called in the riot squad. That answer your question?"

At the sound of a whistle, the line broke into a trot, swept past the Tech Center and plunged into the free-for-all in the plaza. The van speeded up to follow the police, and Copeland ran a few steps alongside before giving up. "Happy New Year," he muttered, standing alone in the middle of the street. He asked himself, "What about Bombay?" and shrugged. When he turned around, Jody was gone.

He returned to the Tech Center entrance, thinking she might have sought shelter inside, but she'd vanished. Another deserter, he thought, like his wife and son. Like Doc. Donald the moneymaker was like a glowing fire. Get close, get warm. Get too close, get burned. In the end they all ran away. He felt miserable.

The subway station was closed. The ticket agent told him no

trains were stopping because of the riot in the plaza. He didn't want to ride the subway anyway. Old Blue and more of Doc's torment were waiting in his house, and he had to go there, but he didn't have to be in a hurry. He buttoned his overcoat and began the long trek across the Brooklyn Bridge to the fabled isle of Manhattan.

On Nassau Street, the members of the Midnight Club sat in a circle on the floor and held hands.

"Did Doc get the codes?" Ronnie asked.

"I don't think so," Bo answered. "He would have called."

"Can we divert the subway generators to the metro feeds?"

Adrian shook his head. "Even if we could, there isn't enough power. No."

A beeping alarm sounded on Bo's monitor. He detached himself from the circle and checked out his screen that duplicated the main ConEd system operator's screen. The operator was receiving a priority message from the federal Nuclear Regulatory Commission.

"Here we go," Bo announced. "The fun and games begin."

The NRC had just ordered ConEd and every other utility company in America to shut down all 108 nuclear power plants across the country.

11

**BROWN-OUT IN CHICAGO AFTER NRC ORDERS
REACTOR SHUT DOWN
MOSCOW FREEZES AT TWENTY BELOW
NAVY ORDERS ALL SHIPS TO PORT
LIGHTS ON, WATER OFF, IN HOLY LAND
PRESIDENT TO ADDRESS NATION AT NINE TONIGHT**

The headlines on the final afternoon editions were enough, Doc thought, stopping at a busy newsstand. People lined up to buy papers as soon as they were dropped off, and he wondered how the truck drivers got through the impossible traffic. That would remain a mystery forever. Just for fun he bought a copy of *Wooden Boat*, a journal that made as much sense as the *Daily News*. Perhaps, after this was over, he'd get a retro life with a girlfriend, a dog, and a nice old Chris Craft runabout.

"Busy?" he queried the vendor.

"Biggest day ever."

"What do you think of all this?" Doc asked, gesturing toward the headlines blaring disaster.

"Sells papers, pal. Next."

He ambled slowly toward Nassau Street, reluctant to deliver the bad news. No passwords, no overrides, no juice. If Manhattan fizzled, what the hell, he'd tried. Programmers all over the world had battled the bug, tediously scrutinizing computer code, sweating artillery shells over an impossible deadline, and receiving in return neither glamour nor recognition. There would be no ticker tape parade for heroic nerds, although the calamity would be much worse without their efforts. It was Murphy's Law. Maybe the whole damned millennium bug was Murphy's Law.

At 4:15 in the afternoon, the bug was ravaging a swath of the industrialized portion of the planet from Murmansk above the arctic circle, through St. Petersburg and Moscow to the Black Sea and Turkey, the ruins of Troy, the Mediterranean, the cauldron of the Middle East, the Sphinx and Pyramids, and down the East Coast of Africa to the wild winds of the Southern Ocean and the ice sheets of Antarctica.

In the Holy Land, the cradle of Western civilization was under assault by the tiniest of Frankenstein monsters, a handful of missing binary code. In Israel, as Y2K compliant as a tiny nation with many computers could be, nuclear-generated power performed flawlessly, but the water mains to Jerusalem and Tel Aviv shut down. The religious significance of the millennium had overwhelmed the country with a million Christian pilgrims, half the resident population, and the hordes had presented crowd control problems for a week. New Year's Eve fell on the Jewish Sabbath, and on the Sabbath no work was done. No busses, taxis, hotel services, restaurants. Most of the Christian pilgrims were American fundamentalists, and a few inadvertently trod upon local customs, provoking Jewish and Islamic fundamentalists into a three-cornered exchange of holy writ and medieval theology. Radical sects used the crowds and confusion as cover for endless provocations, and when the water failed, panic broke out. Disturbances inside Israel were compounded when the infrastructures of neighboring Syria, Jordan and Lebanon collapsed, and Israel was instantly faced with a host of refugees at her borders for whom there was no room and no water. It would take a Second

Coming to prevent chaos in the Levant, but Doc didn't think divine intervention would alleviate the problem. It didn't the first time. Computers didn't know about God. Computers understood binary machine code and were only as smart as the people who wrote their programming. Less than perfect humans wrote less than perfect code, and the deepest errors didn't reveal themselves until put to the test. The century rollover was the test.

At 5:00, Eastern Europe would be crushed, and at six, Berlin, Rome, Paris and Madrid would go down the millennium tube. The shining stars of the West would face their collective folly, not for the first time. Europe had faced invaders from the East before, Vandal and Moor, Visigoth and Persian. Yet Europe was the heart and soul of technology, having given birth to the compass and the voyages of discovery, the invention of the corporation in the coffeehouses of London, the Industrial Revolution, Madam Curie, Signor Marconi, and the man who defined the 20th Century, Albert Einstein. Europe in the 20th Century had been marked by stunningly sudden and radical changes that caught millions by surprise: the mass slaughter of World War One, the Russian Revolution, the blitzkrieg of the Nazis, the Holocaust, the rise of America and Japan, and the fall of the Soviet Union. Another surprise was one time zone away.

The main European event was scheduled for seven P.M., when the enemy would strike Greenwich, England, a pastoral suburb of London that sat astride the prime meridian, zero degrees longitude. Since the establishment of the Royal Observatory in 1757, local time in Greenwich had been the standard for the world. The atomic clocks in the observatory established GMT, Greenwich Mean Time, formally known as UTC, Universal Time Coordinates, and universally recognized by radio and military people as Zulu time. Every satellite and satellite control station on the planet ran on Zulu time, and when the bug reached the prime meridian, all hell would break loose in the skies as well as on earth.

In New York, the sun turned red over New Jersey and the temperature started to drop. The day was dying and with it the 20th

Century, whacked by a techno-plague that was rising like a malevolent strain of bacteria to attack the machines. Doc had no doubt the machines would win. The bug would kill the rotten software and bad chips and shake out the deadwood in the technology industries. Old, inefficient companies would die, and younger, smarter entrepreneurs would win. The survivors would be stronger, leaner, more savvy and perhaps too powerful. Ineffective governments would be replaced by more responsive political bodies, and in the end, a handful of megacorporations would rule the world. Welcome to the 21st Century.

He walked on, watching people as they emptied the buildings. From Harlem to the Battery, the homeward bound jostled in the subway enduring the crush one more time. The meatware, Doc mused, as he moseyed along lower Broadway. That's what geeks called humans who operated computers they knew nothing about: meatware. Da people. At the moment, a half million were beneath his feet, singing the subterranean homesick blues.

Hell of a day and hell of a century. People would be talking about this one for a long time. Where were you on New Year's Eve 1999? What happened? Let me tell you, it was the damnedest thing. . . . Walking along, eavesdropping on people telling each other zany tales, Doc realized everyone had a story, and together they painted a portrait of the city as the day came to a close.

After the banks closed, stores stopped taking checks, uncertain when they would clear. An hour later retailers stopped taking credit cards. Macy's and Saks closed early, and by midafternoon only businesses accustomed to cash were open. Lines at ATMs stretched for blocks, and when the machines ran out of money, people were just out of luck.

At Grand Central Station, where an old-fashioned swing band was setting up for a New Year's Eve of elegant ballroom dancing, the main concourse was packed with harried commuters trying to escape the city. Just as the band was striking up the first Duke Ellington tune, the Metro North reservations computer crashed when it attempted to book seats on trains after midnight. The resulting confusion caused the nearest thing to a riot that 25,000 well-bred, polite, affluent Americans can evoke. To the mellow rhythm of "Tuxedo Junction," commuters stormed the platforms and crowded like cattle onto trains. Ten minutes later, the same thing happened at Penn Station, without the music, and in a spirit of charity and grace, the railroad put on extra trains and stopped checking tickets.

The phones had been screwed up since early morning. Each time the bug hit a new country, every immigrant or visitor from that nation tried to call home. Since New York contained ethnic pockets from every country on earth, long-distance lines were jammed all day. When Bombay went up in flames, wails of agony wafted over the Indian community on the Lower East Side of Manhattan as twenty thousand Indians tried to phone their relatives. While Malaysians, Laotians, Koreans and Pakistanis fretted about their homelands and waited for calls to get through, they formed vigilante committees to protect their families and businesses when the devastation reached New York. Early in the day, Brooklyn's huge Russian enclaves had lost their collective minds when the bug hit the Rodina, Mother Russia, and thousands besieged the consulate in Manhattan and filled Orthodox churches, praying for the salvation of the homeland. Many more Russians, Russian Jews, and natives of former Soviet republics began a wild celebration as martial law was extended to all of Russia. Fueled by vodka, a thousand deranged Russians acted out their mad passions at Coney Island by fighting with the police.

The reality of the bug had sent thousands of businesses careening toward full-blown panic. The constant chatter about Y2K in the preceding months had gone right over many people's heads, and then wham! Suddenly, on the last day, with television reporting malfunctioning computers from the Bronx to Katmandu, meatware types decided to find out for themselves if they had a problem with their machines. Y2K tests for personal computers were readily available on the Internet, and several TV stations broadcast instructions on how to find them. Inexperienced operators followed the instructions, downloaded the programs and ran them. Snap, crackle, pop. Thousands of machines failed BIOS tests, often because of operator error, turbocharging the panic level. In a real estate office on East 37th Street, a salesman went from cubicle to cubicle methodically smashing the monitors because he believed they were the computers. People shot their machines, incinerated them, threw them out of windows, and ran over them with Ford Explorers. In traditional New York style, hundreds of disgruntled computer owners hauled their machines onto the sidewalks and abandoned them, creating an instant industry as enterprising souls promptly collected the discarded hardware, all of it perfectly good since the problems were in the software, the BIOS chips, or the internal clocks.

Minicomputers, mainframes, and supercomputers fared no better than the smaller machines. In the physics department at Columbia University, a last-minute check of an eight-million-dollar Cray used for nuclear research turned up a flaw in the embedded chip that ran the built-in air-conditioners. The test killed the heat exchangers and fried the processors. Other computers died more conventional deaths. Someone pulled the plug, walked away and had a stiff drink.

A hellish mob of commuters packed the tunnels and bridges, but suburbanites pouring into the city for New Year's Eve still outnumbered those trying to leave. The party was definitely on. In a metropolitan region of twenty-five million, you could throw a millennium party in a firestorm and a half million would show up. Manhattan was expecting four million to be in the streets at midnight, and the city was doing nothing to encourage people to stay home.

In preparation for the official fireworks, the city had erected grandstands and VIP tents in Battery Park, a waterfront patch of green near the World Trade Center and Nassau Street. By sundown revelers occupied every seat. In one of the tents a caterer turned on a big 35-inch Sony TV, which immediately blasted out the latest news, presented by a bemused reporter in a bush-jacket broadcasting from Africa.

"At this very moment the millennium bug, as I'm sure we're all sick of hearing it called, has passed over the Arabian Peninsula, the Horn of Africa, and right here, the historic city of Khartoum in the Sudan where the Blue Nile and White Nile meet. As you can see, the lights are on and the river is flowing placidly, as oblivious to catastrophes in other parts of the world as it has since time immemorial. However, north of here, Baghdad has suffered a blackout, and reports from Saudi Arabia indicate a failure of military communications throughout the king . . ."

"Enough of this shit, already."

The news was abruptly cut off by a cadre of drunks who picked up the TV, carried it out of the tent and dumped it into the harbor. Thousands cheered, the applause punctuated by an M-80 firecracker that detonated—*boom!*—with raucous irreverence.

Across the length and breadth of the island, not an empty stool was to be found at any bar. Every restaurant table was surrounded by diners. When anyone with a reservation didn't show, a dozen replacements were waiting on the sidewalk. Times Square was hip to hip and shoulder to shoulder for five blocks in every direction from the corner of Broadway and 42nd as 750,000 people tried to figure out what to do with themselves for the next seven and a half hours. High above the crowd, 24 giant TV screens originally intended to show millennium celebrations in every time zone projected video from the Western Hemisphere and from Times Square itself. Bad news was not allowed to spoil the party, and feeds from every country already hit by the bug had been cut. It was starting to get cold. Police were everywhere, on horses, motorbikes, bicycles, and afoot, and spent most of their energy keeping traffic lanes open for emergency vehicles. Sirens keened, the youthful crowd blew horns, sang songs, and drank, and two rock bands flailed away, the music barely distinguishable from the din.

At Bellevue, where the latest wave of patients consisted of conventional car wrecks and gunshot wounds, Bill Packard persuaded the chief resident to summon a meeting of the medical staff who were cautioned against using automated equipment. Exhausted, Packard found a cot in a staff room and lay down for a nap. He couldn't sleep. Instead, he went down to the basement, found the building engineers, and had them perform a thorough readiness check on the generators.

On the Upper West Side, Captain Ed Garcia strolled through the Millennium Religious Sanctuary of the 24th Precinct that he'd created. The Archbishop of New York was celebrating Mass in Central Park, and a coven of witches was holding a circle on 99th Street. At least two dozen preachers held forth, creating a veritable religious marketplace of zealotry. A cheerful committee of Upper West Side residents armed with clipboards circulated among the evangelicals and awarded style points for oratory, fervor and biblical accuracy. A gospel choir was singing on Amsterdam Avenue, and a flock of Buddhist monks beamed serenity and good will on Central Park West.

In midtown, bubbles of chaos rippled out of hotels as managers realized many guests with expensive New Year's Eve reservations would never arrive. The stranded were offered their old rooms at exorbitant prices, a seeming godsend until many learned their credit cards were rejected. Since most Asian banks had closed down all electronic data processing, their cardholders were stuck wherever they were. In the surreal light of dusk, deliriously excited partygoers stood toe to toe on crowded sidewalks. The schizophrenic nature of the moment was captured in Times Square where two sets of chanting youth faced each other across Broadway. The crowd on the west side mindlessly repeated, "Two Thou-sand, Two Thou-sand," and their rivals on the east side countered with, "Lights out, good night, the millennium bug is gonna bite." A drunken woman wandered into the street between the two groups, wobbled back and forth, listening first to one side and then the other. Then she ceremoniously tilted a bottle of Jim Beam high in the air, missed her mouth, poured whiskey all over herself and slowly, inch by inch, keeled over backwards onto the asphalt. Aloof and haughty, Mickey Mouse, the unofficial mayor of Times Square, peered down from above with a timeless, silly grin. His digital clock read 4:32.

Under a gray and darkening sky, a chain reaction of automated computer controls sent bursts of electricity to the streetlights, and block by block, sector by sector, haloes of light cascaded down the broad avenues. In the twilight the electrician's artifice unveiled a more intimate Manhattan. Like the graceful flowering of a night garden, neon glowed beneath the first stars, a splendid array of 20th Century art, a feast of cocktail glasses and bright marquees, the signs of life. Downtown, the towering skyscrapers emitted a stately sheen as though aware of their solemn majesty.

In the neighborhoods, a TV in every apartment cast a blue light into the dusk. The only way to escape the news was to watch college football or old movies on TNT. Even those stations ran banner headlines across the bottom of the screen, and there was no relief. Doc stopped in a deli on Canal Street for a sandwich, and the TV was on behind the counter with the Sunkist Lemon Bowl from Tampa, the stands half empty, the game desultory, the announcers talking about the brown-out in Chicago.

By a quarter to five it was dark and the city underwent a subtle change, grew more mysterious, more willful and full of desire. Doc could feel the difference when he walked out of the deli, bagged sandwich in hand. The early night people hit the streets to offer exotic forms of commerce to the holiday crowds, and as night descended the odor of sex and drugs charged the atmosphere with illicit thrills. The party was heating up as the fearful drank and smoked and swallowed pills to numb themselves against the coming storm. The fearless ingested everything available because it was expected. On New Year's Eve the rules were always suspended, but on this New Year's Eve the rules were tossed aside and trampled.

When Doc arrived on Wall Street, a busload of Japanese tourists clustered under the iron lions for a group photo. They tried to smile, but news from home had spoiled their holiday in New York. The photographer peered through the lens, backed away, looked again, and said something in Japanese. Doc edged closer and saw the camera was a fancy new digital. He knew what had happened. A chip in the lens running on Japanese time had rolled over to the millennium and malfunctioned, killing the camera.

The bug was invisible, ubiquitous and serendipitous. The next camera off the line might have a different chip, or the configuration of the software burned into the chip might be different, or the chip itself might be assembled from different components, black boxes within black boxes. Doc laughed aloud, startling the tourists who couldn't fathom why a bearded lunatic in engineer's boots and hunting cap with ear flaps was hooting and sniggering in their direction.

"The world is nuts," he yelled. "I'm nuts. You're nuts. Everybody's nuts, and that's what's so wonderful. Ha ha ha ha ha."

The first floor of Copeland Investments on Nassau Street was almost empty, the sales people and account execs long gone. Doc found the remnants of a party, champagne bottles and paper cups, and one saleswoman who remained in her cubicle, her phone miraculously working, speaking German into her headset, then switching to English, then back to German.

"That's right, *Herr* Jager, the basic package for a bank your size is five dollars per line of code, and a bank your size has about forty million lines of code. Yes. We can have a team of consultants there next week. Of course. We can charter a plane or you can send your plane. Yes. That's right. *Ja. Ja. Bitte, Herr* Jager."

Doc drew his finger across his neck and whispered, "Go home, Maria. You don't need to be here."

She waved at him, winking, pointing at the phone and nodding enthusiastically as she said, "*Ja. Ja. Nein. Ja. Bitte. Auf wiedersehn, Herr* Jager. Yes. Good-bye."

She hung up and beamed. "How d'ya like that? Bingo. Hamburg. Wow!"

Leaning against the cubicle wall, Doc asked, "When did Copeland raise the rate to five bucks per line?"

"This morning. Herr Jager doesn't care. He's desperate."

"It's been three bucks for a year," Doc observed. "But you know, you're right. The clients will pay."

The stillness in the office was offset by the sound of firecrackers in Battery Park. The din of distant merriment moved through the night air like an echo from the past New Year's Eves, simple parties and rowdy fun. Outside, pools of light around doorways and lamp posts mollified the darkness. On the sidewalks shadowy figures hurried toward the festival and its promise of warmth.

"You're a good trooper, Maria. Go home."

"Whew!" She grinned like a Cheshire cat. "Hamburg."

"Congratulations," he said cheerfully. "Hope you make the sale."

Maria wrinkled her brow and looked thoughtful. "I wonder if Donald would let me use the plane tomorrow," she said. "If I went, I could close right away."

"Maria," he said gently, "the airports are closed."

"Excuse me?"

"No planes in or out for a few days."

"You're kidding."

"Afraid not."

She blinked, leaned over and looked past Doc at the empty office. "Where is everybody?"

"It's New Year's Eve. Don't you have a party to go to?"

"Ohmygod. What time is it?"

"Almost five."

"Ohmygod ohmygod. I've been on the phone two hours. I'm late I'm late I'm late."

She grabbed her purse, pulled out a compact and examined her makeup. "What about the airports? What's going on in the world anyway, Doc?"

He stroked his beard, processing millions of possible answers, one for each calamity that had rocked the world. Of China's eighteen million computers, fifteen million were dead. Runs on banks had spread across South America. The Russians were still rioting in Brooklyn. In five minutes the bug would slam into Eastern Europe. Etcetera etcetera. Maria would find out soon enough for herself.

He winked and recited, " 'The pump don't work 'cause the vandal took the handle.' Bobby Dylan said that. Happy New Year, Maria."

She wrinkled her nose and said, "Huh?"

Copeland's office was empty and smelled like a smoke bomb. The poor bastard, Doc thought. With people like Maria working for him, he'd make more money than he'd ever dreamed possible. Customers all over the world suddenly wanted Y2K software to fix their broken machines, but with the phone lines jammed, most calls from overseas couldn't get through. Eventually the phones would start working again. Hours, days, weeks maybe, but they'd be back. The millennium disaster would fade into history, and Donald Copeland would be one of the big winners.

On the second floor the customer support staff was trying to communicate with banking clients all over the world. Direct lines to Chase and other local banks were open, but the international staff was through for the day. Busy phone lines had shut them down. Two or three dozed in their cubicles, and the rest were drinking a New Year's toast in the back of the room. Doc looked at the roster board and saw half the swing shift wasn't coming in. Annie, the supervisor, threw up her hands and said nothing. Doc understood. There was nothing to say.

"Heard from Donald?" Doc asked.

"No one's seen him for hours. I think he might have gone over to the Tech Center."

"I think he's gone from there," Doc said. "What're you doing tonight?"

"Manning the fort. What else? My relief isn't coming in anyway. Marty's drunk. He admitted as much on the phone, and I told him to stay home."

"You're an angel of mercy, Annie."

"Ha! No way, pal. What would I go home to? The TV? I got that here."

"What's on?"

"Berlin."

On Annie's TV a CNN reporter was standing in the middle of a broad avenue with fireworks bursting over his head. Seminude people in Mardi Gras costumes danced around him. Off camera but close by, a band played a rendition of "When the Saints Go Marching In," and the reporter had to shout into his mike. The camera panned down to a wide yellow stripe that ran across the street from one sidewalk to the other.

"This stripe under my feet on Freidrichstrasse marked the border between East and West Berlin," the reporter said, "and where I'm surrounded by a marvelous New Year's Eve celebration—right here was the exact spot of Checkpoint Charlie, the place where East and West faced off during the Cold War. Fifty feet to the west, as you can see, the guard tower still exists where American soldiers with machine guns stared down their Russian counterparts in an identical tower on the other side. In those days, when you walked through the barricades and razor wire, both sides trained their guns and binoculars on you, front and back. It was spooky and frightening and now it's gone. There are few traces of Checkpoint Charlie today, only the guard tower and a bit of yellow paint on the asphalt. The Cold War is over and the hot war between East and West never happened. It was a big scare that came to nothing, and that's exactly how people here in Berlin feel about the millennium bug to-night."

"What about everything that's happened today to the east?" asked the voice of the anchorwoman. "Japan has suffered. China and India and Russia . . ."

"People in Berlin are saying it can never happen here."

"Didn't Germany close the banks and stock and financial markets early today?"

"Yes, as a precaution."

"Well, Alexis, you've got fifteen minutes to find out who was right."

The reporter held up a flashlight and a bottle of water. "I'm ready no matter what happens. This is Alexis Kosigian for CNN news in Berlin."

The director cut to the studio in Atlanta and the anchorwoman. "And where are we going next?" she asked. "Moscow and Paul Delaney in Red Square."

A talking head surrounded by snow flurries popped up on the screen. St. Basil's cathedral appeared pristine and immaculate above a squad of soldiers in winter uniforms marching across the square, the tattoo of their footsteps a chilling rhythm of despair.

"This is Red Square, empty. The world's largest public plaza is deserted. In the background, you can see the bright onion domes of the Kremlin picked out by spotlights surrounded by darkness. The lights are out in Moscow. In her long history Moscow has been ravaged by Ivan the Terrible, abandoned by Peter the Great, occu-pied by Napoleon and bombarded by Hitler, and in the last ten years she's struggled to make it in the bewildering world of free enter-prise. And now? This may be the knock-out blow. We have reports of looting in many parts of the city, and unconfirmed reports that many of the looters are the police themselves. The army has been brought in to bring the police under control, and no one knows what's going to happen. Communications are failing all over the place, and the assumption here is that nothing works. We do know the army is having trouble fueling its tanks. Apparently the diesel pumps at the army depots stopped working a few minutes after midnight."

"Are cellphones working?" asked the anchorwoman.

"No."

"Do you know if the hot line between the Kremlin and the White House is working?"

"I don't know, but the lights are on inside the Kremlin compound which has its own generators and power supply. I would guess the hot line is open, but as I said, I don't want to assume anything is working. I think I contradicted myself, but this whole situation is contradictory. Information is at a premium because there isn't much of it. We have one report from the far northern city of Murmansk. We understand a detachment of Russian Naval *spetznatz* special forces are holding the operators of the local nuclear power plant at gunpoint, forcing them to keep the plant operating, but we can't confirm that report because we can't get through to anyone in Murmansk. Wait a minute now. What? When? Now? Okay, Jane, they just told us we can go inside the Kremlin and that's what we've been waiting for. That's all for now. This is Paul Delaney for CNN in Moscow."

Doc turned away without listening to the anchorwoman's comments. Like everybody else, the Russians would learn that the millennium bug merely exacerbated older, deeper problems and brought them into focus. It was a catalyst, a watershed event that would weed out weakness in the technological gene pool.

Doc made his way up to the third floor, passed through the security doors, and told the Midnight Club what they'd already guessed.

"The passwords are locked in an isolated PC and Sarah has no access. End of story."

"You just told us her name, Doc," Bo observed.

"Yeah, well, her name is Sarah McFadden. I said I might go down there with a pistol and make her son of a bitch supervisor turn on the computer. Fat chance."

"So if the primary goes down, he punches in the password, the override kicks over to the backup and then that fails. Presto, magic, we're in the dark."

"Looks that way," Doc said.

"I called Northern Lights in Vermont and told them to get out to their substations and start checking chips, and this guy on the phone, some supervisor says, 'Who the fuck are you? Whaddaya mean check the fucking chips? We paid some assholes from Burlington to do that.' Did you check their work? I asked. 'Who the fuck are you?!' I love this guy. Guys like that are the reason this whole thing is going down. Guys like him are going to make me richer than rich."

"You'll be a lot richer if you figure out a way to get those passwords and keep the lights on in New York," Doc said.

"What about Plan B?"

"We can't count on Mayor Rudy," Doc said. "He might tell us to go fuck ourselves."

Bo turned back to his screens, and Doc looked up to check the time. There were at least a hundred clocks in the room, counting all the clocks in the computers, but the one everyone checked was a big Southern Pacific Railroad station clock Adrian had found in an antique store. It had a big analog face with easy to read numbers and long, elegant hands that gracefully swept away the seconds, minutes and hours. It was ten minutes after five.

"What're you gonna do after?" Carolyn asked Ronnie for the 500th time that week.

"Carolyn, please. I'm not interested in after. This is now."

"I'm just nervous. These phone lines are getting some heavy use. Close to overload."

On Carolyn's screens an array of charts monitored the core loads in telephone trunk lines, and it seemed as though everyone in New

York was on the phone. Besides voice traffic, an enormous load of data traffic burdened the lines as millions dialed up the Internet. The T-4 lines were humming as processing centers all over New York frantically transmitted data to other sites for safekeeping. An equal amount was coming into the city, pushing the capacity of myriad systems to the limit.

Adrian seemed to be pissed off, which was no surprise to Doc. Lately, the kid had started wearing a motorman's uniform and had taken his identification with the subway to an extreme. He thought of it as his private railroad, and he didn't like the people who ran it. At the moment, all the trains were late, the platforms over-crowded, the system a mess, and he was upset.

"What's the matter now?"

"These idiots," Adrian said. "They put all these extra trains on, and they're using old equipment that keeps breaking down. I've got five stalls right now."

"How long have you been sitting there?" Doc asked. "When did you sleep last?"

"I don't remember."

"Why don't you take a nap, Adrian?"

"No way. Fuck that. Leave me alone."

Doc gave him a pat on the back and sat down next to Judd in front of the big TV in the lounge.

"Who's turn is it now?" Doc asked.

"Deutschland," Judd said. "Germany got creamed. Everything in the East went down and took Berlin with it. Some of the West has power, but they shut down all the nuclear plants."

"Poland?"

"Gone."

"Romania, Hungary, Bulgaria?"

"Gone. In Budapest they had seven planes in the air when the air traffic control radars crashed. Six got down, but the pilot of the last one lost it on the runway and hit two of the others. How are things outside?"

"Bizarre, as expected. How are things here?" Doc gestured toward the cubicles.

"Tense, as expected."

"And you? How are you?" Doc asked.

"It ain't the end of the world, y'know," Judd said. "Just the end of a lot of software that was already dead but didn't know it."

"You got that right, pal."

On television the same reporter from Berlin was still standing in Freidrichstrasse in a pool of light generated by the network truck. The hiss and boom of fireworks peppered his commentary as he breathlessly described the bedlam around him.

"People just don't know what to do. Berlin is always rowdy on New Year's Eve. People fire off illegal fireworks and illegal firearms, but I think just now everyone who was hoarding firecrackers has set them off. The noise is deafening. People are running—I don't know to or from what—and I have no idea of the situation beyond what I can actually see, which isn't much. I understand the phones are working in some places and not in others. Apparently, the power outage occurred because the old power plants in the sector that was once East Berlin went down only a few seconds after midnight. I've been told the software in the computers in those old plants was pirated American software, but I can't verify that. Communications are very, very bad right now. This is Alexis Kosigian, reporting for CNN from Berlin."

The network went to a commercial for United Airlines, which Doc thought ironic since not a single United plane was in the air. Judd flipped to CBS, and a shot of the vast plaza in front of Saint Peter's Cathedral in Rome filled the screen. Hundreds of thousands held candles in a moment of silent prayer. A light rain was falling on Vatican City, and the people were bundled up against the cold. A tremendous feeling of deep spirituality welled up from the television, and for once the commentator was quiet. After the chaos of Berlin, the silence was sobering.

The camera slowly panned up the façade of Saint Peter's to the balcony. Pope John Paul II, adorned in white vestments and surrounded by cardinals in red, approached the rostrum. Swiss Guards stood hard by, pikes in hand, ready to protect His Holiness from harm.

The director cut to a close-up as the Pope raised his arms to deliver a benediction in Italian with a disembodied voiceover in English.

"As we enter the Third Millennium of the Christian era . . ."

John Paul II suddenly dropped his arms with a quizzical look on his face. Behind him, one of the cardinals fell backward, clutching his throat. Shouts tumbled from the balcony and the voice of the commentator burst from the speakers.

"There's a sudden commotion on the balcony of Saint Peter's, ladies and gentlemen, and I don't know exactly what happened. Just a moment, I'm hearing from the pool reporter on the balcony that Cardinal De Lignière of France has been shot. He was standing just behind John Paul and slightly to the right. I'm assuming that someone has tried to assassinate the Pope and missed. I didn't hear a shot. I don't think anyone heard a shot. This is a terrible, terrible thing that's happened here in Rome. Now medical people are bending over the cardinal and His Holiness is administering the last rites. This has all happened in a matter of seconds. From the pool reporter I'm hearing the cardinal is dead. Cardinal De Lignière of Lyons is dead. The front of the balcony is obscured by a line of Swiss Guards . . ."

"Holy shit," Judd exclaimed. "I can't fucking believe it."

Carolyn and Ronnie came running from across the room. "What happened? What happened?"

"Somebody took a shot at the Pope," Judd said.

"Jesus," Carolyn said, shaking her head in horrified wonder.

"They missed. They killed somebody else."

"Change the channel," Doc suggested. "Maybe somebody else knows more."

Judd flipped through the channels, almost all of which had instantly gone to Rome.

"Over a billion people have seen this on television . . ."

"One of the tightest security systems in the world seems to have been penetrated . . ."

"Of all the unexpected things on a momentous day . . ."

"The Pope is struggling with the Swiss Guards . . ."

"People are looking up at the roofs of the buildings on the far side of the square . . ."

Bo walked in, looked at the TV for a few seconds, shook his head, and went back to his screens.

Doc's cellphone rang and he answered.

"Doc? This is Jody Maxwell. Where are you? I need to talk to you."

"Where are you, Jody?"

"I'm standing outside your office."

"I'll be right there."

12

Jody was sitting on the corridor floor, a puddle of woe, blowing a defiant plume of menthol at the smoke detector.

"There she is," Doc quipped. "Ms. Tough As Nails."

"Hi, Doc."

Her voice was small but vibrant, laden with emotions almost out of control. In the distance, barely audible, a clarinet solo from Battery Park cut through the night, echoing a mournful song of the city.

He squatted down beside her and placed his hand on her shoulder. "You look like you could use a drink."

"You know," she said, lapsing into the nasal Long Island accent of her childhood, "I like my job. I wanted this job. This place is crazy, but I like it here. Donald is an asshole, but he's our asshole, you know what I mean? I can tell him when he's full of shit, which is every day. If I did that with any other boss in this town, I'd be fired. And you, you're not like anybody I ever met. You're—I don't know what, but you make this place human." She crushed her cigarette into the carpet, lit another and asked, "Am I going to have a job on Tuesday morning?"

"Sure. Why do you ask?"

"Will this company even exist? People are freezing in Warsaw.

My grandfather came from Warsaw. What I'm trying to say is that the world may not exist."

"Hey," Doc said, "a fella just told me it's not the end of the world, it just seems that way. Look on the bright side. It can only happen once, like bubonic plague. It either kills you, or you're immune."

"You're such a joker, always with the smart remark."

"That bother you?"

"No, I s'pose not."

"I'm glad you see it that way," he said. "Folks are gonna need a few jokes tomorrow. People can be amazingly inventive during a crisis. That's how computers got invented in the first place, during the Second World War, and what's happening today is a war. Wars end. Even the Hundred Years War ended. France won. England lost."

Doc wagged his eyebrows and grinned.

"I didn't sign up for a war," she said.

"Nobody did, but we got one anyway. Heard the latest?" Doc asked. "Someone tried to kill the Pope."

She gasped. "No. Where? In Rome?"

"In Saint Peter's Square with a million people assembled for a millennium service and half the world watching on TV. The half that still has TV."

"Is he all right?"

"Yeah, but someone else was killed. A cardinal."

"Oh, Christ, just what the world needs today. Why?"

"We'll probably never know. C'mon." He helped her to her feet, unlocked the door to his office, went directly to the liquor cabinet and poured her a vodka.

"Thanks."

"Have a seat."

"Thanks."

"You said you needed to talk, Jody, so what's on your mind? The big world crisis or something else?"

"Something else."

"Yeah?"

"Donald. And you."

Doc raised his eyebrows and waited. She sighed and fidgeted, biting her lip and swirling her drink, ritually enacting the physical clichés of one compelled to say something unpleasant. Finally she blurted. "Are you trying to rob Chase Manhattan?"

He cracked up, laughing long and loud, the hilarity giving him a moment of welcome relief.

"What makes you ask that?" he asked.

Jody recounted her adventures with Copeland in Brooklyn, and Doc listened with a twinkle in his eye. When she finished, he asked, "Do you really think I'd rob the bank?"

"No, but you're kind of a mystery, Doc. You've got your secret room and those weird people—everybody knows about it, but nobody knows what you do in there. Donald thinks you're robbing the bank, and this morning I thought he was going to have a heart attack. I swear."

He liked her. It occurred to him that he might like her a lot, but he'd had no time for lust, let alone romance. She sipped her drink, and he hesitated before deciding not to have one with her.

"To answer your question, there is no robbery," he said. "It was all a game I played with Donnie, only he took it seriously. I tricked him, and I've been doing it for years." He told her how the idea of robbing the bank had evolved, and how Copeland had been fooled into believing the robbery was actually going to come off.

"So it's only a game?" Jody said, wanting to believe him. "A mind fuck?"

"Correctamento. It's payback for Donnie's greed, that's all. There is no robbery and never was."

"You mean you set it up so His Donaldness would get his come-uppance?"

"Yep. It's all in fun and harmless, a practical joke."

"You dog."

"Yep."

"I love it."

"Thank you," he said. "I rather like it myself. Today I sent him on a wild goose chase just to keep him out of my hair. He should be home any time now."

"You're sure he'll go there?"

"Oh, yes. No doubt."

"Then where will you send him?"

"That's a secret," Doc answered with another chuckle, and she laughed with him.

He stopped laughing and decided to have one vodka after all. He poured himself a shot over ice and looked at her. Her fancy business suit was stained and wrinkled. The stress of living through a calamitous day showed all over her round and pretty face with the nose straightened by expensive cosmetic surgery and big eyes a little red. She was exhausted and running on adrenaline.

"Do you have somewhere to go tonight? A party?" he asked.

"I'm not going. My sister's having a party, but I'm not in a party mood."

"Where's that?"

"Long Island. Garden City."

"Hard to get there, anyway," Doc said.

"I couldn't even get through on the phone."

He leaned closer to her and quietly asked, "Are you afraid?"

"Yes."

"Of what?"

"I don't know. The world's a mess and our turn is coming."

"If you stay here, you'll be safe. We have a generator in the basement."

"I know. That's why I came back here. Do you think we'll need it?"

Doc shrugged. "Nobody can say. Good engineers always plan for failure, you know. Nobody knows more about electric power than the people who make it work. They're doing the best they can."

"Come off it, Doc. I know bullshit when I hear it."

"It's not bullshit, it's true. They're trying—people all over the world are trying, but no one has ever experienced anything like this. This is a unique event."

"Donald said he knew this was coming."

"He did, and since you work here and you're smart, you did, too. You just didn't want to believe it. The entire world has been living in a state of denial."

"There just isn't anything anyone can do about it. I feel so helpless and I hate that."

Helpless. Doc could understand that. People often felt helpless when confronted with computers because the complexity was beyond their ken. The individual machines were complex and the way they were connected was more complex, and that made people feel impotent and defenseless.

Doc had established the Midnight Club in order to show the world that people were not helpless, that fighting even in a losing cause can raise the spirit and proclaim hope as a viable alternative to surrender. Sooner or later the world had to know about the attempt, win or lose. Someone had to know the truth. At least one person outside the Midnight Club had to see and believe that not everyone was helpless. Right there and then he elected Jody.

"Well," he said, "maybe something can be done about it."

"What? Wave a magic wand? I wish."

"Suppose," he said, "suppose I told you that a few minutes after midnight, New York was going to black out along with the rest of the Northeast grid. Everything from Virginia to Maine and east to Ohio was going down, without a doubt."

"After everything else that's happened today, I'd believe you."

"It might happen, it might not, nobody really knows, but some of it is certain to happen. Now, suppose there was a way to keep the lights on in Manhattan no matter what happens anywhere else."

"That would be a miracle."

"No miracles, but people sometimes try to do the impossible just for the hell of it. How'd you like to visit the mysterious secret room?"

"No," she said. "Really?"

"C'mon."

He led her toward the rear of the building, through the conventional computer lab, and stopped between the two sets of security doors to call Bo on an intercom.

"I'm bringing in a visitor."

"You're what? Are you out of your mind?"

"Don't get excited. We need a witness."

"For what?"

"Posterity, Bo. Mere Posterity."

"We have cameras and recorders all over the place. Who is this person?"

"A Copeland employee, Jody Maxwell. Relax. We're coming in now."

Doc unlocked the last door and ushered Jody into the lounge. With no idea what to expect, she stood inside the entrance, slack-jawed, wide-eyed and blinking at a 42-inch TV surrounded by comfortable chairs and sofas resting on Persian carpets. On one side, doors led to a bathroom, kitchen and bedroom, and low partitions separated the lounge from the work space. Clocks were everywhere, old clocks, new clocks, digital and analog, large and small. It was 6:30. High on one wall a series of 24 digital clocks displayed every time zone, and beneath them the IBM, air conditioner and telephone switching station were connected to the workstations by color-coded cables and conduit pipes suspended from the ceiling.

The Midnight Club assembled nervously in the lounge, unused to strangers in their midst. Bo folded his arms across his chest in a posture of distaste, but the others didn't appear upset, just surprised.

Doc provided the introductions. "This is Bo, this is Carolyn, that's Ronnie in the hardhat, and Judd is the guy in the Midnight Club

T-shirt. That's Adrian over there in the motorman's uniform. Ladies and gentlemen, this is Jody Maxwell. I'm sure you've seen her around. Jody is going to operate the video cameras and record what happens here tonight. We'll be too busy, and I thought we could use some help."

"Hello," Jody squeaked, trying to maintain her composure. "My God, I had no idea."

"You weren't supposed to," Doc said. "We've maintained tight security for a long time."

An awkward silence persisted until Ronnie said, "We've never had a visitor before. It's weird."

Carolyn got over her shock at the intrusion and offered her hand. "Hi, Jody. I guess we're as surprised as you are. Looks like you've had a hard day."

Dazed, Jody shook Carolyn's hand, her head swiveling as she tried to understand the meaning of dozens of screens, the big computer, and the industrial-strength pile of technology she recognized as a telephone installation.

"You're the public relations director, aren't you?" Bo asked.

"That's right."

"Oh, that's just great. Real good, Doc. How the hell is she going to even understand what we're going to do?"

"I can write COBOL," Jody blurted. "I'm an ex-nerd."

"You're shitting me," Bo sputtered.

"Do I have to prove it?"

Watching this exchange, Doc applauded silently as Jody held her own, and loudly clapped his hands when Bo shrugged and relented.

"You're the chief geek, Doc," Bo said, offering his hand to Jody. "Welcome to the Midnight Club."

"Thanks."

"I haven't told her anything yet," Doc explained. "What we're going to try to do, Jody, is maintain Manhattan as a viable dwelling place, just in case a total breakdown threatens the city."

"My God," was all Jody could mumble.

"I must emphasize try," Doc continued, "because we have no idea if our system is gonna work. All we've done is replace hardware and software with other hardware and software. We can't replace embedded chips. At best, we have a bare-bones system to maintain a minimum of electric power, water, telephone service, and transport, but there are vulnerabilities and weaknesses beyond our control. In some cases, we've alerted the responsible authorities as to where the vulnerable systems are, and they've made the corrections without knowing the source of their information. On a few occasions, we broke into facilities and made the fixes ourselves, but we didn't do too much of that. We didn't want to get caught, as you can understand."

Jody stared wide-eyed at him and at everything in the room. "This is incredible," she stammered. "I don't know what to say."

"Carolyn, why don't you give Jody a tour and make her feel comfortable?"

Jody shook hands with Ronnie and Judd, and then, awestruck, moved from cubicle to cubicle and listened to Carolyn's description of the system.

Adrian grunted when introduced and kept his eyes on his screens.

"Adrian's workstation is a replica of an operations control station at the MTA's dispatch command center on Jay Street in Brooklyn," Carolyn said. "The center is supposed to be certified Y2K compliant, but Adrian has his doubts. Don't you, Adrian?"

Another grunt. Over the last couple of years Jody had caught glimpses of Adrian in the neighborhood and thought he was a bicycle messenger. His motorman's cap covered his hair, which this week was bright red.

"We love Adrian," Carolyn said, rolling her eyes and continuing her explanation. "Adrian is going to keep the subway running if the MTA can't. It's a very difficult situation to assess, you see. Railroads are leery of computers, with good reason, but events in Asia and Europe have proved they're vulnerable. On the other hand, the MTA has been onto Y2K since early in the game. If any system anywhere has a chance of making it, it's the New York City subway."

Carolyn moved on to Judd's station, a neat workbench laden with tools, equipment for testing and monitoring hardware, short-wave radios, ham receivers and transmitters, police scanners and a battery of TVs and computer monitors. Oscilloscopes and displays flashed from dozens of screens.

"Judd keeps all our gear in tiptop shape and he's also our webmaster," Carolyn said. "He's been keeping abreast of the situation all day on the Net."

Carolyn pointed to a bank of eight PCs logged on to dedicated Usenets where frantic engineers were exchanging information as rapidly as possible.

"Information is a little spotty right now because a lot of phones aren't working," Carolyn explained. "Some are, some aren't, and communications will get much worse at Zulu time."

"Zulu time, what's that?" Jody asked.

"Midnight, GMT. In about seventeen minutes. That's when we expect the European Internet to go down, but for now some of it is working."

Judd pointed to one of the screens. "This group is all railroad managers and it's weird because the guys all write in their native languages or terrible English. It seems that in Italy, the trains stopped because computers date- and time-stamped every activity by the train controllers, and when the stamping application failed, the operations centers went down. In Germany and France, they lost electric power. In the Netherlands, computers in the locomotive cabs failed, stopping the engines. In Austria, radio communications with the train engineers failed when the transmitters went down. None of this was supposed to happen, but all of it did. They've been very lucky everywhere except China, where they had some bad accidents. Everywhere else, the trains just stopped, and that's bad enough. No trains, no coal, no grain shipments, no parts to assembly plants. It's gonna be a mess."

He gestured toward the screens and ticked them off, "Water supply systems, nuclear power, telecommunications, air traffic control, NATO—Ronnie hacked into their net, that was fun. Let's see, this one is already logged onto mission control at Space Command, another of Ronnie's masterpieces, and this last one is dedicated to our own Northeast power grid. Welcome to Y2K central."

"This is incredible," Jody said. "All this time and nobody had a clue what was going on in here."

"Doc has been a fanatic about security, until now."

"Oh, shit," Judd groaned.

"What happened now?"

"Look at this," Judd said, tapping the monitor for nuclear power. "One of the networks reported that Russian troops broke into a nuclear power plant and are forcing the engineers to keep it running, but they don't know the half of it. A bunch of Russian marines broke into the power plant, Kola 2 in Murmansk, killed the security guards, and now one engineer has locked himself into a security room where he can see what's happening on security monitors. He has a computer and he's on the Net writing broken English. He's got a direct satellite connection so he's not dependent on local phones, which are out. He doesn't know what's going on, really, except the marines have killed everyone in the control room and the plant is starting to malfunction. They have sensors that monitor the heat in heat exchangers and pumps and pipes, and the computer application compares the temperatures with other temperatures from specific times and dates, like five minutes ago, but it can't read the dates and has nothing to compare to. Therefore, it assumes a failure and is trying to shut the plant down. The reactor wants to scram, which is to say, control rods are inserted into the pressure vessel to stop the chain reaction in the fuel rods. No chain reaction, no heat, no steam, no turbines, no power. Only thing is, the control rods stopped halfway down because the computer that controls their motion is confused and receiving contradictory orders. Radioactive steam is building up in the pipes under tremendous pressure. It's gonna blow. This is why virtually every other reactor on the planet has been shut down under controlled conditions. At least I hope so. There are a lot of uncounted military reactors."

Jody wrinkled her nose. "I don't think I understood a word you said, but it sounds bad."

"Much worse than Chernobyl," Judd said.

She bent over and read a few lines.

> We should have did before this fix code.
> Probe in high pressure valve two day ago
> fail test but superior say no money to replace.
> I am to shoot myself but have no gun.

Realizing the man in Murmansk was describing the machine that was going to kill him, Jody clutched her blouse. "Oh, God."

"There's a billion stories on the naked planet," Judd said. "This is just one."

"What's gonna happen is gonna happen," Carolyn said. "We can't get sentimental and still take care of business."

They moved on to Ronnie's station, where her screens showed the flow of water into the city. Demand was normal for a Friday evening. People were taking showers and getting ready for the big night. Upstream, the reservoirs were full and operating as smoothly as possible for the oldest sanitary water supply system in the world, but the control center in Queens was in a frenzy. Having seen water supplies fall apart all over the world, the operators knew they were faced with a serious problem.

Ronnie shook her head and pointed to a stack of water bottles in the corner. "We have a tank on the roof with five thousand gallons, and another thousand in bottles in the basement. We're gonna need 'em. This is a lost cause."

"You never know," Carolyn cautioned.

"Yes, you do," Ronnie shot back. "I do. I know. There's not going to be a problem getting water into the city. It's a gravity system. The problem is going to be getting the drainage and sewage out."

"Ronnie's an optimist, you see," Carolyn said, directing Jody to Bo's ConEd station.

"I apologize for being rude," Bo said to Jody.

"Bo's nervous because this is the main event," Carolyn drawled. "The Consolidated Edison Electrocution Society of Greater New York, founded by his very own self, Thomas Edison, renowned inventor of the electric chair. This is the hot seat, and Bo is the man who's gonna sit right here and save New York. Howd'ya like that? If he fails, we fry him. Ain't that right, Bo?"

"I ain't gonna save nothin' if we don't hear from Deep Volt."

"That's right," Carolyn said. "We have a little glitch."

Donald Copeland had tried to cross Times Square and walk home that way but couldn't get through the crowds. He'd wandered across town in a daze, losing track of time in the process—*tempus fugit, yea brother.* His $12,000 Rolex was gone. He remembered stopping in the middle of the Brooklyn Bridge, taking it off and cocking his arm, but then he'd shoved the watch into his pocket and walked on. Things were a little jumbled after that. People lined up at groceries and delicatessens, and signs in every store declared "Cash Only." On Fifth Avenue somewhere in the twenties he'd come across a kid selling cans of beer for $10, and he'd traded the watch for a Miller Genuine Draft. He didn't want to know what time it was. It was dark. New York was crazy. The kid was happy. Unbelievable crowds packed every block in midtown. Fights. Drunks. Cops. People having sex in cars. It was Nero's Rome gone mad. On a TV in a store window he saw John Paul II's Rome gone equally mad. A millennium crazy had taken a potshot at the Pope, and as Copeland watched, the Italian police cornered the assassin who shot three cops and then killed himself. He saw a report that seemed to announce a severe nuclear accident in Russia, but he wasn't sure. Pressured by time to deliver the news raw and unedited, many disasters were being reported that never occurred, or reported with wild inaccuracy, making things look much worse than they actually were. None of the reporters understood or explained technical details, and there was no way to separate fact from fiction.

Without knowing quite how he got there, he found himself at 38th and Ninth Avenue in front of a saloon called the Mad Hatter's Sports Bar and Grill. A hand-printed banner stretched over the doorway: "End of the World Party Tonight." Two young women in blue jeans and flashy jewelry pushed through the doors, giving him a snapshot of the crowded interior: TVs, laughter, a tambourine. He loosened his tie, unbuttoned the top button on his shirt and miraculously found an empty stool at the bar.

Three bartenders were working at a furious pace, splashing liquor into glasses, squeezing lemons, grinding ice in blenders. Sweaty waitresses loaded trays and figured tabs without taking an eye off the eight large screens scattered around the large room.

"Scotch over," he shouted over the racket. "Make it a double."

As disastrous events around the world unfolded on TV, the youthful, drunken crowd was cheering. The screens presented Paris, the City of Light, in the dark. In the French capital, spotlights run by generators punched holes in the sky above the Champs-Élysées. The Arc de Triomphe glowed in the lonesome blue light of the Tomb of the Unknown Soldier. The grand boulevard was a stream of car lights, but the buildings were black, the streetlights mere poles in the pavement. The camera caught the frightened eyes of a policeman trying to direct traffic at the moment he gave up and ran away, losing his *képi* in the process. Hysterical people were running in every direction. The shot from the center of the city was replaced by a succession of talking heads and then a shot of the Stade de France in the Parisian suburb of St. Denis. Built for the World Cup in 1998, the stadium was ablaze and surrounded by wildly careening automobile lights.

The delirious bar crowd exploded in laughter and cheers and chanted, "Fuck the French. Fuck the French." It was weird and perverse and Copeland thought it made as much sense as anything else. A moment later, the director cut to an address by the President of France, who looked bewildered and badly shaken under the improvised lights. The bar crowd booed. Someone shouted, "No politicians! No politicians!" and a bartender flipped through the channels. Car wrecks, burning chemical plants, sinking barges in a river, families huddled in the freezing snow. Train traffic across the continent had slowed to a crawl, and all military air traffic in Western Europe was grounded after six members of a German Air Force squadron flew their F-16s into a Bavarian mountain. Hundreds of ships in the Mediterranean and Baltic Seas were adrift. North Sea oil rigs stopped pumping and one was afire.

A hullabaloo started in the back of the room, and everyone turned to look as a shirtless young man squirted lighter fluid on a laptop computer and set it on fire.

"Oh, shit," shouted the chief bartender. "That's too much! Put that out!"

Old Blue was waiting fifty blocks north with another message from hell. Copeland had to go home. As he turned back to his drink, he was suddenly face-to-face with a pair of sultry brown eyes, full lips and firm breasts pressed against his chest.

"Happy New Year," she said. "Isn't it wonderful? My name is Helen. Who are you?"

"Father Time," he said, dropping his eyes to her cleavage.

"Are you wicked?" she asked. "Are you a bad boy?"

"I have to go home," he said.

"To the little wife and kiddies? It's New Year's Eve. Give in to temptation. Be wicked."

She kissed him, plunging her tongue into his mouth and grabbing his crotch, which caused him to spill his drink down her back.

"Oh, *Jesus*," she screamed and broke away.

"Sorry."

"Fuck *you.*"

He stumbled outside, took a deep breath, and started to walk. The crowds swirled around him. Are you wicked? What kind of question was that? What kind of person asked a question like that? He glanced into a bookstore and saw an entire window filled with books on wolves: zoology books, ecology books, Russian folk tales, *Never Cry Wolf, The Call of the Wild, Peter and the Wolf.* He had a sudden urge to howl, looked up and saw a half-moon rising above Manhattan. He opened his mouth and wailed as long and loud as he could. No one noticed because the entire world was wailing with him.

In the Millennium Religious Sanctuary of the 24th Precinct, Captain Ed Garcia had a little more than he'd bargained for. When he'd told the fire commander that he wanted to attract every religious nut in New York and thus contain them in one place, he'd meant it figuratively. In the spirit of the moment, he'd forgotten that in New York, no matter what you said, enough people would take you at your word to fill a football stadium. After dark, the nature of the crowds changed. The bands stopped playing and families went home to escape the cold. Hundreds of drunks spilled over from midtown and began to arrive along with hard-core religious fanatics of every stripe. Half the loudmouth preachers in New York showed up to further their private agendas, and the oratory became increasingly vehement as zealots mistook the idea of a religious sanctuary for a license to denounce everyone who didn't share their beliefs. Stoked on television and booze, the night crowds were not inclined to share anything.

"You caused this, you sinners. This is God's retribution for your evil ways."

"I didn't cause nothin', you butthead."

"You're going to hell."

"Ain't this it? Shit, man, you're here. That's bad enough."

In place of the ecumenical supermarket Garcia had envisioned, the captain had blacks and whites using the Bible as a weapon in their endless strife; anti-Semites turning the Gospel into virulent poison in their relentless persecution of Jews; and Catholics and Protestants bringing their ancient feuds to the Upper West Side. In the most culturally diverse of cities, each verbal attack prompted a quick response from the offended parties, and it didn't take long before everyone was offended. Jeers and whistles turned to fisticuffs and blows, and in New York City at the end of the 20th Century, Garcia knew automatic assault weapons could appear at any moment.

At Garcia's orders, the cops changed into bullet-proof vests and riot gear and showed no tolerance for the intolerant. Locked in his holding cells upstairs were two gentlemen in white robes claiming to be Jesus, seven members of the Aryan Nation charged with attempted homicide, six members of the vicious 129th Street Bloods arrested for possession of weapons, and more mean drunks than anyone cared to count. Downstairs, the lobby overflowed with people lodging complaints, looking for missing friends and relatives, and even a few who wanted into jail because they were afraid the lights were going out and they'd heard the precinct had a generator.

The assassination attempt on the Pope heightened the religious hysteria. Fortunately, the archbishop had returned to Saint Patrick's Cathedral before an anti-Catholic evangelical minister standing on a chair in the middle of the avenue denounced the Pope as the Antichrist.

Shoddily dressed, eyes burning with hatred, he thundered into a bullhorn, "What happened tonight in Rome is a sign from God for us to *burn the papist churches to the ground*," and before he could utter another word, a body flew from the crowd and tackled him, bringing both men down hard on the asphalt.

"In Ireland I'd kill you," screamed the assailant, and this statement provoked a pack of Irish Protestant hoodlums who jumped to the preacher's defense. Out of the blue, Amsterdam Avenue turned into the High Road in Belfast. Eight cops waded into the brawl, arrested four drunken men, took away three handguns, and dispatched one crazed preacher in an ambulance.

Angry at seeing his sweet idea turned into garbage, Garcia issued orders to shut down amplification equipment and vigorously confiscate weapons. He assembled a force of thirty officers, and a few minutes before seven a line of jittery cops with Garcia in command started a slow sweep up Amsterdam Avenue.

A bottle flew out of the crowd and smashed at the captain's feet. Garcia looked into the angry faces and recognized no one from his precinct. He knew his people, the good, the bad, and the worst, and now his street was filled with strangers, *auslanders*, and almost all white. He wondered what happened to the preacher who'd started it all. He wondered why religion so quickly turned to prejudice and condemnation. Cosmic questions with no time for answers. The Millennium Religious Sanctuary of the 24th Precinct had become an oasis for rowdy drunks.

He sent an order down the line: "Gas masks."

The cops moved forward and the people resisted. "Let 'em have it," he commanded, and a cloud of tear gas swept over the crowd.

13

Doc had placed video cameras around the room to record the Midnight Club's grand experiment, and with Jody needing something to do, he thought footage from a hand-held camera would add a touch of style to the documentation. He scrounged through cabinets until he found a decent Sony autofocus.

"Ever use one of these things?" he asked her.

"Not for years."

He gave her a quick lesson, saying quietly, "Just make a video-tape and save your questions for later."

"Gotcha."

She looked through the viewfinder and panned the room. "Is it on?" she asked.

"See the display?"

"Yeah."

"Then it's on."

"You sure?"

"Just squeeze the trigger and shoot."

He turned on a soft flood, sat down in a comfortable captain's chair in the lounge, and faced the camera. Jody looked through the viewfinder and focused on Doc looking cheerfully professorial in a freshly donned tweed coat and tie.

"When I start to talk, you hold on me, and when I move around, follow and shoot anything interesting. We can always edit this later. All right?"

"Okay."

"What we're doing now is pretty well scripted," he said. "This is practice for what will happen later tonight. Ready, Jody?"

"Yeah."

"Music ready?"

"Ready."

Doc looked directly at the camera and began. "It's three minutes to midnight, Greenwich Mean Time, December 31, 1999," he began. "In one hundred eighty seconds Big Ben will strike twelve over the River Thames and the 20th Century will end in Great Britain. In the London suburb of Greenwich, former home of the Royal Observatory and for that reason home of the prime meridian, zero degrees longitude, Her Majesty's Government are celebrating the imminent arrival of the new millennium in the Millennium Jubilee Dome, centerpiece of Europe's grandest millennium festival.

"Meanwhile, in the skies above, at this very moment, eight thousand nine hundred fifty-four objects are orbiting the earth. One is the moon, and almost eight thousand are bits of space debris, dead satellites, and used rocket parts. The rest are unmanned artificial satellites that are vital components of global communication systems. Satellites are essential for the national defense of many nations, for television broadcasting, corporate data transfers and international bank exchanges. Satellites bring us the weather and the news, and provide universal standards for date and time that allow telephone companies to connect with one another.

"All the satellites in the sky are controlled by radio transmissions from some 75 ground control stations on earth. The radio signals, called uplinks and downlinks, are processed by computers, and as we know, all computers are not equal. More important, all software is not equal. Some satellite companies use cutting-edge technology and advanced, thoroughly Y2K compliant software. However, in most satellite systems, especially those that have been around for several decades, very old software is used to process the streams of data to and from the satellites. Many military and older commercial ground stations use old computer programs for a very good reason. They work. They've always worked, and in the risk-adverse environment of satellite control, anything that works is kept. In the early days of orbital flight, satellite control programs were often scribbled on scraps of paper, translated manually into machine code, and the 'documentation' was tossed away in the excitement of finding something that did the job. When the crucial test of success was passed, fully operational code migrated into program after program, application after application, and much of that original code is still in use in every country that maintains a presence in the sky. With no documentation, the most diligent, conscientious Y2K remediation will never find the millions of millennium bug flaws that lurk in the old code. Workarounds, patches, kludges and new software have eradicated many problems in satellite ground control systems, but since satellites never take a day off, ground control stations can't shut down for thorough software testing. In every space installation on the planet, operators and engineers flying the birds know what is coming, and they know it will happen at midnight, Zulu time."

He stopped his lecture to yell at Judd standing by the audio controls, "Hit it!"

The thundering notes of the cannon chorus of "The 1812 Overture" boomed through the speakers as the Midnight Club geared up for the first major event to affect them directly.

Judd counted down, "Four, three, two, one . . . Zulu time!"

"Zulu time!" Doc hollered.

"Zulu time!" chorused the rest of the Midnight Club.

Startled by the explosion of sound, Jody took her eye away from the viewfinder, recovered, and started walking around and shooting.

Adrian got into the spirit of the moment by walking over to watch

Judd's screens, one of which was wired into internal communications at the United States Air Force Space Command's Consolidated Space Operations Center at Falcon Air Force Base in Colorado Springs.

"You ain't never gonna see this on TV," Adrian declared.

Judd now took up the running commentary, "50th Space Wing at Falcon has the mission of day-to-day operations of Department of Defense satellites. They have about ninety spacecraft under their control, and they connect to the satellites through nine ground stations in places like Thule, Greenland, Hawaii and Diego Garcia Island in the Indian Ocean. At least they did until now. Checking systems. DSP, commonly known as the air defense early radar warning system, holding. Local air traffic control at Colorado Springs, going, going, gone. The radars are down. DMSP, defense meteorological satellite program—gone. Checking links to ground stations, checking hard-wired ground links, okay, satellite links okay—wait a minute—the DCSC bird is drifting off course—wait—wait—not responding to station-keeping command—now more birds are drifting, drifting, Defense Communications System is down. Early warning radars are now down, all satellite telcom links are down. Telemetry links are down. Link to Naval Observatory is down, GPS sats not responding, uplink is down. GPS is dead. The signals stopped completely, their screens have all gone blank. Space Command is dead. Jesus Christ, for all I can tell, the Air Force is dead."

The music ended and a heavy silence invaded the room.

"Fuck," Adrian swore.

"Not in my wildest dreams," Ronnie declared.

"Well," Doc said, "looks like nobody can start a war today. Carolyn, civilian telcom?"

Carolyn was watching screens that monitored nonmilitary communications in and out of New York.

"All civilian telcoms set their clocks with GPS because then they're all on the same page. When the GPS satellites stopped working, the phone companies began losing synchronicity. All have backup systems and run on their own clocks, but those clocks are going to be different. Differences measured in nanoseconds are creeping into the protocols the computers use to talk to one another, and they all will react in different ways. A few will adjust the time difference because the programmer was smart enough to foresee a time difference as a possible problem. Most programmers weren't that smart, and most computers simply will shut down all connections with any systems that don't match their time and date. GPS has a backup system broadcasting the time over the air, and that system is not working in New York. I don't know why and I don't know about other places. We don't know what the effects will be, but we're going to find out. With GPS down, Bell Atlantic and AT&T have synchronized their clocks. Okay, here we go. Trouble in the Midwest. MCI just lost half their satellites and is routing everything to the ground. GTE is dead, their traffic flow is zero. AT&T is good. MCI is wavering. Everyone is routing everything to the ground and we're having overloads. Hold on, hold on, GPS just came back up. Judd, confirm?"

"They got a signal up, and now, now, shit, it's gone again."

The receiver display screen was blank.

Judd said, "The Russian system just went down, too."

"Test your lines, Carolyn," Doc commanded.

"Already done. Lines clear."

"Bo. ConEd's phones?"

"They're good."

"Carolyn, confirm."

"Confirmed. They can talk."

"Okay. What's the situation in London?"

"Lights out in Central London. Lights on in Greenwich because they isolated themselves from the grid. Lights out in Birmingham, Manchester, Liverpool; lights on in Devon and Cornwall. Lights out, Edinburgh, Glasgow. Lights on in York."

"Someone check the TV."

Every station offered nothing more than talking heads in studios.

In shock, the anchormen and women had ashen faces and quivering jowls.

"We've just lost all our satellite connects," said ABC.

"There seems to be a problem with our connection in London," said CBS.

". . . TV, telephones, data transfers, Internet connections to the rest of the world . . ."

". . . the Millennium Dome is still brightly lit, but everything else . . ."

". . . and here in New York another riot has broken out as police tried to shut down the Religious Sanctuary on the Upper West Side. We're going now to Washington and a statement by the Secretary of Defense."

The screen went black and a moment later returned to the studio in New York. "We've lost contact with Washington," said the anchor. "We're trying to get an audio line open. Frankly, I don't care anymore. I'm going home to take care of my family." With that, he stood up from his chair and walked hurriedly out of the studio. The camera held on his empty chair.

"Judd!"

"I have eight screens down, four up."

"Carolyn."

"My lines are still good."

"TEOTWAWKI," Adrian shouted.

"What's that mean?" Jody asked.

"The End Of The World As We Know It," Doc replied. "Adrian's a pessimist. A bunch of computers is not the world, Adrian. Remember that. Somebody put on some music. We have a long way to go. I'd sure like to know what happened to the reactor in Murmansk. Judd?"

"His satellite connection is gone. I've lost him. I got short wave, but I can't understand Russian."

"See if you can get Norway on-line. They have a new communication satellite system that had a chance to make it. If their radiation detection system is working, they'll know right away when that reactor blows. Murmansk is fucked. The entire Kola Peninsula is fucked. The Arctic Ocean is fucked. Sometimes I wonder why God made Russians."

"How about some music?" Ronnie hollered. "We don't have time to get depressed."

David Bowie came through the speakers, singing the wistful, haunting lyrics to "Major Tom."

Uptown, Jonathon Spillman couldn't take his eyes off the nightmare pouring through his TV. The millennium bug had stomped through Europe like Godzilla, crushing everything in its path. The 20th Century was over for them, ending much the way it started, in darkness and fear. Did anyone ever learn from the past? Apparently not. Witness today, thought Jonathon Spillman, sitting in the living room of his third-floor apartment with a shotgun across his knees.

The riot in his grocery store that morning seemed like a long time ago. Since then the bug had circled more than half the globe and plunged into the Atlantic. Brazil was next, and soon enough, New York. An invisible tidal wave as tall as the sky was silently rolling toward America. There was panic in Cincinnati, chaos in L.A. The survivalists in Montana and New Mexico had retreated to their bunkers. Spillman knew all about those crazy bastards. He'd seen them on TV, but now his TV was reduced from sixty-five channels to twelve, all local stations. Satellites down. Uplinks or downlinks or some damned thing. He felt numb. Shirley was in the bedroom sobbing, holding her tears in check every five minutes to call her mother in Queens, but all she got was a busy signal.

"Stay off the phone!" he hollered. "It's only for emergencies."

She came out, eyes red and face puffy. "If this isn't an emergency, then I don't know what is," she bawled, close to hysteria.

"Nothing has happened to us, so for God's sake calm down."

"Whaddaya mean *nothing*? What about your store?"

"I'm all right, you're all right, so just calm down."

"Calm down? *Calm down?* Everything is ruined and all you can think of to say is, 'calm down'!"

"Well, what the hell good does it do to cry about it? That doesn't solve anything."

She ran back into the bedroom and slammed the door.

"Boo hoo," he said to himself. "Shit."

The door bell rang. Spillman grabbed his shotgun, cracked it to make sure it was loaded, and went into the vestibule to the intercom.

"Who's there?"

"Copeland."

"What are you doing here, Donnie?"

"Are you gonna ask stupid questions or let me in?"

"You by yourself?"

"Yes, God damn it, I'm alone, but I won't be for long if you don't open the fucking door."

Spillman buzzed him in, waited for the elevator and checked through the peephole before letting him into the apartment.

"What's that for?" Copeland asked about the shotgun.

"You never know."

"Good God, Jon. Put that thing away before you shoot yourself. Is Shirley here?"

"Yes."

"She okay?"

"No. She's out of her mind. What're you doing here?"

"I lost my keys. I need to get my spares from you so I can get into my house."

"Sure," Spillman said, walking back toward the kitchen. "How'd you lose your keys?"

"I don't know."

"What's it like outside?"

"It's a fucking zoo. Crazy people all over. I just walked here all the way from downtown Brooklyn."

"Are you kidding?"

"No."

"What were you doing in Brooklyn?"

"Business at the Tech Center."

Spillman rooted around in a drawer until he found Copeland's emergency keys. "All the satellites just broke down," he said. "Say bye-bye to the rest of the world."

"*All* the satellites?"

"I don't know. There's no way to tell."

"I expected that," Copeland said. "Some newer systems should be working."

"What's gonna happen here, Donnie? The truth."

"You want the truth? The absolute truth?"

"Yeah."

"Nobody knows."

"Fuck you. That's no answer."

"Look," Copeland said, eyeing the shotgun, "wanna walk across the street with me? Just to be safe?"

"You mean go outside?"

"Yeah."

"I dunno. I saw on TV that Ed has his hands full over on Amsterdam. Did you see that when you were walking over here?"

"No. I stayed away from there. Anyway, we're not going over there. Just across the street."

"Okay. Lemme tell Shirley."

The bedroom door was locked.

"Shirley?" he called, knocking softly on the door. "Donald is here. I'm going across the street with him for a few minutes. I'll be right back."

"Nooo. No no no." The door opened a crack. "Don't leave me here alone."

"I'm just going to walk across the street. I'll be right back."

"It'll be all right, Shirley," Copeland said, and she slammed the door again, yelping, "You can't see me like this."

"Christ," Spillman said. "Let's go."

Three floors below they surveyed the street like commandos. As little boys they'd played this game a thousand times.

"Whaddya see?" Spillman asked.

"Sidewalks clear."

"Let's go. You first. I'll cover you."

"Wait. There's a guy coming down the block."

A New Year's Eve drunk wobbled along the sidewalk, singing off-key in Spanish, *"No me puedo amar sin tí."* He stopped to light a string of firecrackers and let the string dangle, fuse hissing like an angry snake before he tossed it into the street.

Spillman shuddered. "I hate that," he snarled. "I just fucking hate that."

"Shut up," Copeland snapped.

The drunk paused in front of the building and saw them. "Happy New Year," he saluted them, then saw the shotgun and laughed. "Happy New Year. Shoot 'em up, cowboy!" and walked on, laughing.

"See," Copeland said. "Don't be paranoid."

"All right."

"I'm gonna go now."

"Okay. Go!"

Copeland sprinted across the street, ran up the stairs to his front door and waved at Spillman to follow. In a crouch, holding the shotgun with both hands, Spillman scuttled between parked cars. At the far end of the block the drunk heard their footsteps and turned to see Spillman fly up Copeland's stairs. He shook his head and continued his journey toward Riverside Park and the placid, black Hudson River, singing, *"Busqué la verdad en la tequila."*

"Want to come in?" Copeland asked. "We could both use a drink."

"Why not? I'm sure in no hurry to go home."

"That bad?"

"She's fuckin' crazy, man. She's in bed with her Official Millennium Barbie."

Copeland used one key to open an electronic pad, punched in a code, closed the pad, keyed a second lock and opened the door. Micro came running, spinning in circles with excitement. With the dog at his heels, Copeland opened a closet and reset the alarm. Before he could emerge from the closet, every light in the house started to blink.

"What the fuck?" he growled. He reached for a light switch and snapped it up and down with no effect.

"What's going on?" Spillman asked.

"I don't know."

Spillman turned around to go back outside, but the door wouldn't open.

"What the hell?"

He kicked the door and jiggled the latch to no avail. Copeland tried the key and it wouldn't turn. Then the sound system came on, and from speakers in every room they heard Doc's voice.

"Hello, Donald. You're locked in. Get used to the idea. I called up Old Blue and he thought it would be easy to seal you in. Old Blue and I became pretty good friends while he was here on Nassau Street. We stay in touch. You know how it is with old friends. You have grates on all your windows, but you're a resourceful guy and without a doubt you can escape. But if I were you, I'd relax and have a drink. You can't call out on your phones, so you might as well try and get it over with."

Copeland ran into the kitchen and saw Doc's face on TV.

"This is a videotape," Doc said. "Thirty seconds after you keyed the door it started the VCR in the kitchen, where you're probably watching me now. I hope you're alone, but if you're not, your guests will have to stay with you. I'll be calling in a few minutes. Enjoy the show."

"What is this?" Spillman said. "What's going on? Isn't that Doc Downs?"

"Give me that shotgun."

"Why? What're you gonna do?"

"I'm gonna kill my TV. C'mon!"

Copeland took the gun, pointed the muzzle at the TV and pulled the trigger. *Pow!* The cathode ray tube imploded with a loud bang. Sparks flew. Bedlam. Yelping dog. The kitchen was a cloud of acrid smoke, the TV a singed wreck. Copeland's eyes blazed with righteous ferocity as Spillman recovered from his surprise and started to laugh.

"God damn, Donnie! I always wanted to do that. Wow."

Copeland rubbed his shoulder where the recoil had pressed his flesh. "I'm fucked," he muttered.

Doc's voice emanated once more from the speakers. "You can shoot all the TVs in the house if you have enough ammunition, Donnie, but then you'll miss the show."

"Can you hear me, you son of a bitch?"

"Of course. The place is bugged. Cameras, too. Want to know where they are? None in the bathrooms."

"Donnie, what the fuck is going on here?" Spillman cried. "What is this?"

"Do you want to explain, or shall I?" Doc asked. "Perhaps Mr. Spillman would be entertained by the saga of Butch and Sundance and the Chase Manhattan Bank."

"Donnie, what the hell is he talking about?"

"Jonathon," Copeland said. "You're a good guy, a decent man. We've been friends for a long time. Can I use your shotgun to kill myself?"

"Hell, no. Give it back."

Copeland took a step backward, but Spillman didn't hesitate. He grabbed the weapon and snatched it away.

"Wha'd you get yourself into, Donnie? What's this guy talkin' about?"

Copeland shot back, "Aren't you worried about Shirley? She'll go nuts if you don't call and don't come back."

"So what? She's already nuts. I want to know why we're locked in your house."

"Do you think we should try all the doors and windows?"

"Donald, later. Tell me what's going on here."

"Tell him!" Doc demanded, his voice registering somewhere between Big Brother and God.

Copeland squirmed. Looking back and forth between the shattered TV and his friend, he spit out the words. "We robbed the fucking bank."

"You what?"

"You heard me."

Spillman blinked a few times. "Wait a minute. Of course. You had access to all the codes, the most sensitive accounts, everything. You didn't. C'mon, man. You didn't. You fox. You son of a bitch." He punched Copeland in the shoulder. "Yeah! Rob the fucking bank. Why the fuck not?"

"Donald!" Doc said curtly.

"Yes?"

"No one robbed the bank."

"Say what?"

"Donnie, you might as well know right now, the whole thing was a hoax. There was no robbery and never was. I put you on for all these years. That's all there is to it."

"No."

"Yes."

Spillman thought his friend was going to have a seizure. His eyes bulged, his face turned red, he breathed deeply several times and then a calm spread over his features and he sagged against the kitchen counter.

Spillman searched the ceiling for a camera and guessed it was inside an air conditioning vent high in the corner. He pointed.

Copeland looked up and said to Doc, "A hoax? A put on?"

"Yep."

"A practical joke?"

"Yep."

"What about Chase? Did you put a virus into their systems?"

"Of course not."

"You did all this just to fuck with my head?"

"Yep."

"You bastard."

"You can see it that way if you like, but we never could have pulled it off. We would have been caught. Simple as that. Plus we didn't need the money. I'm sorry to disappoint you. You can't be the biggest bank robber of all time, but those are the breaks. You can't gloat, and you can't feel guilty, either. You're clean, Donnie boy. You may be a greedy prick, but you're legal. You should thank me. Don't worry. Business is fine. Earlier this evening Maria Maranello sold a package to Hamburg Private GmBH for I don't know how many millions. Since most satellites are down and power is off in Hamburg, I don't know exactly how you'll wrap up that contract, but I'm sure you'll find a way."

Copeland sat down on a counter stool, resigned and defeated. Spillman poured a pair of scotches and without a toast they drained their glasses.

"Atta boy," Doc said. "Drink up. Things aren't as bad as you think."

"Hamburg Private?"

"At five dollars per line of code, your new rate. Believe me, Donald, you don't need Chase's money. There's a videotape in the machine in the living room. I think you'll find it interesting and worth your time. You're going to have your minds blown, gentlemen, and after you've seen it, we'll talk again. Enjoy the show. It's called the Midnight Club."

14

The great city began to convulse. Riptides of fear and anxiety criss-crossed the island as the phone system broke down, the Internet collapsed and network television vanished. The loss of the GPS and communications satellites was only a harbinger of things to come. Few understood how deeply these delicate space mechanisms affected their lives, but everyone knew their phones didn't work properly. Local TV was broadcasting over the air, but millions of televisions no longer had aerials. Sticking to their New Year's Eve schedules, New York 1 had Barbra Streisand with an upbeat show live from Madison Square Garden, and WABC had Nebraska and Alabama in the M&M's Official Millennium Bowl from Giants' Stadium. Concerts and football seemed to have lost their cachet. People wanted news, but just as the graphic TV images of devastation in Europe had built to a peak, they'd abruptly ceased, leaving millions on the edges of their seats wondering what happened next. The bug was racing across the Atlantic in silence, making its approach that much more terrifying.

Time was all that mattered. The 20th Century had only a few hours to live, and in New York everyone was staring at the clock. The seconds ticked away; minutes spun off and disappeared into the past; hours lasted forever. Time was thick, like oil. You could rub it between your fingers and taste it.

The magnificent skyscrapers glistened as always. Surrounded by the towering walls of steel and glass, Doc stood with Jody on the roof of the building on Nassau Street, and with great passion told her the tale of Christopher Marlowe's *Dr. Faustus*. The good doctor sold his soul to the devil for knowledge, women and a song. Near midnight, as Mephistopheles was coming to collect his due, Faustus cried,

> *Stand still you ever-moving spheres of heaven,*
> *That time may cease and midnight never come.*

"I like Mephistopheles," Doc declared. "He's a lot more clever than Cinderella."

"I like Cinderella," Jody said. "Shut up and kiss me."

Startled, Doc felt awkward and clumsy. Kiss? Here? Now? What is this, a reality check? And then he abandoned himself to the moment, gently took her in his arms and kissed her.

Fireworks exploded over a barge on the East River. The bands played on. The city shuddered and had another drink.

"C'mon, Doc," she breathed, and led him downstairs into the building, past the equally surprised members of the Midnight Club, and straight into the bedroom.

A few minutes after eight o'clock, a small group of demonstrators appeared with signs and slogans at Gracie Mansion, the mayor's residence at East 88th and East End Avenue. With no media present, the chants were half-hearted and had no chance of reaching the mayor's ear. "What do you want us to do?" the mayor's spokesperson asked the people. Confused and afraid, the demonstrators had no coherent plan of action. Barely distinguishable from the New Year's Eve crowds surging through the streets, their chants and shouts inaudible above the din of horns and noisemakers, the futility of protesting was readily apparent. His Honor's harried spokesperson had more enthusiasm for the demonstration than the demonstrators.

She didn't mind being out in the cold engaging in a little give and take with a bunch of cranks because anything was better than being locked in with the mayor. Rudy Giuliani had been out of his mind ever since returning from Washington late in the afternoon.

Inside the mansion, Mayor Giuliani screamed in frustration at his advisors and aides. Stuck in the mansion by impossible traffic, he was reduced to communicating with the outside world by motorcycle messenger and radio. The streets were impassable, even to him, and he was forbidden the use of his helicopter—nothing could fly, although he wondered who the hell would stop him if he could get to the heliport.

Staring out his office window he could see the huge Con Edison Ravenswood power plant across the river in Queens. Big Allis, queen of the grid. Rudy knew the truth. He'd promised no problems with the lights. He's sworn to his public that everything would be okay. He'd guaranteed no interruption of the biggest party the world had ever seen, but things were already fucked up beyond belief. He wanted a meeting with the CEO of Con Edison, Mr. Peter Wilcox, but that gentleman was nowhere to be found. The mayor was livid. Shit. He didn't feel good, either. Outside, the city growled at him. Fuck, this thing was bigger than New York, bigger than him even, and he couldn't stand that. It really pissed him off. His people really pissed him off. They were supposed to take care of this. The city had paid half a billion dollars and they'd better be fuckin' well ready.

"And if the fuckin' phones don't work *now,* what the fuck is going to happen at midnight? I want answers!" he shouted at an aide who hunched his shoulders and looked at his feet.

"Take it easy, Mr. Mayor. Your blood pressure."

"Did you get a list of chemical plants and all that crap like I told you to?"

"Yes, Your Honor."

"Did they all get the message to shut down?"

"I don't know, Mr. Mayor. I had one hundred and sixty-seven locations and twenty messengers."

"My God," said the mayor. "I can't believe this. I just can't fucking believe this. *No fucking telephones!* Ow!"

"Mr. Mayor?"

"Damn. Something's wrong with my arm."

"Mr. Mayor? Rudy? Jesus Christ."

At 8:45 Bill Packard was ready to leave the hospital and get drunk. He'd done his bit. Sensible people throughout the hospital had seen the wisdom of doing things right and didn't need him anymore. Nurses were placing yellow stickers on dangerous machines in every ward. He was exhausted and thought two or three drinks would put him under. On the other hand, he mused, he could go over to the 24th Precinct house, surprise his pal Ed and take a gander at the zoo that place must be.

Still wearing his white coat and stethoscope, Packard was standing outside the emergency room doors smoking a cigarette, something he hadn't done in years. Two nurses and an ambulance driver were smoking a few yards away. Off to his right, the drive curved around to First Avenue, but no ambulances had come in for at least an hour. Not even flashing lights and sirens could get through the streets. To his left, the East River sparkled with reflected light. Above the low, rumbling din of night he heard a motor launch close by. A moment later, two paramedics with a stretcher rushed out the doors and headed toward the river where a small pier for police boats served the hospital. Presently, the paramedics, a man on the stretcher, and four bodyguards with headsets returned from the pier.

Packard watched the stretcher wheel past. Lying unconscious on his back with a respirator over the lower half of his face was Mayor Rudy Giuliani. Then the stretcher was through the doors and a guy with a bad suit, tinted glasses, and a headset was standing less than a foot away, eyeballing Dr. Packard as though he were a cockroach.

"Who are you?" the guy demanded.

"Looks like your man was having trouble breathing," Packard answered mildly.

"That's none of your business."

"I'm a cardiac surgeon. Do you want me to examine him?"

"No way."

In no mood to be intimidated by political creeps, Packard blew smoke in the guy's face. The man hesitated, then backed off and said, "Sorry, Doctor. We don't want any publicity right now. You know what I mean? He has his own doctor. He's gonna be okay. Can I get your name?"

Before Packard could answer "No" the man was distracted by a voice in his headset.

"What?" he exclaimed into his tiny microphone. "You're shitting me."

The other security types were interrogating the nurses and driver. Three police motorcycles roared up the drive, and the cops congregated to one side, radios crackling, the night air condensing in macho puffs as they spoke among themselves.

The bodyguard was responding to his caller with a sense of urgency. "I don't know where the hell the damned doctor is. He was supposed to meet us at the door. No. Wait a minute, I got one right here." He tapped Packard on the shoulder and said, "You're a heart guy? That's what you said, right? Come with me."

Streetwise, Packard wasn't about to be drafted without his consent. "Ask me nice and I'll think about it," he said as a way of opening negotiations.

"Okay, pal. Whaddya want?"

"What I want," Packard said, "is for you to keep the hell away from me and let me do my job. That's what I want. Otherwise, I'll let the son of a bitch croak."

Doc and Jody lay in bed, cuddling and listening to the radio, when the President addressed the nation at 9:00 P.M. No one in New

York saw him on TV. The President started with an excessively long explanation of the millennium bug and date-sensitive computers, and then notified his audience that some of our global neighbors had already experienced problems.

"We are much better prepared for the crisis than any other nation," said the President in his most reassuring tone. "We've spent trillions of dollars. The smartest people in America have been working on this problem, and we're confident in their ability. Some things will go wrong, that's certain, but we'll get things working again as soon as humanly possible."

He politely asked everyone to go home and remain calm. Cooperate with your neighbors. Don't loot, he said, because that's not neighborly. He called on the governors of the fifty states and Puerto Rico to shoulder the responsibility of using the National Guard to maintain order.

"Your local authorities know your situation better than we do here in Washington," the President said. "Trust your public officials."

"Why do we have a president, then?" Jody asked.

Doc considered his answer for a moment and then replied, "Nobody remembers."

By 9:30 traffic in and out of Manhattan had reached critical mass. Nothing moved across the bridges or through the tunnels. After being stuck in traffic for hours, hundreds of people ran out of gas and abandoned their cars, ultimately immobilizing every traffic lane and isolating the island. Gridlock seized midtown and the bridge and tunnel approaches, and elsewhere on the island vehicles crept along, drivers making liberal use of their horns while passing bottles of champagne back and forth between cars.

True to the Broadway tradition that the show must go on, the festivities around Times Square continued as planned. Bands played, choirs sang, the 24 monster video screens displayed extravagant party scenes from around the city. Revelers in the street were treated to galas at the World Trade Center, the Plaza, and the Metropolitan Museum of Art. Diamonds glittered in the bright lights. Senators and judges in tuxedos smiled for the cameras, projecting an illusion of power and security.

The planned night regatta of tall ships commenced on schedule under the first round of fireworks along the Hudson River. The fleet of sailing vessels all had modern navigational equipment that depended on the GPS satellites that were no longer transmitting, but this posed no problem for experienced sailors. However, one of the ships near the front of the line, the Mexican training sloop *Emiliano Zapata*, was under the command of a young lieutenant who owed his billet to political connections rather than maritime skill, and he promptly rammed the Greek ship *Marathon* just off the 23rd Street sports complex. Under exploding rockets and pyrotechnic magic, the ships behind the two colliding craft maneuvered frantically to avoid a waterborne accordion crash, and presently the stately procession of nautical heritage was in complete disarray. The river turned white with churning foam from propellers thrust into reverse, and small boats escorting the ships were suddenly tossed into a maelstrom of right-of-way violations and abrupt maneuvers. In the midst of the chaos on the river, the Coast Guard discovered their GPS-driven radar system that controlled ship traffic in the harbor was malfunctioning. The radars were giving false positions when checked against simple hand-held radars. Ghosts and reflections were being displayed as solid objects. When the radar operators began reporting their difficulties to the captains and the pilots of the 37 ships underway between the Atlantic Ocean and the piers in New York, they learned to their horror that thirty vessels had lost their radars as well. The average ship of modern construction contained over 300 embedded chips and at least two dozen date-sensitive chip controllers, and almost every operation on board from propulsion to emission monitoring was automated and computerized. With most ships' clocks set to GMT, midnight in London marked the century rollover for the ships' computers, and ten ships immediately lost propulsion power. Their engines stopped. Four of the ten suffered failures in all their computer-controlled systems and were adrift without radar, communications, or steering.

The fireworks never stopped. The bursting balls and star clusters had no balky silicon transistors to impede their moment of glory. As a result, people in tall buildings could watch the Brownian movement of ships as the confusion in the harbor developed in slow motion. A huge container ship ran aground on Liberty Island, another rammed a pier at the foot of Broad Street just under the Brooklyn Bridge, and an automobile ship full of new Mercedes-Benzes smashed into the western support of the Verrazano-Narrows Bridge. The bridge held. The bow of the ship started taking on water. The steel containers had been expertly sealed by skilled craftsmen in the old country and kept the cars dry.

Spellbound, Copeland and Spillman watched Doc's videotape, and when it ended Copeland rewound it and started it again. From the opening shots of Con Edison's Manhattan power plants, he realized he was being presented with the greatest business opportunity of his life. Doc had recorded the work of the Midnight Club, and then edited the footage down to a forty-five-minute presentation of the plan to save New York. The Midnight Club had refined the principles Doc had developed while writing the Copeland 2000 software packages for the banks and adapted them for electric utilities. After midnight, when the Midnight Club knew which parts worked and which didn't, they'd be able to debug the programs and in very short order create a viable, eminently saleable product. The software was incredibly valuable.

"Do you know what this means?" Copeland asked Spillman.

"No," Spillman said. "I dunno. A nifty way to keep the lights on?"

"Christ almighty, Jonathon, it means that while this son of a bitch was fucking with my head all day, he was maneuvering me here to watch this tape. These freaks are going to make me more money than Chase ever did."

"Will that help us get out of this house?" Spillman asked.

"Who cares? What are you going to do if you get out? Go back to Shirley?"

Back down on Nassau Street, "The Future's So Bright, I Gotta Wear Shades," was blasting through the speakers. At 10:30 Doc was lying on a couch in the lounge, hands tucked behind his head, the football game on with the sound off. He was imagining the world as seen from space, the glorious blue of the sea, the white clouds, the polar caps. People were invisible, too small to be of significance. They hadn't been around long enough to make a significant mark and weren't nearly as important as they thought. Humans couldn't destroy the planet if they tried; they could only destroy themselves and perhaps a few other species, which they did every day, anyway.

Feeling serene, Doc tried to find a balance in the tumultuous events of the day. In the end the millennium bug would be remembered as a large hiccough in humanity's long, grappling struggle with the issue of the collective mind. People invented things: the wheel, the compass, the steam engine, the telephone, the controlled chain reaction, the computer. Other people found ways to use them that the inventors never dreamed of. It happened. Anything a human being could do, another human could understand and duplicate. Technology was wonderful and inevitable, but the organization of technological resources was never as advanced as the gadgets themselves. In time, microtechnology would open the heavens, plunder the depths of the earth, discover the chemical secrets of life, and find new sources of renewable energy, but not yet. High-tech was new. Computing was still in its infancy and having teething problems. By its very nature new technology broke new ground and was always experimental, which meant sometimes it broke. Sometimes the experiments didn't work out, but people learned. In this case the lesson would be hard won, but they usually were. The world that emerged from this event would be leaner, stronger, and more efficient, if not more just, equitable and fair.

The world would be different in the morning. His universe certainly was going to be different with Jody in it. He had a hard time remembering his last romance, or even the last time he got laid. No doubt it took the edge off and made him feel better. Lying next to him she'd felt like liquid silk, and when he licked the sweat between her breasts, she'd thrown back her head and laughed with pure joy.

For Jody, at the very moment when her world was imploding, when everything that could possibly go wrong did go wrong, she'd found salvation. She'd found Doc. The world was falling apart and he was spouting poetry, having a grand old time.

"Why me, Doc?" she asked. "You kept this secret for so long."

"You can handle it," he said. "Besides, you're cute. Do you like old boats?"

When they'd emerged disheveled and a little embarrassed from the bedroom, Ronnie had presented Jody with a Midnight Club T-shirt while the rest of the club whistled and applauded.

"You're one of us now," Ronnie said. "You proved Doc is a human being."

"You weren't sure?"

"Nope."

"Hey, Doc," Judd said. "Rudy had a heart attack."

"No shit?"

"They took him by boat to Bellevue, and he's there now. His guys are yapping about it on their radios. Want to listen?"

"Pass. I'm gonna watch the Millennium Bowl."

Jody picked up the video camera and resumed taping events in the room. Judd looked at the lens and began explaining the current satellite situation.

"As near as we can tell," he said to the camera, "world-wide we have twelve ground control command centers flying 87 satellites out of 864. Three more ground stations have partial control of another 40 birds. The AT&T installation at Basking Ridge about twenty miles from here in New Jersey is fully operational. This is very good news. We have a total of 127 birds, including 53 communication sats with operational transponders, providing some communications. We're not dead in the water here. It just looks that way."

Jody moved on to Carolyn who was watching her telephone screens and drinking a mint julep.

"When I was a little girl there was one phone company, Ma Bell, and a single monolithic structure meant everyone was always on the same page. With a zillion telephone companies, connections often fail even in the best of times. Bell Atlantic and AT&T are functioning properly and with each other, but their voice and data lines are suffering from more traffic than the systems can handle. Since every other telephone company is equally overloaded and the connections among them are malfunctioning, the surviving systems have to take drastic measures to ensure their integrity and survival. There isn't a damned thing any telephone company can do about overloads except cut off exchanges, and Bell Atlantic is doing that."

"Can you do it?"

"Yes, but I don't want to decide who goes down and who doesn't. Who do you think the phone companies are shutting off first? Harlem? Bedford-Stuyvesant? Guess again. They're doing in the Russians in Brooklyn."

"How are the Russians in Russia doing?" Jody asked. "Would you know?"

"Ask Ronnie."

Jody swung the camera around.

"Russia is toast," Ronnie said. "The north and far east are cut off, but they have some communications in the Moscow–Petersburg corridor. Some of their phone systems are old and don't have so many computers, and they're all right. They have land lines that connect to AT&T in Helsinki and the AT&T satellite up- and downlinks are functional. There's traffic, probably diplomatic and other high priority stuff, from Russia to New York."

"Through Finland."

"Right, but they're on emergency generators because the power is out in Helsinki."

"What happened to the nuclear reactor in Murmansk?"

Ronnie turned away from her screens and looked at Jody and the camera. "You don't know? It must have happened while you were in the bedroom. Just before we lost contact with them, the Norwegian Ministry of Defense radiation monitoring station on the Kola Peninsula detected a uranium isotope in the atmosphere that could only come from a chain reaction exposed to the open air. The implication, unverified, is that the Kola 2 nuclear generating plant near the Arctic city of Murmansk has suffered a catastrophic nuclear accident much worse than Chernobyl. It's also possible a reactor melted down in one or more of the Russian Navy ships stationed in Murmansk. The possibilities are unpleasant to consider."

"Consider them," Jody said. "Tell the camera all about it."

Ronnie began a dissertation on the effects of the nuclear contamination of the Arctic Ocean. Meanwhile, on the far side of the planet, the Tokyo Electric Company restored full power, enabling the Japanese to discover sixty percent of their mainframes were malfunctioning. The central banking system was dead, although several private banks had survived. A single year-old Japanese military communication satellite system had survived, providing domestic telephony for the self-defense forces.

The clocks ticked over. Doc's cellphone rang.

"This must be the only phone in New York that's working," Packard said.

"Well, actually, that's not true," Doc said. "What's up?"

"You aren't gonna believe who just showed up here."

"The mayor," Doc said.

"How'd you know?"

"I have a good police scanner. What's the matter with him?"

"A mild heart attack. We did an angiogram and now we're gonna do a bypass."

"Tonight?"

"Yes."

"Will he live for another hour without it?"

"Sure."

"Can he talk?"

"Rudy doesn't talk. He shouts, only right now he's scared to death."

"Does he know you have a working phone?"

"No."

"Good," Doc said. "I need a favor, and I have something to give in return. Here's the deal. A call will come from Copeland. He knows the mayor, at least he says he does. They probably had lunch a couple times. I'll call Donnie and you sit tight and wait for him to call you. And yes, I can make the phones work. That's my gift for the mayor. Bye."

Click. Dial tone. Nebraska 34–Alabama 21. China returned to the abacus. A revolution appeared imminent in Indonesia. Doc punched in the number, and Copeland answered on the first ring.

"Hi there, Donald. Enjoying the videotape?"

"Doc, I gotta tell ya," Copeland said breathlessly, "this is fucking great. This is fantastic. This is the most amazing software I've ever seen. It's a work of art."

"Thank you, Donald. I'm glad you like it."

"If you can keep the lights on in New York—Christ. Do you know what you have here, if it works? Jesus, even if it doesn't work. It hardly matters."

"I think so, yes."

"It's worth a fortune. It's practically a revolution."

"I thought you'd come around and see it that way, Donnie. You have a nose for money."

"I want in."

"Do you now? Interesting. What about you, Mr. Spillman? Do you want in, too?"

"Uh, yeah. Damn straight. How do I do that?"

"See, Donnie, they're already lining up. The package is configured for electric utilities, and they'll be your market. The bank software is working just fine, and this is better. It's more systemic. It
accounts for all the different ways the multiple systems interconnect. One of my crew wrote it. His name is Bo Daniels and he deserves a medal, as well as a bunch of your dough."

"I want in," Copeland repeated. "What's the price?"

"Care to make an offer, Donnie? You taught me to always make
the other guy name a number first. You're the other guy. Shoot,
baby."

"You're enjoying this, right?"

"Immensely."

"You fucked me around all day. Hell, you fucked me around for
five years, and now you're springing this on me."

"Your insight is remarkably clear. How much, Donnie?"

"Twenty mil."

"Nah."

"Thirty."

"Hmm."

"Thirty-five."

"I have a lot of people to take care of here, Donald. A whole
crew."

"Fifty. Fifty million dollars and all rights."

"Okay. Now we're in the ball park. And by the way, you know
the mayor, right?"

"Yeah. I know Rudy. So what? We're doin' business here."

"Did you know he had a heart attack tonight?"

"What?"

"He's in Bellevue and Bill Packard is about to open him up and
do a bypass. How d'ya like that? Now, I have a little problem. We
have a nice software package that might save ConEd's ass tonight,
but we'll never know unless I get something out of ConEd right

now. I need override codes. That's it, Donnie. That's the ticket to fame and fortune, the price of admission, yada yada. You know the mayor, and you also know the CEO of ConEd, isn't that right?"

"Peter Wilcox? He's an acquaintance, that's all."

"You know where he's supposed to be tonight?"

"At a party at the World Trade Center."

"Give the mayor his cellphone number. Do what you have to do, Donnie. Get me the override codes."

"Jesus. Can you get me a phone line?"

"You got it. Call Bill at the hospital on his office line. He's waiting."

"Explain to me exactly what these are again, these override codes, so I'll know exactly what the hell I'm talking about."

Doc explained and hung up. He turned to the Midnight Club and asked, "Boys and girls, how does fifty million dollars sound to you?"

Adrian swiveled around and squinted at Doc. The number was interesting enough to distract him from his screens.

"Your share will be about four and a half million, Adrian," Doc said. "That's on top of your bonus, and before taxes."

The kid smiled for the first time in two years. "There won't be an IRS," he said.

"Yes, there will be," Doc retorted. "Don't fool yourself. They may not have computers, but they'll find a way to take your money without them."

Uptown on 85th Street, Copeland stared at the cellular phone in his hand and had second thoughts. This *could* be Doc's ultimate trick. What did he actually have? A nice videotape, a view through a security camera of a bunch of freaks in a room full of high-tech hardware: an IBM s/390, workstations and computers everywhere, more monitors than he could count, jabbering police scanners and short-wave radios broadcasting in Russian and Chinese. All of this was on Nassau Street? Christ almighty. How could he not know? It could all be faked.

"What do you think, Jonathon? Is this bullshit?"

"I don't know, man, but you know what? I don't care. What I see is a man who is making war on a vicious enemy while everyone else is running around like chickens with their heads cut off. If it's bullshit, it's the most magnificent bullshit I've ever witnessed. Give him what he wants. Do what he says. The world is completely fucked, and there's nothing left to lose. Call the mayor."

Copeland dialed and Packard answered, "Yeah."

"Copeland here."

"You talk to Doc?"

"Yeah."

"He said you'd call, but he wouldn't tell me what it was about."

"You ain't gonna believe it, but I think it's true. It's called the Midnight Club."

Copeland explained and Packard listened, at first with skepticism, and then with the realization that the computer on Nassau Street could very well be the difference between darkness and light in Manhattan.

"So put the mayor on," Copeland pleaded. "Make him take the call."

Packard carried his cellphone down the corridor to the mayor's private room. Rudy was in bed, dressed in a hospital gown with an IV in his arm. "Mr. Mayor, I've got a call for you."

"You have a phone that works? Who is it?"

"Donald Copeland."

"The investment guy from Wall Street? He did Y2K for Chase, right?"

"That's him."

"You know him?" the mayor asked the doctor.

"Since we were kids."

"How'd he know I was here?"

"Your security people are talking up a storm on their radios. Anyone with a good tuner can listen in."

"Of all the people I could talk to with a real phone, why should I talk to Donald Copeland? Because he has a fancy radio?"

"He says he knows how to keep the lights on, Mr. Mayor. I think you should listen to him."

"The lights?"

"You know, incandescent bulbs, fluorescent tubes, neon."

"You're a real wise-ass, Dr. Packard."

"I take that as a compliment, Mr. Mayor, but I'm snotty to all my patients. Don't feel special. Listen, you don't know me. There's no reason to listen to me. I'm here to take care of your heart, not advise you on executive decisions, but you should take this phone call."

"Gimme the phone," the mayor snapped, grabbing the instrument. "Copeland?"

"Your Honor, I'm sorry to hear—"

"Cut the crap. Whaddya want?"

"Mr. Mayor, you're very well aware that Con Edison is connected to the Northeast grid, which includes many power companies. At least two of them, one in Vermont and one upstate are not Y2K compliant and are going to bring the entire grid down. Con Edison is not prepared to deal with the rolling blackout when it comes at a few minutes after midnight, but my company is prepared. We're willing to provide this service free of charge and keep the lights on in Manhattan. Con Edison has other problems we can solve. Communications, for starters. We've already done a ton of work on their phone lines. ConEd doesn't know what we've done, and Bell Atlantic doesn't know, but we did it anyway. Right now the ConEd people are talking to one another while you can't."

"Are you shitting me?"

"No, sir. We can do the same for you. Listen, we've already fed ConEd an enormous amount of information to help them in their Y2K efforts, and you can verify that, but you don't have time right now. You must understand, Mr. Mayor, this is the only chance we have to keep the lights on in the city, but to do it we need your help."

"This sounds like a crock of shit to me, Copeland."

"We've spent twelve million dollars, Mr. Mayor, as an act of civic duty. We know Con Edison's computers will fail, and we know our computer won't. We can save ConEd and save New York."

"Tell it to me again," the mayor said. "Explain to me what you think you can do, and what you think will happen if you don't. Spell it out."

When Copeland finished, the mayor understood perfectly well that if Copeland's people could do half of what he claimed, and he authorized them to do it, then he could take the credit. If they failed, things were going to be so fucked up no one would remember or even know about the Midnight Club.

"I've been trying to find Peter Wilcox, the CEO of ConEd, all night," Rudy confessed. "I don't know where he is, and his phone doesn't work."

"I know how to reach Wilcox," Copeland said. "When you get him, you tell him to talk to the supervisor of the command center on West End Avenue whose name is Sarah McFadden. We need the override codes on a disk, and we'll send a heavyweight cop to be the messenger. I'm gonna have the cop call you. His name is Ed Garcia, precinct commander of the Two-Four in Manhattan. That's how we want to do it."

Rudy listened and weighed the risks. He was thinking he was about to have heart surgery and might never wake up. Did he want to leave behind a city in chaos, or a city that gleamed in the night, alone and proud? It was a hell of a chance to take and he might never know the result.

"Okay," he said. "I'll do it. Then this Aztec asshole friend of yours is going to cut out my heart."

15

The eleventh hour. D minus sixty and counting.

At 10:00 the bug had crashed into Brazil and Venezuela, mowing down oil wells, pipelines, and refineries like blades of steel wheat. Supply chains were broken at the source. Mines, railroads and chemical plants, the basic industries on which an economy is built, teetered on the brink of ruin across the plains and mountains of South America. The first systems to crash were often pollution controls. When date-sensitive sensor controls failed, gaseous and liquid effluvia either spewed into the air and water, or backed up the operation and shut it down before other computer systems had a chance to go haywire. In South America, as in most of the Third World, the millennium bug savaged the coastal cities and industries, with minimal if not positive effects up-country in the hinterlands. No doubt the rain forests would benefit as logging and industrial expansion ceased when trucks ran out of fuel.

Now, in the penultimate hour, the millennium bug struck the far northeastern provinces of Canada. The invisible alien had arrived in North America and was slipping across the frozen tundra at a thousand miles per hour, a silent arrow pointed at the most heavily industrialized, computerized, automated concentration of machinery in the world, New York City.

The residents of the outer boroughs had seen blackouts and riots from Vladivostok to Dublin all day on TV. At the last moment thousands decided their neighborhoods were not where they wanted to be when the millennium bug slammed into New York like a freight train. Afraid of their city, panicky New Yorkers from Brooklyn and Queens migrated east on Long Island, where few were prepared to welcome them with open arms. From the Bronx, people headed north into Westchester County and Connecticut, overwhelming the suburbs, cleaning out convenience stores and emptying fuel tanks at every gas station within fifty miles of the city limits. Few of the locusts exiting the city had a destination or adequate supplies for a cold night in the open. By nine o'clock, desperate authorities in towns around New York were calling on the governor and state police for help, but the phone lines were overwhelmed and useless.

In Manhattan many chose this hour to pray. From Harlem to the Bowery, churches, mosques, and temples opened their doors and filled with fearful worshippers. Since it was the Sabbath, Friday night services had concluded in the city's many Jewish synagogues, with far larger congregations than usual. Many of the suddenly devout remained for hours in the temples to offer more prayer and discuss how to deal with the coming hardship. The millennium and the event that marked its passing transcended Christianity and the two-thousandth anniversary of the birth of Christ. The catastrophe touched everyone, rich and poor, believer and nonbeliever. The bug knew nothing of sacred writing, prophecy, original sin, reincarnation, or a Messiah, but in every neighborhood men and women of all faiths sought the wisdom of holy writ. They read the Torah, the Gospels, the Koran, the Tibetan Book of the Dead, and in the ancient texts found the courage and strength to see them through the night.

A miracle was happening in the Millennium Religious Sanctuary of the 24th Precinct. The flow of people flocking to the houses of worship overflowed into this now famous haven. Thousands of religious seekers arrived seeking solace in the community of their brethren. Whole congregations arrived with their ministers, who quickly organized a communal mass prayer to commence a minute before midnight. After walking miles from faraway places like Rye and Yonkers, people who'd struggled all day and night to be part of the sanctuary were not about to let rowdy drunks spoil the most significant religious experience of their lives. By sheer numbers, the righteous pushed the revelers downtown toward Times Square.

Ed Garcia didn't know which way the wind would blow next. One minute he had an Irish civil war, then a riot, then a mystical convention. What was that old adage? Be careful what you wish for; it may come true.

He was pacing around his office, drinking coffee and worrying himself sick over what he was supposed to do if the lights went out. What would happen to all these people? What would happen to everyone in Times Square? There were three or four million New Year's Eve lunatics down there. He had at least fifty thousand in his precinct, maybe more. He couldn't get an accurate count. Garcia had never seen the city this crazy, and he'd seen a lifetime of crazy. What passed for normal in New York would be crazy anywhere else, and he'd seen political mêlées, race riots, Superbowls, violent labor strikes and police brutality, but not all at once. The prisoners in his overcrowded jail were frightened, traffic had the city in a death grip, TV was fucked up, the phones were fucked up, and it wasn't yet midnight.

He pulled open a desk drawer, fondled a bottle of good single malt scotch, sighed and put it back.

The phone rang and he jumped, staring at the device as though it were an inanimate object that suddenly had come alive. Gingerly, he picked it up.

"Two-Four precinct," he said. "Captain Garcia."

"Hi, Ed. Copeland here."

"Donald. Jeez. I mean, I'm surprised the phone rang. All day it never shuts up, but tonight, well, you know."

"You think you got problems? I'm locked in my house."

"You're what?"

"Yeah, I'm locked in. The fucking computer won't let me out."

"That monster in your basement? That's pretty funny, Donnie, considering everything. You bettah off anyway. It's nuts outside."

"Look, Ed, I need a favor. I need a cop I can trust. I want you to call this number I'm gonna give you, and you'll recognize the voice at the other end."

"Oh, yeah? You're sounding kinda mysterious, Donnie, and I'm busy. I got every religious nut in New York up here. My jail is full. My cops are half out of their minds. Cut to the chase, boy."

"Ed, you're gonna call the mayor, and he's going to order you to go to the Con Edison command center on 65th Street and West End and pick up a computer disk that you're gonna take to my building on Nassau Street."

"The mayor?"

"Yeah, Giuliani himself."

"You're puttin' me on."

"No, sir. Lemme give you the number."

"Wait a minute. Suppose this is true, how do I get there? The city is a parking lot."

"The mayor will send a motorcycle and the guy will take you on his bike."

"How'm I gonna make a call if the damned phone doesn't work?"

"It'll work."

"How d'ya know it'll work?"

"*It'll work*. God damn."

"You got a magic phone wand?"

"I'm callin' you, right?"

"Right."

"Okay. It'll work."

"Gimme the number."

"It's Bill Packard's number at Bellevue. You got it?"

"Yeah. Why would I call the mayor there?"

"Because that's where he is, Ed. He had a heart attack."

"Rudy?"

"He's the only mayor we got."

"Is he dead?"

"How could he talk to you if he was dead? C'mon."

"He wants me to be a messenger boy? No wonder I hate the son of a bitch."

"Leave politics out of this, Ed. This is more important."

"What's this about, anyway?"

"Rudy can tell you if he wants. Just call him, and maybe later you can come by and get me out of my house."

Garcia laughed at that. "Nah," he said. "I'm gonna leave you there. You can't get into trouble that way."

"Jonathon is with me and we're both locked in. Shirley is across the street and doesn't know he's here. She's probably gone bananas."

"If your phone is workin', why can't he call her?"

"Jesus Christ, Ed. I can call you, I can call Packard, but I can't call just anybody."

"Why not?"

"Stop with the questions and just call Bill's number, all right?"

"Give me a hint. Give me a reason to remember you ever called me."

"You think this is a New Year's Eve prank?"

"It crossed my mind, yes."

"Ed, we're trying to keep the lights on in New York. For God's sake. The clock is ticking."

After forty years, Garcia knew when a guy was bullshitting and when he wasn't, and in his inimitable, overblown, melodramatic way, he knew Copeland was telling the truth.

"The lights," Garcia said.

"You got it. We're staring at a blackout with only one chance of avoiding it."

"How the fuck . . . ?"

"Don't ask. I don't have all night to explain. Call the mayor. Now."

"Okay, I'll call."

Click. Dial tone. Never had that hum sounded friendlier. Garcia looked up Packard's number and punched it in.

"Packard."

"Bill? This is Ed. Copeland says you got the mayor there."

"Hold on. Heeeeere's Rudy."

"You're diabolical, you know," Jody said to Doc.

"I told you I liked Mephistopheles."

"You lucked out having the mayor in captivity at Bellevue."

Doc shrugged. "Maybe, but I knew he'd be stuck someplace like Gracie Mansion, or City Hall, or in his car. His security is useless, so he's easy to track. Politicians aren't very bright, as a general rule. They're just like everybody else."

"So you planned to get him involved no matter what?"

"This is Plan B. It would've been cleaner to get the overrides from Sarah, but as it is, we might have better cooperation from ConEd. Maybe. Maybe maybe maybe. I hope so."

"Were you planning to spring this on Copeland all along?"

He winked and chuckled and put on his Ignatius J. Reilly hunting cap with ear flaps. "Yep," he snorted. "That was Plan A. You can always count on greed as a motivator. Works like a charm. I locked him in his house so I'd know where he was if I needed him. I didn't want him to get lost."

After 11:00, people in Times Square started to count down the minutes. The buzz and clamor grew ever more intense, the ululation of millions of voices swelling in volume to tribal levels. Car horns never ceased. No traffic moved on the north–south avenues, with very little movement on the side streets. Firecrackers exploded nonstop from one end of the island to the other. Home-made rockets and black-market Roman candles lit up the sky with streaks of flame and bursts of pyrotechnic rainbows.

Throughout the city, shopkeepers and merchants prepared to defend their business from looters in case the lights went out. In heavily ethnic neighborhoods, among the Greeks, Hassidic Jews, and West Indians in Brooklyn, Koreans, Indians, and Italians in Queens, middle-class blacks in Harlem and the Bronx, activists organized neighborhood patrols to protect their enclaves from anarchy. Spread dangerously thin, overwhelmed by rowdy drunks, traffic snarls and poor communications, the police deployed as many officers as possible in commercial districts, and looked the other way when confronted by shopkeepers with shotguns.

The city trembled with fear and anticipation.

At 11:13 Doc played Johnny Cash's "The Midnight Special" and then was banished from music duties by Carolyn who wanted The Last Poets.

> *The Big Apple is outta sight.*
> *But you ain't never had a bite.*
> *Wake up, niggers, or you're all through.*

A million clocks ticked over, minute by minute. At 11:14 Ed Garcia climbed aboard a Kawasaki police special behind a veteran sergeant biker cop, one of the mayor's elite messengers.

"You know where you're going?"

"Just hang on, captain," cautioned the driver.

The sergeant started slowly, winding through stalled cars and crowds in front of the station, and headed west toward the Hudson with spurts of speed, heavy brakes and delicate balance. West End Avenue was jammed as far south as the eye could see, so the sergeant continued to Riverside Park and zipped down a bicycle trail, scattering startled pedestrians with blaring siren and lights for 35 blocks to 65th Street. To Garcia, the park was a blur, the ride a psychedelic roller coaster, the night a deluge of sensory overload. Fireworks like magical hallucinations lit the sky, their booms lost in the racket from the city and the shriek of the motorcycle engine. To his right, the lights of pleasure craft filled the river, serene and marvelous in the sparkling night. Ahead, open pavement stretched in the headlight's beam and the bike accelerated like a catapult. Garcia gripped the driver's waist with one hand, glancing every few seconds at his watch as it bounced in front of his eyes. He was transported to a dreamlike trance. His mind stopped processing the surge of data and just let it all in, the city, the noise, the wind and cold, the smell of the driver's leather jacket, the motorcycle throbbing between his legs like a controlled chain reaction.

The bike wheeled onto 65th Street and back into traffic, the sergeant expertly weaving around cars and vans. Firecrackers, horns, men in tuxedos, the whole New Year's Eve chorus of people doing extraordinary things: standing on top of cars, pissing in the gutter, drinking champagne from a shoe.

Wearing a white supervisor's hardhat, Sarah McFadden was waiting on the sidewalk in the middle of a crowd of revelers.

"Are you Ms. McFadden?" Garcia asked.

"Yes, sir."

"Lemme see some ID."

Sarah flashed a photo badge on a necklace and leaned close to the motorcycle. "You give this to Doc Downs and nobody else. It took a phone call from the mayor, but here it is. I hope."

"Save it," Garcia snapped. "Gimme the disk. Doc'll call you when he gets it."

They spurted away into the traffic. The driver tried the West Side Highway, 11th and 12th Avenues, but the lanes between the lanes were blocked. People were out of their cars, drinking and singing in the street. Lights, sirens, driving on sidewalks, they inched downtown. At 42nd they caught a glimpse of the video screens and giant marquees in Times Square. Inside his helmet Garcia could hear nothing over the whine of the engine and the siren, but he could feel the city trembling under the wheels. At 11:30 they made it to 34th Street.

At 11:32 an anesthesiologist rendered Mayor Giuliani unconscious.

At 11:39 the President of the United States met with the members of the National Security Council who could make it to the White House.

At 11:42 Eastern time, 8:42 on the West Coast, the associated utilities of the Northwest grid agreed to isolate themselves from one another and deconstruct the grid. Elsewhere in the nation, including the Northeast, the grids determined to stand or fall together.

At 11:44 Ronnie and Judd went into the bedroom and shut the door. Doc fired up a joint, Carolyn danced, Adrian played with his trains, Bo fidgeted and paced, and Jody, having become one with her camera, shot everything.

At 11:45 on 85th Street, Copeland and Spillman watched Barbra Streisand belt out a love song to New York City live and direct from Madison Square Garden.

Across the rivers, America waited and watched the clock.

The congestion thinned below the Village, and the motorcycle got up to speed on Lower Broadway. Garcia arrived in front of the building on Nassau Street with fourteen minutes to spare.

Doc and Bo were waiting in the street. Bo immediately rushed upstairs with the disk while Doc stayed to invite the police captain to come in.

"I really can't. I have to get back and take care of my precinct," Garcia said.

"You can probably do that better from here," Doc told him. "Come on."

The driver twisted his throttle and said, "What's it gonna be, captain?"

"I gotta go back, Doc. I'm gonna let Copeland out of his house. Did you know he was locked in?"

Doc laughed and waved and went inside.

Upstairs, Bo inserted the Zip disk into the drive, checked the directory on the screen, and loaded seven files into seven systems that would run simultaneously on the IBM, one for each of five power plants, one for the command center on 65th, and one for the grid interconnect switching station at the East River plant. Then he linked the IBM to the seven locations. When Doc walked in, Bo was ready to take over the system with the push of a button.

One small screen in Bo's console was wired into ConEd's security and surveillance system. Doc saw fifty people on the verge of panic in a huge room reminiscent of Houston's Mission Control. Sarah was in the foreground, sitting at the master operator's station, wearing a headset and looking anxiously up at the big screen above the security camera.

Doc put on a headset and called her.

"Doc here."

"You got the disk?"

"Yes, ma'am. The codes are installed and we're ready to go."

"You have some heavyweight friends, Doc. I never suspected that."

"Sarah, the only friend I need now is you. I expect you have a lot of anxious people there," he said without stating directly that he could see them.

"You might say that," Sarah replied. "They heard me talk to the mayor and Peter Wilcox because I put the calls on the speakers, and they know I gave the override codes to a police captain on Wilcox's orders."

"Do they understand your system will crash and burn unless we do this?" Doc asked.

"Some do, some don't. Most of them think I'm out of my mind, and maybe they're right. I am out of my mind, but I'm going through with this anyway."

"I, for one, am extremely grateful," Doc said. "Now, I'm going to turn you over to a young man named Bo Daniels. It was Bo who found the Y2K solution for your load factor applications. He found the bad chips in the feeder valves at Waterside that I told you about. Most of the data I've given you in the past two years came from Bo. All right?"

"Whatever you say, Doc."

Doc unplugged his headset, took it off, and nodded to Bo. "It's all yours. Drive carefully."

"Sarah?" Bo said. "Hello."

"Hello, Bo. You nervous?"

"Yes."

"Me, too."

"Okay," Bo said. "We're both nervous, but can we get acquainted later? I have the overrides installed for the five plants, the command center, and the interconnect at East River, and I need to run them *right now*."

Sarah punched keys on her terminal and said, "You're in command."

"Ravenswood," Bo said crisply.

"Check. She's yours."

"Waterside."

"Check."

"East River."

"Check."

"59th Street Station."

"Check."

"74th Street Station."

"Check."

"West End."

"Check."

"Interconnects."

"Check."

"Going to the interconnects now. We're going to disconnect ConEd from the grid."

"Thank God," Sarah exclaimed. "That's exactly what I believed we should've done two hours ago. The chief thought I was nuts."

"So we're on the same page?" Bo asked.

"Same page, same paragraph. Let's do it," Sarah said. "Show me what you got, Bo. Every other company on the grid is going to scream bloody murder, but that's too damned bad. Let's knock 'em down."

"Ready?"

"Ready."

"Pleasant Valley."

"Disconnect. Check."

"Ramapo–Landentown."

"Disconnect. Check."

"Farragut."

"Disconnect. Check."

"Goethals."

"Disconnect. Check."

"Jamaica."

"Disconnect. Okay."

Bo took a deep breath and exhaled slowly. "That's all of them. I don't see any leakage, do you?"

"No, sir. We're on our own now. We just violated every rule the public utilities commission ever wrote. I'm popping circuit breakers all over the place," Sarah announced. "Hold on. Rerouting all 345kV lines. All right. We're isolated. My phones are ringing. I think a lot of pissed off people upstate are already calling me."

"Don't answer," Bo replied, turning up both thumbs and winking at Doc.

"Wait a minute. I'm trying to reroute the 345s, and, and, they're already rerouted."

"That's right," Bo said. "I don't trust your distribution controls."

"I guess you know what you're doing."

"Thanks," Bo said, "but I'm going to need a lot of help before this night is over."

Bo began firing technical questions at Sarah, and Doc went into the lounge to watch a little Barbra Streisand. It was 11:55. If the day were to end now, he thought it would pass muster. He had a new lady-friend whom he liked a lot. He'd made fifty million bucks for his little band of outlaws. He'd found a way to get the damned overrides, and Bo was in command of Con Edison with a shot at finding out if his system could run the plants and generate enough juice to keep the lights on.

The members of the Midnight Club were glued to their stations. Jody moved among them, recording these last minutes. She crouched down beside Ronnie, catching a close-up of a sweaty temple, then stood and panned the room, taking in all the clocks.

Doc lit a cigarette and noticed his hands were trembling.

After building toward a crescendo all day and night, during the last five minutes the city's frenzy launched into a cosmic realm. The bands played louder, people danced harder, the religious prayed more fervently and an enormous tintinnabulation radiated from Manhattan like the swelling rise of a long drum solo. It was a cold night and yet people were in a sweat because no one could keep still. The tension forced everyone into motion, into acts of sexual passion, wanton destruction, into confessing their sins at the top of their lungs. People smashed their clocks and turned up their stereos to ear-shattering volume. Thousands fired gunshots into the air to mark the passing of the 20th Century.

In the still air of a surgical theater Bill Packard opened Rudy Giuliani's chest and saved his life.

At 11:58 the frenzy suddenly stopped and the city turned eerily quiet, as though the entire population understood the moment. It was here.

At 11:59 the ecumenical council of the Millennium Religious Sanctuary of the 24th Precinct led their flock in prayer.

"Our Father who art in Heaven, hallowed be Thy name . . ."

The ball began to drop in Times Square. In silence the crowd watched the descent.

On Nassau Street Bo had installed the overrides. Con Edison was isolated from the grid whose other members were screaming foul. The screens were live with real feeds from the command center, and Bo and Sarah were rapidly reconfiguring their five precious power plants to shoulder the load.

"I'm holding my breath," Ronnie shouted.

Wilson Picket blew out the last bars of "The Midnight Hour." Doc threw open a window and looked up at the World Trade Center whose twin towers framed the moon. He kissed Jody, this time without prompting.

The last seconds of the 20th Century were counted down like a rocket launch. Five, four, three, two, one.

Midnight.

PART THREE

January 1, 2000

PART THREE

16

The ball in Times Square descended halfway and stopped, as if time itself were suspended. Twelve thousand rhinestones and 180 halogen lights glistened and sparkled, but the sphere was immobilized. The crowd gasped. The twenty-four giant video screens went blank and the crowd gasped again. Then, with no preamble, the screens suddenly came alive with film of a monstrous subway train rushing headlong at the camera, coming closer and closer, blue sparks flying, the thundering roar of steel wheels on steel rails exploding through the sound system. The unexpected terror of the film slammed the crowd like a howitzer. A half million people were screaming when the hurtling train suddenly stopped in a blurry freeze-frame. In giant script, splashed in crimson across the front of the cab were the words, "Adrian 2000."

The screens faded to black. A pair of dumbstruck operators in the main video truck thrashed at their controls, shrieking their astonishment, when images from live cameras around 42nd Street popped back onto the screens as they'd been programmed to do. Scheduled events moved resolutely on. Bands played "Auld Lang Syne," fireworks erupted from the Hudson River and Central Park, the world did not end, Christ did not appear in the 24th Precinct or anywhere else, and the ball completed its descent in stately fashion.

The crowd uttered a huge sigh of relief, thinking the moment had passed with nothing more than a trick. If that was the worst the dread millennium bug could do, party on!

The 21st Century commenced in the Eastern time zone. People in Manhattan danced and laughed away their fears and trepidations. To them, Y2K had been a hoax. It was all a big nonevent.

On the edge of the crowd, a five-year-old, bundled up against the cold and perched on his father's shoulders, pointed up at Mickey Mouse's big digital clock.

"Look, Daddy!"

The display read, "8:01 A.M. January 5, 1980."

On Nassau Street, Doc had watched the finale of Barbra's show from the Garden. After Barbra blew kisses and gushed, "Happy New Year! Happy New Year, everybody!" New York 1 had switched coverage to Times Square, and Doc had witnessed Adrian's prank.

Laughing so hard he fell out of his chair, he lay on the floor and shouted across the room, "Adrian, you're beautiful!"

The kid was irrepressible, God bless him. Doc picked himself up, crossed the room, and gave the boy a pat on the back.

"Way to go, Adrian. Nice hack."

Adrian shrugged, fixated on his monitor that displayed a duplicate of the big screen in the MTA dispatch center. Red and green lights twinkled and jumped from one electrical block to the next, showing the movement of trains in 238 miles of tunnels.

Doc glanced at the clocks. 12:02. The Eastern time zone was toast but didn't know it yet. He went from station to station, offering murmurs of encouragement. He'd done his part, preparing the Midnight Club for their moment of glory, but this was like nuclear war. There was no way to practice.

"Ronnie? How's the water supply?"

"Okay coming in. Going out not so good. Six of fourteen treatment plants are down, and three more are on the brink."

"Carolyn? Phones?"

"MCI and GTE are down. Bell and AT&T are up. Military hardened land lines are up. State police dedicated lines are down. All our lines are up."

"Judd? The Web?"

"Internet is dead. There is no Web. DARPA is still up, but spotty."

"Bo?"

"I'm going to lose two plants in Queens and one in the Bronx."

Bo's fingers trembled above his keyboard and sweat poured down his temples.

"How's Sarah?" Doc asked.

"Terrified."

Doc lit a Camel. On Bo's main screen, the flow of electricity through the grid of which Con Edison was no longer a part was measured by a flickering chart. The grid had been under heavy load since nuclear-fueled plants were taken off-line earlier in the day, and all the plants were straining to provide extra power for all the cities illuminated for millennium celebrations.

An array of smaller screens displayed the output from each of ConEd's ten remaining power plants, three of which were faltering.

"Steady as she goes," Bo said into his headset. "Steady, steady, oh shit."

Spikes appeared on several of the smaller screens, and a huge downward spike flashed on the big monitor.

"It's coming! It's coming! Hold onto your hat, Sarah."

"Oh my God."

"You're going to lose Astoria, Hudson Avenue and Narrows right now," Bo said rapidly, naming the three failing Con Edison power plants. "I'm initiating the isolation of Manhattan. We can't wait. Astoria has lost all boiler controls in number three and she's about to blow sky high."

"I can see that."

"Well, shut the damned plant down!" Bo demanded. "Do it!"

"I'm trying," Sarah answered, her stress radiating from Bo's headset. "I'm losing my phones to the six outer plants."

"Shit," Bo shouted. "Carolyn! Her phones are going down."

"I can't do a damned thing about their dedicated lines, Bo. I've been telling them for months to check their telcom switches, but they didn't. They're toast."

"We're all toast," Sarah said dejectedly.

"Not yet," Bo said as he launched a program that reconfigured the transmission and distribution of electricity from the five plants he hoped were compliant through 53 substations to Manhattan and thin slices of Brooklyn and Queens along the East River waterfront. The isolation of the island was complete. The rest of New York had to stand or fall on its own.

Ten seconds later a high-pressure boiler exploded in Astoria Generator Three, killing four workers instantly and wounding five more. Astoria tripped and went off-line. In the Hudson Avenue plant, supposedly Y2K compliant voltage controls had been remediated by a programmer asleep at the compiler. He'd missed thousands of date-fields because they'd been named "Zorro" by the original programmer. When Zorro met the 21st Century, the devilish swordsman corrupted the compliant code and sent false readings to the operators' screens. Well-trained and prepared for false readings that fell outside the parameters of possibility, the plant operator disconnected the sensors and shifted voltage control to a backup system. The last thing he saw on his screen was the infected backup system tripping the plant and shutting down everything, including his monitor.

At the Narrows plant, a bizarre reading from emission controls immediately tripped the plant, shut down the generators, and took it off-line. Staten Island and the southern half of Brooklyn suffered a brownout. Twenty seconds later, the first jolt of weird voltages rippled over the grid. The Northeast grid experienced failures and anomalies every day, but it had never endured hundreds of simultaneous malfunctions. When twenty-seven power plants north and west of the city failed immediately, all for different reasons, voltage across the grid suddenly dropped, causing widespread brownouts that lasted a few seconds. The remaining plants struggled to pick up the slack, but the failure of defective high-voltage regulators two hundred miles north in Vermont sent an uncontrollable power surge over the transmission lines that swept across the grid like a hurricane. To protect hardware from the surge, circuit breakers tripped power plants, transmission lines, and distribution substations, and in a minute and forty-three seconds, five hundred thousand square miles from Maine to the District of Columbia and east to Ohio blacked out. The Northeast grid crashed.

Three minutes later the Southeast grid flamed out along with Eastern Canada, the Yucatan peninsula and the islands of the Caribbean. The race with the most implacable of deadlines was lost. It was as though the Atlantic Ocean had overflowed its shores and swallowed North America.

In Washington, where 750,000 millennium celebrants had gathered in the Mall, the city turned as dark as the granite facade of the Vietnam memorial. Emergency generators popped on in the White House, but the millennium bug had decapitated the nation. Deep underground, the President was in a communications bunker talking to the military and the CIA, but he couldn't talk to Philadelphia, Atlanta, Charlotte, or Mobile. He couldn't call across town, for that matter.

America's long night of darkness began with sirens screaming down Pennsylvania Avenue. From Maine to Florida, the leaderless, disorganized nation entered the 21st Century in a state of total disarray.

The millennium bug had come home.

———

Unique and dazzling, New York was ablaze with light. The party continued in Times Square where the delirious crowd, oblivious to events elsewhere, celebrated the glorious arrival of the new millennium. The news that the entire world was dark beyond the Hudson passed quickly by word of mouth. Many dismissed it as a rumor. "And if it's true," one drunk bellowed to another, "who cares?"

In the 24th Precinct, the prayer that ended the 20th Century greeted the new millennium with a rousing, "Hallelujah."

At Bellevue, Packard sewed up the mayor's chest and took a straw poll of the nurses. "So," he asked, "will you guys vote for Rudy again?"

On 85th Street, Donald Copeland heard a knock on his door. When he twisted the knob, to his surprise the door swung open and revealed Ed Garcia standing on the porch.

"I thought you guys were locked in," the captain said, and when Copeland didn't respond, he added, "We got lights. How 'bout that."

Copeland blinked. A cash register was jingling between his ears and he appeared more than a little bewildered. He blinked a few more times before he said, "Come in. Let's have a drink. Happy New Year."

On Nassau Street, cool, unflappable Bo rushed to the bathroom and puked, leaving his seat vacant and headset dangling.

Three miles north, Sarah McFadden had closed her eyes, clasped her hands together, hurriedly mumbled a prayer, and listened for the hum of emergency generators that never came. All she heard was the buzz of excited people in the command center. She opened her eyes. The lights were on.

"Bo?" she said anxiously.

Doc turned on a speaker phone and said, "This is Doc. Bo will be right back."

"Oh my God," she uttered. "Whatever that young man did, it worked."

"I'm going to reserve judgment on that," Doc replied, reading

Bo's screens. "You have problems at Ravenswood. Big Allis is not happy."

"I'm on to that. Just let me catch my breath."

Sheepishly, Bo emerged from the bathroom wiping his mouth.

"Sorry," he apologized.

Doc wrapped him in a bear hug. Ronnie, Carolyn and Jody took turns hugging and kissing the embarrassed young man. Adrian, naturally, didn't move from his station. Judd added a hug and handshake and declared, "We're the only place within a thousand miles that has lights, Bo. You did it, man. All right."

Bo broke free and plugged in his headset.

"Sarah?"

"We have trouble at Ravenswood."

"Let's get on it. I have a set of diagnostics configured for each of the five plants. If they don't work, we'll try something else."

The Midnight Club returned to their stations, astonished at Bo's success. With no way to test the system under battlefield conditions, Doc's plan and Bo's code had had a one in a million chance to succeed. Even if the code were perfect, the plan still should have failed because of embedded chips in the vast tangle of systems. As it was, Bo's applications kept the lights on in Manhattan. Across the East River, downtown Brooklyn remained brightly lit because power had to reach Jay Street to keep the subway running. A strip of Queens around the Ravenswood power plant near the Queensboro Bridge had lights thanks to proximity to Big Allis. The rest of New York was as dark as Moscow.

Let there be light, Doc thought, as he ran downstairs to the second floor where Annie and the customer support staff were working with the banks.

"Did Chase make it?" he demanded. "They should have power at the Tech Center."

"They do," Annie said. "They're okay."

"The credit unions?"

"Everyone is okay, Doc. Relax."

Annie pulled him over to one of the staff screens where a techie in a headset was in multimedia communication with the Chase Y2K team at the Tech Center. Doc could see that the bank's core computers had survived the century rollover and were performing, if not flawlessly, at least as well as they ever did.

"Is the microwave circuit to Chase okay?" Doc asked.

"Yeah, communication is fine, and the 2000 software is cool," said the techie, a kid in a Princeton sweatshirt, "but the Metro Tech building is like full of bugs. The swing shift is locked in and the night shift locked out."

Doc grinned, amused.

"Did you do that on purpose?" Annie asked, playfully punching Doc in the shoulder.

Doc punched her back and said, "I'll never tell."

"I hear the lights went out in Boston," the techie remarked.

"Yep."

"And in Philly."

"Yep."

"Everywhere except here. Isn't that like, strange?"

"Nope. How're your phones?"

"It's really weird. Our phones are good, but everyone we call is like really surprised because they can't call out on their phones, and no one else can call them, either. It's like the phone gods smiled on us. We can call some places and not others. There's like no phones in Washington or Toronto. I knew this was going to be like, bizarre, but this is bizarre bizarre."

Doc stuck his fingers in his mouth and whistled, causing the staff to glance up from their screens. Thirty heads sprouted like cabbages above the cubicle dividers.

"Annie tells me Chase and all our clients survived the millennium crunch," Doc announced. "You're veteran troopers, and you've earned an honest victory tonight. I'm not going to make a ridiculous speech. I just want to say that everyone in this room will receive a bonus of $20,000. Thank you."

The whistles and cheers lasted only a moment before everyone went back to work.

As they walked toward the door, Doc said, "Your people are doing terrific work, Annie. They're all great."

"Now that the big moment has come and gone," she said, "people are wondering about their jobs. The bonuses are nice, but they want to know if their jobs will be here next week."

"Annie, tell them this isn't the end. It's only the beginning. Our people don't have to worry about their jobs. We have to worry about paying them enough to keep them."

"How bad is it, Doc?"

"Depends on your point of view. You might say the collapse of civilization is not a bad thing if you think civilization is on the wrong track."

"Don't be such a smart-ass."

"Okay, let's see," he said, "Around town, Brooklyn Union Gas has lost control of pressure regulators in the natural gas pipes and shut down. All broadcast TV has gone belly up, and two cable stations are the only TV right now. I think three radio stations are broadcasting music. Only a few Bell Atlantic and AT&T telephone lines are working, including yours. Police radios are working. In the outer boroughs, emergency generators are providing electricity to some buildings and hospitals. The subway is running."

"Is there looting?"

"Too soon to tell."

"How do you know?"

"I have a good police scanner," he answered with a shrug. "I like toys."

Computer malfunctions were instantaneous, but effects required several nanoseconds to manifest. Inside billions of silicon wafers, the flow of electrons responded to binary instructions the only way possible, taking the path of least resistance. The machines peeled off trillions of calculations in those first slim fractions of a second, following instructions written by human beings, and many of those humans were defective units. Because of human error, complacency, poor management, bad fixes and inadequate testing, three million computers in New York malfunctioned before the century was one second old.

Not all malfunctions were fatal, and many were rapidly fixed once they became apparent. A somewhat lesser number of machines survived with no malfunctions, but wide area networks of compliant machines were inoperable because phone systems were down. The ratio between effort put into Y2K remediation and survival was direct and merciless. Solid, meticulous, grueling inspection of applications, function point by function point and thorough conversion to four-digit date fields paid off. Sloppy, hurried patches and kludges failed. Curiously, the little things people had worried about—household appliances, cars and elevators had only minor problems. People had been so concerned about elevators that they'd been fixed. VCRs that displayed a two-digit date worked fine anyway. In a few cars digital dash displays went crazy, but the motors ran and the antilock brakes worked. It was not the small, personal systems that failed but rather the large, complex, next-to-invisible and taken-for-granted systems that comprised the infrastructure not only of the city and nation but the global economy that failed. It was the Big Picture right in front of everybody's eyes that disintegrated. All the major banks in New York survived but couldn't communicate with one another. Supply lines were disrupted at every link. Warehouse inventory controls were screwed up. Ship and rail traffic was crippled. Every single manufacturing plant, refinery, chemical fabricator and automated assembly line had a problem somewhere.

On the East Coast, only in New York and in those places with emergency generators did people have an opportunity to learn if their systems were good or bad. In the three time zones to the west, after learning of the calamitous events in the east, people woke up from a thirty-year snooze and initiated frantic efforts to prepare for the coming disaster. All remaining power grids and co-operatives initiated disconnects, the companies separating from one another and standing alone. Every energy worker who could be found was pulled in and given a crash course in manual work-arounds to keep the plants up and running when equipment failed. The governors of eighteen states called out the National Guard, and thousands of earnest young men and women, largely from rural areas, were sent to patrol cities to prevent rioting and looting. In Milwaukee and Little Rock, the sudden military presence provoked the very rioting it was supposed to prevent. All over the West, sur-vivalists hunkered down in their fallout shelters, the idea of indi-vidualism taken to the extreme. In most places, however, faced with a foreseeable crisis, people acted like intelligent, sensible members of a community and figured out ways to help one another. In small towns, people rallied to organize disaster relief, setting up shelters in high school gyms and rigging generators for grocery stores. From Chicago west, city officials called off the millennium parties, and police started moving people off the streets. Plant managers rushed to their facilities and turned everything off. Desperate shoppers stripped urban groceries bare.

As the millennium bug began its journey across North America, it was a little after 5:00 in the morning in London, 8:00 in Moscow and just past noon in Beijing. After shrinking for five hundred years, the world had suddenly expanded. The fragile network of telecom-munications that had once unified the planet collapsed. Factories in China that supplied half of America's toys lost their computerized records. Chinese banks that handled the transactions were dead. The ship that carried the teddy bears was lost at sea. The oil refinery that produced the diesel fuel for the truck that carried the bears to Toys-R-Us was shut down. The teddy bears were okay. Neither they nor the workers who sewed them had chips.

The planet had a bad hangover, but the lights were on in New York.

On Jay Street in Brooklyn, in the command center of the most thoroughly Y2K compliant transit system in the world, where every computer application had been thoroughly checked, corrected and tested, where every embedded chip had been identified, tracked down, checked, tested, and replaced, where every dispatcher, operator, manager, yard boss, supervisor, motorman, and track sweeper had had Y2K drummed into his head until he was sick of it, the twenty-foot-long, eight-foot-high master screen of the entire system blinked out at 12:02. Two seconds later 187 subway trains stopped where they were.

When the screens went down, every signal in the system defaulted to red and stopped all the trains. The dispatchers at their terminals stared at the big screen in stunned silence. The terminals included new programmable logic processors that time-stamped and recorded every keystroke and sent the data to twenty brand-new chips in the screen that were not supposed to be date sensitive. To save money the MTA had purchased generic chips with a subassembly that had two-digit date codes burned into a circuit in the chip-within-a chip. The chip vendor had not known the subassembly existed, and the screens had passed a full-blown rollover test under simulated conditions. Powering down after the test, something that never occurred under real conditions, and then powering back up had activated all the circuits in the subassemblies in the poorly manufactured chips. A second test would have caught the malfunction, but since the first was a success, a second test had never been performed.

The radios worked, giving the dispatchers and towermen contact with the motormen, all of whom started talking at once. The communal blood pressure of the entire subway system stepped up a notch. The lights flickered in the tunnels and in the command center. Deep within the subterranean bowels of the city, the bug had fired another salvo.

"Where's Adrian?" Doc asked when he returned from downstairs. He looked in the bathroom and kitchen and scratched his head. "Where's Adrian?" he asked again.

"What?" Judd exclaimed.

"Where's Adrian? He's gone."

Mesmerized by their screens, too busy to pay attention to anyone else, no one had seen him leave.

Jody had been all over the room with her video camera, and Doc had her flash through the last three minutes of tape.

"There," he said, "you have Ronnie in the frame and there's Adrian in the background opening a drawer and pulling out a bunch of circuit boards."

"Chips?" Jody asked.

"Yeah."

He studied the subway schematic on Adrian's monitor and saw right away that none of the trains was moving.

"Bo," he shouted. "Status of 59th Street."

The Con Edison power plant on 59th was dedicated to the subway and provided power to the entire system.

"59th is online," Bo reported.

"Then what the hell's the matter with the subway?"

Carolyn got up from her seat and started pushing buttons on Adrian's panels. "Gee, Doc, didn't you ever learn how to run Adrian's terminal?"

"I guess not."

Carolyn brought up a live image from a security camera at the Metropolitan Transit Authority's dispatch center on Jay Street. The big screen was down. Unable to see where the trains were or the status of the signals, the dispatchers were starting to move trains one by one by radio.

Since Adrian's screen showed the locations of the trains, somewhere in his duplicate system was an operating circuit they didn't have on Jay Street. Clearly, he'd taken a pile of circuit boards and was on his way to Brooklyn to repair their system himself.

"My God," Doc said. "Oh, Christ. Poor sweet Adrian."

"What can he do?" Jody asked.

"He can probably fix their system and get the trains running, but he'll have a hell of a time convincing them of that. Imagine these hard-headed, no-nonsense MTA guys confronted by Adrian with eyes like mandalas and waving a circuit board. They'll think he's out of his mind. I have to go after him."

Judd walked away from his station and pulled on a windbreaker.

"Doc," he said, "you'll never catch him. I'll get him."

Doc raised his eyebrows. "He's my responsibility," he insisted. "Christ. He'll go through the A train tunnel from Fulton Street under the river and right to Jay Street. It's the second stop in Brooklyn."

"You think he'll go through a subway tunnel?" Jody exclaimed, horrified.

"He does it all the time," Judd said.

"I'll find him and drag his ass back," Judd declared, and went out the door without further argument.

"Peopleware," Carolyn sneered and went back to her station. "The human factor."

"Shit," Doc swore. "This is crazy."

He bolted for the door, ran down the stairs and raced toward the Fulton Street subway station three blocks away. Running at a marathoner's pace, Judd was two blocks ahead, and Doc was in no shape for an heroic sprint to Brooklyn. After a block he slowed down and jogged along at a steady cadence, surprised to discover many anxious business people in winter Gore-Tex and down clothing who'd returned to the financial district to see what their computers would do. He could hear cheers and shrieks of delight from some offices, and groans of defeat and disaster from others. The cleansing of the technological gene pool was underway.

He ducked into the subway station and found a Brooklyn-bound train sitting motionless on the tracks, doors open. People milled around and watched the frenzied scene from Times Square on the TVs suspended over the platforms. At the front of the train, the motorman was talking to a transit cop who leaned over the tracks and pointed down the tunnel. Doc ran past them and jumped down onto the tracks as the cop shouted, "Not another one! What's the matter with these people?"

"Aren't you going after them?" the motorman asked.

"Hell, no. You think I'm nuts?"

"What do they say upstairs?"

"They're workin' on the screen. Fuckin' computers."

Doc pounded doggedly ahead, out of breath, stopping frequently to rest with hands on knees. Jogging through a subway tunnel with a live third rail was not his ideal way to spend New Year's Eve. Footsteps echoed through the dimly lit tunnel, and red signal lights marched down the right of way. A few hundred yards ahead, Judd was gaining on his quarry. Almost to Brooklyn, Adrian looked back, heard Judd, and started running faster.

Adrian had short-circuited the moment he saw the MTA screens blow out. Suddenly, he was a man with a mission, convinced he was the only person alive who knew what was wrong with the subway and how to fix it. He'd slipped away from Nassau Street without saying anything because, in the hot furnace of his twisted mind, he believed the Midnight Club would try to stop him. They tolerated him, he believed, but didn't really respect him and now were proving it by chasing him.

The tunnel passed under the river, bored into Brooklyn Heights, and curved south toward the High Street station. As Adrian rounded the bend, the station came into view where a Manhattan-bound train was stopped, headlights shining brightly. Pudgy and slow, Adrian knew the intricacies of the tunnels and had explored the A train route many times. Just around the curve, he ducked into a service passageway, and when Judd came around the bend, Adrian had disappeared.

"Adrian!" Judd called out.

Doc heard Judd's shout and stopped.

"Adrian, come out," Judd hollered. "We'll take the circuit boards to the dispatchers together."

Walking cautiously around the bend, Doc saw Judd and then Adrian in the shadows, out of Judd's view, looking distraught.

Suddenly, the train in the station closed its doors and moved, the sound scaring Doc half to death. The roadbed vibrated, the train motors roared, the wheels screeched, and the air brakes hissed. Doc ran ahead, grabbed Judd, and pulled him into the passageway with Adrian just as the first Brooklyn train whooshed by from the other direction.

"You knucklehead," Doc yelled at Adrian who couldn't hear him. The trains moved on, and the three managed to get onto the platform without drawing attention.

Adrian said nothing, folded his arms across his chest, slouched down on the bench and stared at the ceiling. He'd honed his disdain for the MTA dispatchers and towermen since the day he'd arrived in New York, calling them idiots who didn't know how to run a railroad, but the idiots had repaired their screens and put the system back into operation.

With a fair idea of Adrian's thoughts, Judd pointed up the tracks toward Jay Street and said, "They were just lucky, that's all."

"You were trying to do the right thing," Doc added. "It's all right."

Another Manhattan train pulled in, packed to the windows with passengers. The errant members of the Midnight Club squeezed through the doors and passed back under the river.

At Fulton Street, financial district types rushed toward the exits, in a hurry to find out if they were winners or losers in the computer lottery. When the train pulled out, Doc and Judd were on the platform but Adrian was still aboard, heading for Times Square. He smirked as he slipped away, and waved his fingers bye-bye.

———

Doc and Judd emerged from the station onto sidewalks littered with PCs that had failed the rollover. On Wall Street three men in a van were collecting discarded CPUs and monitors.

"Urban farming," Doc commented. "It'll become quite popular in the next few weeks."

As they turned onto Nassau Street, the stars had disappeared, the sky had clouded over, and snow began to fall.

17

The unthinkable had occurred. From the skyscrapers of Manhattan one could see the silhouette of the Statue of Liberty surrounded by a panorama of darkness. Across the Hudson, the lightless Jersey shore was a wall of brick and stone dusted with snow; to the south Staten Island had become a black hole in the Upper Bay; to the east, beyond Brooklyn and Queens, Long Island stretched like a primeval prairie. Here and there automobile lights flickered like lost stars in the gloom, and a few ships' lights dotted the harbor. On Governor's Island a generator lighted the Coast Guard Station where technicians worked frantically on the radars' computers.

A stillness fell over the world beyond the slim, illuminated island of Manhattan. At the moment the power stopped, the hum of transmission wires fell silent. TVs, radios, stereos, and machinery of all types stopped making noise. Drivers stopped in traffic to marvel at the transformation. Life was reduced to fundamental elements. Bugs. Wind. Snow.

Unable to look out, people had to search within themselves for the means of survival. It was a rude awakening, but an awakening nonetheless. Natural selection immediately came into play. The strong and intelligent survived; the weak and witless perished.

Despite millions of hours and billions of dollars spent in preparation for Y2K, the USA had proved as vulnerable to the millennium bug as the rest of the world. All airports were closed. Rail traffic slowed to a crawl. Food supplies were disrupted. People panicked, drove into the woods, ran out of gas and froze. In some cities New Year's Eve parties and millennium celebrations dissolved into local chaos. Riots erupted in Washington and Tampa, but not in Boston or Philadelphia. Even in the District of Columbia, which suffered the most, the pointless violence petered out after a few hours. Everywhere, the deranged used the cover of darkness to steal and pillage and commit crimes of personal vengeance, but the vast majority of Americans were neither criminals nor anarchists. They neither panicked nor huddled terrified in their homes. They responded as they did to storm, earthquake, flood or attack by hostile aliens. In standard American fashion, they'd ignored the coming disaster until it was too late, but once it happened, they galvanized into action and fought back.

If the morning of December 31, 1999 had resembled Black Thursday, October 24, 1929, when the stock market crashed and precipitated the Great Depression, then the first hours of January 1, 2000 resembled December 7, 1941, the day Pearl Harbor was attacked. In 1941 the USA had not been prepared to go to war, but when war came to them, the American people put aside their squabbles and differences and brought their enormous energy to bear on one concerted effort. Millions had volunteered immediately and risked their lives for the communal good.

In January 2000, America was divided over dozens of political, social and religious issues, and partisans argued across wide chasms with deep historical roots. It was difficult to sustain a republic founded on the belief that all had equal rights when in practice the opposite was true. People disagreed, sometimes violently, on race, abortion, drugs, sex, religion, campaign contributions and industrial deregulation. The political process and the Constitution itself were under attack from the left, the right and even the center. Millions hadn't believed a word uttered by the government since

Vietnam and Watergate destroyed all credibility. America was far from perfect, and would never be perfect, fair or just; nevertheless, striving toward the ideal, even if it was ultimately unobtainable, was preferable to surrendering to tyranny or chaos. When the lights went out, priorities were suddenly thrown into proper perspective. Ideological and religious dogma didn't solve immediate problems. Agendas were worthless. It was neighbors helping neighbors that did the trick.

The Y2K work already completed gave the nation a head start and a great advantage over the rest of the world, but if the American people wanted a resolution to the crisis, the only option was to knuckle down and do the work. They didn't hesitate.

Blasted by the millennium bug, this was a chance to rise like a phoenix from the ashes and strike back. When the phones went down, a half-million phone workers showed up, ready to go. In mines and factories, railroad yards, fuel depots and laboratories, people arrived in the middle of the night to get things working again. They didn't have much success at first, but they didn't give up. Every power plant swarmed with engineers searching out problems, jerry-rigging repairs, plotting workarounds and solutions. The problems were immense, the damage seemingly unfathomable, but piece by piece, chip by chip, the process of recovery was started.

New York had endured major blackouts in 1965 and 1977. After the 1965 episode, people told fond stories of how many babies were born nine months later. People had been afraid but not terrified, and the city had survived with good humor and high spirits. By 1977 the city had changed dramatically. In twelve short years New York had become grim and dangerous, reeking of poverty and crime, boiling with anger and frustration, and the blackout spawned stories of violence and urban chaos. Urban legend held that looting had started within ten minutes. The 1977 incident had occurred on a hot summer day when the city was already close to exploding with racial tension. Most of the looting was nothing more than a massive crime of opportunity. Squalor, poverty and racial oppression add up to a lot of angry, hotheaded young men, and it was they who looted in a spasm of rage.

Now, in 2000, massive immigration had changed the demographics once again. In the last quarter of the 20th Century so many new faces had arrived that no ethnic group had a majority. Everyone belonged to a minority. Except for the homeless and most desperate immigrants, New York's poor didn't look poor. Fed at McDonald's and dressed by Kmart, they had TVs and cars and minimum wage jobs that kept their heads one inch above water. The urban poor were the legacy of an economy that had evolved from labor-intensive manufacturing to a service economy and automated high technology, leaving huge segments of the population without the skills needed to thrive in a techno-world. The prosperity from high technology and the global economy was concentrated in fewer and fewer hands, creating the most inequitable distribution of wealth since the Second World War. Economic conditions and three centuries of vicious racism had set the stage for riots and looting of epic proportions, and America expected the ghettos to explode if the lights went out.

Unlike previous power failures, the great American blackout of January 1, 2000 didn't come as a surprise. Millions celebrating in the street were caught unprepared, and hundreds of thousands already had panicked and left the city, but many more millions had considered the possibility of a blackout and taken elementary precautions against chaos and anarchy. The long campaign by community leaders to prepare the most squalid ghettos had convinced the populace that burning down the place where they lived was not effective urban renewal. Smashing windows and looting TVs didn't exact revenge against real oppressors. In 2000, hoodlums had cellphones and computers and knew Y2K was coming, and they understood that looting would bring heat they didn't need. The word had spread through the ghettos and barrios: don't take that TV. If the power goes out, it won't work anyway.

Perhaps the most prepared organization in New York was the Mafia, who'd seized on Y2K like a mongoose on a python. The advantages of surviving a crisis was never lost on them. Every business remotely connected to the well-being of the Cosa Nostra had an expensive, well-managed Y2K compliance program, and on New Year's Eve enjoyed the protection of armed security guards.

Despite the preparations and warnings not everyone got the message. After a day of watching blackouts around the globe, opportunistic looters in Queens, Brooklyn and the Bronx had picked their targets, electronics being the most popular followed by jewelry and apparel. When the lights went out, dedicated criminals were joined by mobs of drunken New Year's Eve revelers who smashed into the first electronics stores within fifteen seconds. The crazed, disorganized looters were caught in the act by the police, deterred by armed merchants and confronted by angry and determined community patrols. Inevitably, fear and itchy trigger fingers resulted in dozens of looters being blown away, the violent percussions lost in the din of firecrackers and the traditional New Year's Eve blasting away with firearms. Looting in the boroughs was brutally snuffed out within an hour.

Armies of frightened people had been fleeing New York all day. By one in the morning almost three hundred thousand were scattered in all directions and lost in the dark. When they learned that the lights had remained on in Manhattan, the exodus reversed and people streamed back toward the light, as they had in Tokyo. The already overcrowded island was inundated again from all directions. The subways were jammed. People walked across the bridges and arrived from New Jersey and Staten Island in fleets of boats. At that moment, the citizens of Manhattan confounded every stereotype of New York as a cold and heartless city.

New York threw open its doors. Starting in midtown, hotels graciously opened their lobbies and banquet rooms to shelter the stranded. When Macy's unlocked the doors and let five thousand freezing visitors in out of the cold, Saks and Bloomingdale's followed. Countless churches and office buildings, National Guard armories, subway stations, theaters and schools were turned into impromptu shelters.

Starting in the Millennium Religious Sanctuary of the 24th Precinct, citizens began taking strangers into their homes. They made coffee, sat in over-crowded living rooms, and exchanged stories from an extraordinary day. From Morningside Heights to Battery Park, people surprised themselves as much as their guests with their generosity and hospitality. For many, these acts of kindness were difficult and not without trepidation, yet the people of New York opened their hearts and somehow made it through the night.

At 1:00 the global blackout reached the Central time zone. In Chicago, Dallas, and Mexico City, the muscle and sinew of North America succumbed to the millennium bug with, by now, predictable results. Fortunately, the disassembly of the western grids meant Biloxi, Wichita Falls, Green Bay, Duluth and the entire state of Nebraska had power. Along the entire length of the Mississippi River, only steamboats had lights. In New Orleans, the antique craft chugged along the riverfront without a care, rip-roaring New Year's Eve parties in full swing.

At 2:00 A.M., midnight Mountain standard time, Jesus did not appear in Hermosillo, Mexico. Electric power, however, disappeared. Several hundred miles north, the lights blinked out in Denver but stayed on in Colorado Springs. Space Command was well lit all night as information technicians tried to restore control to the GPS satellites. Around 7:00 in the morning, Zulu time, the GPS backup system that broadcast the time signal through a series of ground level transmitters was restored. The few phone companies with compliant equipment were able to reconnect and begin the slow rebuilding of their vast networks.

By 2:30 A.M. Sarah had disaster recovery teams in each of the three failed power plants. Line engineers had inspected every substation, tested hardware and made repairs, and by 3:00, power was restored to Brooklyn and Queens. The influx of refugees to Manhattan slackened, and the newly lit areas began to absorb the flow from Long Island.

On Nassau Street the Midnight Club was exhausted and running on sheer exhilaration. Judd tinkered with the radios, tuning into shortwave and ham broadcasts and recording everything. On military frequencies, National Guard units were generating a great deal of radio traffic as the militia tried to prepare for any contingency. Civil disorder had clocked in at much lower levels than expected, but anything could happen over the next few days.

Across the room Bo was running diagnostics on Big Allis, Number Three at Ravenswood, trying to bring the system's most powerful generator back on-line. Ronnie had the Department of Environmental Protection on the phone and was explaining where to look for faulty chips in the sewage treatment plants. Jody had put aside her camera and was sitting with Doc on the couch, drinking champagne, holding hands and watching the last few minutes of *Breathless* on videotape. When the movie ended, Doc flipped through the channels and discovered ABC had resumed local broadcasting from the studio on West 65th Street.

"Be careful if you're driving in Queens," the anchorman was saying. "Traffic lights are performing erratically."

"Too bad they don't have a satellite link," Judd said. "They could tell us about all the National Guardsmen who reported to Fort Dix that nobody knows what to do with."

"I can give them a satellite," Carolyn said. "I happen to have one right here."

"Hmmm," Doc said. "Jody, get your camera."

"I am the Phone Goddess," Carolyn said. "Watch this."

She called ABC, got the newsroom producer on the line, impressed him with the fact that his phones were working, explained that she was with the company that had saved Con Edison and Chase Manhattan and asked, "How'd you like to be connected to functioning satellites? I can give you links to your trucks in the city and a link to Europe as a bonus."

The ABC producer almost choked on his bagel. "Oh, God, yes yes yes. How much?"

"Ten million for the rights and two hundred grand a day for ten days minimum."

"Oh, Jesus. That's a lot of money. I'll have to get that cleared."

"I have phones. I have a satellite. You have zilch. Welcome to the new order."

"Okay. It's a deal."

"Who's your bank?"

"Chase."

"How convenient," Carolyn said. "I'll give you a nice phone line and a useful number at Chase. If you actually have ten million dollars, you can have it transferred to the account number I'm going to give you. When I hear from them, I'll get right back to you."

Next, Carolyn called AT&T and asked the system manager if she were willing to lease transponders to ABC for a nice premium, say five million in advance and a hundred thousand a day for a minimum of ten days. Negotiations. Callbacks. Finally ABC said yes, the bank called and said the money was transferred and Carolyn winked at Doc who winked back.

"You planned this," Jody stated.

"I worked out a few scenarios in advance, just in case. ABC is across the street from the ConEd command center. I had to have clean phone lines into ConEd, and since Carolyn was right there, she did a little work on ABC's phones. Better than Bell Atlantic. Better than their own people."

"What other little surprises do you have?"

"If I told you, they wouldn't be surprises, would they?"

A few minutes later ABC had a live link to a truck at Bellevue Hospital where the crew had tracked the mayor with police scanners.

Bill Packard stood inside the emergency room doors watching the ABC video truck. At first the crew was hanging around gazing longingly at the sky, and then something got them excited. They huddled inside the truck, started the generator and rotated the dish. Then they fired up lights, camera, sound and a reporter who stood in front of the emergency entrance and delivered a piece on the mayor.

Rudy was asleep in a private room, diligently attended by a bevy of doctors and nurses and guarded by guys with headsets. Having negotiated the traffic, ABC was on the job, and Packard had no desire to be part of their show. He walked through the hospital to the entrance on First Avenue, hit the streets and caught the subway.

When he changed trains at Penn Station, the pedestrian tunnels were packed with people camping out. Somewhere in the maze of tunnels an enchanting flamenco guitar turned the air to froth. New Year's Eve litter collected in corners: gold glitter, silver stars, crumpled funny hats. The parties continued in tight clusters of stranded suburbanites staking out concrete and tile turf. At three in the morning the food kiosks enjoyed a brisk trade, but the newsstands had no papers. Packard asked a vendor what was up.

"I dunno. I got no papers. That's all I know."

"Right."

Packard started to walk away when a blind guitarist called out, "Hey, mister."

"Yeah?"

"The presses at all the papers went down behind Y2K, and I heard the trucks are stuck in the garages because their dispatch computers are spewing out gibberish."

He played a flourish of Spanish chords and smiled.

"You're a fountain of information," Packard said, giving him five dollars. "Play on."

As Bill Packard was riding the train up the West Side, the millennium bug reached the West Coast. Seattle, Portland, San Francisco, Las Vegas, San Diego, San Jose and Los Angeles bit the millennium dust. Miraculously, Oakland remained alight. In California, years of earthquake education helped families and individuals to prepare, but communities, cities and governments were devastated by computer malfunctions. Silicon Valley imploded. The heart and soul of American technology was left to reap what it had sown.

Thirty minutes after leaving the hospital, Packard stepped into the 24th Precinct on West 100th Street, a loony bin sideshow movie set police station full of millennium crazies and exasperated cops.

Ed Garcia was asleep at his desk, head cradled in the crook of his elbow.

"Ed!"

"Wha . . . ? Oh, Christ, Bill."

"Sentries found asleep at their posts will be shot."

The captain chuckled. "So shoot me. You do the mayor?"

"Yeah."

"He gonna live?"

"Yeah."

"You gonna vote for him?"

"You know, I asked the nurses that," Packard said, turning his thumb down. "How many people are still in the park?"

"I don't know. A few thousand. The drunks will freeze. They moved a lot of them into the armory over on the East Side, but some just refuse to leave."

"You gonna stay here all night?"

Garcia nodded his head, yawned and rubbed his eyes. "I got Jesus downstairs with a broken arm. You wanna look at him?"

"You bastard."

"Yeah? Why'd you come over here? To drink champagne? I got your champagne. I got three cases of Mumms looted from Spillman's store this afternoon. How d'ya like that? I'm takin' it home. Fuckin' all right. Hahahahaha."

"How'd Jesus break his arm?"

"Nailing himself to a cross. He missed. Hey, man, I got Jesus three times over, I got Mary, I think I got Pontius Pilate. I don't know what I got. Mohammed, I got him. I definitely got Buddha. I may have a bunch of Krishnas, but I think we let them go. I got the Irish Republican Army, the Jewish Defense League and Free Puerto Rico. It's real ecumenical around here right now. Mostly, though, I got drunks. We'd toss them out, but they'd freeze."

"Sounds like just another Friday night in the Big Apple. Happy New Year."

"You gonna check out my broken Jesus?"

"Okay. You got any tetanus vaccine around here?"

Jonathon Spillman finally walked across 85th Street to see if Shirley was all right. Unlocking his apartment, he heard voices, peeked into the living room and saw two Jehovah's Witnesses asleep in chairs and three huddled in prayer.

Shirley was in the kitchen making coffee. At first Spillman wasn't sure he recognized her. He'd left an hysterical, sobbing woman who'd locked herself in the bedroom, and now his kitchen was occupied by a blissed-out millennium hostess.

"Hi," he said, picking up a copy of *The Watchtower*. "Who are these people?"

"The trains aren't running."

"The trains?"

"To Philadelphia. It's too far to walk so I asked them in. Mrs. Finklestein has Baptists."

"Don't you want to know where I was?"

"No. Yes. Where were you?"

"Across the street."

"Oh. That's nice."

"Shirley, have you been into the Prozac?"

"Mm hmm. You know, Jon, you have a store full of food you can't sell. Have you thought of giving it away?"

Spillman could hardly believe his ears. Shirley's idea of charity was sending five dollars to Israel to plant a tree. She'd never given a homeless beggar a second glance, let alone a quarter.

"Are you serious?"

"Are you going to let it rot?"

It was a strange night that turned spouses into strangers and strangers into best friends. If the world was upside down, Spillman thought, you had to stand on your head.

"I'll need help," he said.

"I'm sure the Witnesses would be delighted. And Mrs. Finklestein's Baptists."

While Shirley roused the millennium faithful from the entire building and explained to them the Jewish concept of *mitzvah,* or doing good, Spillman ran back across the street and made Copeland come along to the grocery store.

"C'mon. You don't want to sit in your house all night, anyway."

"Yes, I do. I'm happy to sit here with my dog and watch TV. ABC is back on the air."

"Come on, Donnie. We're gonna give away the store."

"You're fuckin' crazy, you know that?"

The Jehovah's Witnesses, the Baptists, some Methodists from Newark, a half dozen Upper West Side Jews and a couple of Buddhists marched up Broadway to the Safeway. Spillman found aprons for everybody. Cans and boxes from the riot still lay in the aisles. The Baptists immediately began straightening everything out.

"Here's what we'll do," Spillman announced. "Open up two bags and put them in a cart. They can fill the bags and carry them away. Don't let too many in the store at one time. And don't let anybody go to sleep and block the aisles."

"How much is your inventory worth?" Copeland asked.

"A couple of million, maybe. Safeway can afford it."

The lines formed quickly, and by four in the morning they wrapped around the block.

For once it was quiet on the third floor of the old building on Nassau Street. No music, no police scanners, no blaring TV.

Ronnie was curled up asleep on one of the couches. Carolyn walked over and methodically shut down Adrian's terminal. She sang softly, "I . . . bin working . . . on the raaaailroad . . . all . . . the livelong . . . daaaay."

Bo stood up and stretched. "Anybody hungry?" he asked.

"I'm too damn tired to eat," Judd said, heading toward the kitchen. "Besides, all we got are some Pop-Tarts."

"I could go for some pizza," Bo said.

"Hey!" Judd shouted from the kitchen. "Look at this."

He came out with a bucket of caviar in one hand and a bottle of Mumms in the other.

"Where'd this come from? Doc?"

"I think they went back in the bedroom," Carolyn said.

Judd knocked on the bedroom door and it swung open. The room was empty. On the bed were five briefcases labeled "Bo," "Ronnie," "Adrian," "Carolyn" and "Judd."

Judd went in, picked up the briefcase with his name and opened it.

"Holy shit," he swore to himself, and walked out to show the others.

"You'd better wake Ronnie up," he said. "She'll want to know what a million dollars in cash looks like."

They walked lazily through the snowfall, footsteps gently echoing off the walls, and Doc told Jody his plan to sand and varnish an old speedboat, rebuild the old Caddy V8 or maybe buy a brand-new engine. He told her about a beautiful lake in Wisconsin with a stone house on a peninsula surrounded by pines. He liked to putter around and fish for bass and pike all day, then play cards and bullshit all night. Did that sound good to her?

"Are there mosquitoes?" she asked.

"Fierce mosquitoes. You bathe in bug spray."

"Would a small-block Chevy fit into the engine bay?"

His jaw dropped. "Oh, man," he said. "This must be a fairy tale."

At the corner of Beaver and Williams they entered the splendid old-fashioned bar at Delmonico's. While the world was crashing into the 21st Century, Doc felt like retreating to the 19th, to the old New York of wood paneling and leaded glass.

The bartender greeted them with a smile. "Evenin', Doc."

"Howdy, Nick. Two double fifty-year Macallans, straight up."

"Got cash?"

Doc laid a hundred-dollar bill on the bar.

"Yes, sir. What happened to your cash register?"

"Locked up, wouldn't open after midnight," the bartender said. "I tried to pry it open with a crowbar, but I didn't want to wreck it."

"What's the mood around here?" Doc asked.

"It ain't happy new year."

Businessmen and women clustered around tiny tables, deeply engaged in earnest conversation. By the looks on their faces, they'd all taken Y2K hits of considerable magnitude. Their Asian and European markets were gone, and no one knew for how long. Transportation was a mess. Fuel supplies were uncertain. The meager news that filtered in from outside the city was almost all bad.

"Did you know that George Washington fought the first battle of the Revolution a few miles from here, right over in Brooklyn?" Doc asked, and when Jody said yes, she'd paid attention in the eighth grade, Doc continued anyway. "Did you know he got whipped by the British something fierce and retreated to right here? He camped right where this bar is today, and then the British came over and kicked his ass again. The Redcoats held New York to the end of the war, but the New Yorkers didn't mind. They were only interested in business, faithless sons of bitches that they were. Washington was in bad shape. His army was in rags and deserting, tired of getting beat up by the Brits, but old George never gave up. The point is, these guys are crying in their beer because they've taken a whipping. So will they get up tomorrow and carry on the fight, or are they gonna cave?"

"I don't know," Jody said.

"I don't, either," Doc said. "That's why I'm going to the lake as soon as things settle down and I can get gas."

"Did he really camp right here?"

"No," he said, deadpan. "I made that part up."

18

Time neither accelerated nor slowed down, but rather ticked along as it always had, complex and perhaps unknowable even by Stephen Hawking. A pink sun rose over Brooklyn. Six inches of snow blanketed New York, and Bernie's Delicatessen was open.

"You think there's gonna be a Superbowl?" Spillman asked.

"I dunno," Packard said. "I don't think anybody'll play this weekend."

"Wouldn't you know it?" Copeland sneered, disgusted. "The first time the Jets get into the playoffs in twenty years, and this has to happen."

Ed Garcia came in, tossed his hat and briefcase on the table and sat down heavily.

"Any of you guys get any sleep?" he asked, unbuttoning his tunic. "Don't answer. I don't wanna know."

Bernie hollered at the captain, "You gonna eat?"

"Yeah, gimme a minute, will ya?"

"Jeez. Take it easy. Hey, any you guys see the fireworks?"

"They got some fireworks over in Jersey City," Garcia said. "Some chemical plant is on fire."

"Only one?"

"Far as I know."

"Hear what happened in Frisco?" Spillman asked.

"Nah, what?"

"Some guys robbed the Bank of America. Sixty million bucks."

Copeland went white. "Where'd you hear that?" he demanded. "Who knows what's going on in California?"

"I heard it, that's all. From a guy."

"From a guy, from a guy. Oh, that's great. That's called a rumor."

"Oh, fuck you." Spillman turned from Copeland. "Hey, Bernie, gimme sausage and scrambled and a side of white toast."

"Sausage and scrambled. Toast dry?"

"Yeah. And turn on the TV."

"Always with the TV. Get a life."

"How's your Jesus?" Packard asked Garcia.

"Out of his mind, if he ever had one. You hear from your old lady in Maine?"

"No. No phones. I'm going up there today if I can."

"You got gas?"

"Full tank."

Bernie turned on the TV, flipped through a number of whited out channels until he landed on ABC.

"Hey, Donnie, look. That's your building."

In the dim light of dawn ABC had a truck in front of Copeland Investments on Nassau Street. The camera panned over the dark red brick facade, while a reporter's voice narrated a brief introduction.

"The story is emerging this morning about a small group of computer experts in this building who kept the lights on in Manhattan. Consolidated Edison has revealed that a team of programmers here at Copeland 2000, led by Donald Copeland and working in partnership with ConEd and Mayor Rudolph Giuliani . . ."

Copeland beamed. Bernie scrambled eggs. The voice on TV called him the Man Who Saved New York. The reporter interviewed Bo and Carolyn, both wearing Midnight Club T-shirts. Break for commercial. Chase Manhattan. Year 2000. We're ready.

Author Note

The author would like to thank the following people for their invaluable contributions to this work: Mike Phillips of San Francisco for first mentioning Y2K as a subject worth writing about; Nick Ellison, my agent, for suggesting the millennium as a topic of wide interest; Daniel Starer of Research for Writers, New York City, for his extraordinary ability to provide a nuclear reactor on demand; Professor Charles Shapiro of the Physics Department of San Francisco State University for teaching me to understand Dan's reactor; radio guru Peter Gerba for his patient explanations of telecommunications; architect William Rosenblum of New York for his descriptions of many New York buildings; business adventurer Peter Winslow for his detailed analysis of life in Manhattan; day trader Barry Shapiro and entrepreneur Mark Lediard for making sense of Y2K, the stock markets and financial institutions. Lastly, and most gratefully, I would like to thank my editor, Jim Fitzgerald, for finding a thousand flaws, providing the big fix and making this book Y2K compliant.

**Turn the page
for an excerpt
from Colin Harrison's
exciting new novel,
<u>Afterburn</u>—**

AVAILABLE SOON IN HARDCOVER
FROM FARRAR, STRAUS & GIROUX . . .

CHINA CLUB,
HONG KONG

He would survive. Yes, Charlie promised himself, he'd survive *this*, too—his ninth formal Chinese banquet in as many evenings, yet another bowl of shark-fin soup being passed to him by the endless waiters in red uniforms, who stood obsequiously against the silk wallpaper pretending not to hear the self-satisfied ravings of those they served. Except for his fellow *gweilos*—British Petroleum's Asia man, a mischievous German from Lufthansa, and two young American executives from Kodak and Citigroup—the other dozen men at the huge mahogany table were all Chinese. Mostly in their fifties, the men represented the big corporate players—Bank of Asia, Hong Kong Telecom, China Motors—and each, Charlie noted, had arrived at the age of cleverness. Of course, at fifty-eight he himself was old enough that no one should be able to guess what he was thinking unless he wanted them to, even Ellie. In his call to her that morning— it being evening in New York City—he'd tried not to sound too worried about their daughter Julia. "It's all going to be *fine*, sweetie," he'd promised, gazing out at the choppy haze of Hong Kong's harbor, where the heavy traffic of tankers and freighters pressed China's claim—everything from photocopiers to baseball caps flowing out into the world, everything from oil refineries to contact lenses flowing in. "She'll get pregnant, I'm sure," he'd told Ellie. But he wasn't sure. No, not at all. In fact, it looked as if it was going to be easier for him to build his electronics factory in Shanghai than for his daughter to hatch a baby.

"We gather in friendship," announced the Chinese host, Mr. Ming, the vice-chairman of the Bank of Asia. Having agreed to lend Charlie fifty-two million U.S. dollars to build his Shanghai factory,

Mr. Ming in no way could be described as a friend; the relationship was one of overlord and indentured. But Charlie smiled along with the others as the banker stood and presented in high British English an analysis of southeastern China's economy that was so shallow, optimistic, and full of euphemism that no one, especially the central ministries in Beijing, might object. The Chinese executives nodded politely as Mr. Ming spoke, touching their napkins to their lips, smiling vaguely. Of course, they nursed secret worries—worries that corresponded to whether they were entrepreneurs (who had built shipping lines or real-estate empires or garment factories) or the managers of institutional power (who controlled billions of dollars not their own). And yet, Charlie decided, the men were finally more like one another than unlike; each long ago had learned to sell high (1997) and buy low (1998), and had passed the threshold of unspendable wealth, such riches conforming them in their behaviors; each owned more houses or paintings or Rolls-Royces than could be admired or used at once. Each played golf or tennis passably well; each possessed a forty-million-dollar yacht or a forty-million-dollar home atop Victoria's Peak, or a forty-million-dollar wife. Each had a slender young Filipino or Russian or Czech mistress tucked away in one of Hong Kong's luxury apartment buildings—licking her lips if requested— or was betting against the Hong Kong dollar while insisting on its firmness—any of the costly mischief in which rich men indulge.

The men at the table, in fact, as much as any men, sat as money incarnate, particularly the American dollar, the euro, and the Japanese yen—all simultaneously, and all hedged against fluctuations of the others. But although the men were money, money was not them; money assumed any shape or color or politics, it could be fire or stone or dream, it could summon armies or bind atoms, and, indifferent to the sufferings of the mortal soul, it could leave or arrive at any time. And on this exact night, Charlie thought, setting his ivory chopsticks neatly upon the lacquered plate, he could see that although money had assumed the shapes of the men in the room, it existed in differing densities and volumes and brightnesses. Whereas Charlie was a man of perhaps thirty or thirty-three million dollars of wealth, that sum amounted to shoe-shine change in the present company. No, sir, money, in *that* room, in *that* moment, was understood as inconsequential in sums less than one hundred million dollars, and of political importance only when five times more. Money, in fact, found its greatest compression and gravity in the form of the tiny man sitting silently across from Charlie—Sir Henry Lai, the Oxford-educated Chinese gambling mogul, owner of a fleet of jet-foil ferries, a dozen hotels, and most of the casinos of Macao and Vietnam. Worth billions—and billions more.

But, Charlie wondered, perhaps he was wrong. He could think of one shape that money had not *yet* assumed, although quite a bit of it had been spent, perhaps a hundred thousand dollars in all. Money animated the dapper Chinese businessman across from him, but could it arrive in the world as Charlie's own grandchild? This was the question he feared most, this was the question that had eaten at him and at Ellie for years now, and which would soon be answered: In a few hours, Julia would tell them once and forever if she was capable of having a baby.

She had suffered through cycle upon cycle of disappointment—hundreds of shots of fertility drugs followed by the needle-recovery of the eggs, the inspection of the eggs, the selection of the eggs, the insemination of the eggs, the implantation of the eggs, the anticipation of the eggs. She'd been trying for seven years. Now Julia, a woman of only thirty-five, a little gray already salting her hair, was due to get the final word. At 11:00 a.m. Manhattan time, she'd sit in her law office and be told the results of this, the last in-vitro attempt. Her *ninth*. Three more than the doctor preferred to do. Seven more than the insurance company would pay for. Good news would be that one of the reinserted fertilized eggs had decided to cling to the wall of Julia's uterus. Bad news: There was no chance of conception; egg donorship or adoption must now be considered. And if *that* was the news, well then, that was really goddamn something. It would mean not just that his only daughter was heart-broken, but that, genetically speaking, he, Charlie Ravich, was finished, that his own fishy little spermatozoa—one of which, wiggling into Ellie's egg a generation prior, had become his daughter—had run aground, that he'd come to the end of the line; that, in a sense, he was already dead.

And now, as if mocking his very thoughts, came the fish, twenty pounds of it, head still on, its eyes cooked out and replaced with flowered radishes, its mouth agape in macabre broiled amusement. Charlie looked at his plate. He always lost weight in China, undone by the soy and oils and crusted skin of birds, the rich liverish stink of turtle meat. All that duck tongue and pig ear and fish lip. Expensive as hell, every meal. And carrying with it the odor of doom.

Then the conversation turned, as it also did so often in Shanghai and Beijing, to the question of America's mistreatment of the Chinese. "What I do not understand are the American senators," Sir Henry Lai was saying in his softly refined voice. "They say they *understand* that we only want for China to be China." Every syllable was flawless English, but of course Lai also spoke Mandarin and Cantonese. Sir Henry Lai was reported to be in serious talks with Gaming Technologies, the huge American gambling and hotel conglomerate that clutched big pieces of Las Vegas, the Mississippi casino towns, and Atlantic City. Did Sir Henry know when China would allow Western-style casinos to be built within its borders? Certainly he knew the right officials in Beijing, and perhaps this was reason enough that GT's stock price had ballooned up seventy percent in the last three months as Sir Henry's interest in the company had become known. Lai smiled benignly. Then frowned. "These senators say that all they want is for international trade to progress without interruption, and then they go back to Congress and raise their fists and call China all kinds of names. Is this not true?"

The others nodded sagely, apparently giving consideration, but not ignoring whatever delicacy remained pinched in their chopsticks.

"Wait, I have an answer to that," announced the young fellow from Citigroup. "Mr. Lai, I trust we may speak frankly here. You need to remember that the American senators are full of—excuse my language—full of shit. When they're standing up on the Senate floor saying all of this stuff, this means nothing, *absolutely* nothing!"

"Ah, this is very difficult for the Chinese people to understand." Sir Henry scowled. "In China we believe our leaders. So we become scared when we see American senators complaining about China."

"You're being coy with us, Mr. Lai," interrupted Charlie, looking up with a smile, "for we—some of us—know that you have visited the United States dozens of times and have met many U.S. senators personally." Not to mention a few Third World dictators. He paused, while amusement passed into Lai's dark eyes. "Nonetheless," Charlie continued, looking about the table, "for the others who have not enjoyed Mr. Lai's deep friendships with American politicians, I would have to say my colleague here is right. The speeches in the American Senate are pure grandstanding. They're made for the American public—"

"The *bloodthirsty* American public, you mean!" interrupted the Citigroup man, who, Charlie suddenly understood, had drunk too much. "Those old guys up there know most voters can't find China on a globe. That's no joke. It's shocking, the American ignorance of China."

"We shall have to educate your people," Sir Henry Lai offered diplomatically, apparently not wishing the stridency of the conversation to continue. He gave a polite, cold-blooded laugh.

"But it is, yes, my understanding that the Americans could sink the Chinese Navy in several days?" barked the German from Lufthansa.

"That may be true," answered Charlie, "but sooner or later the American people are going to recognize the hemispheric primacy of China, that—"

"Wait, wait!" Lai interrupted good-naturedly. "You agree with our German friend about the Chinese Navy?"

The question was a direct appeal to the nationalism of the other Chinese around the table.

"Can the U.S. Air Force destroy the Chinese Navy in a matter of days?" repeated Charlie. "Yes. Absolutely yes."

Sir Henry Lai smiled. "You are knowledgeable about these topics, Mr."—he glanced down at the business cards arrayed in front of his plate—"Mr. Ravich. Of the Teknetrix Corporation, I see. What do you know about war, Mr. Ravich?" he asked. "Please, tell me. I am curious."

The Chinese billionaire stared at him with eyebrows lifted, face a smug, florid mask, and if Charlie had been younger or genuinely insulted, he might have recalled aloud his war years before becoming a businessman, but he understood that generally it was to one's advantage not to appear to have an advantage. And anyway, the conversation was merely a form of sport: Lai didn't give a good goddamn about the Chinese Navy, which he probably despised; what he cared about was whether or not he should soon spend eight hundred million dollars on GT stock—play the corporation that played the players.

But Lai pressed. "What do you know about this?"

"Just what I read in the papers," Charlie replied with humility.

"See? There! I tell you!" Lai eased back in his silk suit, running a fat little palm over his thinning hair. "This is a very dangerous problem, my friends. People say many things about China and America, but they have no direct knowledge, no real—"

Mercifully, the boys in red uniforms and brass buttons began setting down spoons and bringing around coffee. Charlie excused himself and headed for the gentlemen's restroom. Please God, he thought, it's a small favor, really. One egg clinging to a warm pink wall. He and Ellie should have had another child, should have at least tried, after Ben. Ellie had been forty-two. Too much grief at the time, too late now.

In the men's room, a sarcophagus of black and silver marble, he nodded at the wizened Chinese attendant, who stood up with alert servility. Charlie chose the second stall and locked the heavy marble door behind him. The door and walls extended in smooth veined slabs from the floor to within a foot of the ceiling. The photo-electric eye over the toilet sensed his movement and the bowl flushed prematurely. He was developing an old man's interest in his bowels. He shat then, with the private pleasure of it. He was starting to smell Chinese to himself. Happened on every trip to the East.

And then, as he finished, he heard the old attendant greeting another man in Cantonese.

"Evening, sir."

"Yes."

The stall door next to Charlie's opened, shut, was locked. The man was breathing as if he had hurried. Then came some loud coughing, an oddly tiny splash, and the muffled silky sound of the man slumping heavily against the wall he shared with Charlie.

"Sir?" The attendant knocked on Charlie's door. "You open door?

Charlie buckled his pants and slid the lock free. The old man's face loomed close, eyes large, breath stinking.

"Not me!" Charlie said. "The next one!"

"No have key! Climb!" The old attendant pushed past Charlie, stepped up on the toilet seat, and stretched high against the glassy marble. His bony hands pawed the stone uselessly. Now the man in the adjacent stall was moaning in Chinese, begging for help. Charlie pulled the attendant down and stood on the toilet seat himself. With his arms outstretched he could reach the top of the wall, and he sucked in a breath and hoisted himself. Grimacing, he pulled himself up high enough so that his nose touched the top edge of the wall. But before being able to look over, he fell back.

"Go!" he ordered the attendant. "Get help, get a key!"

The man in the stall groaned, his respiration a song of pain. Charlie stepped up on the seat again, this time jumping exactly at the moment he pulled with his arms, and then *yes*, he was up, right up there, hooking one leg over the wall, his head just high enough to peer down and see Sir Henry Lai slumped on the floor, his face a rictus of purpled flesh, his pants around his ankles, a piss stain spreading across his silk boxers. His hands clutched weakly at his tie, the veins of his neck swollen like blue pencils. His eyes, not squeezed shut but open, stared up at the underside of the spotless toilet bowl, into which, Charlie could see from above, a small silver pillbox had fallen, top open, the white pills inside of it scattered and sunk and melting away.

"Hang on," breathed Charlie. "They're coming. Hang on." He tried to pull himself through the opening between the wall and ceiling, but it was no good; he could get his head through but not his shoulders or torso. Now Sir Henry Lai coughed rhythmically, as if uttering some last strange code—"Haa-cah . . . Haaa! Haaa!"—and convulsed, his eyes peering in pained wonderment straight into Charlie's, then widening as his mouth filled with a reddish soup of undigested shrimp and pigeon and turtle that surged up over his lips and ran down both of his cheeks before draining back into his windpipe. He was too far gone to cough the vomit out of his lungs, and the tension in his hands eased—he was dying of a heart attack and asphyxiation at the same moment.

The attendant hurried back in with Sir Henry's bodyguard. They pounded on the stall door with something, cracking the marble. The beautiful veined stone broke away in pieces, some falling on Sir Henry Lai's shoes. Charlie looked back at his face. Henry Lai was dead.

The men stepped into the stall and Charlie knew he was of no further use. He dropped back to the floor, picked up his jacket, and walked out of the men's restroom, expecting a commotion outside. A waiter sailed past; the assembled businessmen didn't know what had happened.

Mr. Ming watched him enter.

"I must leave you," Charlie said graciously. "I'm very sorry. My daughter is due to call me tonight with important news."

"Good news, I trust."

The only news bankers liked. "Perhaps. She's going to tell me if she is pregnant."

"I hope you are blessed." Mr. Ming smiled, teeth white as Ellie's estrogen pills.

Charlie nodded warmly. "We're going to build a terrific factory, too. Should be on-line by the end of the year."

"We are scheduled for lunch in about two weeks in New York?"

"Absolutely," said Charlie. Every minute now was important.

Mr. Ming bent closer, his voice softening. "And you will tell me then about the quad-port transformer you are developing?"

His secret new datacom switch, which would smoke the competition? No. "Yes." Charlie smiled. "Sure deal."

"Excellent," pronounced Mr. Ming. "Have a good flight."

The stairs to the lobby spiraled along backlit cabinets of jade dragons and coral boats and who cared what else. Don't run, Charlie told himself, don't appear to be in a hurry. In London, seven hours behind Hong Kong, the stock market was still open. He pointed to his coat for the attendant then nodded at the first taxi waiting outside.

"FCC," he told the driver.

"Foreign Correspondents' Club?"

"Right away."

It was the only place open at night in Hong Kong where he knew he could get access to a Bloomberg box—that magical electronic screen that displayed every stock and bond price in every market around the globe. He pulled out his cell phone and called his broker in London.

"Jane, this is Charlie Ravich," he said when she answered. "I want to set up a huge put play. Drop everything."

"This is not like you."

"This is not like anything. Sell all my Microsoft now at the market price, sell all the Ford, the Merck, all the Lucent. Market orders all of them. Please, right now, before London closes."

"All right now, for the tape, you are requesting we sell eight thousand shares of—"

"Yes, yes, I agree," he blurted.

Jane was off the line, getting another broker to carry out the orders. "Zoom-de-doom," she said when she returned. "Let it rip."

"This is going to add up to about one-point-oh-seven million," he said. "I'm buying puts on Gaming Technologies, the gambling company. It's American but trades in London."

"Yes." Now her voice held interest. "*Yes.*"

"How many puts of GT can I buy with that?"

She was shouting orders to her clerks. "Wait . . ." she said. "Yes? Very good. I have your account on my screen . . ." He heard keys clicking. "We have . . . one million seventy thousand, U.S., plus change. Now then, Gaming Technologies is selling at sixty-six even a share—"

"How many puts can I buy with one-point-oh-seven?"

"Oh, I would say a huge number, Charlie."

"How many?"

"About . . . one-point-six million shares."

"That's huge."

"You want to protect that bet?" she asked.

"No."

"If you say so."

"Buy the puts, Jane."

"I am, Charlie, *please*. The price is stable. Yes, take this one . . ." she was saying to a clerk. "Give me puts on GT at market, immediately. Yes. One-point-six million at the money. *Yes.* At the money. The line was silent a moment. "You sure, Charlie?"

"This is a bullet to the moon, Jane."

"Biggest bet of your life, Charlie?"

"Oh, Jane, not even close."

Outside his cab a silky red Rolls glided past. "Got it?" he asked.

"Not quite. You going to tell me the play, Charlie?"

"When it goes through, Jane."

"We'll get the order back in a minute or two."

Die on the shitter, Charlie thought. Could happen to anyone. Happened to Elvis Presley, matter of fact.

"Charlie?"

"Yes."

"We have your puts. One-point-six million, GT, at the price of sixty-six." He heard the keys clicking.

"*Now* tell me?" Jane pleaded.

"I will," Charlie said. "Just give me the confirmation for the tape."

While she repeated the price and the volume of the order, he looked out the window to see how close the taxi was to the FCC. He'd first visited the club in 1970, when it was full of drunken television and newspaper journalists, CIA people, Army intelligence, retired British admirals who had gone native and crazy Texans provisioning the war; since then, the rest of Hong Kong had been built up and torn down and built up all over again, but the FCC still stood, tucked away on a side street.

"I just want to get my times right," Charlie told Jane when she was done. "It's now a few minutes after 9:00 p.m. on Tuesday in Hong Kong. What time are you in London?"

"Just after 2:00 p.m."

"London markets are open about an hour more?"

"Yes," Jane said.

"New York starts trading in half an hour."

"Yes."

"I need you to stay in your office and handle New York for me." She sighed. "I'm due to pick up my son from school."

"Need a car, a new car?"

"Everybody needs a new car."

"Just stay there a few more hours, Jane. You can pick out a Mercedes tomorrow morning and charge it to my account."

"You're a charmer, Charlie."

"I'm serious. Charge my account."

"Okay, will you *please* tell me?"

Of course he would, but because he needed to get the news moving. "Sir Henry Lai just died. Maybe fifteen minutes ago."

"Sir Henry Lai . . ."

"The Macao gambling billionaire who was in deep talks with GT—"

"Yes! Yes!" Jane cried. "Are you sure?"

"Yes."

"It's not just a rumor?"

"Jane, you don't trust old Charlie Ravich?"

"It's dropping! Oh! Down to sixty-four," she cried. "There it goes! There go ninety thousand shares! Somebody else got the word out! Sixty-three and a—Charlie, oh Jesus, you beat it by maybe a minute."

He told her he'd call again shortly and stepped out of the cab, into the club, a place so informal that the clerk just gave him a nod; people strode in all day long to have drinks in the main bar. Inside sat several dozen men and women drinking and smoking, many of them American and British journalists, others small-time local businessmen who long ago had slid into alcoholism, burned out, boiled over, or given up.

He ordered a whiskey and sat down in front of the Bloomberg box, fiddling with it until he found the correct menu for real-time London equities. He was up millions and the New York Stock Exchange had not even opened yet. Ha! The big American shareholders of GT, or, more particularly, their analysts and advisers and market watchers, most of them punks in their thirties, were still tying their shoes and kissing the mirror and soon—very soon!—they'd be saying hello to the receptionist sitting down at their screens. Minutes away! When they found out that Sir Henry Lai had collapsed and died in the China Club in Hong Kong at 8:45 p.m. Hong Kong time, they would assume, Charlie hoped, that because Lai ran an Asian-style, family-owned corporation, and because as its patriarch he dominated its governance, any possible deal with GT was off, indefinitely. They would then reconsider the price of GT, still absurdly stratospheric and dump it fast. Maybe. He ordered another drink, then called Jane.

"GT is down five points," she told him. "New York is about to open."

"But I don't see *panic* yet. Where's the volume selling?"

"You're not going to see it here, not with New York opening. I'll be sitting right here."

"Excellent, Jane. Thank you."

"Not at all. Call me when you're ready to close it out."

He hung up, looked into the screen. The real-time price of GT was hovering at fifty-nine dollars a share. No notice had moved over the information services yet. Not Bloomberg, not Reuters.

He went back to the bar, pushed his way past a couple of journalists.

"Another?" the bartender asked.

"Yes, sir. A double," he answered loudly. "I just got very bad news."

"Sorry to hear that." The bartender did not look up.

"Yes." Charlie nodded solemnly. "Sir Henry Lai died tonight, heart attack at the China Club. A terrible thing." He slid one hundred Hong Kong dollars across the bar. Several of the journalists peered at him.

"Pardon me," asked one, a tall Englishman with a riot of red hair. "Did I hear you say Sir Henry Lai has *died*?"

Charlie nodded. "Not an hour ago. I just happened to be standing there, at the China Club." He tasted his drink. "Please excuse me."

He returned to the Bloomberg screen. The Englishman, he noticed, had slipped away to a pay phone in the corner. The New York Stock Exchange, casino to the world, had been open a minute. He waited. Three, four, five minutes. And then, finally, came what he'd been waiting for, Sir Henry Lai's epitaph: GT's price began shrinking as its volume exploded—half a million shares, price fifty-eight, fifty-six, two million shares, fifty-five and a half. He watched. Four million shares now. The stock would bottom and bounce. He'd wait until the volume slowed. At fifty-five and a quarter he pulled his phone out of his pocket and called Jane. At fifty-five and seven-eighths he bought back the shares he'd sold at sixty-six, for a profit of a bit more than ten dollars a share. Major money. Sixteen million before taxes. Big money. Real money. Elvis money.

It was almost eleven when he arrived back at his hotel. The Sikh doorman, a vestige from the days of the British Empire, nodded a greeting. Inside the immense lobby a piano player pushed along a little tune that made Charlie feel mournful, and he sat down in one of the deep chairs that faced the harbor. So much ship traffic, hundreds of barges and freighters and, farther out, the supertankers. To the east sprawled the new airport—they had filled in the ocean there, hiring half of all the world's deep-water dredging equipment to do it. History in all this. He was looking at ships moving across the dark waters, but he might as well be looking at the twenty-first century itself, looking at his own countrymen who could not find factory jobs. The poor fucks had no idea what was coming at them, not a clue. China was a juggernaut, an immense, seething mass. It was building aircraft carriers, it was buying Taiwan. It shrugged off turmoil in Western stock markets. Currency fluctuations, inflation, deflation, volatility—none of these things compared to the fact that China had eight hundred and fifty million people under the age of thirty-five. They wanted everything Americans now took for granted, including the right to piss on the shoes of any other country in the world.

But ha! There might be some consolation! He pushed back in the seat, slipped on his half-frame glasses, and did the math on a hotel napkin. After commissions and taxes, his evening's activities had netted him close to eight million dollars—a sum grotesque not so much for its size but for the speed and ease with which he had seized it— two phone calls!—and, most of all, for its mockery of human toil. Well, it was a grotesque world now. He'd done nothing but understand what the theorists called a market inefficiency and what everyone else knew as inside information. If he was a ghoul, wrenching dollars from Sir Henry Lai's vomit-filled mouth, then at least the money would go to good use. He'd put all of it in a bypass trust for Julia's child. The funds could pay for clothes and school and pediatrician's bills and whatever else. It could pay for a *life*. He remembered his father buying used car tires from the garage of the Minnesota Highway Patrol for a dollar-fifty. No such thing as steel-belted radials in 1956. You cross borders of time, and if people don't come with you, you lose them and they you. Now it was an age when a fifty-eight-year-old American executive could net eight million bucks by watching a man choke to death. His father would never have understood it, and he suspected that Ellie couldn't, either. Not really. There was something in her head lately. Maybe it was because of Julia, but maybe not. She bought expensive vegetables she let rot in the refrigerator, she took Charlie's blood-pressure pills by mistake, she left the phone off the hook. He wanted to be patient with her but could not. She drove him nuts.

He sat in the hotel lobby for an hour more, reading every article in the *International Herald Tribune*. Finally, at midnight, he decided not to wait for Julia's call and pulled his phone from his pocket and dialed her Manhattan office.

"Tell me, sweetie," he said once he got past the secretary.

"Oh, Daddy . . ."

"Yes?"

A pause. And then she cried.

"Okay, now," he breathed, closing his eyes. "Okay."

She gathered herself. "All right. I'm fine. It's okay. You don't have to have children to have a fulfilling life. I can handle this."

"Tell me what they said."

"They said I'll probably never have my own children, they think the odds are—all I know is that I'll never hold my *own* baby, never, just something I'll never, ever do."

"Oh, sweetie."

"We really thought it was going to work. You know? I've had a lot of faith with this thing. They have these new egg-handling techniques, makes them glue to the walls of the uterus."

They were both silent a moment.

"I mean, you kind of expect that *technology* will work," Julia went on, her voice thoughtful. They can clone human beings—they can do all of these things and they can't—" She stopped.

The day had piled up on him, and he was trying to remember all that Julia had explained to him about eggs and tubes and hormone levels. "Sweetie," he tried, "the problem is not exactly the eggs?"

"My eggs are pretty lousy, *also*. You're wondering if we could put *my* egg in another woman, right?"

"No, not—well, maybe yes," he sighed.

"They don't think it would work. The eggs aren't that viable."

"And your tubes—"

She gave a bitter laugh. "I'm *barren*, Daddy. I can't make good eggs, and I can't hatch eggs, mine or anyone else's."

He watched the lights of a tanker slide along the oily water outside. "I know it's too early to start discussing adoption, but—"

"He doesn't want to do it. At least he says he won't," she sobbed.

"Wait, sweetie," Charlie responded, hearing her despair, "Brian is just—Adopting a child is—"

"No, no, *no*, Daddy, Brian doesn't *want* a little Guatemalan baby or a Lithuanian baby or anybody else's baby but his own. It's about his own goddamn *penis*. If it doesn't come out of *his* penis, then it's no good."

Her husband's view made sense to him, but he couldn't say that now. "Julia, I'm sure Brian—"

"I *would* have adopted a little baby a year ago, two years ago! But I put up with all this shit, all these hormones and needles in my butt and doctors pushing things up me, *for him*. And now those *years* are—Oh, I'm sorry, Daddy, I have a client. I'll talk to you when you come back. I'm very—I have a lot of calls here. Bye."

He listened to the satellite crackle in the phone, then the announcement in Chinese to hang up. His flight was at eight the next morning, New York seventeen hours away, and as always, he wanted to get home, and yet didn't, for as soon as he arrived, he would miss China. The place got to him, like a recurrent dream, or a fever—forced possibilities into his mind, whispered ideas he didn't want to hear. Like the eight million. It was perfectly legal yet also a kind of contraband. If he wanted, Ellie would never see the money; She had long since ceased to be interested in his financial gamesmanship, so long as there was enough money for Belgian chocolates for the elevator man at Christmas, fresh flowers twice a week, and the farmhouse in Tuscany. But like a flash of unexpected lightning, the new money illuminated certain questions begging for years at the edge of his consciousness. He had been rich for a long time, but now he was rich enough to fuck with fate. Had he been waiting for this moment? Yes, waiting until he knew about Julia, waiting until he was certain.

He called Martha Wainwright, his personal lawyer. "Martha, I've finally decided to do it," he said when she answered.

"Oh, Christ, Charlie, don't tell me that."

"Yes. Fact, I just made a little extra money in a stock deal. Makes the whole thing that much easier."

"Don't do it, Charlie."

"I just got the word from my daughter, Martha. If she could have children, it would be a different story."

"This is bullshit, Charlie. Male bullshit."

"Is that your legal opinion or your political one?"

"I'm going to argue with you when you get back," she warned.

"Fine—I expect that. For now, please just put the ad in the magazines and get all the documents ready."

"I think you are a complete jerk for doing this."

"We understand things differently, Martha."

"Yes, because *you* are addicted to testosterone."

"Most men are, Martha. That's what makes us such assholes."

"You having erection problems, Charlie? Is *that* what this is about?"

"You got the wrong guy, Martha. My dick is like an old dog."

"How's that? Sleeps all the time?"

"Slow but dependable," he lied. "Comes when you call it."

She sighed. "Why don't you just let me hire a couple of strippers to sit on your face? That'd be *infinitely* cheaper."

"That's not what this is about, Martha."

"Oh, Charlie."

"I'm serious, I really am."

"Ellie will be terribly hurt."

"She doesn't need to know."

"She'll find out, believe me. They always do." Martha's voice was distraught. "She'll find out you're advertising for a woman to have your baby, and then she'll just flip out, Charlie."

"Not if you do your job well."

"You really this afraid of death?"

"Not death, Martha, oblivion. Oblivion is the thing that really kills me."

"You're better than this, Charlie."

"The ad, just put in the ad."

He hung up. In a few days the notice would sneak into the back pages of New York's weeklies, a discreet little box in the personals, specifying the arrangement he sought and the benefits he offered. Martha would begin screening the applications. He'd see who responded. You never knew who was out there.

———

He sat quietly then, a saddened but prosperous American executive in a good suit, his gray hair neatly barbered, and followed the ships out on the water. One of the hotel's Eurasian prostitutes, watched him from across the lobby as she sipped a watered-down drink. Perhaps sensing a certain opportune grief in the stillness of his posture, she slipped over the marble floor and bent close to ask softly if he would like some company, but he shook his head no—although not, she would see, without a bit of lonely gratitude, not without a quick hungered glance of his eyes into hers—and he continued to sit calmly, with that stillness to him. Noticing this, one would have thought not that in one evening he had watched a man die, or made millions, or lied to his banker, or worried that his flesh might never go forward, but that he was privately toasting what was left of the century, wondering what revelation it might yet bring.